A NATURAL HISTORY
OF DRAGONS

BY MARIE BRENNAN

A Natural History of Dragons

Midnight Never Come
In Ashes Lie
A Star Shall Fall
With Fate Conspire

Warrior
Witch

A NATURAL HISTORY OF
DRAGONS

A MEMOIR BY LADY TRENT

Marie Brennan

TOR®

A TOM DOHERTY ASSOCIATES BOOK

NEW YORK

A NATURAL HISTORY OF DRAGONS

Copyright © 2013 by Bryn Neuenschwander

Interior illustrations by Todd Lockwood

Maps by Rhys Davies

Design by Greg Collins

A Tor Book
Published by Tom Doherty Associates, LLC
175 Fifth Avenue
New York, NY 10010

www.tor-forge.com

Tor® is a registered trademark of Tom Doherty Associates, LLC.

The Library of Congress has cataloged the hardcover edition as follows:

Brennan, Marie.
    A natural history of dragons : a memoir by Lady Trent / Marie
Brennan.—First edition.
        p. cm.
    "A Tom Doherty Associates Book."
    ISBN 978-0-7653-3196-0 (hardcover)
    ISBN 978-1-4299-5631-4 (e-book)
    1. Women scientists—Fiction. 2. Dragons—Fiction. I. Title.
PS3602.R453N38 2013
813'.6—dc23

                                                            2012038819

ISBN 978-0-7653-7507-0 (trade paperback)

Tor books may be purchased for educational, business, or promotional use. For information on bulk purchases, please contact Macmillan Corporate and Premium Sales Department at 1-800-221-7945, extension 5442, or write specialmarkets@macmillan.com.

First Edition: February 2013
First Trade Paperback Edition: February 2014

Printed in the United States of America

Anthiope

Scirland

Niddey

7. 8.

Siaure

Svaltan

Bulskevo

1.

Ielej

Zmayet

Rzegi

2.

Eiverheim

Tashal

Gillae

Vystrana

3.

Maraño

4.

5.

Cape

Thiessin

Heuvaar

6.

Chiavora

Curxo

Prania

Uwahse

Sea of Alsukir

Isnats

Kesa

Seghaye

Akhia

Nichaea

Haggad

1. Kupelyi
2. Minsurgrad
3. Ziveyjak
4. Drustanev
5. Sanverio
6. Trinque-Liranz
7. Falchester
8. Sennsmouth

Rhys Davies 2012

Drustanev
and environs

Staulerns

to boyar's lodge

to cavern

hunt

Gritelkin's house
Astimir's house
tabernacle
sauna

ruins

Rhys Davies 2012

PREFACE

Not a day goes by that the post does not bring me at least one letter from a young person (or sometimes one not so young) who wishes to follow in my footsteps and become a dragon naturalist. Nowadays, of course, the field is quite respectable, with university courses and intellectual societies putting out fat volumes titled *Proceedings of* some meeting or other. Those interested in respectable things, however, attend my lectures. The ones who write to me invariably want to hear about my adventures: my escape from captivity in the swamps of Mouleen, or my role in the great Battle of Keonga, or (most frequently) my flight to the inhospitable heights of the Mrtyahaima peaks, the only place on earth where the secrets of dragonkind could be unlocked.

Even the most dedicated of letter-writers could not hope to answer all these queries personally. I have therefore accepted the offer from Messrs. Carrigdon & Rudge to publish a series of memoirs chronicling the more interesting portions of my life. By and large these shall focus on those expeditions which led to the discovery for which I have become so famous, but there shall also be occasional digressions into matters more entertaining, personal, or even (yes) salacious. One benefit of being an old woman now, and moreover one who has been called a "national treasure," is that there are very few who can tell me what I may and may not write.

Be warned, then: the collected volumes of this series will contain frozen mountains, foetid swamps, hostile foreigners, hostile fellow countrymen, the occasional hostile family member, bad decisions, misadventures in orienteering, diseases of an unromantic sort, and a plenitude of mud. You continue at your own risk. It is not for the faint of heart—no more so than the study of dragons itself. But such study offers rewards beyond compare: to stand in a dragon's presence, even for the briefest of moments—even at the risk of one's life—is a delight that, once experienced, can never be forgotten. If my humble words convey even a fraction of that wonder, I will rest content.

We must, of course, begin at the beginning, before the series of discoveries and innovations that transformed the world into the one you, dear reader, know so well. In this ancient and nearly forgotten age lie the modest origins of my immodest career: my childhood and my first foreign expedition, to the mountains of Vystrana. The basic facts of this expedition have long since become common knowledge, but there is much more to the tale than you have heard.

Isabella, Lady Trent
Casselthwaite, Linshire
11 Floris, 5658

PART ONE

~~~

In which the memoirist
forms a youthful obsession with dragons,
and engineers an opportunity
to pursue that obsession

A Sparkling (actual size)

ONE

Greenie — An unfortunate incident with a dove —
My obsession with wings — My family — The influence
of Sir Richard Edgeworth

When I was seven, I found a sparkling lying dead on a bench at the edge of the woods which formed the back boundary of our garden, that the groundskeeper had not yet cleared away. With much excitement, I brought it for my mother to see, but by the time I reached her it had mostly collapsed into ash in my hands. Mama exclaimed in distaste and sent me to wash.

Our cook, a tall and gangly woman who nonetheless produced the most amazing soups and soufflés (thus putting the lie to the notion that one cannot trust a slender cook) was the one who showed me the secret of preserving sparklings after death. She kept one on her dresser top, which she brought out for me to see when I arrived in her kitchen, much cast down from the loss of the sparkling and from my mother's chastisement. "However did you keep it?" I asked her, wiping away my tears. "Mine fell all to pieces."

"Vinegar," she said, and that one word set me upon the path that led to where I stand today.

If found soon enough after death, a sparkling (as many of the readers of this volume no doubt know) may be preserved by embalming it in vinegar. I sailed forth into our gardens in determined search, a jar of vinegar crammed into one of my dress pockets so the skirt hung all askew. The first one I found lost its right wing in the process of preservation, but before the week was out I had an intact specimen: a sparkling an inch and a half in length, his scales a deep emerald in color. With the boundless ingenuity of a child, I named him Greenie, and he sits on a shelf in my study to this day, tiny wings outspread.

Sparklings were not the only things I collected in those days. I was forever bringing home other insects and beetles (for back then we classified sparklings as an insect species that simply resembled dragons, which today we know to be untrue), and many other things besides: interesting rocks, discarded bird feathers, fragments of eggshell, bones of all kinds. Mama threw fits until I formed a pact with my maid, that she would not breathe a word of my treasures, and I would give her an extra hour a week during which she could sit down and rest her feet. Thereafter my collections hid in cigar boxes and the like, tucked safely into my closets where my mother would not go.

No doubt some of my inclinations came about because I was the sole daughter in a set of six children. Surrounded as I was by boys, and with our house rather isolated in the countryside of Tamshire, I quite believed that collecting odd things was what children did, regardless of sex. My mother's attempts to educate me otherwise left little mark, I fear. Some of my interest also came from my father, who like any gentleman in those days kept himself moderately informed of developments in all fields: law, theology, economics, natural history, and more.

The remainder of it, I fancy, was inborn curiosity. I would sit in the kitchens (where I was permitted to be, if not encouraged, only because it meant I was not outside getting dirty and ruining my dresses), and ask the cook questions as she stripped a chicken carcass for the soup. "Why do chickens have wishbones?" I asked her one day.

One of the kitchen maids answered me in the fatuous tones of an adult addressing a child. "To make wishes on!" she said brightly, handing me one that had already been dried. "You take one side of it—"

"I know what we *do* with them," I said impatiently, cutting her off without much tact. "That's not what chickens have them for, though, or surely the chicken would have wished not to end up in the pot for our supper."

"Heavens, child, I don't know what they grow them for," the cook said. "But you find them in all kinds of birds—chickens, turkeys, geese, pigeons, and the like."

The notion that all birds should share this feature was intriguing, something I had never before considered. My curiosity soon drove me to an act which I blush to think upon today, not for the act itself (as I have done similar things many times since then, if in a more meticulous and scholarly fashion), but for the surreptitious and naive manner in which I carried it out.

In my wanderings one day, I found a dove which had fallen dead under a hedgerow. I immediately remembered what the cook had said, that all birds had wishbones. She had not named doves in her list, but doves were birds, were they not? Perhaps I might learn what they were for, as I could not learn when I watched the footman carve up a goose at the dinner table.

I took the dove's body and hid it behind the hayrick next to the barn, then stole inside and pinched a penknife from Andrew, the brother immediately senior to me, without him knowing. Once outside again, I settled down to my study of the dove.

I was organized, if not perfectly sensible, in my approach to the work. I had seen the maids plucking birds for the cook, so I understood that the first step was to remove the feathers—a task which proved harder than I had expected, and appallingly messy. It did afford me a chance, though, to see how the shaft of the feather fitted into its follicle (a word I did not know at the time), and the different kinds of feathers.

When the bird was more or less naked, I spent some time moving its wings and feet about, seeing how they operated—and, in truth, steeling myself for what I had determined to do next. Eventually curiosity won out over squeamishness, and I took my brother's penknife, set it against the skin of the bird's belly, and cut.

The smell was tremendous—in retrospect, I'm sure I perforated the bowel—but my fascination held. I examined the gobbets of flesh that came out, unsure what most of them were, for to me livers and kidneys were things I had only ever seen on a supper plate. I recognized the intestines, however, and made a judicious guess at the lungs and heart. Squeamishness overcome, I continued my work, peeling back the skin, prying away muscles, seeing how it all connected. I uncovered the bones, one by one, marveling at the delicacy of the wings, the wide keel of the sternum.

I had just discovered the wishbone when I heard a shout behind me, and turned to see a stableboy staring at me in horror.

While he bolted off, I began frantically trying to cover my mess, dragging hay over the dismembered body of the dove, but so distressed was I that the main result was to make myself look even worse than before. By the time Mama arrived on the scene, I was covered in blood and bits of dove-flesh, feathers and hay, and more than a few tears.

I will not tax my readers with a detailed description of the treatment I received at that point; the more adventurous among you have no doubt experienced similar chastisement after your own escapades. In the end I found myself in my father's study, standing clean and shamefaced on his Akhian carpet.

"Isabella," he said, his voice forbidding, "what possessed you to do such a thing?"

Out it all came, in a flood of words, about the dove I had found (I assured him, over and over again, that it had been dead when I came upon it, that I most certainly had not killed it), and about my curiosity regarding the wishbone—on and on I went, until Papa came forward and knelt before me, putting one hand on my shoulder and stopping me at last.

"You wanted to know how it worked?" he asked.

I nodded, not trusting myself to speak again lest the flood pick up where it had left off.

He sighed. "Your behaviour was not appropriate for a young lady. Do you understand that?" I nodded. "Let's make certain you remember it, then." With one hand he turned me about, and with the other he administered three brisk smacks to my bottom that started the tears afresh. When I had myself under control once more, I found that he had left me to compose myself and gone to the wall of his study. The shelves there were lined with books, some, I fancied, weighing as much as I did myself. (This was pure fancy, of course; the weightiest book in my library now, my own *De draconum varietatibus*, weighs a mere ten pounds.)

The volume he took down was much lighter, if rather thicker than one would normally give to a seven-year-old child. He pressed it into my hands, saying, "Your lady mother would not be happy to see you with this, I imagine, but I had rather you learn it from a book than from experimentation. Run along, now, and don't show that to her."

I curtseyed and fled.

Like Greenie, that book still sits on my shelf. My father had given me Gotherham's *Avian Anatomy*, and though our understanding of the subject has improved a great deal since Gotherham's day, it was a good introduction for me at the time. The text was only half comprehensible to me, but I devoured the half I could understand and contemplated the rest in fascinated perplexity. Best of all were the diagrams, thin, meticulous draw-ings of avian skeletons and musculature. From this book I learned that the function of the wishbone (or, more properly, the *fur-cula*) is to strengthen the thoracic skeleton of birds and provide attachment points for wing muscles.

It seemed so simple, so obvious: all birds had wishbones, be-cause all birds flew. (At the time I was not aware of ostriches, and neither was Gotherham.) Hardly a brilliant conclusion in the field of natural history, but to me it was brilliant indeed, and opened up a world I had never considered before: a world in which one could observe patterns and their circumstances, and from these derive information not obvious to the unaided eye.

Wings, truly, were my first obsession. I did not much discrim-inate in those days as to whether the wings in question belonged to a dove or a sparkling or a butterfly; the point was that these be-ings flew, and for that I adored them. I might mention, however, that although Mr. Gotherham's text concerns itself with birds, he does make the occasional, tantalizing reference to analogous structures or behaviours in dragonkind. Since (as I have said be-fore) sparklings were then classed as a variety of insect, this might count as my first introduction to the wonder of dragons.

I should speak at least in passing of my family, for without them I would not have become the woman I am today.

Of my mother I expect you have some sense already; she was an upright and proper woman of her class, and did the best she could to teach me ladylike ways, but no one can achieve the impossible. Any faults in my character must not be laid at her feet. As for my father, his business interests kept him often from home, and so to me he was a more distant figure, and perhaps more tolerant because of it; he had the luxury of seeing my misbehaviours as charming quirks of his daughter's nature, while my mother faced the messes and ruined clothing those quirks produced. I looked upon him as one might upon a minor pagan god, earnestly desiring his goodwill, but never quite certain how to propitiate him.

Where siblings are concerned, I was the fourth in a set of six children, and, as I have said, the only daughter. Most of my brothers, while of personal significance to me, will not feature much in this tale; their lives have not been much intertwined with my career.

The exception is Andrew, whom I have already mentioned; he is the one from whom I pinched the penknife. He, more than any, was my earnest partner in all the things of which my mother despaired. When Andrew heard of my bloody endeavours behind the hayrick, he was impressed as only an eight-year-old boy can be, and insisted I keep the knife as a trophy of my deeds. That, I no longer have; it deserves a place of honor alongside Greenie and Gotherham, but I lost it in the swamps of Mouleen. Not before it saved my life, however, cutting me free of the vines in which my Labane captors had bound me, and so I am forever grateful to Andrew for the gift.

I am also grateful for his assistance during our childhood years, exercising a boy's privileges on my behalf. When our father was out of town, Andrew would borrow books out of his study for my use. Texts I myself would never have been permitted thus found their way into my room, where I hid them between the mattresses and behind my wardrobe. My new maid had too great a terror of being found off her feet to agree to the old deal, but she was amenable to sweets, and so we settled on a new arrangement, and I read long into the night on more than one occasion.

The books he took on my behalf, of course, were nearly all of natural history. My horizons expanded from their winged beginnings to creatures of all kinds: mammals and fish, insects and reptiles, plants of a hundred sorts, for in those days our knowledge was still general enough that one person might be expected to familiarize himself (or in my case, herself) with the entire field.

Some of the books mentioned dragons. They never did so in more than passing asides, brief paragraphs that did little more than develop my appetite for information. In several places, however, I came across references to a particular work: Sir Richard Edgeworth's *A Natural History of Dragons*. Carrigdon & Rudge were soon to be reprinting it, as I learned from their autumn catalogue; I risked a great deal by sneaking into my father's study so as to leave that pamphlet open to the page announcing the reprint. It described *A Natural History of Dragons* as "the most indispensable reference on dragonkind available in our tongue"; surely that would be enough to entice my father's eye.

My gamble paid off, for it was in the next delivery of books we received. I could not have it right away—Andrew would not borrow anything our father had yet to read—and I nearly went mad with waiting. Early in winter, though, Andrew passed me the book in a corridor, saying, "He finished it yesterday. Don't let anyone see you with it."

I was on my way to the parlor for my weekly lesson on the pianoforte, and if I went back up to my room I would be late. Instead I hurried onward, and concealed the book under a cushion mere heartbeats before my teacher entered. I gave him my best curtsy, and thereafter struggled mightily not to look toward the divan, from which I could feel the unread book taunting me. (I would say my playing suffered from the distraction, but it is difficult for something so dire to grow worse. Although I appreciate music, to this day I could not carry a tune if you tied it around my wrist for safekeeping.)

Once I escaped from my lesson, I began in on the book straight-away, and hardly paused except to hide it when necessary. I imagine it is not so well-known today as it was then, having been supplanted by other, more complete works, so it may be difficult for my readers to imagine how wondrous it seemed to me at the time. Edgeworth's identifying criteria for "true dragons" were a useful starting point for many of us, and his listing of qualifying species is all the more impressive for having been assembled through correspondence with missionaries and traders, rather than through firsthand observation. He also addressed the issue of "lesser dragonkind," namely, those creatures such as wyverns which failed one criterion or another, yet appeared (by the theories of the period) to be branches of the same family tree.

The influence this book had upon me may be expressed by saying that I read it straight through four times, for once was certainly not enough. Just as some girl-children of that age go mad for horses and equestrian pursuits, so did I become dragon-mad. That phrase described me well, for it led not only to the premier focus of my adult life (which has included more than a few actions here and there that might be deemed deranged), but more directly to the action I engaged in shortly after my fourteenth birthday.

TWO

Blackmail — Reckless stupidity — An even more unfortunate incident with a wolf-drake — The near loss of off-the-shoulder dresses

We knew disgracefully little of dragons in those days, as there were no true dragons in Scirland, and the field of natural history was only beginning to turn its attentions abroad. I was very conversant, though, with the available information on those lesser cousins of dragons which may still be found in our own lands, and no command nor sum of money could have persuaded me to pass up an opportunity to learn more firsthand.

So when word came that a wolf-drake had been sighted on our property, not once but several times, by several different witnesses, and that it had been savaging sheep, you may well imagine how my interest soared. The name, of course, is a fanciful one; there is nothing wolflike about them, save their tendency to view livestock as their rightful meal. They are scarce in Scirland now, and were not abundant then; no one had sighted one in our region for a generation.

How could I forgo the chance?

First, however, I had to contrive a way to see the beast. Papa immediately set about organizing a hunt, just as he would have for a wolf that made a nuisance of itself. Had I asked for permission to ride along, though—as Andrew did, without success—I would absolutely have been denied. I had enough sense to realize

that riding out on my own in hopes of sighting the wolf-drake
would be fruitless, and highly dangerous if it were not; gaining
my desire, therefore, would require more serious effort.

Credit—or perhaps blame—for what followed belongs at least
in part to one Amanda Lewis, whose family were our nearest
neighbors during my youth. My father and Mr. Lewis were good
friends, but the same could not be said of my mother and Mrs.
Lewis, and this created a degree of tension whenever social occasions threw us together—especially given Mama's disapproval of
their daughter.

Amanda was one year my senior, and the only girl of near age
and equal status anywhere in the Tam River Valley. To my mother's unending distress, she was also what young people nowadays
would call *wing*—very improper in what Amanda thought to be
fashionable ways. (I have never been wing; my impropriety has
always been decidedly unfashionable.) But as I had no one else
with whom to socialize, Mama could hardly forbid me to visit
the Lewises, and so Amanda was my closest friend until marriage
took us both away.

On the day we learned of the wolf-drake, I walked two miles to
her house to share the news, and my situation immediately fired
her fruitful imagination. Clutching a book to her chest, Amanda
drew in a delighted breath and said, eyes sparkling with mischief,
"Oh, but it is *easy*! You must dress yourself as a boy and ride with
them!"

Lest it be thought that I slander the name of my childhood
friend by laying this incident at her feet, I must assure you that I,
not she, was the one who found a way to put her idea into practice. This has often been the way with me: notions too mad for
another to take seriously are the very notions I seize upon and
enact, often in the most organized and sensible fashion. (I say this
not out of pride, for it is a very stupid habit that has nearly gotten

me killed more than once, but out of honesty. If you do not understand what my husband has called my deranged practicality, very little of my life will make the slightest bit of sense.)

So Manda's declaration was the spark; the tinder and kindling which built it into a blaze were entirely my doing. It went thusly.

There were a number of lads who did odd jobs around our estate, mostly out of doors. I was not generally on close terms with these, but there was one, Jim, over whom I had a hold. Specifically, I had once come upon him in highly compromising circumstances with one of our downstairs maids. I myself had been on my way to hide a small and fascinating skull I could not identify, but as I had it concealed in my skirts, Jim did not know my own compromising circumstances. He therefore owed me a favor, and I determined that now was the time to redeem it.

Bringing me along on the hunt was, of course, an offense for which he could be turned out with no references. I could have achieved the same by telling of his dalliances with the maid, though, and while I would not have done so, I led him to believe I would. You may think it dreadful of me, and I blush now to recall my blackmail, but I will not pretend I had such scruples then. Jim, I insisted, must bring me on the hunt.

Here the chilly distance between my mother and Mrs. Lewis served my purposes very well. Amanda told Mama that she had invited me to her house for an afternoon and evening, to be returned on the morrow, and Mama, little desirous of corresponding with her neighbor, gave permission without asking questions. Therefore, on the morning the hunt was to begin, Amanda stopped by our estate with a manservant, on the pretense that I would be spending a few days with her family.

A small distance down the road, we reined in, and I inclined my head at her from my saddle while her manservant looked on, mystified. "Thank you, Manda."

Her eyes fairly danced. "You must tell me *all* about it when it's over!"

"Certainly," I replied, though I knew she would probably grow tired of the story in short order, unless I contrived to have a thrilling romance while on the hunt. Amanda's taste in reading ran to sensational novels, not natural history.

I left her to deal with the manservant by whatever means she found appropriate, and rode by back ways to the field where the hunt was gathering. Jim was waiting for me by a sheltered spring, as we had arranged.

"I've told them you're my cousin, here for a visit," he said, handing over a stack of clothing. "It's a madhouse down there—people in from all over. No one will think it strange if you join us."

"I'll be just a moment," I told him, and shifted to a spot where he could not see me. Casting looks over my shoulder all the time in case he should have followed me, I changed out of my own riding habit and into the much rougher boy's clothing he had brought me. (Words cannot express, I might add, how alien it was to wear trousers for the first time; I felt half naked. I have worn them on many occasions since—trousers being far more practical for dragon-chasing than skirts—but it took me many years to adjust.)

To his credit, Jim blushed when he saw me dressed so scandalously. He was a good lad. But he helped me bundle my hair up under a cap, and with it hidden, I believe I made a passable boy. I was not done growing then, and was all coltish arms and legs, with not much to speak of yet in the way of hips or breasts.

(And why is it, I ask you, that my editor should complain to me of such words when I have written several books discussing dragon anatomy and reproduction in far more frank terms? He will not wish to leave this aside in, I predict, but I shall make him. There are advantages to my age and status.)

The most startling part of the morning, though, came when Jim handed me a gun. He saw the look on my face and said, "You don't know how to use one, do you?"

"Why should I?" was my reply, and said in a rather sharper tone than he deserved. After all, I was the one who had insisted on dressing in boy's clothes; it was hardly fair that I should act the offended lady now.

He took it in stride. "Well, it's pretty simple—you put the stock up against your shoulder, point it in the direction . . ." His voice trailed off. I suspect he, like I, was imagining the potential consequences of me actually firing a gun in the midst of a chaotic hunt.

"Let's just leave it unloaded, shall we?" I asked, and he said, "Yes, let's."

Which was how I came to ride in the hunt for the wolf-drake, disguised as a boy, my hair under a cap and an unloaded rifle in my hand, on my mare Bossy, who had been rubbed all over with dust to conceal her glossy coat. Jim was right to call it a madhouse; despite Papa's best efforts, it was a disorganized thing, with far too many people there. Few men wanted to miss their chance to hunt a wolf-drake.

The day was quite fine, and I could barely contain my excitement as we rode. The areas in which the wolf-drake had been sighted were not terribly far from our manor house, which was why Papa had moved so quickly to organize the hunt, but we still had some distance to go.

Our estate consisted mostly of rocky, hilly soil, suitable more for sheep than anything else, though we had some tenant farmers in the Tam River Valley; the manor house stood just on the north edge of that valley. If one were to ride east or west, the terrain was gentler, but our path led us north, where the land sloped up quickly into an area too steep to be worth clearing. There, pine trees still ruled, and in their shade the wolf-drake was said to be hiding.

I stuck to Jim's side like a burr and affected to be shy, so as not to have to answer any more questions than necessary. I did not trust my voice to pass, even though I was clearly supposed to be a beardless boy. Jim served me well in this regard, talking enough that no one else could get a word in edgewise—though perhaps his nerves were the ones talking. He had reason enough to be worried.

We reached the northern woods a short time after noon, at which point the leaders began to organize the hunt. "Quick, head for Simpkin," I said, urging Jim away from my father and other men who might know me.

I gathered, from the fragments of speech I overheard, that the preparations for this hunt had begun well in advance of today. We congregated some distance downwind of a copse of trees that gave off an undeniable stink of carrion; it seemed that Papa's huntsmen had been placing carcasses there for several days, to lure the wolf-drake to a predetermined spot. Some brave souls had ventured forth that morning to examine the copse, and found signs that the creature lay within.

What followed was quite a confusing tangle to me, knowing nothing as I did of hunting. Men held wolfhounds and mastiffs on leashes, each dog muzzled so it would not bark and give our presence away. They seemed very uneasy to me; dogs that will hunt wolves without fear may still balk at approaching any sort of dragonkind. Nonetheless, their handlers chivvied and cuffed them to prearranged positions, through which I understood the wolf-drake was to be driven. An arc of local men was sent out with unlit torches, at a great distance from the wood; when the time came, they were to light their brands and approach the creature's shelter, provoking it to flight.

This, at least, was the intention. Wolf-drakes are cunning beasts; no one could be certain that it would oblige us by fleeing into our trap. Thus the arrangement of riders, myself and Jim included, at other points in the area: if the creature bolted, we would have to chase it down.

Astute readers will correctly surmise that I would not have troubled to mention this last point had the hunt gone according to plan.

My first sight of the wolf-drake came as a furious blur of movement streaking out of the wood. I do not know what precisely the hounds had been intended to do at that moment, but they never had a chance to do it; the drake was upon them too quickly.

Rare as the species was, the hunters had underestimated reports of its speed. The creature leapt upon one of the mastiffs, and there was an abrupt, shocking spray of blood. The other dogs hesitated before rushing into the fight, and their delay undid all our careful plans; the lines of the hunt were broken, and now we gave chase.

I have always been a good rider, for in those days it was not uncommon for the daughters of country gentry to learn to sit a horse both sidesaddle and astride. Never in my rambles with Bossy around my family's estate, however, had I experienced anything like this.

Jim goaded his horse forward, and mine followed by instinct, wanting (as horses do) not to be left alone. Soon we were galloping across the rocky slope, at a pace far faster than Mama would have deemed safe. The wolf-drake was a distant figure, already well ahead, and only the quick thinking of some of the local men kept it from escaping us entirely; they blocked its path with fire and sent it veering southward again, whereupon we angled across to intercept it.

The dogs were running as if to avenge the death of their

brother, the wolfhounds leading far in the front. They harried the wolf-drake back and forth while hunting horns gave their cries and directed the groups of horsemen about. All too soon, however, we reached another patch of the woodlands, and I understood why they had initially chosen that isolated copse in which to lay their bait: once in the main stretch of woods, finding and trapping the drake would be much more difficult.

Despite the best efforts of the hunters and hounds, the creature reached the shelter of the woods. One of Papa's huntsmen, a fellow as stony-faced as the hills around us, spat onto the ground, and I reminded myself that he did not know he was in the presence of a lady. "Won't run so fast now," he said, eyeing the shadows into which it had vanished. "But we'll have a devil of a time digging it out."

This afforded us our first chance to catch our breath since the chase had begun. Some of the men had brief, incomprehensible conversations out of which the only information I could sift was that we were now to use certain techniques common to boar-hunting. Since I knew no more of this than I did of wolf-hunting, the change did not mean much to me, but the mastiffs were brought up and the wolfhounds called back. The situation called now for strength more than speed.

The pines in this area were old and tall enough that we could often ride beneath their branches without ducking, and the carpet of their needles meant the ground was startlingly bare, except where a tree had fallen and created a gap in which other plants might grow. I soon lost sight of much of the hunt, but Jim stayed with me, and the rest of our group to either side. Through the trees we heard occasional shouts, and blares of the horns telling us nothing had been sighted yet.

Then a frenzy of barking . . . then nothing.

We paused where we were, as much to consider our path as

anything else, for a tangle of underbrush blotted the ground in front of us. I looked at Jim, and he back at me. "I should take you home, miss," he said in a voice too low for others to hear, though no one was nearby. "This really isn't safe anymore."

For the first time, I felt like agreeing. My entire purpose in coming had been to see the drake alive and at first hand, rather than as a dead trophy, but I understood now how unlikely that was. The blurred frenzy that savaged one of the dogs might well be the best glimpse I got all day.

As I pondered this, Jim suddenly shouted and drove his horse straight at me.

Bossy reared up and shrieked—a dreadful sound—and then lurched over sideways, spilling me from my saddle. She missed falling on my leg by a hairbreadth. I scrambled to a sitting position in the dry needles, my breath knocked out of me, and Jim half whimpered, half groaned in a way I had never heard before.

What drew my attention, though, was a long, rumbling snarl.

In lands where wolf-drakes are still numerous, it is common knowledge that they prefer female prey. Unfortunately, this was a detail we had forgotten, and which Sir Richard Edgeworth had not included in his otherwise splendid book.

I looked across at the wolf-drake, crouching atop a large outcropping of stone. Its scaled hide was a dull brown that fitted in well with our surroundings, and its eyes a disturbing crimson. The low-slung body featured powerful legs ending in scythelike claws and a long, flexible tail that moved hypnotically back and forth, like a cat's. Just behind its shoulders, a pair of vestigial wings shifted and settled.

I could not look away from it. My right hand groped blindly in the needles for the gun I had dropped, but did not find it. Panic built in my throat. The wolf-drake's claws tightened on the stone. I fumbled with my left hand, reaching out and further out,

The Wolf-Drake

and there! My fingers wrapped around the stock of a gun. I dragged it toward me, raising it as I had seen the men do, and the wolf-drake tensed, and as I brought the rifle up it leapt toward me and only as my finger tightened on the trigger did I remember, *we had not loaded my gun.*

A deafening bang went off in my ears, and the wolf-drake landed just to the side of me, claws shearing through shirt and shoulder like knives through butter.

I screamed and rolled away, dropping the gun again, the gun that must have been Jim's, because it certainly *had* been loaded. What had happened to Jim? The wolf-drake was pivoting to face me again, its bulk more agile than it looked, and though there was blood on its hide now—I had struck it a glancing blow—it was far from defeated.

Here I should write something heroic, but in truth, the thought that went through my head was: *This is what you came for, and it is the last thing you will ever see.*

More gunshots went off, these not directly in my ears but still loud enough that I screamed again and curled into a ball, terrified that the shots would hit me, that the wolf-drake would leap again, that one way or another I was going to die.

Instead I heard a frenzy of snarling, a horse's agonized scream, men shouting and horns blowing, and then, after a moment or two, a blessed sound I recognized, for it was the same horn call they used when returning home from a successful hunt: *prey down.*

Then there were men around me, and I uncurled only to realize that my cap had fallen off at some point in the struggle, and my hair come loose from the ribbon that had bound it atop my head. There seemed to be brown strands everywhere, waving like banners as if to advertise, Here! Look! A girl!

Which was, more or less, what I heard the men saying. (But with rather more profanity.)

More shouts, and then my father was there, staring down at me in horror: the minor pagan god, appalled at what his worshipper had done. I stared back at him, I think; this is the point at which things become somewhat muzzy, for I know I went into shock. Papa picked me up, and I asked about Jim, but no one answered me. Soon I was on Papa's horse, still cradled in his arms, riding out of the woods and across the rocky hillside to a shepherd's cottage.

A physician had accompanied the hunt, to minister to both the dogs and the men; he arrived shortly after we did. I was not his first patient, though. I heard Jim's voice moaning from the other side of the small room, but I could not see him through the press of other people.

"Don't hurt him," I said to no one in particular, though rationally I knew the physician must be trying to help him. "Don't blame him. I made him do it. And he protected me; he got in the way when the wolf-drake attacked." This I had pieced together after the fact.

The injuries Jim suffered through his heroic move were one of two things that kept him from being ignominiously sacked. The other—though I can take little pride in it—was my tireless defense, insisting that he was not to be blamed for bringing me on the hunt. Now, far too late, my guilt boiled up, and I fear I kept harping on the point long after my father had agreed to keep him on.

All of that came later, though. Once finished with Jim, the physician came to me, and banished everyone but my father and the now-sleeping Jim out of the hut, for the wound was on my shoulder and it would not be appropriate for others to be there while it was bared. (This I thought foolish, even at the time, for young ladies may wear off-the-shoulder dresses, which show just as much flesh as his ministrations did.)

I was given brandy to drink, which I had never had before, and its fire nearly made my eyes start out of my head. They made me drink more, though, and after I had enough in me, they poured some over the wounds in my shoulder to cleanse them. This made me cry, but thanks to the brandy I no longer particularly cared that I was crying. By the time the physician began to stitch me up, I was not aware of much at all, except him telling Papa in a low voice, "The claws were sharp, so the flesh is not too ragged. And she's young and strong. If infection does not threaten, it will heal well."

Through lips gone very thick and uncooperative, I tried to mumble something about how I wanted to wear off-the-shoulder dresses, but I do not believe it came out very clearly, and then I was asleep.

Mama had vapors upon my return, of course, but no one questioned me immediately, because they judged that I needed quiet rest to recover from my ordeal. This was not entirely a mercy; it meant that I had many hours in which to imagine what they would say to me when the time came. And while I may not have Amanda's vivid imagination, given enough time, mine does more than adequately well.

When I was finally permitted to get out of bed, put on a dressing gown, and go out into my sitting room (two days after I deemed myself ready to do so), I found Papa waiting for me.

I had prepared for this; those two days had their benefits as well as their drawbacks. "Is Jim recovering?" I asked before Papa could say anything, for no one had told me anything about him.

Papa's face pulled further into its grave lines behind his beard. "He will. He took quite a wound, though."

"I am sorry for it," I said honestly. "Were it not for him, I might be dead. It isn't his fault I was there, you know."

Sighing, Papa gestured for me to sit down. I settled onto a chair rather than the love seat he indicated, not wanting to look as though I might need to use it as a fainting couch. "I know," he said, a world of weariness in his voice. "Madness like that could never have been *his* idea to begin with. He should have refused, of course, and reported it to me—"

"I wouldn't let him," I broke in, eager to martyr myself. "You mustn't—"

"Blame him, I know. You've said it many times before."

I had the sense to close my mouth rather than continue to protest.

Papa sighed again as he looked across at me. The late-morning light was coming through the windows and lighting up all the roses embroidered into my upholstery; in his sober grey suit, my father looked terribly out of place. I could not remember the last time he had come into my sitting room, if indeed he ever had.

"What am I going to do with you, Isabella?" he asked.

I bowed my head and tried to look meek.

"I can imagine the story you will tell me, if I give you half a chance. You wanted to see the wolf-drake, yes? Alive, preferably, instead of safely dead. I suppose I have Sir Richard Edgeworth to blame for this."

My head shot up at that, and no doubt my guilt was written all over my face.

He nodded. "Oh, I keep a closer eye on my library than you seem to think. The catalogue, so carefully folded back, and then one book covered in rather less dust than it ought to be. Which your mother would take as an indication that we should sack the maid—but I do not mind a little dust. Especially when it alerts me to my daughter's clandestine activities."

Inexplicably, this made my eyes fill with tears, as if skulking about in his library were a thing to be repented of more than my wolf-drake escapade. Mama's disappointment was a familiar thing, but his, I found, could not be borne. "I'm sorry, Papa."

Silence stretched out. Crawling with shame, I wondered how many of the maids were eavesdropping at the keyholes.

At last Papa straightened and looked me in the eye. "I have to think of your future, Isabella," he said. "As do you. You won't be a girl forever. In a few years, we must find a husband for you, and that will not be easy if you persist in making trouble for yourself. Do you understand?"

No gentleman would want a wife covered in scars from misadventures with dangerous beasts. No gentleman would take on a woman who would be a disgrace to him. No gentleman would marry me, if I kept on this way.

For a few trembling, defiant moments, I wanted to tell my father that I would live a spinster, then, and everything else be damned. (Yes, I thought of it in those terms; do you think fourteen-year-old girls have never heard men swear?) These were the things I loved. Why should I give them up for the company of a man who would leave me to run the household and otherwise bore myself into porridge?

But I was not so lacking in common sense as to believe defiance would result in happiness, for me or anyone else. The world simply did not work that way.

Or so it seemed to me, at the wise old age of fourteen.

I therefore pressed my lips together, gathering my strength. Under the bandages that swathed it, my shoulder twinged.

"Yes, Papa," I said. "I understand."

THREE

The grey years — Horses and drawing — Six names for my Season — The king's menagerie — An awkward conversation there — The prospect of a friend — My Season continues — Another awkward conversation, with good results

I will spare you anything like a lengthy account of the two years that followed. Suffice it to say that I forever after referred to them as "the grey years," for attempting to force myself into the mold of a proper young woman, against my true inclinations, drained nearly all color from my life.

My collections of oddments from the natural world went away, tipped out onto the ground of the small wood behind our house. The cards I had written up to label various items were burned, with great (not to say melodramatic) ceremony. No more would I bring home anything dirtier than the occasional flower picked from the gardens.

Only Greenie remained, tucked away where Mama would not find him. That was one treasure I could not bring myself to forswear.

I would be a liar, though, if I pretended that I gave up on my passions entirely. Horses were an acceptable pastime, if dragons were not, and so, in company with Amanda Lewis, I turned my attentions to them. They had no wings—a fault I never quite forgave them for—but I learned a great deal about them in those two years: the various breeds and their conformations; patterns of coloration; the different gaits, both those that occurred naturally and those that could be taught. I kept extensive diaries in a cipher Mama could not read, noting therein a thousand details of equine nature, from appearance to movement, behaviour, and more.

Horses, as it happens, led indirectly to a new and unexpected source of pleasure. While my shoulder was healing—and indeed, for a long time afterward—I was considered too delicate to ride, but I could not stand to be in the house all the time. I therefore had the servants place a chair by the paddock on fine days, and there I sat to sketch.

People often say kind and utterly misguided things about my "talent" for art. The truth is, I have no talent, and never did. If any of my youthful sketches survived, I would show them as proof; they were as clumsy as any beginner's. But drawing was a suitable accomplishment for a young lady—one of the few I enjoyed—and I am nothing if not stubborn. So, through determined practice, I learned the rules of perspective and shadow, and how to render what I saw with charcoal or pen. Andrew, bored by this turn of events, abandoned me for a time, but he could be persuaded to tell me when the horse doctor was coming to treat injuries or birth foals; and so I learned anatomy. Mama, relieved to see me take up something like a ladylike pastime, turned a blind eye to these excursions.

At the time, this seemed a sorry replacement for my grand adventures, which were (I thought) over for good. With the wisdom of age, though, I have come to be grateful for the fruit of those grey years. They honed my eye and taught me to keep notes on what I saw: two skills which have formed the basis of all my accomplishments since.

For all that, though, they were two very dull, very tedious years.

Their end came with my sixteenth birthday, and my official transition from "girl" to "young woman." Mama therefore looked to my future—or rather I should say, put into action the plans she had been forming since I was born. She had great ambitions for my marriage: Sir Daniel Hendemore's only daughter should not wed any of the gentlemen in the Tam River Valley, but go to Falchester and make her debut in Society, where she might attract the eye of someone very fine indeed.

My patience with martyrdom would not have extended quite so far as to endure this peaceably, were it not for a startling conversation I had with my father shortly before I was to be dragged to Falchester.

We had this encounter in his study, where I trained my eyes away from the shelves with their old, forbidden friends. My father leaned back in his chair and steepled his fingers before him.

"It is not my intention," he said, "to force you into unhappiness, Isabella."

"I know that, Papa," I replied: the picture of daughterly demureness.

Perhaps a smile quirked his mouth inside its beard; perhaps I simply imagined it. "You do that very well," he said, index fingers tap-tapping against each other. "Indeed, you've become quite a credit to us, Isabella. I know these years have not been easy on you, though."

To this I did not respond, having nothing ladylike to say. I valued his approval too much to cast it aside.

After a pause, he said, "Matchmakers have gone out of fashion these days; we seem to think we can do better without professional aid. But I have taken the liberty of paying one to assemble a small list, which you will find on the table at your side."

Mystified, I found the paper and unfolded it, revealing six names.

"A husband willing to fund a library for his bookish wife is not so easy to obtain; most would see it as a pointless expense. You might, however, find one willing to *share* his library. The gentlemen on that list are all amateur scholars, with well-stocked studies." Papa's eyes gleamed at me from beneath his brows, and the lines around them threatened to crinkle up. "I have it on good authority that the ones I have underlined possess copies of *A Natural History of Dragons*."

As I had not allowed myself to think that name for two years, it struck me with roughly the same force I imagine accompanies the name of a girlhood love, not seen for ages. For a moment, I understood Manda and her sensational novels.

Before I succeeded in finding words, Papa went on. "I have not secured any of them for you; that task remains for you and your mother, who would not thank me for my interference. They are all eligible, however, and should you snare one, I promise my consent."

He rose from his chair in time to catch me as I came flying around his desk to envelop him in a hug. A laugh of startled delight won its way free of me. After our conversation in my sitting room, I had demoted my father from minor pagan god to well-meaning ogre—but it seemed that my dutiful efforts these two years past had paid dividends.

Six names. Surely one of them would bring me joy.

The hunt for spouses is an activity on a par with fox-hunting or hawking, though the weapons and *dramatis personae* differ. Just as grizzled old men know the habits of hares and quail, so do elegant society gossips know every titbit about the year's eligible men and women. Horses feature in both pursuits: in one as modes of transportation, and in the other as means of display. The fields and forests of the countryside are changed out for drawing rooms, ballrooms, and every other sort of room where a social event might be arranged and the eye of a potential spouse might be caught.

So did Society descend upon Falchester, and the horns sounded the beginning of the hunt.

Gossip about such matters ages badly; who said what to whom and where is swiftly forgotten, replaced by fresher meat. At my advanced years, such minutiae of my youth rank somewhere between the Gostershire tax rolls and the complaints of one's hypochondriac great-aunt for their interest to the modern audience. I shall trouble you only with the part that had lasting effect, which is the day I went to the king's menagerie.

I was not supposed to go. Mama's scrupulous plans called for me to be seen riding in the park that afternoon; she intended to make a virtue of my country upbringing, by displaying my skill in the saddle. But she, poor woman, had come down with a stomach ailment (I suspect bad fish at Renwick's the night before), and could not accompany me.

By a stroke of luck, Andrew was in town at the time, and came by to discharge his filial duty by commiserating with our mother. He was not yet hunting a wife; at that time he was idling his way through university, changing his mind every other week as to whether he would prefer to join the army and shoot at people in foreign places. But he was still my best ally among my brothers, and so when Mama fretted about the disruption of her plans, he offered to be my escort for the day.

She did not consider this ideal—he might be mistaken for a suitor of mine, by those who did not know him—but I had no other chaperon arranged. (Amanda, who had come out and promptly wed the previous year, was housebound by the expectation of her first child, and could not be there to assist.) Andrew's offer was better than my wasting the time at home, and so she agreed, with reluctance.

Andrew caught my arm as soon as we were away from her

door. "Don't put on riding clothes," he said, *sotto voce*. "We're going to the menagerie."

I blinked at him, surprised but not uncooperative. I enjoyed riding, but out in the countryside; trotting around the park in boring circles held little appeal. "But we shan't get in."

"Yes, we shall," he said, his eye gleaming with conspiratorial pleasure. "The Countess of Granby has arranged for the tour, and I am permitted a guest."

I knew little of the menagerie, except that the king's late father had established it on spacious grounds downstream from Falchester, and the son had spared no expense to see it stocked with every exotic creature that could be persuaded to survive in captivity. It existed primarily for the entertainment of the royal family, with occasional public days, which I, growing up in rural Tamshire, had no chance to experience. As Andrew could well guess, a tour would be a rare treat for me.

Our guide was Mr. Swargin, the king's naturalist. Under his direction, the menagerie was organized according to broad type: birds in one place, mammals in another, reptiles in a third, and so on. Stuffed and mounted specimens of those creatures that had passed on stood alongside the cages of those that still lived. The king possessed parrots, platypi, and piranhas; cuckoos, camels, and chameleons. I attempted to restrain my enthusiasm; learning is an admirable thing, in women as well as men, but only when it is of the right kind. (That is, of course, society's opinion; not my own. I am glad to say it has changed somewhat since my day.) As a young lady, I should show interest only in songbirds and other such dainty creatures, lest I brand myself as ink-nosed.

The tour was disappointing in its organization, for people wandered in and out of the various gardens and glass-walled rooms, few paying even the slightest attention to Mr. Swargin's speeches. I wished very much to listen to him, but didn't dare single myself out by being the only one to attend to his words, and so I caught only snatches before we stopped before a pair of very grand doors.

"In here," the naturalist said, in ringing tones that drew more eyes than usual, "we keep the crowning jewels of His Majesty's collection, only recently acquired. I beg the ladies to have a care, for many find the creatures within to be frightening."

One may measure the extent to which I had cut myself off from my old interests that I did not have the slightest clue what the king had acquired, that lay beyond those doors.

Mr. Swargin opened them, and we filed through into a large room enclosed by a dome of glass panels that let in the afternoon sunlight. We stood on a walkway that circled the room's perimeter and overlooked a deep, sand-floored pit divided by heavy grates into three large pie-slice enclosures.

Within those enclosures were three dragons.

Forgetting myself entirely, I rushed to the rail. In the pit below me, a creature with scales of a faded topaz gold turned its long snout upward to look back at me. From behind my left shoulder, I heard a muffled exclamation, and then someone having a fainting spell. Some of the more adventurous gentlemen came to the railing and murmured amongst themselves, but I had no eyes for them—only for the dragon in the pit.

A dull clanking sounded as it turned its head away from me, and I saw that a heavy collar bound its neck, connecting to a thick chain that ended at the wall. The gratings between the sections of the pit, I noticed, were doubled; in between each pair there was a gap, so the dragons could not snap at one another through the bars.

With slow, fascinated steps, I made my way around the room. The enclosure to the right held a muddy green lump, likewise

AKHIAN DESERT DRAKE

chained, that did not look up as I passed. The third dragon was a spindly thing, white-scaled and pink-eyed: an albino.

Mr. Swargin waited at the rail by the entrance. Sparing him a glance, I saw that he watched everyone with careful eyes as they circulated about the room. He had warned us, at the outset of the tour, not to throw anything or make noises at the beasts; I suspected that was a particular concern here.

The golden dragon had retired to the farthest corner of its enclosure to gnaw on a large bone mostly stripped of meat. I studied the beast carefully, noting certain features of its anatomy, comparing its size against what appeared to be a cow femur. "Mr. Swargin," I said, my eyes still on the dragon, "these aren't juveniles, are they? They're runts."

"I beg your pardon?" the naturalist responded, turning to me.

"I might be wrong—I've only Edgeworth to go by, really, and he's sadly lacking in illustrations—but my understanding was that species of true dragon do not develop the full ruff behind their heads until adulthood. I could not get a good view of the green one the next cage over—is that a Moulish swamp-wyrm?—but these cannot be full-grown adults, and considering the difficulties of keeping dragons in a menagerie, it seems to me that it might be simpler to collect runt specimens, rather than to deal with the eventual maturation of juveniles. Of course, maturation takes a long time, so one could—"

At that point I realized what I was doing, and shut my mouth with a snap. Far too late, I fear; someone had already overheard. From the other side of me, I heard another voice say, "The albino is certainly a runt, and I cannot determine its species."

If you wish, gentle reader, you may augment your mental tableau with dramatic orchestral accompaniment. I suggest something in a minor and ominous key, as that is what went through my own head as I realized just how thoroughly I had outed myself as ink-nosed. Heavy with dread, I dragged my eyes away from the gold dragon and up to the gentleman who had spoken.

A pair of trim feet in polished leather shoes; that was what I saw first. Then a goodly length of leg; then narrow hips and a waist not yet thickened by age. One long-fingered hand, resting on the sculpted bronze of the railing. Shoulders acceptably broad, without being so wide as to produce that triangular appearance I find unattractive, though it appeals to some ladies. A long oval of a face, with firm lips, a straight nose, good cheekbones, spectacles in front of clear hazel eyes, topped off with a neatly trimmed cap of brown hair.

Another lady, perhaps, might have been able to tell you what he was wearing. For my own part, I viewed him with a naturalist's eye, seeing size, conformation, coloration. And identifying marks: the handkerchief tucked into his breast pocket was embroidered with a coat of arms, *argent, three arrows in hand sable*.

The Camherst coat of arms, belonging to a wealthy baronet. The age and the spectacles made this the baronet's second son: one Jacob Camherst, twenty-three years of age, educated at Ennsbury, and well situated with investments. The matchmaker who gave his name to my father had marked him as an outside chance at best; he would make an agreeable if not spectacular catch someday, but he showed no inclination yet to wed.

Which was the one thing that saved me from utter mortification. I had not jeopardized any of my good prospects—provided I did not give Mr. Camherst reason to gossip about me to anyone else.

"I beg your pardon," the gentleman said, focusing on me. "I didn't mean to interrupt."

He hadn't interrupted; I'd stopped myself before he could. The stopping, however, had left me tongue-tied, a state from which I was saved only by the arrival of my wayward sibling. "Of course not; that's a brother's job," Andrew said, swooping in to offer his hand for Mr. Camherst to shake. "Andrew Hendemore. My father is Sir Daniel, of Norringale in Tamshire. This is my sister, Isabella."

My social graces were not the best in those days—nor are they the best now; they have been improved only by the greater dignity of years—but two years of practice had rescued them from complete disgrace; I managed a credible curtsy despite the mixture of panic and yearning unsettling my heart. Panic for the man, yearning for the dragons; most young ladies would feel the reverse. "Charmed," I said, as Mr. Camherst took my hand and kissed the air above my fingers.

He gave his name in reply, but then turned his attention away from me and back to Mr. Swargin. "The albino, sir?"

"A Vystrani rock-wyrm," the naturalist said. "They are naturally grey in coloration, of course, but you are correct; that one is a true albino, as you can see by the eyes."

Andrew was making comical faces behind Mr. Camherst's back. I knew what he wanted; it would amuse him greatly to watch me babble on further about dragons. Mama would have fits merely knowing I had been here, though. Any report of my conduct must be above reproach. If I were wise, I would take my leave of Mr. Camherst and Mr. Swargin, before temptation became too much.

I was not, of course, wise. Just as Manda Lewis's impressions of the world had been informed by her reading—leading her to expect balls, duels, and conveniently timed thunderstorms out of life—so, too, had mine; but what I expected was intellectual commerce between equals. I had, you understand, read a great many works by men, who regularly experience such things, and had not realized the unlikelihood of such things for me. In my naive, sixteen-year-old way, I thought Jacob Camherst and I might be *friends*.

Mr. Swargin closed the matter by including me in his reply to Mr. Camherst. "Miss Hendemore is correct; all three are runt specimens. The green is a Moulish swamp-wyrm, and the gold, a desert drake from the south of Akhia. His Majesty would very much like to have full-grown adults, but they could not possibly be kept within a menagerie. No doubt you've noticed the gratings that keep them apart from one another, and at that, we've had to keep a muzzle on the swamp-wyrm. He will persist in breathing at everything, and while the other two endure it better than we humans do, no one enjoys it very much."

"Extraordinary breath," Mr. Camherst murmured, looking across at the motionless lump of the green dragon.

I recognized the phrase from *A Natural History of Dragons;* it was the term Edgeworth had coined to describe the sixth and final characteristic he considered diagnostic of the true dragon. All such species could expel *something* additional with their breath, whether it was the legendary fire or otherwise.

The general theory for young ladies at the time was that curiosity was considered more attractive to young men than knowledge. Armed with this dubious advice, I ventured a question to which I already knew the answer. "What does it breathe?"

To my disappointment, Mr. Swargin answered in Mr. Camherst's place. "A noxious fume, miss," he said. "Very unpleasant, and harsh on the lungs. At feeding times, we lower large boards into the gaps you see, between the pens; that keeps the worst of it away from the other two when we unmuzzle the Moulish for his meal."

"I imagine the albino would have a hard time of it, in particular," Mr. Camherst said.

"Surprisingly not, sir. For a runt and an albino, it's quite robust; don't let its appearance fool you. The Akhian has the worst of it— but then, she's a bit of a dramatic thing."

She. For the first time, I noticed that Mr. Swargin was using gendered pronouns to refer to the dragons. The Akhian, the gold dragon currently pacing at my feet, was a female. I tried not to stare. Thank heavens the Moulish was curled up, so I didn't embarrass myself trying to spot anything.

An anomaly distracted me. The Akhian was female, and the Moulish male, but for the Vystrani, Mr. Swargin said "it." I voiced this thought to the naturalist, only realizing that it might be considered inappropriate after I had already said, "What sex is the albino?"

"None, miss," Mr. Swargin said. Mr. Camherst had turned back to listen; I hoped he didn't think me scandalous for asking. "Rockwyrms don't . . ." His eyes slid toward me. "They don't develop such characteristics," he continued, apparently amending the phrase he would have used, "until maturity. The Vystrani remains immature, and therefore neuter."

This was fascinating, and I wanted to ask more. I wasn't sure how to feel when Mr. Swargin spotted one fellow leaning over the railing by the swamp-wyrm's pen and said abruptly, "Pardon me," rushing over to intervene. It saved me from the chance to ask further inappropriate questions . . . but it left me alone with Mr. Camherst.

And with my brother—who would have done splendidly as a young lady, at least where the matter of curiosity versus knowledge was concerned. He knew no more of dragons than your average young man, which is to say, that they were huge and scaly and had wings, which was very pleasing to the part of him that was still an eight-year-old boy. He began to question Mr. Camherst himself, which gave us sufficient reason to remain in the man's company until the time came for us to retire to the lawn outside of (and, I might add, upwind of) the menagerie. By then I had managed to address a small handful of other remarks to the man, rendering myself agreeable enough that he obtained a lemonade for me before the ebb and flow of socialization carried him away.

(Or perhaps it was not my conversation that charmed the man, although I'm sure he was glad to have someone take an interest in him for some reason other than his wealth. I recall very little of what I wore that day, but I do know I had changed from the bony girl who went after a wolf-drake, and the dresses sewn for my Season did intriguing things with my bosom.)

Mama was displeased to hear where I had gone, and only somewhat mollified by a suitably edited account of my introduction to Mr. Camherst. His fortune and breeding were both acceptable, but she sniffed at my enthusiasm for his company. "Don't waste your time where it will do no good, Isabella. I know of the man, from Mrs. Rustin. He isn't looking for a wife."

I knew better than to tell her I wasn't looking for a husband, not in this instance. In truth, a part of me felt rather wistfully that it was a pity Mr. Camherst was not on the market. I felt no rushing swell of adoration for him, such as Manda Lewis dreamed of— but he was acceptably handsome, acceptably personable, and acceptably rich; Mama might dream of me snaring a certain bachelor viscount, but she would not instruct me to say no if Mr. Camherst offered. I hoped whatever husband I caught in the end would permit me a friendship with him; he seemed a very nice man.

That was not the end of my search for a husband, of course. There were dances and card parties, sherry breakfasts and afternoon teas: all the whirling life that accompanies a Season in Falchester. There were also gossiping mamas, discreet inquiries into familial finances, and scandalous tales of heritable dementia: all the backstage machination that accompanies the hunt for spouses. Frankly, I prefer the worst of the trials and initiations I've been required to endure in pursuit of my research. But despite my naive intentions, I found myself more and more in the pleasing company of Mr. Camherst. This culminated in a certain evening at Renwick's, when he asked if he could call on us the following afternoon at our hired house in Westbury Square.

Even such a dullard as I could not miss what he meant by the request. I barely had time to stammer out permission before Mama whisked me home and put me to bed with orders that I should not be roused before ten, as it would not do for me to look tired the next day. (This was something of a problem for me, as I woke at eight and was not permitted to rise for two hours. I had unwelcome memories of my convalescence from my torn shoulder.)

As soon as the clocks chimed ten, however, everything went into motion. I was bathed and dressed with more than the usual care, and my hair styled to perfection. We ate a tense late breakfast, during which I almost snapped at Mama to take her nerves elsewhere. I cannot pretend I was entirely composed myself, but certainly her jittery behaviour put me more on edge.

Following the meal, I was sent upstairs to change from morning clothes into more respectable afternoon dress. Mama came with me, and chose and discarded four possible gowns before the doorbell rang. Looking harried, she reverted to her second selection, ordered my maid to dress me as quickly as possible, and rushed downstairs.

The caller was, as expected, Mr. Camherst, and when I was quite as primped and polished as I could be, I made my way to the sitting room.

Mama was there with him, occupied in polite chatter, but she rose with alacrity when I appeared. "I will leave you two to talk," she said, and closed the doors behind her as she departed.

I was alone in a room with an unmarried man. Had I needed any further proof of what was about to occur, that would have done nicely.

"Miss Hendemore," Mr. Camherst said, stepping forward to take my hand. "I trust you are well?"

"Yes, quite," I said, marveling inwardly at the inanity of small talk in a situation such as this.

As if he heard my thoughts, Mr. Camherst hesitated, then smiled at me while we settled into our chairs. There was, I recall, a hint of apprehension in his eyes. "I'm afraid I don't know the finer points of how this is done—I had not really considered it in advance—but I don't imagine either of us would benefit over-much from my delaying. As I'm sure you've guessed by now, I have come here today to ask you to marry me."

Saying it with so little drama might be the most merciful thing I ever saw him do, but it still took my breath quite away. When I regained the ability to speak, unfortunately, my words were not at all what they should have been.

"Why? I mean—that is—" I blushed a vivid red and struggled to form a coherent sentence. "I apologize, Mr. Camherst—"

"Please, call me Jacob."

"—I don't mean to be rude, and I *am*, dreadfully. It's just that—" I managed, somehow, to meet his hazel eyes. "All of this has been so strange, the process of finding a husband, and now that the moment's come, I can't help but wonder *why*. Why do you wish to marry me? Why me, and not some other? Which is not to say that I think you should *look* for some other—" I quelled myself, shook my head, and said lamely, "I will stop there, before I embarrass myself any worse than I already have."

Belatedly, it occurred to me to pray Mama was not listening at the keyhole with the maids.

Mr. Camherst was, understandably, taken aback by my words. "Miss Hendemore—"

"Please, call me Isabella."

"I cannot think how to answer that question without being a little blunt. Given how we've begun, though, perhaps it's only appropriate."

He paused there, and I tried not to squirm.

"You've read Sir Richard Edgeworth's *A Natural History of Dragons*, haven't you?"

"Heaven preserve me," I said, quite involuntarily. "Mama will have fits if I answer that question."

I succeeded in provoking a fleeting laugh, though it hadn't been my goal. "Miss Hendemore—Isabella—you are not the first young lady to set her cap for me. But I do believe you are the first one to do so, not because of my wealth, but because of my hobby. Unless I'm very much mistaken, you came to Falchester not in search of a husband, but in search of someone with an interest in natural history, and that was the primary quality that recommended me to you."

If Mama *was* eavesdropping, she would never let me hear the end of this . . . but at that precise moment, I could not imagine lying to the man who might become my husband, even if the frank truth might cause him to cry off.

I took a deep breath and unclenched my hands from each other, my fingers cramping at the release. "Mr. Camherst—Jacob—" The name felt strange on my tongue, and intimate. Had it been the same for him? "Natural history has been a passion of mine since I was a small child. It is not a ladylike passion, I fear, and there are few husbands in the world who would tolerate it in their wives. I do not know if you would be one such. But I know, at least, that you would keep a library on the subject, and I hoped that I might be allowed to read from it."

He regarded me with a bemused expression. "You want me for my *library*."

Put so baldly, it sounded ridiculous. "Oh dear—I don't mean to insult you—"

This time his laugh was more full-bodied. "It's the strangest insult I've ever suffered, if indeed I would give it that name. So Edgeworth, then—"

"I was eleven," I admitted. "The first time. I've read it dozens of times since."

"I see," he said. "I didn't hear quite everything you said to Swargin, but I thought I recognized the name. And you *did* identify the swamp-wyrm; of that I was sure."

"Those dragons," I said wretchedly. "I was sure I had made a mull of my entire future, gabbling away like that in public."

He smiled, and the sight caused my heart to flutter a little, most ludicrously. "Not a mull of it—not then, anyway. But there was that other time . . ."

My heart changed from fluttering to lurching. "Other time?" I racked my memory for other occasions on which I had disgraced myself. There were so many!

"Yes, that time just a moment ago, when I asked you to marry me." His smile widened. "You still haven't given me an answer."

So I hadn't, and after I got over my moment of horrified self-castigation, I swallowed and returned his smile. Miraculously, my voice worked on the first try. "Yes," I said. "If you haven't run off by now, you're quite possibly the only man in Scirland who would have me. How could I do anything but agree?"

Prey down, the horns sounded in my head. And this time, I was decidedly the victor.

FOUR

P apa gave his consent to my wedding, and I saw true joy in his eye when I returned home after the Season's end. I teared up unexpectedly, and could not muster the words to thank him for pointing me at such a chance for happiness, but I believe he understood.

The wedding took place that autumn, just after my seventeenth birthday. It was a lavish affair; with only the one daughter, my parents could afford to dower me well and send me off in grand style. We had several truly august personages in attendance, too, thanks to the connections of the Camherst family, which were somewhat better than my own.

My clearest recollections of the day ought to be of my husband, and many of them are, but the one I wish to share concerns my father instead. A bride has few if any quiet moments to herself during the course of her wedding day, but that evening, Papa drew me aside and presented me with a small wrapped package. "We have other gifts for you and your husband as a couple," he said, "but this one, my dear Isabella, is for you."

I suspected what it was even before I removed the paper; my fingers knew the shape inside so well. I did not begin crying, though, until I actually saw the cover of Sir Richard Edgeworth's *A Natural History of Dragons*.

"I purchased that book for you," Papa said, "despite knowing it might result in trouble. As it has led you to happiness, I believe you should have it."

With a fine disregard for the damage my tears were doing to my cosmetics, and also the possibility of leaving stains on him, I threw my arms about my father and hugged him for dear life.

As absurd as it may sound, I think that was the moment at which I realized I was truly leaving. This is something the gentleman readers of this memoir may not understand, but the ladies will know it all too well. If they are married, they have been through it already, and if not, I am sure they have devoted some thought to the matter. To marry means to leave one home for another, and often one *place* for another. My own experience was not so disconcerting as that of royal brides who depart for another country, but from my family's estate in Tamshire, on which I had spent virtually all of my young life, I now left behind everything I knew and removed to Jacob's house outside of Falchester.

Jacob. I have made a deliberate choice, in the writing of this, to refer to him as Mr. Camherst until now, for that was how I thought of him at the time, and for some while after. Weeks, perhaps months, passed before it felt natural to call him by his given name. We spent a fair amount of time together during our courtship and engagement, but even so, moving into his household as his wife felt distressingly intimate, and no amount of telling myself that such intimacy was now quite expected made it less strange. Only time could do that—time in which he would cease to be a half stranger to me, and become, not only my husband, but a kind of friend, as I had once hoped.

For his own part, I think Jacob had to adjust to me as well. He did not live a rowdy bachelor's life, but he *had* been a bachelor, and was unused to having a woman ordering certain parts of his existence. Nor, I think, did he quite know what to do with me.

He offered for me that afternoon in Westbury Square because he liked the notion of a wife with whom he could converse about more than the guest list for a dinner party—but what to do with her once she was installed in his house?

In the end, he left me much to my own devices. I had free run of his library and could request certain purchases of him, if there was a title I desired that he had no interest in. Edgeworth and a few other volumes I kept for my own, in my private sitting room. With so much material to read, I must confess that I occasionally neglected my social duties as his wife, failing to arrange the sorts of dinner parties and other events that are expected of our class. Jacob spoke to me about it, and I promised to mend my ways; unfortunately, tragedy soon intervened.

Almost a year after our wedding, I found myself with child, but miscarried after a short time. This left me in a depression for several months, during which I ceased correspondence with nearly all family and friends; I could not even bring myself to write to Manda Lewis, with her healthy son and another on the way. Despite reassurances, I could not shake off a guilty conviction that I had failed in one of my primary obligations as a wife. Jacob did what he could to comfort me, but eventually buried himself in business interests for a time—I was not exactly pleasant company, prone to crying fits as I was. To console myself one rainy afternoon when even books could not hold my attention, I took out one of the few childhood possessions I had brought with me from home: my carefully preserved Greenie.

Jacob found me thus, with the vinegar-soaked sparkling cradled in my hands.

"May I see that?" he asked gently. I started; I had not heard him enter my private sitting room. The motion tipped Greenie over my fingers, and I cried out, but Jacob caught him as he fell, and with such a delicate touch that he was not damaged.

Jacob inspected the sparkling with a close eye. "Vinegar. Who taught you that?"

"The cook," I said. "I used to collect things, when I was young. All kinds of things, really—rocks and feathers and so on—but sparklings especially. He was the only one I kept, though, when—"

I stopped myself, but Jacob prompted me onward. "When?"

Then I told him about the wolf-drake; he had, of course, seen the scars on my shoulder, but I had been vague about their origins, citing only a "youthful misadventure." My husband might be tolerant of my interests, but I had not wanted to expose my childhood foolishness so thoroughly. He settled himself onto the sofa with me as I talked, and laid Greenie on my knee. I picked the sparkling up and described the aftermath of that incident, the grey years, and how I had disposed of my collections, keeping only this one relic.

When I finished, Jacob reached forward and wiped away the few tears that had fallen during my recitation. "Sparklings, eh?" he said. "I must concur with your father on the subject of wolf-drakes—I should not like to see you injured—but sparklings seem harmless enough. If you wish to collect them again, I will not stop you."

Only in silly novels does the sun actually come out at the speaking of such words, but to me, it felt like it did.

The weather continued foul for several days, but that gave time for a crate of vinegar to arrive. The cook eyed me strangely when I came to collect it from the kitchens, but I did not care; having this purpose in my life, however small, helped fend off the malaise that had burdened me for so long.

Jacob affectionately referred to what followed as the Great Sparkling Inquiry. The woodlands around Pasterway, the town outside Falchester in which we lived, were a breeding ground for sparklings, and in the summer and fall one could not take an evening walk without encountering them. I began by collecting the recently deceased, preserving them in vinegar, but soon moved on to butterfly nets and cricket cages, so that I might observe and sketch living specimens. The gardener's shed was given over to my use, as we did not keep much of a garden and therefore did not need many tools, and I soon filled it to the roof beams.

Many might laugh at me for my fascination—and in fact many did; this was not an eccentricity we could keep entirely quiet—but I rapidly learned that there is far more to sparklings than my childish eye had seen. They differ in size, color, and conformation between males and females, and there is more than one breed; I identified three in the vicinity of Pasterway, though I have since revised that analysis. I learned their behaviours and habits, and poured much unsuccessful effort into coaxing them to breed in captivity.

Earth-shaking discoveries they were not, but the simple fact that I made them lifted me out of my depression and back into the realm of social life. I went out once more, and hosted gatherings at our house; Jacob spent more time at home. With their delicate tails and scintillating wings, sparklings healed the damage my heart had suffered.

In a sense, therefore, sparklings led me to my life's work not once but twice: first when they seeded my childhood interest in natural history, and again when they brought me back to myself following the miscarriage. Had I not recovered then, I would not have met Maxwell Oscott, Earl of Hilford, and heard of his Vystrani expedition.

Even before my miscarriage, I went to Renwick's less often than before; it is not the best place for recreation if you are not on the catch for a spouse or shepherding a relative through the process.

Jacob's younger brother, though, had decided to advertise himself as an eligible bachelor, and Jacob had promised to help look out a suitable wife for him.

It was not the best choice for my first truly public outing since my miscarriage. The press of people threatened to become overwhelming, and I had occasion to be glad that entry to the upper rooms was so closely regulated. True crowds, I fear, might have done me in.

As it was, I spent the evening reacquainting myself with Society, the ladies' comments alternating between solicitous concern for my well-being and pointed barbs about my recent hobby. I endured these latter in polite silence, mostly for Jacob's sake; left to my own devices, I would have loved to shock the earrings off some of the women I spoke to with a few well-chosen details about my sparkling breeding programme.

My one respite came from Miss Natalie Oscott, a merry-hearted young woman I met early in the evening, and found to be quite a congenial soul. Very nearly the first words I heard her speak were a comment on the historical scholarship of Madame Précillon, and when the ebb and flow of socialization left the two of us alone for a time, I found she had quite as much ink on her nose as I. When she offered to introduce me to her grandfather, I was glad to accept.

"He doesn't often come here," Miss Oscott said over her shoulder, leading me through the crowd, "but my cousin Georgia has designs on a husband, and Grandpapa insisted on meeting the fellow—ah, there you are. Have you put the fear of Heaven into the young man yet?"

"The fear of *me*, which is quite sufficient," Lord Hilford said, pecking his granddaughter upon the cheek. He was not a tall man, balding and stocky of build, though without the large gut commonly observed among the older peerage. I could imagine him as quite fearsome to a prospective suitor, though he greeted me pleasantly enough. It transpired that he knew Jacob's father, Sir Joseph, and he congratulated me upon my marriage. "Must have missed the news," he said apologetically. "I've not been in Scirland much these last few years. Puts me quite behind the news, I'm afraid."

"You've been abroad, then?" I asked.

Miss Oscott laughed. "Grandpapa's hardly ever at home. Too busy visiting exotic places."

Lord Hilford drew himself up with an air of aggrieved dignity, looking down at his granddaughter—or attempting to, for she was scarcely an inch shorter than he. "I'll have you know, my girl, that the last six months were entirely for my health. My physician advised me to take the sea waters on Prania."

"And the sea-snakes that can only be found off the coasts of Prania had *nothing* to do with it, I'm sure."

Her words spurred my memory. "Didn't you present to the Philosophers' Colloquium about those creatures?"

He dismissed this with a wave of his hand. "Nothing terribly important. I spent six months swimming and being dosed with vile tonics I didn't need in the slightest; the lecture was my attempt to get something of value out of the experience. I do travel for research, though, as my granddaughter has so pointedly indicated."

"That must be pleasant," I sighed. "Jacob and I had hoped to take a tour after our wedding, but circumstances interfered. Where have your travels led you?"

As I had surmised from Miss Oscott's evident fondness for her grandfather, it did not take much encouragement to get Lord Hilford started in talking about his research. He puffed up a little and hooked his thumbs into the pockets of his waistcoat. "Here and there. After so many years, the places do pile up. I was with the army in my youth, during our wars in Akhia, but the desert doesn't agree with me; the sun is too harsh." One hand came away from its perch to rub at his hairless pate. "Not enough to protect me up top, you see, and I went bald at a young age.

"Nor am I much of a sailor," he went on, "so it's the mainland for me, I fear. In fact, I think the climate of Prania did more harm to my joints than good. Rheumatism, you know. I intend to try the mountains next—a research expedition to Vystrana."

There are any number of animals in Vystrana that one could go to study, but in truth, my mind went straight to the creature I had seen a few years before, in the king's menagerie. "Dragons?"

Lord Hilford raised one white eyebrow at me. "Indeed, Mrs. Camherst."

"But—do you not study sea creatures?"

"I have a little of late, but only in pursuit of a side theory of mine, regarding taxonomy. If I'm a poor sailor, what sort of sea-going naturalist would I make, eh?" Lord Hilford shook his head. "No, Mrs. Camherst, my interest is primarily in dragons. We know very little of them, compared to other creatures—it's a terrible shortcoming in our learning."

It called to mind a fellow Jacob and I had dined with once. "Do you know Lord Shalney, by any chance?"

His laugh turned out to be the basso version of Miss Oscott's. "Verner? Certainly. I take it you've heard his diatribe on our lack of dragon knowledge, then."

"Shortly after my wedding," I admitted. "Vystrana, you say?"

"There's a breed of dragons there—we call them rock-wyrms, though the locals call them *balaur*. Not a native word; it may be a loan from Bulskoi or Zmayin. Relatively approachable, as dragons go, and one doesn't have to endure too much in the way of dreadful weather to find them, at least in the proper season. I often wonder what it is about dragons that makes them prefer extreme climates—or is it just that we've pushed them back as we've spread out? Were there once simple field- and meadow-dragons that liked their living more comfortable? I couldn't say, but Vystrana seems a reasonable place to try and observe the ones we have."

I was a better hand at concealing my enthusiasm these days than I had once been. I like to believe the expression I presented to Lord Hilford was one of polite interest, rather than the quivering excitement I held within. "I am sure my husband will look forward to reading about your findings." He would have to wait, though—first for Lord Hilford to conduct his expedition, then for him to issue his report, and finally for me to snatch it out of the mail and devour every word before giving it to him. Jacob found dragons interesting, make no mistake, but not with my degree of passion. He could read it after I was done.

"Grandpapa brought a dragon back from Vystrana once," Miss Oscott put in. "He gave it as a personal gift to the king."

"The albino?" I asked, looking to Lord Hilford.

He nodded, beaming at the memory of his own accomplishment—as well he might, given the difficulties involved. "You saw my little drake, I take it?"

"In the king's menagerie." I blushed a little, wishing I could do it as prettily as some ladies, and admitted to him, "Jacob and I met there, in fact. Not just in the menagerie, but in the dragon room itself. It made me so very low when I heard the Vystrani had died."

The earl looked philosophical. "Yes, well, don't blame Swargin; he did his best. They rarely thrive away from their homelands. Most efforts to transport dragons fail outright, of course, and then they do poorly in captivity. The imperial dragon-men of Yelang claim they've been able to propagate some of their local breeds, but I have my doubts. My little white outlasted that Akhian, though!"

I remembered Mr. Swargin talking about the desert-drake's

delicate constitution. I had hoped for her to survive, but she had succumbed to a pulmonary illness even before my wedding. "Was that one your acquisition as well, my lord?"

"Only in part. I did help capture her—and swore blind after that I would never go to the desert again—but the Duke of Conchett was the one who presented her to the king."

Not one dragon captured and brought into captivity, but two. My estimation of Lord Hilford was climbing steadily, and had not been low to begin with. "And the Moulish swamp-wyrm?"

He laughed outright. "Nothing could persuade me to attach my name to that thing. Ill-tempered and as intractable as they come, and an ugly example of the breed to boot. Not that Moulish dragons are ever what one might call attractive, mind you. But I'm certain its breath contributed to the ill health of the Akhian—of course, our climate also had much to do with it; I'll put blame where blame is due—and it bit my little white more than once, when it got out of the control of its keepers. No, Mrs. Camherst, the Moulish beast was *not* my doing."

"I hope I haven't offended," I said, though I rather doubted I had.

"Not in the least. You do an old man's sense of self-importance good, asking so much about dragons."

I returned his smile, and resolved to find some way to thank Miss Oscott for her part in bringing me to her grandfather's acquaintance. "I wish you luck in your Vystrani expedition. When is it scheduled to depart?"

He waved one hand again, a gesture I was beginning to suspect was habitual. "Not until next year. Hard to arrange things from Prania, especially when you're being laid low by sea journeys and vile tonics, and I have some relations who insist they like me and would like to see me once in a while." He gave his granddaughter a mock-suspicious look. "Either that, or they're luring me home so they can whack me over the head and get the inheritance at last."

Miss Oscott put on a look of airy innocence, and we all laughed. Then, not wanting to impose more than I already had on the earl's time, I bid them a good evening and made my way once again through the crowds of Renwick's.

Locating Jacob took some time. When I succeeded at last, I found him in a foul temper, owing to unspecified fraternal antics. It put something of a damper on my bubbling enthusiasm; this was clearly not a good time to bring up Lord Hilford and his expedition. Instead we made our departure from the hall, and went to the house Jacob kept in town, where we stayed on our Falchester trips. Feeling somewhat deflated, I prepared for bed, then lay for nearly an hour in the dark, staring at the ceiling and thinking of Vystrana.

FIVE

Advantageous correspondence — An unwise request — I speak my mind — An unproductive morning — The risk of lunacy — What other people might say

Judging by the number of letters we received at our house over the next two months, Lord Hilford was more than happy to correspond with my husband about his lecture and everything else under the sun. Jacob read bits of these out loud to me, mostly anecdotes of natural history, but occasionally the earl's biting observations about the trials of spending time with family. I gathered that he was glad for the excuse to closet himself away from them for an hour or two and engage his mind with the questions of a colleague.

I cultivated that connection with every wile I possessed, for I had awoken the morning after Renwick's utterly possessed by a single notion: that Jacob should join the expedition. By now I had every confidence that we would hear all the details, not merely those digested for lectures and articles; but it was not enough. Jacob must go, and I could live the experience vicariously through him.

Or so I thought at the time.

Over a quiet dinner one night, I found I had achieved my goal. "Isabella," Jacob said during the main course, "would you object if I went abroad?"

I did not drop my fork, though my hand forgot to mind it for a moment. "Abroad?"

"Lord Hilford's planning an expedition—" Jacob stopped

himself mid-sentence and eyed me across the tureen of stewed carrots. "But I don't need to remind you of that, do I? You've orchestrated it very well, I must say."

"Orchestrated?" I made a valiant attempt at an innocent expression. "Lord Hilford had that expedition in mind long before I met him."

"But not that I should be a part of it. Admit it, Isabella; you've been nudging me toward him and his Vystrani escapade, since— when? Certainly since the beginning of summer. As far back as Renwick's?"

"Not that early," I said, avoiding a lie by the narrowest of margins. The hour of sleeplessness *after* Renwick's did not count as *at* Renwick's.

"It can't have been long after that. I can't say I object, precisely; Hilford's fast become a good friend. You could have been more open about it, though."

I studied my husband at the other end of the table and replied with more honesty than I'd intended. "Would you have listened, had I been blunt? Had I told you from the start what I had in mind—that you should deliberately seek out and befriend a peer of the realm, for the purposes of worming your way into his foreign expedition?"

Jacob frowned. "When you put it like that, it sounds dreadfully presumptuous."

"Precisely. And it *would* have been presumptuous, had you had any such intention—which means you probably wouldn't have done it at all. Therefore, I approached it more subtly."

The twitch of his eyebrow said he was not persuaded by my logic. "Meaning you had that intention on my behalf."

"Isn't that a wife's duty?" I offered him an innocent smile.

My husband put down his fork and leaned back in his chair, gazing at me in bemusement. "You're outrageous, Isabella."

"Outrageous? Me? Do you see me wearing scandalously low-cut gowns to the opera, like the Marchioness of Priscin? Do you see me publishing books of poetry and pretending they aren't mine, like Lady Hannah Spring? Do you—"

"Enough!" Jacob laughed and cut me off. "I'm afraid to hear what other pieces of Society gossip you may have picked up. Since you have admitted to your meddling, I imagine you would *not* object to me going abroad with Hilford." He looked rueful and picked his fork up again. "I wouldn't be surprised if you booted me out the door."

"And risk damage to my shoe?" I imitated the tone of the most vapid beauty in Society. Jacob smiled, and ate in silence for a few minutes. The footman came in and cleared away the plates, then brought in the pudding.

For once, I had little appetite for it, and the heavy bread sat like a raisin-studded lump in my stomach. I picked at it for a little while, not really eating much, while across from me Jacob dug into his own.

When I realized the source of my suddenly dismal mood, it escaped my lips before I could stop it.

"I want to go with you."

Jacob paused, a forkful of pudding already in his mouth, staring across at me. Slowly, he drew the fork out, and laid it on his plate while he chewed and swallowed. "To Vystrana."

"Yes." I wished I had kept silent. If there were any chance of success, it would not come this way, with my desire stated so bluntly.

Jacob's expression showed me I was not wrong. "Isabella . . . it's out of the question, and you know it."

So I did, and yet . . .

"Please," I said. The word came out softly, and heartfelt. "I've been fascinated by them since I was a girl. You *know* that, Jacob. To sit idly at home, while others go and see them in person—"

"Isabella—"

"To see *real* ones, I mean; adults instead of runts. Adult dragons, living in the wild, not chained in a pit for the king's favourites to gawk at. I've read about them—you of all people know how much—but words are *nothing.* Engravings give the illusion of reality, but how many of the engravers have even seen the subjects they depict? This might be my only chance, Jacob."

I stopped and swallowed. The pudding I had eaten felt like it might come back up again, did I relax my guard against it.

"Isabella." His voice was also soft, but intense. I could not look up at him, staring fixedly at my plate instead. "I know your interest, and I have sympathy for it—believe me, I do! But you cannot ask me to take my wife abroad in this manner. A tour, certainly, going to civilized places, but the mountains of Vystrana are not civilized.

"You've read about it, I know. Try to imagine what you've read made real. The peasants there eke out their existence; do you think they will have a comfortable hotel for us to stay in? Servants who are more than local girls hired on for our stay, who—who actually understand how to care for people rather than for sheep? It will not be a pleasant existence, Isabella."

"Do you think I care?" I slammed my fork down, heedless of the scene I was making. "I don't need luxury, Jacob; I don't need pampering. I'm not afraid of dirt and drafts and—and washing my own clothing. Or yours, for that matter. I could be useful; would it not be advantageous to have someone to make accurate drawings? Think of me as a secretary. I can keep your notes, organize your papers, make certain that you and Lord Hilford have what you need when you go out to observe."

Jacob shook his head. "While you sit in the rented cottage, content to be left behind?"

"I didn't say I would be content."

"And you wouldn't be. I'd find you out there in boy's clothes, masquerading as a shepherd, before a fortnight was done."

Heat stained my cheeks. It might have been anger, embarrassment, or a little of both. "That is not fair."

"I'm just being pragmatic, Isabella. You've made headstrong decisions before, and they got you hurt. Don't ask me to stand by and let you be hurt again."

I took a deep, slow breath, hoping it would calm me down. The air caught in my throat, raggedly. I *would not* cry. Why was I crying?

"Please," I repeated, knowing I had said it already, but unable to avoid repeating it. "Please . . . don't leave me behind."

Silence followed my words. My gaze had drifted downward again, and I could not bear to lift it, to look at him while I said this. "Don't leave me here alone. You'll be gone for months, a year perhaps—and what will I do with myself?"

His answer was gentle. "You have friends. Invite one of them to come stay with you for a time. Or go visit your family; I am sure they would be glad to have you." A soft sound that might have been a laugh. "Continue your work with sparklings, if it makes you happy."

"But it *doesn't*! It isn't enough. Jacob, please. I don't blame you for going away so much when I was in my depression, but if you go away for so long, I'll feel—"

The words stuck in my mouth. No matter how hard I tried, I could not bring myself to enunciate it, to tell him the depth of fear and inadequacy the prospect of his absence created in my heart.

More silence, while I tried to breathe. Then at last Jacob spoke, in level, almost grim tones.

"I did not mind when you set out to snare me in Falchester, Isabella. And I did not mind when you put me in Lord Hilford's path. But I will not let you maneuver me into this one—*especially* not with that."

All desire for tears vanished in a surge of white-hot rage. My gaze snapped up to meet his, and my chair skidded backward on the rug as I stood, palms flat on the table, feet widely braced.

"Don't you *dare*," I spat, not caring how loud my voice became. "Don't you *dare* accuse me of using this to maneuver you. I spoke my heart, and nothing more. Have you any concept what it feels like, to endure the loss I have? You may not blame me, but others do; whether you think of it this way or not, they whisper that I have failed as your wife. If you leave, what will they say then? How will we feel toward one another, when you come back? Can you promise me it would not create distance between us? And while you're gone, I will be sitting here, trying to keep myself occupied with frivolity and artifice, an endless round of dances and card games and things I don't give a *damn* about, knowing all the while that my one opportunity to see true dragons has come and gone, leaving me behind."

My words exhausted, I stood, panting, staring at Jacob's white face. That face blurred alarmingly, and I could not think of anything to say in the aftermath of my tirade, anything that would begin to atone for the anger I had just shown him. A lady, quite simply, did not speak so to her husband.

There was nothing I could say. Nor could I bear to remain there in silence.

Turning sharply, almost stumbling over my chair, I fled the room.

* * *

Jacob did not pursue me, nor did he come to my bedchamber that night. (We had slept apart since my miscarriage, that I might not trouble him with my restlessness.) I rose at my usual hour the next morning, but dressed slowly, not eager to go downstairs and face him after my outburst of the previous night. My state was not helped by my uncertainty as to how I felt about that outburst. I did not know whether to regret it or not.

My cowardice eventually lost out to my will, and I went down, only to discover that Jacob had gone riding, and the servants could not tell me when he would return. This did nothing to improve my mood.

I sat down to answer correspondence, but my handwriting was atrocious, a reflection of my feelings that day, and I soon gave it up in disgust. The day being fine, I went out into the garden, but as I have said before it was a small place, and not one that could keep me occupied for long. At length I went down to the shed where I kept my sparklings and my notes, though I was not much in a mood to work.

Once inside, I sank onto a stool and gazed sightlessly over the neat ranks of my vinegar-soaked sparklings. Each stood on a card labeled in my tidiest handwriting, recounting when and where it had been collected, its length, its wingspan, and how much it weighed. They were organized into categories based on my research, grouped according to the subtypes I was beginning to identify. One stood on my working-table, submerged in a jar of vinegar, awaiting my latest effort at dissection. I picked up the surgeon's scalpel I had been using for that task, and put it down. Hardly a pastime for a lady.

Yet it was the closest thing I could arrange to the work I truly wanted to be doing. My childhood obsession, buried for years after the incident with the wolf-drake, had put up shoots during the tour of the menagerie, and now those shoots had burst into full flower. I wanted both to see dragons, and to *understand* them. I wanted to stretch the wings of my mind and see how far I could fly.

I wanted, in short, the intellectual life of a gentleman—or as close to it as I could come.

I picked up a sparkling, my fingers gentle despite my frustration, and studied the minute perfection of its scales. The tiny head with its ridges, no less fierce for being so small, and the elegant wings. They did not look precisely like dragons, but they spat infinitesimal sparks: the origin of their name and, I thought, a means of attracting mates, much like a firefly's glow.

That thought made me lower than ever, and I put the sparkling down, turning to a book I had left open. It showed an anatomical drawing of a wyvern, which I believed might be a larger relative of the sparkling—a notion which, if true, would make them not insects at all.

A shadow fell across the page, obscuring the diagram.

It might have been a servant, but even before the silence stretched out long past the time when a servant would have announced his business, I knew it was not. I recognized my husband's step.

"I thought I might find you here," Jacob said after a brief silence.

"You almost didn't," I replied, my voice pleasingly steady despite the turmoil inside. "I was about to go inside and make another attempt at answering letters."

I heard Jacob move a few steps around the interior of the shed, and suspected he was studying my shelves. "I had no idea you had collected so many."

I could not think of a response that would not sound antagonistic, and so I kept quiet.

Jacob, I think, had been hoping I would make small talk, perhaps help him find a graceful way into the conversation we could not avoid. Faced with my silence, he sighed. "I'm sorry for what I said last night," he told me, his voice heavy. "The implication that you were . . . using our loss against me, as a way to get what you wanted. I should not have said that."

"No, you should not have." My words came out harder than I meant them to. I sighed, echoing him. "But I forgive you. It's true; I *have* maneuvered you before."

My husband came forward to lean gingerly on the edge of my working-table, careful not to disturb anything on it. He gazed down at me, and when I made myself look up, I could not read his expression.

"Tell me truly," Jacob said. "If I go to Vystrana without you—with travel time, it will take the better part of a year. What will you do?"

Go mad in white linen . . . but I would not say that to him. Though true, it was not the sort of answer he deserved. I considered it for a moment, then said, "I would likely visit my family, at least to start. I would rather be in the countryside than engaging in empty rounds about Society. Here, I would have to endure too much gossip and false sympathy, and I fear I would hit someone and make a true disgrace of myself."

The corner of Jacob's mouth quirked. "And then?"

"In truth? I don't know. Go to the coast, perhaps, or see if I might convince you to finance a trip for me somewhere foreign. People would think it less strange if I went to a spa for my health. But that would not keep me occupied; it would just remove my boredom to somewhere further from the public eye."

"Are you that bored?"

I met his gaze directly. "You have no idea. At least when men visit with friends, it is acceptable for them to talk about more than fashion and perhaps the occasional silly novel. I cannot talk to ladies about the latest lectures at the Philosophers' Colloquium, and men will not include me in their conversations. You allow me to read whatever I wish, and that spares my sanity. But books alone cannot keep me company for a year."

He absorbed this, then nodded. "Very well. I've listened to your side. Will you hear mine?"

"I owe you at least that much."

His eyes roved across the ordered ranks of my sparklings as he spoke. "You would be thought odd for going on an expedition to Vystrana; I would be thought a monster. I care little for those who would tell me I should keep my wife in line; I have not made a habit of keeping you on a leash. But there are others who would ask what sort of gentleman would subject his wife to such hardship."

"Even if your wife volunteered for it?"

"That does not enter into it. It is my duty to protect you and keep you safe. Protection and safety do not include ventures of this sort."

I folded my hands into my lap, noting irrelevantly that I had begun biting my nails again. It was a habit I have spent my life trying and failing to break. "Then the question, I suppose, is how much those criticisms concern you."

"No."

I glanced up at Jacob again, and saw the quirk in his mouth grow to a rueful smile.

"The question," he said, "is whether that concern is important enough to warrant making my wife miserable."

Hardly daring to breathe, I waited for him to go on. Whatever else he might say, I knew one thing: that I had been luckier than I knew, the day Andrew invited me to go with him to the king's menagerie. How many other gentlemen would even have made such a statement?

Jacob's hazel eyes fixed on me, and then he shook his head. My heart sank, though I tried not to show it.

"I am the greatest lunatic in Scirland," he said, "but I cannot bear to deny you. Not with you looking at me like that."

His words took a moment to sink in, so convinced was I that I had lost my case. "You mean—"

Jacob held up a cautioning hand. "I mean that I will write to Hilford. The expedition is his; I can't go adding people on my own whim. But yes, Isabella—I mean that *I*, at least, will not stand in your way. On the condition—!" His words broke off as I surged to my feet and threw my arms about him. "On the condition," he continued when I released him enough to breathe, "that you promise me, no mad antics. No putting yourself in the path of a hungry wolf-drake. Nothing that will make me regret saying this today."

"I promise to try and keep myself safe."

"That isn't quite the same thing, you know," he said, but my kiss stopped any other objections he might have had.

SIX

Lord Hilford's visit — A vow never to be birdbrained — Preparations for departure

Trrue to his word, Jacob wrote to Lord Hilford that very afternoon. This began a week of nervous waiting, wherein I replayed every interaction I had ever had with the earl. He seemed to tolerate, even appreciate, the company of his granddaughter Natalie, who had something of a mad streak in her; surely that boded well for my own chances? But I was not family—and so my thoughts went, round and round, dragging up every factor, every ounce of information that might influence his decision.

When a letter came notifying us that he would call at our house on his way to Falchester in a week's time, I did not know what to make of it. Jacob gave me the letter to read, and I pored over every word, but it said nothing of Jacob's unusual request. Was he favorably inclined to it? Unfavorably? Had he even received our letter? I dreaded that last prospect; how awkward it would be to bring it up if he had no prior warning!

Nonetheless, he was coming, and we had to prepare. I made certain the house was ready to receive its visitor, devoting far more of my time and energy to domestic tasks than I ordinarily did. (I fear I drove the maids quite to distraction with my interference.) I carefully selected the gown I would wear, when the time came. I reminded myself to be on my best behaviour.

I tried not to invent contingency plans for what I would do if he said no. That way lay all manner of schemes that would turn my husband's hair grey with fright.

Lord Hilford arrived in a comfortable carriage pulled by a splendid pair of matched greys. I praised the horses as he entered our house, using it as a source of comfortable small talk while we were out in public places. It helped me to hide my nerves.

"You are here to see my husband, I imagine?" I said when he was done handing his hat and gloves to the footman.

"Hmmm," the earl said. "I rather think I had better speak with you both."

This made my heart skip a beat. "Please, have a seat in the drawing room," I said, indicating the way, as if he could somehow lose his orientation in our smallish front hall. "Jacob will be down in a moment. Would you like tea?"

Fortunately my husband was prompt; I might have died of nerves else. He greeted Lord Hilford, and when everyone was settled in with tea and biscuits, the earl cut straight to his point.

"I received your letter, Camherst," he said to Jacob, "and read it over two or three times. Rather surprising to me, you must understand. Eventually I decided the only sensible way to handle it was to come here and speak to you in person—you and your wife both. If you don't mind?"

Jacob made sounds of demurral, and as he did so, I realized Lord Hilford was asking permission to question me directly. I sat bolt upright in my chair as the earl turned his sharp-eyed attention to me.

"Mrs. Camherst," he said. His booming voice was almost too much for our small drawing room. "Let me see if I understand. You wish to accompany us to Vystrana, where you imagine you will keep your husband's notes—or mine as well; the letter was a trifle unclear—provide us with accurate drawings, and otherwise be some manner of assistant to us in our studies and daily living?"

I had expected this question, and so even under his gimlet eye, I did not squirm. "Yes, my lord."

"Your husband's a sensible enough fellow. I can't imagine he's neglected to describe to you the sorts of hardships and difficulties we're likely to suffer."

"I am well aware of them, my lord. Both from my husband, and from my own reading."

He took a sip of tea. It hid his lower face from me momentarily, which I think might have been his intent; I could not tell what he thought of my statement. "You are a well-read woman, I take it."

"As much as I can be."

"Hmmm. I'll want to pick your brain on that more later. In the meantime, though—you know the difficulties, apparently in good detail, and despite that, you still wish to be a part of the expedition."

There was no room for prevarication, for the kinds of social niceties that might have softened the blunter edges of my desire. All I could do was say, "Yes, I do."

He eyed me for several heartbeats. I fought not to reach for my tea and avoid his gaze thereby.

"Well," Lord Hilford said abruptly, turning to Jacob, "that seems clear enough. Either she's birdbrained *and* you failed to make the situation clear to her—in which case she'll be entirely your problem; I wash my hands of her—or she knows precisely what she's letting herself in for. At the very least, she might be a civilizing influence. Might even be of some use—in which case I take full credit for bringing her along, and commandeer her services in filing my own notes. I stuff them in a box most days; makes for a devil of a time finding anything when I need it."

I vowed on the spot to show no behaviour that might possibly be construed as birdbrained, from then until the end of time.

"You—you're certain?" Jacob stammered, glancing from me to Lord Hilford and back again.

"Don't go questioning me, Camherst, unless you want me re-considering my decision. Make sure she knows what she needs to *before* we get to Vystrana; fat lot of use she'll be filing notes if she can't tell a hatchling from a lizard. But I doubt that will be a problem." Lord Hilford's eyes twinkled at me, so briefly I might have imagined it.

We rushed to thank him, but he waved it all off with one hand. "My plans are all being turned on their heads anyway; what's one more change?"

"What do you mean?" Jacob asked.

Lord Hilford's good humour was overshadowed by a scowl. "Politics. The tsar of Bulskevo has decided again that he doesn't like Scirlings. Which is a problem, when we're dependent on him for iron . . . but that is neither here nor there. What matters is that the boyar of Ziveyjak—which is where I captured that albino runt—is a boot-licking court toady who won't do anything the tsar might frown at. So I've been refused permission to return to Ziveyjak next year."

"Oh no!" I said, dismayed. "Will the expedition be delayed, then?"

"And wait for the tsar to like us again? He'd change his mind before I got halfway to Vystrana. Damned temperamental man—my apologies, Mrs. Camherst." Lord Hilford waved one hand, dismissing the tsar. "No, I've found a new location. Stroke of luck, actually; a Chiavoran colleague of mine put me in touch with a Vystrani fellow called Jindrik Gritelkin, who went to university in Trinque-Liranz. Gritelkin has invited us to come to his village."

"Doesn't *his* boyar mind?" Jacob asked.

Lord Hilford shook his head. "Not all of them swear off contact with foreigners every time the tsar gets up on the wrong side of the bed. And Gritelkin's a razesh—sort of a local agent for the boyar. He can settle things for us. But we'll have time enough to talk about this later. It's late in the day; I should look into finding a hotel—" We pressed him to stay, and he acquiesced. I summoned servants to get him situated in a guest room, and told the cook to plan for one extra at dinner.

That was the first of several dinners Maxwell Oscott took at our house during the months we spent preparing for the Vystrani expedition. Whether he dined at our house, or we at his, we talked of little else, and the earl made good on his promise (or perhaps threat) to pick my brain about my readings. Initially I tried to gloss over details, downplaying my interest into something a little more acceptable, but he had a knack for getting people to talk, and in truth—as perceptive readers may have noticed—I have a difficult time resisting the chance to discuss my passions. The incident with the wolf-drake I successfully kept to myself, but before that first night was out, Lord Hilford knew about both my childhood interest in Sir Richard Edgeworth's work and my recent endeavours on the Great Sparkling Inquiry. He spoke approvingly of my anatomical drawings, and showed particular engagement with my notion that sparklings were not insects, but diminutive wyvern cousins. We argued the point with great enthusiasm through the following months.

I did not get on so well with Thomas Wilker, Lord Hilford's assistant and protégé. To be honest, we rather scorned each other. Mr. Wilker tried very hard, but with imperfect success, to hide the Niddey accent of his birth; he was the son of a quarryman who used to supply Lord Hilford with fossils of strange animals, and I thought him a bit of a tufthunter, eager to attach himself to a man who could help him climb into Society. For his own part, he did not think much of my scant learning, and clearly only forebore to complain out of deference to his patron's decision.

Fortunately, he and I were rarely in each other's company, as our spheres of preparation for the expedition were entirely separate.

Mr. Wilker and Lord Hilford undertook the work of planning the expedition itself, arranging transportation, lodgings, scientific equipment, and permissions from a variety of foreign officials. To me fell the duty of renting out our Pasterway house, stabling our horses, and arranging references for the servants who would not stay on. Jacob's task was a sobering one: he set his business affairs in order, which included meeting with his solicitor to make certain his will was prepared. The perils we faced were unfortunately quite real.

By far the least pleasant aspect of our remaining time in Scirland, though, came from the society gossips.

Before the news became public, Jacob and I had a sober conversation about what we could expect by way of reaction from acquaintances and strangers alike.

"I don't particularly care what they say," I admitted to him one afternoon in late Fructis as we walked in the garden. "I have the chance to go abroad and see dragons; I do not think anything they say could steal that happiness from me."

Jacob sighed. "Isabella, my dear—I am sure it feels that way now, when you are to go see dragons, but do remember that we will be *returning* to Scirland when the expedition is done. If you snub society ladies now, you will have to face them again later."

"Perhaps I could bring back a dragon to frighten them with. Just a small one, nothing extravagant; Lord Hilford has caught them before."

"Isabella—"

I laughed and twirled a few steps down the path, arms wide in the sunlight. "Of course I'm not serious, dear. Where would we *keep* a dragon? In my sparkling shed? It would make a dreadful mess, and undo all my careful work."

Despite himself, Jacob laughed. "You're like a little girl who's been told for the first time that she may have a pony."

"Ponies!" I dismissed these with a snort. "Can ponies fly, or breathe particles of ice upon those who vex them? I think not. Ponies, indeed."

"Perhaps I shall tell the society gossips that you have become deranged," Jacob mused, "and that I am installing you in a sanatorium for your own safety. I'm sure they would believe that."

"Tell them I am deranged; tell them I am dead; tell them I have run off to be a dancing girl in Chiavora. I don't *care*."

Jacob paused to straighten a late rose I had bent in my exuberant passing. "We have not been married for so long; perhaps I can pass it off as an overly affectionate attachment to you, that I still cannot bear for you to be parted from my side." He paused for reflection, twirling between his fingers a blossom that had come off in his hand. "It would not be far from the truth."

I came back to his side and planted a kiss on his cheek. "No, I have it. I will put it about that I would not let you go because I do not trust you to be faithful away from me."

"Who would entice my eye to stray? There's a dearth of Chiavoran dancing girls in Vystrana."

"Then say I'm to keep you civilized. You needn't mention the drawings and suchlike at all. Say that, in addition to being gaptoothed, pockmarked, and weak-chinned, the Vystrani peasant girls haven't the slightest idea how to keep a gentleman in the style to which he is accustomed. I will be there to make certain they polish your shoes and don't brew tea out of your tobacco."

"What a pity it is that you haven't shown any interest in charitable work before now. You might be going to teach them their letters, or campaign for better working conditions."

"Only thirty sheep per shepherdess; any more is quite inhumane."

I pray you pardon me a moment of sentimentality when I say that I adored my husband's laugh. Light and melodious, it was all the better when I startled it out of him, and this may go some way to explaining why I so often tried to do so. Partly that was my own nature, of course—but who could fault me for indulging it when I loved its reward so much?

Jacob set his hands on my waist and spun me in the center of the path, so that my skirts swung out behind me and damaged the roses still further. "Civilization it shall be. *Do* try to keep quiet about the dragons, my dear. Talk to Miss Oscott of them if you must, but allow me the public pretense that we are being more well behaved."

I took especial care to maintain that pretense with my family— even with Andrew, who was only half joking when he asked whether Lord Hilford would notice if he clubbed Mr. Wilker over the head and took his place. Papa, I later learned, suspected much of the truth, but for Mama's sake we did not speak of it; she was concerned enough for my safety.

Having done so little traveling in my life, I imagined our luggage for the trip would be akin to that which I packed when Mama and I went to Falchester for my first Season, with fewer evening gowns and more in the way of practical wear. Foreign travel, for those who may not know, more closely resembles moving house. In addition to clothing, scientific equipment, and the materials for my sketches, we brought with us various accoutrements of our daily lives that we hoped would make our lives abroad more comfortable: saddles, lamps, writing desks, and one armchair which Lord Hilford apparently took with him wherever he went. I overheard him advising Jacob to bring with him a good supply of coffee—"As it can't be got for love or money in Vystrana, and the stuff they drink would be more suited to scouring rust from horse tack."

We journeyed together down to the coast at Sennsmouth: myself and Jacob, Lord Hilford and Mr. Wilker, and a variety of friends and relations, including Andrew. I had never been to the port city before, and much entertained my companions by exclaiming over all the new sights, of which the grandest by far was certainly our steamship, the *Magnolia*.

It was a measure of Lord Hilford's wealth that we would travel in such style. When I was born, everyone assumed steam engines would be ubiquitous in the future; but that was before the iron deposits in Scirland were found to be all but exhausted. Coal we still had in abundance, but to build the machines themselves, we had to engage in expensive trade with other lands—or, often as not, try to colonize them, which was the origin of our misadventures in Eriga and elsewhere. To travel in a steamship was, in those days, still a rare and wondrous thing.

Rare and wondrous—and new enough that it was quite prone to trouble. The *Magnolia* carried sails, for use if the engine should fail us. "Just as ancient ships sometimes carried oars," Mr. Wilker said. He had what I saw as a regrettable habit of showing off his learning. "In case the wind should fail."

"We had best hope the engine and wind don't fail together," Jacob said. "I don't see oars anywhere."

Our route would take us around the Cape of De Vrest and through the Sea of Alsukir to the port of Trinque-Liranz in Chiavora, from which we would go north into the Vystrani highlands. Andrew came on board to help settle me in the cabin I would share with Jacob, which lay in the forward part of the ship, along the starboard side. "I hope you aren't prone to seasickness," he said, peering out the porthole that was the room's only source of natural light.

"How should I know whether I am or not?" I replied, hanging a few of my dresses in the tiny wardrobe. "I've never been to sea before."

Andrew had gone to Thiessin last year, as a reward for completing university at last. "I advise not being seasick, if you can avoid it. Not a pleasant experience."

While he continued to potter about the small room, peering into the ingenious little cabinets with which its designers had supplied it, I sank onto one of the two narrow beds. When at length Andrew noticed me sitting there—when he noticed the expression on my face—he became awkward. "Buck up, old girl; seasickness isn't *that* bad."

I took a steadying breath, not certain whether it was tears or a hysterical laugh I was trying to hold back. "Oh, it isn't that. A touch of nerves, nothing more. And a realization that I will not see anything familiar for some time—not my house, not my family, not Scirland itself."

He patted my shoulder. "You'll have Camherst, won't you? Surely that counts for something. I'm sure he'll take care of you."

How could I have explained it to him? My fear was not that I would not be taken care of; it was that I would *need* to be. That my inexperience, my provincial upbringing, would render me little more than a child who had somehow convinced her parents to bring her along to an event she would not enjoy in the slightest. Oh, yes, I believed I would enjoy dragons—but in between me and the great beasts lay a tremendous number of things unknown, and therefore frightening.

This worry may sound ludicrous to those who know the later parts of my life's story, but there on that steamship, at the tender age of nineteen, it was a terrifying thought indeed.

Despite that terror, I took Andrew's hand in my own and squeezed it, making myself smile at him. "I'm sure. And just think of the stories I will have to tell when I return!"

We made a grand sight that sunset, steaming our way out of the harbor at a slow but deliberate pace. Andrew and various other well-wishers stood on the jetty that thrust out into the sea, from which they waved farewell. I waved in response until we drew far enough away that they retired back into Sennsmouth, vanishing among the houses; then I stood on the deck for some time more, watching Scirland dwindle steadily behind us. Around me the crew conducted their duties, and I tried to stay out of their way, until the light was quite dim and Jacob came to take me below.

PART TWO

*In which the expedition
arrives in Vystrana,
but faces difficulties
in commencing its work*

SEVEN

The journey to Vystrana — My first wild dragon — Arrival in Drustanev — A chance to depart

Although it is hard to find now, I encourage any youngsters reading this—by which I mean anyone under the age of forty—to seek out a copy of my first publication, *A Journey to the Mountains of Vystrana*. Not for reasons of quality; it's an insipid little thing, produced because at the time travel writing was considered a suitable genre for young ladies' pens. But that book, which contains a much fuller account of our travel from Scirland to Vystrana, is a window into a time all but forgotten now, in this age of railways, fast ships, and caeligers.

You cannot conceive, if you are young, the slowness and difficulty of travel back then. Nor, I imagine, do you want to; this modern speed has brought many improvements for commerce, diplomacy, and learning, and more. And yet, there is a part of me that misses the old way. Call it an old woman's nostalgia if you like, but our journey to Vystrana served as a useful transition, a separation from the young woman I had been in Scirland, and a preparation for the woman I would be on the expedition. Had it been possible for me to arrive quickly in Vystrana, I think I would not have been ready when I did so.

I believed myself to be ready then; now, with the hindsight brought by greater age, I see myself for the naive and inexperienced young woman I was. We all begin in such a manner, though. There is no quick route to experience.

From our landing in Trinque-Liranz we went upriver to San-verio, where we attached ourselves to a trio of carters taking supplies across the nearby border into Vystrana. For a fee, they packed their wagons high with our belongings, and so we began our climb into the mountains.

It was my first real taste of hardship, though by the standards of such a word, my sufferings were mild indeed. The village we aimed for was very isolated, even for Vystrana; the carters only made the journey because it was more convenient for the local boyar to be supplied from Sanverio than anywhere else. Once or twice we managed beds in a farmhouse, but more often than not we slept in tents, on folding cots that kept us off the ground, but had nothing else to recommend them.

So determined was I not to complain that I did not let myself think of the day when this stage would end. It therefore came as a shock to me one morning when Lord Hilford said, "We should make it there today, if this weather holds."

Blinking in the early sunlight, I said, "Make it where?"

He smiled at me. "The village of Drustanev. Our destination, Mrs. Camherst."

After so much time on the sea and the road, I could hardly believe we would be stopping at last. We loaded ourselves onto the wagons in a hurry, and set out with more energy than usual.

I studied the landscape around me with a newly curious eye. It was uneven territory, valleys of spruce and fir alternating with gentle slopes of grass and windswept ridges of limestone and lichen. Even with the cloudless sky, the air was no more than pleasantly warm. I wondered how far we had risen from the coast. High above I saw a bird floating lazily on the winds; with no point of reference, I could not be sure how large it was, but I rather thought it must be some breed of eagle. Certainly it was not a dragon, though I kept my eyes eagerly open for one.

The weather held fine for most of the morning, but as the afternoon drew on, clouds grew on the mountaintops and rolled in our direction. One of the carters shot at a wolf that was following us too closely, scaring it off. He and his fellows held a brief conversation (in the impenetrable dialect of their native region, not the more refined Chiavoran the rest of us knew), and decided to press on; they judged this a bad area to camp in, even if it meant a wetting before we arrived in Drustanev.

As the wind picked up, I tied my bonnet more firmly to my head. The clouds seemed very low. I had a book out which I had been attempting to read, and for a time I tried to go on doing so, bracing my forearms along the edges of the pages to keep them from flapping about. From the wagon bench at my side, though, Jacob nudged me and said, "You might want to put that away. I fear it will rain soon."

I sighed, but he was right. Closing the book, I turned in my seat and reached over the back of the wagon bench to stow it in a pack that would all too soon prove whether it was as waterproof as advertised or not.

As I did so, a gust of shockingly cold air pulled at my sleeves, and ice stung my face. Wondering if we were in danger of hail, I looked up.

I have little recollection of the next several seconds. Just a moment of frozen staring, and then—with no transition—my voice shrieking "*Get down!*" as I wrapped my arms around my husband and dragged him forward, off the wagon bench.

Two other screams overlaid my own. One, high-pitched and awful, came from our driver as claws snagged him off the wagon and into the air. The other, lower but even more terrible, came from above, as the dragon plummeted from the clouds and raked over our heads.

Jacob and I landed in the wagon traces, the reins and harness tangling our limbs while the horses shied and whinnied their terror. Being on the outside, I tumbled free first, and cried out to see the wagon lurching forward, my husband still caught within. He fell a moment later, directly beneath the wagon, and the wheels passed close enough to leave a track across his coat.

I crawled toward him, hearing shouts from all around us. Frantic glances skyward showed me nothing; the dragon had vanished again. From the slope ahead, though, came the agonized groans of our driver. Just as I reached Jacob, a loud noise cracked the air: a gunshot, as one of the other drivers fired off the rifle he carried against highwaymen or wild animals.

Wild animals. I had not, until that moment, put dragons in that class. I had thought them something apart.

"Stay down, Isabella," Jacob said, shielding me with his own body. I crouched in his shadow, and realized quite irrelevantly that my bonnet had gone astray. The wind was very cold in my hair.

A great flapping, as of sails: the dragon, though we could not see it. Looking under Jacob's arm, I saw Lord Hilford put out a hand and stop his driver, who would have fired at the sound. With nothing to see, there was no point in wasting the round.

Then suddenly there was something to see. Several shots rang out, and I swallowed the protest that tried to leap free of me. This was no vulnerable runt in a menagerie. The dragon was huge, its wingspan far larger than a wagon, with stone-grey hide and wings that kicked up dust with every beat. The guns fired, and the beast made a dreadful noise, aborting its stoop on us and climbing rapidly for the sky. Clouds enveloped it once more, and we waited.

Waited, and waited, until at last Lord Hilford sighed. "I think it's gone."

Jacob helped me to my feet. My bonnet was caught in a low, scrubby bush; I retrieved it and smoothed it out with shaking hands while Mr. Wilker and one of the other men went after the driver the dragon had seized. Its claws had left great gashes in his back and chest, but the worst injury was to his legs, which had broken badly when he fell. Blood seeped out where the bones had breached the skin. If I had not seen a similar injury once to a horse, I might have fainted.

"Make room for him in one of the wagons," Lord Hilford said in Chiavoran, then turned to me. "Mrs. Camherst, if you would—in my green chest there should be some laudanum. Black bottle, in the top rack."

I crammed my bonnet back onto my head and did as he asked. There were bits of grit and rock in my palms, which I picked out as I went, and I had torn my skirt, but seeing the driver, I was acutely aware of how lucky Jacob and I had been. Had I not seen the dragon coming . . .

Rain began to fall. Mr. Wilker bound up our driver's wounds as best he could. We needed to get him to shelter, but first there was his cart to deal with; the horses had quite understandably bolted at the approach of the dragon. They had both gone lame, and the wagon had overturned, spilling our trunks onto the ground and knocking one of them open. Working together, the men retrieved everything while I created a makeshift canopy to keep the rain off the injured man. The laudanum, fortunately, put him into a shallow sleep, and he did no more than moan in protest when we moved onward and the road jolted him where he lay.

In this manner, bedraggled and scarred, we arrived in the village of Drustanev.

I did not see much at first of the building that was to be our home for the next several months. I accompanied the injured driver as some locals carried him inside, and tried to explain in my very bad Vystrani what had happened. I expect that little of what I said even registered on them, between my limited vocabulary, appalling accent, and atrocious grammar, but one thing I did notice: the villagers did not seem surprised to see his wounds. No one could have mistaken them for anything other than dragon-inflicted, even without me repeating that one word over and over again—*balaur, balaur*—and they did not seem surprised.

Relatively approachable, Lord Hilford had called the Vystrani dragons, that first evening at Renwick's when I heard of his expedition. It was not the phrase I would have chosen.

A young woman appeared out of nowhere at my elbow, tugging me away from the men now swarming through the downstairs of the building. Using a flood of incomprehensible Vystrani, she seemed to be trying to convince me to sit down in a quiet place and have vapors over my misfortune. I'm afraid I gravely disappointed her by haring off into the rain, my already-ruined bonnet listing to one side on my head, to make certain our things were being brought inside. It seemed a minor thing to worry about, with howls emanating from a back room where they were trying to set the driver's broken legs, but I was no use there, and could not abide sitting around and doing nothing.

My efforts averted a buildup of trunks in the front hall that would have made passage impossible. By repeating those few parts of my Vystrani vocabulary that were relevant to the situation, accompanied by much gesticulation, I managed to get some of the local servants to shunt our luggage upstairs, to the rooms we would sleep in. Jacob found me in the midst of this, and insisted on examining me for injuries. He exclaimed over my skinned palms and had Mr. Wilker bind them up, although by then they were hardly bleeding at all. For my own part, I conducted a similar examination of Jacob, and was relieved to find that his coat might have been badly torn along the back, but his skin was nothing more than scratched. An inch less into our fall, and the dragon would have caught him like the driver.

The noise in the back room subsided at last, and Lord Hilford appeared, weary and bloodstained. "He's asleep again," the earl said. "Whether he'll survive . . . well, we shall see. Come." We followed him obediently, Jacob, Mr. Wilker, and myself, like very lost and unnerved ducklings, into a room off the front hall.

Someone had made an effort to transform this dark-paneled, low-ceilinged chamber into a sitting room, though whoever had done so appeared to have been operating from a thirdhand description of Scirling customs. There were couches at least, even if they were more like wooden benches with cushions placed along the seat and back, but we sank onto them gratefully. From somewhere Lord Hilford produced a bottle, and there were clay tumblers on a nearby table; he poured a small amount of brandy into four of these and passed them around, even to me. I had not tasted brandy since the physician sewed me up after the wolf-drake, and had to force myself to take a sip, momentarily overwhelmed by the memory.

As the warmth traveled through me, dispelling the chill of the rain, Lord Hilford said heavily, "I am so very sorry, Mrs. Camherst."

I looked up at him. "Sorry? Why to me, more than another?"

"I know I spoke to you of the dangers of this expedition, but I did not anticipate anything like this."

"What the devil got into that thing?" Mr. Wilker demanded, and got a reproving look from Jacob for his language.

"My question exactly," I said, "if in rather more vivid terms than I am permitted to use. I was not under the impression that rock-wyrms tended to attack people."

Lord Hilford scowled and knocked back the remainder of his brandy. "They don't."

"Then I don't blame you for failing to warn me of a danger you could not have expected," I told him. My fingers curled around the clay mug. "By all means, let us be sorry for the poor driver, and pray for his recovery. But I am not the one injured, Lord Hilford; I do not need your apology."

It sounded well, and I meant it as much as I could. Under no circumstances was I going to begin by letting anyone think I would wilt at the first hint of peril. Such wilting could be done later, when there was no one present to see.

I was rewarded with a rueful smile from the earl. "You will tarnish my reputation as a gentleman, Mrs. Camherst, with such gallant courage as that."

"We still have Mr. Wilker's question to answer," I said. It was easier to think of the dragon's attack as a puzzle in need of solving; that gave me something to focus on. "What could provoke such behaviour? It can't have been rabid."

Jacob laid one hand on my forearm. "Isabella, we might leave such questions until morning. Now is not a suitable time."

"If by 'not suitable' you mean that we don't have any answers," Lord Hilford said. He put his empty tumbler down on the scarred surface of the side table. "Or at least I don't. Perhaps the excitement rattled my brains loose, but that was quite unlike anything I have seen from a rock-wyrm before, and I've been close to them many a time. I shall have to ponder it. At any rate, this is the house where we are to be staying; our luggage should be around here somewhere . . ." He stared about the ill-lit room as if the trunks might be lost in the shadows.

"Upstairs," I said. When I rose to my feet, I was pleased to find my knees steady. I had feared the moment of sitting and relative relaxation would have persuaded them to give out. "Though where precisely I sent them, we must discover."

We ascended the stairs in a damp herd, all bumbling against one another in the dark and cramped stairwell. The boards creaked alarmingly beneath my feet, let alone Lord Hilford's,

DRUSTANEV

but held. Once in the corridor above we found that our luggage had gotten all mixed up, despite the tags with our names. By now, however, the hour was grown late enough that we did not care. We pulled out the valises that contained our traveling gear, allocated rooms, and fell into bed with hardly a pause to change out of our wet clothes.

All through the night, I dreamt of the dragon, and fell again and again to the hard Vystrani soil, just out of the range of its claws.

When I awoke the next morning, Jacob was already gone. Morning sunlight showed me the room in better detail than I had seen the previous night, disclosing a bleak and cheerless place. The walls, ceiling, and floor were all of that same dark wood; I stretched out one hand from where I lay and found it was painted with a kind of resin that presumably sealed it against weathering. The ceiling beams were low and heavy, giving the room a claustrophobic feel. Our furniture consisted of a bed without posters or canopy, a wardrobe, a dressing table with a mirror, and nothing else.

The air outside my coverlet was quite chill, as I discovered when I left the bed. Shivering, I made a quick search and pulled on my dressing robe and slippers. These warmed me enough that I could search more thoroughly for a trunk with suitable clothing in it. The previous day's dress was piled on the floor, stained, torn, and utterly beyond repair.

I was lucky enough to find one of the plain, sturdy dresses I had commissioned before leaving Scirland, with buttons I could reach on my own. Just as I finished with the last of them, the door creaked open, and the young woman from the night before poked her head tentatively in.

She was tall and of that build we so politely call "strapping" and applaud when found in peasant folk, with strong features and a wealth of dark hair. She also, at that moment, had an alarmed expression, apparently provoked by the sight of me dressing myself without aid.

From the words that poured out of her mouth, I gathered that she was supposed to be my lady's maid. I had been afraid of that. She would need to be educated in her duties, starting with the purchase of a bell I could use to summon her when I awoke. I laid that aside for the moment, however, and held up my hand to silence her.

When she subsided, I asked, *"Tcha prodvyr e straiz?"* *What is your name?*—or at least, that is what I hoped I had said.

"Dagmira," she replied.

"Dagmira," I said. *"Isabella Camherst eiy. Zhe Mrs. Camherst tchi vek ahlych."* This was a line I had rehearsed many times, until I was certain I pronounced it at least as well as our Chiavoran drivers did. *I am Isabella Camherst. You will call me Mrs. Camherst.* If I was to train this young woman to be my lady's maid, then we would have to start by establishing boundaries. I was her employer, not a child to be chivvied around. Proper respect was essential.

I did not want to reflect that a Vystrani child would know more of the area and local customs than I did, let alone the language.

For my next display of linguistic accomplishment, I asked Dagmira where my husband had gone, and received in return a second flood of words too quick to comprehend. Another attempt, this time prefaced by *setkasti, setkasti—slower, slower—*rewarded me with a more suitable pace, but still far too many words I did not understand. Jacob had gone out; no more could I discern.

Frustrated by this, I gave Dagmira broken instructions to bring to that room all the trunks with mine or Jacob's name on them, and to remove all those with Lord Hilford's or Mr. Wilker's, then went downstairs. The kitchen was cold and empty, the only smell a lingering one of blood from the doctoring of the driver. It drove out any thought I had for breakfast.

Compared with the dank interior of the house, the street outside (if I could dignify the hard-packed dirt path with such a grand name) was painfully bright. I squinted and shielded my eyes until they adjusted. In the distance, I could hear voices chattering in fluent Vystrani, but none were familiar to me.

The exterior of the house was not much more promising. Weather had faded the dark resin to more of a golden color, but it was bereft of decoration, showing just bare planks, broken here and there by narrow windows, and capped by a steeply sloping thatched roof. The bedroom had not exhibited such an angle; there must have been attic space above us. A glance around showed me there were few houses nearby, and those downslope; they appeared to be single story, apart from the presumed attics. Our lodging appeared to be the best Drustanev had to offer.

The path led downward to the rest of the village. Descending, I saw that most of the houses, unlike our own, had low fences enclosing geese-filled yards. Women stood at the gates, spinning thread and chatting with one another, not bothering to disguise the way they watched me. I smiled pleasantly at them as I passed, but my attention was mostly on the familiar wagons drawn up around the village well, with one of our Chiavoran drivers fixing a horse into harness. "Are you leaving so soon?" I asked him, a little surprised.

He glanced over his shoulder at one of the houses. "Soon as they bring Mingelo out. We have to go on to the boyar's lodge."

I knew they still needed to deliver their cargo, but Mingelo was the injured man. "Oh, surely it would be kinder to leave him here to heal, rather than subject him to such a journey."

The driver spat into the dirt, unconcerned with propriety. "They say there's a doctor at the boyar's house. Chiavoran. Better than some Vystrani peasant any day."

Even allowing for partisan national pride, I had to admit his assessment was probably fair; surely the boyar's man would be better educated than the village bonesetter. I pitied Mingelo, though, having to endure the trip.

Jacob found me shortly after that. He, too, had apparently dug clothing out of a chest in random haste; his suit was rather finer than the situation called for. "Isabella, there you are," he said, as if I had been the one to vanish so early this morning. "The drivers have to continue on to the boyar's lodge, but after that, they're going back to Chiavora. You—"

I stopped him with a hand on his wrist, very aware of Vystrani eyes on us. "Please don't," I said in a soft voice, so no one could eavesdrop, even if they spoke Scirling. "Don't ask it of me. You know I will not go, and I don't want to argue in front of these strangers."

His hazel eyes searched mine. The mountain wind disarranged his hair, adding a touch of distress I would have found charming under other circumstances. Only then did it occur to me that I had left without so much as brushing my own, let alone pinning it up. What sort of image was I presenting now, argument or no argument?

Perhaps my own distress charmed him. Jacob sighed, though the worry did not leave his eyes. "Can I at least ask you to keep close to home for now? Hilford is asking questions of the village leader—what's going on with the dragons, and where Gritelkin is. Until we have that settled, please, behave yourself."

I resented the implication that I was misbehaving already, but that faded next to other concerns. I had assumed that Jindrik

Gritelkin, Lord Hilford's local contact, was one of the men rushing about last night. "He's not here?"

"No, he isn't. Will you go back to the house?"

The house, where I would have to face the incomprehensible
Dagmira. "Yes, dear. Please let me know what's going on, when
you can. And what we are supposed to do for food."

"There should be a cook; that's another thing Hilford's asking
about. I think." Jacob tried to smooth his hair back down, only to
have it blown astray again by the wind. "I will arrange for something."

I climbed the stony path back toward our borrowed house,
resolutely not looking back toward the Chiavoran wagons, and
my chance to depart.

EIGHT

An introduction to Drustanev — Mr. Gritelkin's absence —
We attempt to proceed

I have written before about Drustanev, in *A Journey to the Mountains of Vystrana*. If you should happen to own a copy, though, or are intending to buy one (as I encouraged before), I beg you not to pay any attention to what I said there concerning the village, or indeed the Vystrani people as a whole.

The words I wrote then heartily embarrass me now. I was attempting, against my inclination, to conform to the expectations of travel writing, as practiced by young ladies at the time. It is a worse piece of drivel than Mr. Condale's *Wanderings in Central Anthiope*, inspired more by the theatrical convention of colorful, semiprophetic Vystrani characters than by the people I knew in Drustanev. To hear that book tell of it, Vystrana is a land of wailing fiddles, flashing-eyed women, and sweet, strong wines.

Which is to say, a land of the most tedious cliches. I drank more tea in Vystrana than wine, heard fiddles rarely, and never once saw Dagmira's eyes emit anything resembling a flash. You would be better served to read a history book, which will explain to you the many threads woven into the fabric of that nation. The position of their mountains, nearly straddling the neck of Anthiope, has brought most of the peoples on this continent trampling past at one time or another: Chiavorans, Eiversch, Akhians, Bulskoi, and more—those last ruling Vystrana as a client-state for sixty years before our arrival. But those influences have remained largely in the valleys and lowlands, trickling up only piecemeal to the shepherds and hunters in the mountains, where an intense Vystrani identity holds strong.

Young ladies are also expected to wax rhapsodic about the charms of the places they visit. Men, when they write about their travels, are permitted to complain, and to assert the natural superiority of their homelands. While I am relieved that my sex forestalled me from committing to print any sins of the latter sort, I must take this opportunity to say what I could not admit then:

I hated Drustanev.

Not the people; though I rarely understood and often resented them, in the end I am grateful for all of their aid, and their forbearance in permitting us to come among them. And there were points at which the mountains touched my heart with their beauty. But I often detested my physical circumstances, and have never felt the slightest urge to return.

Some of it was a simple matter of climate. The astute among you will have noticed that almost all of my expeditions have been to the warmer regions of the world: Akhia, the Broken Sea, and so forth. (The one notable exception apart from Vystrana—my flight into the Mrtyahaimas—was regrettably unavoidable.) My native companions in those places often expressed amazement at my willingness to endure the heat; in their experience, we Scirlings are a cold-adapted lot, who wither and die without regular applications of chilly fog. But I have always preferred warmth to cold, however excessive it may be, and so the mountains of Vystrana in springtime were hardly to my taste. The wondrous prospect of dragons had convinced me to overlook this impending misery, but now that I was subjected to it, I became very grumpy indeed.

For one thing, "springtime" to the Vystrani means something rather different than it does to us Scirlings. (Or to nearly anyone who may be reading this, be they Erigan or so on—unless I have acquired devotees in Vystrana, which I suppose is possible.) Spring, to the inhabitants of Drustanev, is the time when their lowland cousins drive the flocks of sheep up to the so-called middle pastures, near to the village. This usually happens in early Floris—not long before our arrival—and you may deduce the average local temperature from the fact that the villagers do not shear their sheep until later in the season.

At that time of year, snow still lingers in the steep valleys, especially where spruce and fir grow too thick for the sun to easily penetrate. Fresh falls may occur through the end of Floris or beginning of Graminis; our expedition saw flurries almost into Messis. I have had gentlemen—I use the term loosely—mock me for complaining of having been cold my entire time in Vystrana; to them I say, join me next summer in the deserts of Akhia, and we will see who fares better then. I may be elderly, and I certainly detest the cold, but that does not make me delicate.

Drustanev was a scattered place, houses planted in whatever spot offered enough level ground, with nothing one could particularly call a street running among them. Most appeared absurdly small beneath the tall peaks of their thatched roofs—tall because of the need to shed that abundant snow. The people were, and are, shepherds in the warmer months, and hunters in the winter; they trade fleeces, woven blankets, and hides to the lowlands.

The slopes around their villages have been shaped over time by the centuries of human habitation. Some have been cut into small terraces, suitable for local crops, but the primary alteration is that every ten years or so the men go out and set fire to the forests. I was not privileged to see this event—though I would have enjoyed it, I think, for the heat if nothing else—but I'm told the ashes enrich the soil, creating good pastureland for some time, and afterwards the kind of young forest that attracts deer. Sheep eat the grass, wolves eat the deer, and dragons eat everything that doesn't run away fast enough.

I detested the cold and the isolation, the repetitive food reeking of garlic—but the true root of my suffering was that I was in a foreign land, far from everything familiar, and I adapted very badly. You may think it would be romantic to run away there, like young Thomas in Mrs. Watree's insufferable three-volume novel, and for some of you it might be so; for me, it was not. Looking back on it now, my feelings have faded into a kind of gentle dislike that might almost be called fond, and so I will not harp too much on the misery I felt when I sat down to yet another sour-flavored soup, or looked out the (unglazed) window to see snow falling yet *again*. But it may help to understand a few of my subsequent actions if you bear in mind that I was going half mad in Drustanev, and dragons were the one thing that could distract me from it.

The house we were staying in belonged to Jindrik Gritelkin, who was of the class they call "razesh" in Vystrana—a sort of local agent to the boyar, as Lord Hilford had said. That was the definition of the term; its true meaning, particularly in this locale, took longer for us to discern. Much would have been clearer had Gritelkin been there, but he was not; and that absence was of primary concern on that first full day in Drustanev.

By the time Lord Hilford arrived at the house, with Jacob bearing a hamper of food for our lunch, I had given up on Vystrani and was repeating myself to Dagmira in Scirling, over and over again, louder with every repetition, as if volume would succeed where vocabulary did not. Our trunks were sorted, but the furniture in which to store their contents was lacking, and

Dagmira did not seem to understand this. Moreover, Lord Hilford's beloved chair, that he hauled with him wherever he went, had been damaged when the wagon overturned, and in my frustration I was about ready to scrap the thing for kindling.

Some of my irritation, though, came from hunger, and so I was relieved to find the earl unpacking sausages and bread rolls onto the kitchen table. "If you could acquire chairs, Mrs. Camherst," he said, "we can sit down and talk."

Three chairs and one stool were scrounged from other parts of the house, and we fell like ravening wolves upon our meal, Mr. Wilker nobly taking the stool.

"Gritelkin," Lord Hilford said after the first round of food had vanished, "is not here. He sent a message warning me that now was not an opportune time for research. But knowing how the international post can be, he also took the precaution of traveling to Sanverio in the hopes of intercepting us. It seems that both the message and Gritelkin went astray."

"Do you think he is all right?" I asked. In light of what had happened to our driver, my imagination was creating a variety of unfortunate scenarios for the absent Gritelkin.

"Likely so," the earl said. "The villagers don't see much cause for worry, at any rate. Odds are we missed him on our way into the highlands; it's easy enough to do." The optimism in his tone was only a little forced, but I wondered what he would have said, had a lady not been present.

"What of the dragon?" Mr. Wilker asked. "It's clear this isn't the first time such a thing has happened, but no one will talk to me about it."

Lord Hilford shook his head and reached for another roll. "Nor to me, but you are correct. There have been other attacks. I was able to winkle that much out of the village mayor, Urjash Mazhustin. Not so many that we must fear for our lives every time we step out the front door, but enough that he did not wish to speak of them to a foreigner."

This produced a quiet moment at the table. I wondered, but did not ask, whether anyone else was questioning whether we could even do what we had come for.

Jacob broke the silence. "Do we have any idea what might cause such a thing? Is there a disease akin to rabies that afflicts dragons? Or do they, like wolves, prey on human settlements when times become harsh?"

Lord Hilford's eyes gleamed. "That, Camherst, is an excellent set of questions to answer. I haven't the faintest clue, but we shall address ourselves to the matter forthwith."

I kept silent as our luncheon continued, attending to every word, but striving not to draw attention to myself. This, I remembered firmly, was to be my role here: facilitating their research from this home base in Drustanev. Since no one had yet tried to forbid us our work, the gentlemen were making plans to ask for maps and scout the surrounding area. Gritelkin should have had that information for us—for *them*, I reminded myself—but in his absence, the gentlemen were prepared to fend for themselves.

If you doubt the restraint of my intentions, please remember: I was only nineteen, and not yet Lady Trent, with all the associations that name conjures up. I did not yet even know that dragons were to be my lifelong career. I thought this Vystrani expedition was all I would ever have, and I was determined to do my best in the role allotted to me, as an efficient and effective helpmeet.

Which is a lofty way of saying that I spent the following week butting heads incessantly with Dagmira. My command of Vystrani improved rapidly, through sheer necessity and use, and while I will not claim my grammar was good, at least I acquired the words I needed. It did not help that Dagmira had a way of seizing my hands and kissing them both whenever I produced a new piece of vocabulary. In Vystrana this is a courtesy shown to those of higher rank, but the sardonic manner in which she did it was more like a Chiavoran woman throwing her hands into the air to praise the Lord for a miracle.

Some of the words I searched for, even Dagmira did not seem to know. It soon became apparent that what I considered to be a minimal amount of furniture, just barely enough for us to scrape by, was extravagant by the standards of rural Drustanev, and some of the pieces I wanted (such as a wardrobe, for hanging my dresses) existed nowhere in the village, or even in Dagmira's understanding. To obtain them would require that we have them brought up from Sanverio, which was not worth the time and expense. We would, I supposed with the long-suffering martyr-dom of a gentlewoman in rough circumstances, have to make do.

We were equally short of servants, though that, at least, I had expected. A shockingly pale boy named Iljish served the gentle-men, or rather Jacob and Mr. Wilker (with Mr. Wilker himself playing servant to the earl), and after the first day we had a placid cook whom nothing seemed to disturb, but Dagmira was the one I dealt with most, and I began to suspect that no facility with her language would aid me in breaking through the barrier of her manner. She was not imperturbable—far from it, with her hand-kissing and frequent diatribes too rapid for me to understand—but whether calm or distraught, she seemed utterly unaffected by anything I said to her. It is fortunate that I had not expected or hoped for my maid to be a source of companionship while in Vystrana; I would have been gravely disappointed.

I did not tell Jacob or the others how much of the work around our house I took on personally. The tedious work of cleaning and other such domestic tasks I left to Dagmira, of course, but anything relating to dragons I kept jealously to myself. In the ab-sence of proper shelving, I acquired a number of crates which sufficed for the purpose, and arranged those volumes we had brought with as much care as if I were organizing a grand library. Mr. Wilker had brought a large map of Vystrana and a smaller one of the mountains around Drustanev, which I tacked up onto the walls, bringing a spot of relative brightness into the otherwise grim house.

The sitting room became our working room, as we lacked any place more suitable. I confess I did not mind this, as it meant any conversations we had as a group were liable to be held in there, giving me more time in the one place I felt anything like at home.

As the days passed without sign of the absent Mr. Gritelkin, Jacob and Mr. Wilker began the task of mapping the surrounding countryside. They had not brought surveyor's tools, so their work was imprecise, but Mr. Wilker's childhood collecting fossils on Niddey meant he was more than accustomed to tramping about the countryside (albeit a flatter one) and mapping the area in his mind. A third sheet went up onto the walls, and was taken down each evening for me to add their findings to it, in my best draftswoman's hand. During the day, Lord Hilford paced in front of it, muttering often to himself.

The reason for his muttering was that without Gritelkin's guidance, they had very little notion of where to go looking for dragons. Oh, it was often possible to see them winging through the air; during my morning constitutional around the village, which I undertook so as to have *some* escape from the grim darkness of our house, I glimpsed the beasts gliding about the distant mountain peaks, long-winged shapes instantly distinguishable from those of raptors. But to see them more closely was a much greater challenge.

The Vystrani rock-wyrm, you see, prefers to lair in caves. (This, along with its stony grey hide, gives rise to the name.) Once such a lair is found, the natural historian may track the inhabitant's movements to see where it goes to feed, to water, to attract the attention of other dragons. He may, if he is bold, enter the lair during the dragon's absence to examine its castings and ordure. The lair is a nearly indispensible starting point for such work.

But first it must be found. And one of the reasons Vystrani rock-wyrms love to lair in caves is because they abound in the region, which is largely a karst landform. The primary function of the map my husband was making with Mr. Wilker was to mark the locations of caves. They discovered easily half a dozen each day, though many were too small for dragons; some they discovered on their way home, passing through an area they thought already mapped in its entirety. Jacob found one by the unfortunate expedient of falling down a loose, steep slope, fetching up on a ledge beneath an overhang of brambles that had previously obscured the cave's entrance from their eyes. Intrepid man that he was, he had Mr. Wilker lower down an unbroken lantern so that he could search the interior before finding a route back up. Deep gouges in the stone of the floor said a rock-wyrm had indeed once laired there, but the drift of dead leaves above those gouges betrayed how long ago that had been.

In the dark of night, when I lay on our lumpy, uncomfortable bed and tried to go to sleep, my mind entertained itself with ever wilder visions of how I might solve this puzzle on their behalf. It began with half-reasonable notions: I could sit with a sketch pad at a good vantage point and draw the movements of the dragons, to see if there was a pattern. (And pray none of the dragons spotted me and swooped in for an easy meal: this is why the notion was only half reasonable.) I could make my own search of the mountains, concentrating in areas Jacob and Mr. Wilker had not yet covered. (And pray I didn't fall as my husband had, break my leg, and lie helplessly until a dragon came looking for an easy meal.) I could walk empty-handed into the Vystrani wilderness, trusting to my childhood dream of dragons to guide my steps, as Panachai had been guided by the Lord in the desert, until fate led me to the perfect lair. (Where I would become an easy meal. The deranged side of my mind invented these ideas, but the practical side knew where they would end.)

Then again, I should not speak too readily of practicality. Although I did at last find a solution to our problems, the means by which I arrived at it was nearly as foolhardy as the worst of my dreams.

NINE

A shadow in the night — A foolish response — Staulerens in the mountains — The possibility of aid

There is a peculiarity that comes with living in a rural village, with which my readers—most of who, I imagine, enjoy the benefits of the electric lights that are nowadays everywhere—may be unfamiliar.

In the absence of artificial illumination, one's sleep divides into two distinct periods, with a gap of wakefulness during the dark hours of the night. Experiencing this in Drustanev, I initially attributed it to the lumpiness of the bed, the cold of the room, the general alienness of my surroundings, and so on; it took me some time to discover this was the usual way of things for the villagers. (Jacob's own habits took longer to shift, I think because of the strenuous exercise he received, climbing about the mountains.)

On the night I will now relate to you, I had not yet learned the reason for my wakefulness. All I knew was that I awoke, as I had for several nights running, and could not immediately go back to sleep. Rather than trouble Jacob with my tossing and turning, I rose from the bed, wrapped myself in a thick robe, and tiptoed out to occupy myself elsewhere until drowsiness returned.

It's an odd time, that period of midnight wakefulness, if you are not accustomed to it. The world seems dreamlike at that hour, and the mind subsides into a meditative state; my own thoughts seemed distant to me, like specimens upon the table of my shed back home. I considered reading, as I had the previous two nights, but felt guilty at using yet more candles—especially as I was beginning to suspect that striking a light only postponed my return to sleep.

I went into our workroom, it being the place I was least likely to disturb anyone, but instead of reading I unbarred the shutters and swung them open. Chill air struck my face, simultaneously bringing me further awake and yet strengthening the dreamlike nature of my thoughts. I felt pleasantly detached from myself and, sitting in the dark room, gave myself over to contemplation of the cloudless night sky.

I pray you forgive me if I temporarily postpone the true purpose of this narration to speak about that sky. In Falchester at that time, and in many places these days, the light from human habitation blots out a portion of the stars. *And?* you may ask, wondering why this matters. There are still plenty of stars to be seen. But I remember my childhood home in Tamshire, far enough from the nearest city to be spared this change, and I remember the sky above the mountains of Vystrana. You may think you see plenty of stars, friend reader, but you are wrong. Night is both blacker and more brilliant than you can imagine, and the sky a glory that puts to shame the most splendid jewels at Renwick's. Up in the mountains, where the air is crisper than the humid atmosphere of Scirland, I beheld a beauty I had never before seen.

I am not often a sentimental woman. But whether it was the splendor above me or my odd state of mind—likely both—I found myself nearly overwhelmed. At first I was entranced; then, feeling it was too much, I tore my eyes away and contemplated the far more mundane scene of sleeping Drustanev.

Mundane—except for the light that flared some distance away.

This was not the diamond wink of a star, but the warm, spilling glow of firelight. A door had opened in one of the houses, and two figures appeared in the gap. One, smaller, had the rounded silhouette of a woman, with a shawl thrown over her shoulders. The other was noticeably taller, with clothing in an unfamiliar style, and in the light from inside I saw something even more out of place: yellow hair, pulled back into a very un-Vystrani plait.

The fascination of the stars fled as I sat up, peering through the darkness toward those two. My first, absurd thought was that Mr. Wilker had taken a Drustanev woman for his lover—for lovers those two certainly were, by the way they embraced in the doorway, the man appearing as reluctant to depart as the woman was to let him go. But Mr. Wilker's hair was not so light, nor nearly long enough to braid. The man was no one I had seen in the village; and there were not so many people in Drustanev that I could have overlooked that blond head among them.

I became aware that I was now hanging halfway out the window, its sill pressing uncomfortably across my pelvis, as if closing the distance by two feet would allow me to make out more detail. My interest was not prurient; in fact, I wished the two would stop kissing and move apart so I could see the man's face. But the face was not what mattered, was it? His features would not tell me who he was. I hauled myself back inside, stuffed my feet into the muddy shoes I had left by the door, and slipped outside without a sound.

I would like to tell you I did this because of the dreamlike state brought on by waking in the middle of the night. It is a fine excuse, and there might be some truth in it. The bulk of the blame, however, must fall first upon my impatience, which chafed under the slowness of our research, and second upon my curiosity, which knew even fewer bounds than usual that night.

By the time I made it outside, the door had closed. I halted, clutching up my robe so it would not trail in the half-frozen mud, and soon spotted movement: the man, walking uphill out of the village. Very definitely not a local, and my curiosity grew stronger. I set off after him, darting from house to house so as to have some cover if he looked back.

How far did I intend to follow him? I cannot tell you. Eventually I would have had to ask myself that question, but before I reached that point of awareness, something took the decision entirely out of my hands.

The village was surrounded by a rocky, cleared area, and downhill there were fields, but the woods began not far up the slope. I had gone far enough into their depths to realize that a nightgown and robe do not make good attire for creeping after a man who obviously knows his way through such terrain, and to feel the chill biting at my stockingless ankles. Drustanev was obscured from sight by a screen of trees, and so was most of the light from the sky. I therefore had not the slightest bit of warning before an arm pinned me tight and a hand clamped down over my mouth.

I let out an immediate scream—insofar as I could, muffled as I was. It wasn't yet a cry for help; my thoughts had stopped dead with shock, leaving nothing but pure animal reflex. The man jerked me closer and hissed something unintelligible in my ear. I could not tell if it was Vystrani or some other language; it could have been Scirling, for all my brain was capable of comprehending it. I twisted, trying to get free, and now I *did* try to shout for help, with no particular success. The man snarled wordlessly, a sound of clear threat, and I stopped.

We had managed enough noise between the two of us, though, that my quarry heard and turned back. For the moment or two it took him to reach us, I thought he might prove my savior. As he drew near, unfortunately, my hopes were dashed. He spoke, not to me, but to my captor, and my captor answered him, in a language that was neither Scirling nor Vystrani. They clearly knew each other, and if they were not happy with each other, that still did not mean either one was on my side.

The dreamlike feeling vanished as if it never had been there at all. I stood rigid in my captor's grip, mind racing in useless little circles, like a mouse trapped under a basket. What would they do to me? Kidnapping, murder, an outrage upon my honor—all of those and worse seemed possible. I had faced a wolf-drake and a stooping dragon, but never a human who wished to do me harm, and the one part of my brain that remained detached enough to observe this scene was disgusted at how badly I was handling it.

I am grateful to that little corner of my brain, for it shamed me into better effort. I weighed my options, and found them sadly wanting. I had nothing of value with which to bribe the men into letting me go. We were far enough from the village that I couldn't be certain anyone would hear me scream, if my captor uncovered my mouth long enough for me to try. His grip was strong as a dragon's, and even if I somehow broke free of it, I wouldn't get very far, stumbling through the woods in my nightgown and robe. I found myself wishing, quite irrationally, that I had read more of Manda Lewis's sensational novels—as if those would provide anything like useful guidance in a situation like this.

Perhaps I would have been better off not weighing my options. They both dismayed and distracted me, such that I was taken by surprise when the hand over my mouth vanished, and the man I'd been pursuing stuffed some kind of rag between my teeth. I shouted as loudly as I could—which was not very—and squirmed more, but they soon had me bound, gagged, and blindfolded. Before the kerchief went over my eyes, I caught a glimpse of my captor, who proved to be another light-haired man, taller and more heavily built than the first. Once I was sufficiently trussed up, he threw me over his shoulder, and off we went.

So it was to be kidnapping, then. At least to begin with, and my blood ran cold at the possible sequel.

We soon achieved sufficient distance from the village (or rather *they* did, and I was carried along willy-nilly) that the men felt it was safe to talk at greater length. From the tones, it was clear that my captor, now my bearer, was seriously displeased with the man who had gone to visit his lover, and was reading him quite a lecture. And then, to my surprise, I realized that I was gathering this sense from more than just their tones: I could *understand* them.

Not well, mind you. If my Scirling readers have ever encountered a farmer from the more distant and rural parts of the country, they will have some sense of what I heard that night: familiar words, turned on their heads and decorated with oddly bent vowels. They were not speaking Scirling, of course. But their language, once recognized, was easier for me to grasp than Vystrani: it was an obscure dialect of Eiversch, which I had studied as a girl.

There is, of course, a world of difference between learning to sing a song or read a poem in Eiversch—or any other language—and translating the angry conversation of two strangers while you are slung over the shoulder of one, being carried through the midnight forests of mountainous Vystrana. Now that I recognized the language, though, I was able to follow the general thrust of the argument, which I shall take the liberty of re-creating.

"You're an idiot," my bearer said in disgust—except he used some word I did not know, whose meaning, I suspect, was rather more opprobrious. "I told you not to go back there."

"I didn't think it would do any harm!" the young lover protested. (I had seen his face while they were trussing me, and he could not have been much more than a year or two above my age, if that.)

My bearer snorted and hitched me higher on his shoulder. "You mean you didn't think I would notice. You're lucky I *did*, or this little chit would have followed you all the way back to our camp."

"What does that matter?" the lover asked sullenly. "You're bringing her there yourself."

So he was, and I did not like to think why that might be. But knowledge was my one tool, and so I kept listening.

"I'm not about to let her go running back and raise a cry," my bearer said. "Maybe the locals ignore you going for a tickle with your pretty widow, but this one isn't from around here. I want to know who she is, and what she's doing here. Then we'll decide what to do with her."

For all that "we," he spoke like a leader—of this pair at least, and likely of more. And they hadn't been in the area for long, or they would know of Drustanev's Scirling visitors.

I grunted as the pieces fell into place. Yellow hair, and a dialect recognizable, if only barely, as Eiversch: these fellows must be Staulerens. I could not, in that moment, remember the details of their history, but an army from Eiverheim had marched through these mountains some two hundred years previously, and some, being cut off at war's end with no pay and no way home, had settled in the region. Their descendents, known as Staulerens, lived for the most part on the northern side of the Vystrani mountains, but their young men occasionally crossed south toward Chiavora, for one clandestine (and lucrative) purpose:

Smuggling.

Well, *two* clandestine purposes, if one counted midnight tickles with pretty widows. But smuggling was of primary importance. Brandy or opium, I wondered—not that it much mattered, except insofar as it might tell me whether my captors were more likely to be drunk or drugged when they decided what to do with me. Did smugglers sample their own cargo? I had no idea. Nor any idea what to do with my understanding, except cling tight to it and wait for a chance.

Upside down and blindfolded as I was, I cannot say how long I was carried through the woods. All my blood had rushed to my head, and my bearer's shoulder digging into my lower abdomen became more painful with each step. Furthermore, my clothing was far from sufficient for the nighttime chill; I have known winter days in Scirland that are warmer than a Floris night in Vystrana. Consequently, it came as a complete surprise when my bearer stopped and dumped me without ceremony to the ground.

My first reaction was pure relief, that I could relax my abused stomach muscles and breathe freely. All around me was half-intelligible speech in Eiversch, which I hadn't the wit to attend to. Then a hand snatched the kerchief from my head, and I could see.

Even the small fire burning nearby was too much light at first. I blinked and curled my legs under me, less to hide my bare ankles than to warm them. There were half a dozen men, I saw, all Staulerens, each one more villainous-looking than the last, if only from lack of bathing. My bearer knelt in front of me, kerchief in hand, and addressed me in Vystrani. "Who are you?"

I thought of my shouting matches with Dagmira, my deplorable grammar, and judged it better to take my chances with standard Eiversch. In that tongue, I said, "I'm sorry—I don't speak Vystrani very well. Can you understand me?"

His eyebrows went up, and the others muttered in surprise. "You're from Eiverheim?" my bearer asked.

Judging by the way the others were standing back, letting him question me, he was indeed their leader. I quickly reviewed the formal pronouns in my mind—it is never bad policy to be polite to one's captor—and said, "No, I am from Scirland. But you and your companions are Staulerens, are you not? I thought we might converse more easily in your language."

From what I could gather out of the laughter and muttered jokes between the other men, they thought it grand comedy that I was using formal pronouns for their leader. The man himself grinned. "Scirling, eh? And what are you doing here, in Vystrana?"

During the men's interruption, I had taken swift inventory of my present assets. They consisted of one inadequately warm robe, one even more inadequate nightgown, a pair of shoes. I had other belongings back in Drustanev—but we'd brought equipment more than money, and these men would not want to show their faces to negotiate for my ransom. The pine needles, small stones, and dirt within my reach. Myself.

As I have said before, I am an old woman now, and don't much care whom I shock or offend. I will tell you honestly that I thought of the pretty widow in Drustanev, and I thought of myself: not particularly pretty, but young and healthy (which goes quite far, among men isolated in the mountains), and far from completely attired; and I wondered if I might be able to bargain my charms in exchange for release.

Did you not believe me when I wrote earlier of my deranged practicality? Perhaps this will convince you, then. We are not supposed to speak of such things, of course, but on that cold night, my mind performed an even colder arithmetic: it would be better to comply than to be forced, and compliance might preserve my life in the bargain. If I could bring myself to it, which was by no means certain.

Whether I could or not, such tactics would not be my first resort. I answered the leader's question honestly. "I'm here to study dragons."

By the perplexity in his expression, he thought at first that the differences of language were causing him to misunderstand. I watched him mouth the words, as if tasting them for consonants I might have pronounced wrong, the way Hingese will sometimes say "bear" when they mean "pear." "*Balaur*," I added helpfully, trusting that he would recognize the Vystrani word.

His eyes widened. "Dra— You mean you are here to *hunt* them."

There were at the time big-game hunters who pursued dragons for sport, despite the impossibility of keeping trophies beyond the odd tooth or claw. I shook my head. "No, I mean study. For science."

"*You?*" he said in disbelief, gesturing at my disheveled and female self. (He did *not* use the formal pronoun.)

"Not alone, no," I said, feeling a twinge of guilt for overstating my role. "I am here with companions. A Scirling earl and his assistant, and my—my husband." I stumbled over those last words, remembering my bleak calculations of a moment before.

The leader scratched his beard. "Your husband, eh?"

I wondered frantically whether to issue the usual melodramatic threats—*If you hurt me, he will hunt you to the ends of the earth!*—or to attempt to flirt my way free. Or to claim it was my unclean time; Staulerens, I thought, followed the Temple, even though their brethren back in Eiverheim had since become largely Magisterial. In the end, my conflicting impulses produced a smile.

I cannot describe that smile for you. I have no idea what it looked like to the smuggler; to me it felt like an incoherent blend of hopefulness and desperation. Whatever its appearance, its effect was to make him burst out laughing.

"Good God, woman," he said, proving by his blasphemy that if he *did* follow the Temple, he did not do so very well. "You bat your eyelashes at me and expect me to believe you're here for science?"

"I am!" I said, the confusion of a moment before resolving quite neatly into indignation. "Vystrani rock-wyrms. I came along to do sketches—I'm an artist of sorts—at least, I *would* do sketches if we knew where the dragons were lairing and could get close. But so far—" That last word stretched out comically as inspiration ambushed me. "You must know! Rock-wyrms don't normally attack people, or so Lord Hilford says—despite what happened to us on the way here—but they *are* territorial, and don't like people coming near their lairs. You're smugglers, aren't you? So you must know the mountains very well. Surely *you* know where the dragons are. Oh, if you tell us how to find them, I'm certain Lord Hilford would pay you handsomely. We've wasted so much time already."

By the time I ran out of breath and words, *everyone* was staring. In my excitement, I had risen up onto my knees, gesticulating with my bound hands like a Chiavoran street-seller. There was no chance of my captor doubting me now; I would have to have been a stage actress to feign that kind of demented enthusiasm. What sort of woman, upon being kidnapped by smugglers in the middle of the night, would jump for joy at the thought of questioning them about dragons?

He didn't doubt me, but he didn't entirely believe my words, either, simply because they made no sense. "Why do you care about dragons?"

I'm afraid I stammered in trying to answer; too many replies attempted to come out of my mouth at once. The scrimmage was won by a simple truth, with me from the moment I held little vinegar-soaked Greenie in my palm. "Because they're beautiful. And, and—for *science*, because we know so very little about them. I don't know why Lord Hilford chose Vystrana, except that he hates the desert, and it's relatively close to Scirland, as such things go. But—" I belatedly tried to gather my wits. "We are here for scholarly purposes, I assure you. My father has some Minsurgrad brandy that may very well have come through these mountains by, shall we say, an *unofficial* route; he would not thank me if I interfered with your work."

My unwise reference to that work hardened his face, but it did not produce violence, as it might have done. The leader sat back on his heels, pulling the kerchief through his fingers as if to smooth it out. "You said three others." I nodded. "All here to study the dragons?"

I nodded again, and he glanced over at one of his companions—not the young lover. The other man knelt to mutter in his ear, and between the low volume and the dialect I could not catch a word. The leader scowled, and I tensed. But the scowl, it seemed, was not for me. "Your friends," he said, addressing me. "They can make the dragons stop attacking people?"

My gaze slid past him to the other men. Now that I looked properly, I saw that one leaned on a crutch that looked new-cut, and the clothing of another was stained with an ominous amount of blood, likely not his own. Of course they would be in danger, as much as or more than the people of Drustanev.

Could we make the dragons stop? We had debated possible causes, but without observational data, it was all just speculation. And until we knew the cause, I could only guess at whether we'd be able to affect it.

It is the prerogative of old women to give unlooked-for advice, so let me offer you this, friend reader: when you are lost in the woods and your safe return home depends on telling a Stauleren smuggler that you can help him, that is *not* the time for a scientific evaluation of your chances. It is the time for smiling and saying, "Yes, absolutely."

The leader considered this, then stood without replying and went off to the side, gathering his men with him. No one bothered to keep watch over me; there was no need. What was I going to do, run off into the night? I had no sense of which way Drustanev lay, except "downhill." And there were wolves and bears in these mountains—not to mention angry dragons.

My interlocutor had made some effort to speak distinctly

while addressing me, but in conversation with his men it all dissolved into an incomprehensible smear. Besides, I rather thought it would not do to seem like I was eavesdropping. I occupied myself by trying to straighten my nightgown and robe, then hunching over into the most heat-conserving posture I could achieve.

To my surprise, after a minute or so of this, a rough and smelly blanket was dropped over my shoulders. I looked up in time to see the young lover returning to the group. Even that small gesture of charity gladdened my heart, and changed my perspective on these men. They were not the romanticized figures you think of when you hear the words "Stauleren" or "smuggler"—but neither were they vicious cutthroats, ready to murder at the first opportunity. They were simply men, mostly on the youngish side, who made their living by carting boxes of illicit cargo through the mountains. It is a trade that has gone on for ages in this region, though the boundaries, goods, and carriers have changed with time; as occupations go, it is nearly as venerable as sheep-herding, and the local boyars rarely rouse themselves to stop it.

Even the "leader" seemed a democratic sort, consulting with his fellows before arriving at a decision. This did not take very long, though. Soon they broke up, and he returned to kneel before me. "At first light," he said, "we take you back down to the village. You tell your men we want to meet with them, at the spring below the cliff. Can they find the place?"

I had drawn it on the map myself. "Yes."

"We want money," he said. "And help. Money first; then we tell them where the dragons are. Then they quiet the beasts down. So long as they do that, and don't try to interfere with us, we'll leave you alone."

He hadn't named a figure, but bargaining over the price of my safety was a task I would gladly leave to the gentlemen. "I understand."

The smuggler reached out and untied my hands, then my feet. "Get some sleep."

He turned to go, and the words burst out of me: a deep-seated Scirling impulse toward good manners, entirely out of place in my current surroundings. "I am Isabella Camherst."

He cast a glance back over his shoulder at me, eyebrows raised. Then a hint of a smile lifted the corner of his mouth. "Chatzkel," he said. Only his given name: well, I could not blame a criminal for not wanting to identify himself more than was necessary.

"Thank you," I said, and he went on his way.

By then it was long past the time that my midnight wakefulness should have ended. With my blood still racing, though, and the ground hard and cold beneath me, I did not manage a second sleep that night.

TEN

My triumphant return — A productive meeting — Progress at last in our work

Sunrise, as seen from high on a mountain, is a truly glorious thing.

The light cut like a knife blade through the trees, setting aglow the mist that had gathered in the valleys below. Its cold brilliance hurt my eyes, but I was glad to see it all the same; it meant I would soon be going—

Not *home*. In fact, that sleepless dawn in the mountains brought with it the strongest tide of homesickness I have ever felt. I often miss Scirland during my travels; there is a great deal to be said for the place where one need not *think*, all the time, about the right thing to do or say, but simply behave according to well-worn habit, and that feeling has never been more intense than on my morning with the smugglers. But I had spent enough time in Gritelkin's dark house for it to feel like the closest thing to safety I would find in Vystrana. I very much wanted to return.

My cold-stiffened legs had other ideas. I tried to stand, failed entirely, and turned my back on the men so I could massage my calves and thighs into something resembling life. My feet remained frozen, but I could not bring myself to beg for stockings. No one gave me breakfast, either; I suspected, by their lean and hungry looks, that they had little enough for themselves.

Most of the men stayed behind; the leader and two others formed my escort. Each carried a rifle and a pistol, which I hoped were only for such wildlife as we might encounter on the way. I tried to return the blanket to the young lover with a smile and thanks in Eiversch, but he pressed it back onto me, and in truth I was glad for its warmth as we began our hike.

At first I was also glad to be traveling on my own feet, rather than being carried like a sack of meal. Three falls later, my joy had been firmly tempered. My cold feet were clumsy, and my attire, as I said before, was quite unsuitable; clutching the blanket about myself meant I could not use my hands for balance, until I knotted it around my shoulders like a lumpy shawl. I attempted to question the men about how they survived in the mountains, but was ordered into silence; and so we went down to Drustanev.

Most of the way. Before we came within sight of the village, however, we heard sound echoing up the narrow valley: shouts, and the barking of dogs. One of the men immediately grabbed my arm; the smuggler threw up a silencing hand. I swallowed a moan as my slow, sleep-deprived mind realized what the racket must be.

Jacob had turned out the population of Drustanev to search for me.

Guiltily, I thought what his morning must have been like. He awoke not long after dawn; I was not in bed. He went downstairs, thinking to find me, but found no sign. Dagmira or the cook might have arrived by then, and neither knew where I was. A quick glance would show that I had gone out without dressing. My tracks would lead out of the village, and then . . .

I had seen the care with which the smugglers broke and hid our trail on the way down. They might well have done the same during my abduction, which meant the search would not lead back to their camp. But to my husband, it would look like I had wandered inexplicably out of the village—then vanished.

And the most obvious explanation would be that I had been eaten by a dragon.

My heart ached for the panic I must have caused him. Ached, and then tightened in fear for what might yet go further wrong. "Let me go on alone," I said in an urgent whisper. "You don't wish to be seen, do you? I can find my way from here. And I'll send the men to meet with you as planned."

Daylight had revealed the leader's face more clearly: weather-worn features, with blue Stauleren eyes and a fortnight's growth of beard. That latter did not obscure the clenching of his jaw as he considered me. "You have my word of honor," I said, drawing myself up with as much dignity as I could manage in my current state.

Whether the word of a Scirling gentlewoman meant anything to him, or whether he simply decided it wasn't worth the trouble of keeping me, I do not know. But he waved me on with a curt hand. "Tomorrow," he said as I passed him. "The spring beneath the cliff."

I resolved that *someone* would be there to meet him, if I had to go by myself.

The barking grew louder as I scrambled down toward the searchers, trying to put distance between myself and my erst-while hosts before I drew anyone's attention. When I judged I had gone far enough, I began to shout, and soon they found me.

I will spare you the tedious details of what followed. (Much of it escaped me anyway, owing to my inferior grasp of Vystrani.) For posterity's sake, however, I should note the reactions of two individuals upon my return.

The first, of course, was Jacob, who was leading the search. His first action upon seeing me was to crush me in the tightest em-brace we had ever shared; and if the blanket over my shoulder was damp by the time we parted, I made no comment on it. "Thank the Lord you're safe," he said, and then on the heels of that, "Where in heaven have you been?"

He asked that question several more times before I managed to give him an answer, though not for lack of trying on my part; every time I opened my mouth, he declared anew his relief over my safe return, and soon this was further interrupted by orders to call off the search. We were halfway back to Drustanev—I had to insist to Jacob that I was perfectly capable of walking, or he might have carried me—before I could say, "It's quite a complicated story, and I *will* tell it, but perhaps we should wait until Lord Hilford and Mr. Wilker can also hear. But oh, Jacob—I have solved our problems. I know where the dragons are lairing."

"Dragons!" he exclaimed, stopping dead in a damp meadow. "Isabella, what are you talking about? Were you attacked?"

"No, no," I said, fending off a renewed attempt to check me for injury. He had already catalogued the various scrapes resulting from my falls, and fussed over them as if they were a collection of broken legs. "Rather, *I* don't know; someone else does—"

I remembered that we were surrounded by men from Drustanev, and stopped before I could say any more. We were speaking Scirling, of course, which I doubted any of the villagers understood, but better safe than sorry. Jacob finally agreed to wait for the full story, but I think it was more out of conviction that I was overwrought by my experiences than anything else.

The other noteworthy reaction came later, after I had been fed, doctored, buried under a pile of fire-warmed blankets, and finally permitted to dress. Dagmira undertook this task, and lambasted me up one side and down the other for my stupidity in going out like that.

"There was a *man* lurking about," I said in frustration, trying to stop her tirade. An indiscretion—I had not meant to bring up the man—and one that did no good.

"A man? A man! Of course there was a man," she said furiously. "Everyone knows Reveka has her lover, ever since her husband died. One of those Stauleren smugglers. Anyone could have told you that. No need to go running around the mountains to find out!"

So much for my indiscretion in mentioning him; the smugglers, it seemed, were no secret at all in Drustanev. Except, of course, where the Scirling interlopers were concerned. "*Would* you have told me, if I asked? Would anyone?"

"Of course not," Dagmira snapped. "It's none of your business."

I forebore to point out that then there *was* need to go running about the mountains. My fractured interactions with Dagmira—nothing like so fluent as I represent them here, but for my readers' sakes I will not subject you to a reconstruction of my appalling grammar and circumlocutions—had made it clear to me that the villagers of Drustanev had very little understanding of, let alone sympathy for, our reasons for being there. Gritelkin, I suspected, had not told them much, except that we intended to tramp around the mountains looking for dragons. As a result, we were an intrusion, an imposition upon their lives, and the sooner we were gone the better. As Dagmira said, their affairs were none of our business.

I let her finish dressing me, and went at last to speak with the three men whose affairs very much *were* my business—as mine were theirs.

They let me tell my story in peace, barring the occasional yelp of alarm or disbelief from Jacob. He withheld actual comment until I was done, though, at which point he dropped his face into his hands. "I should never have let you come here," he said through their muffling barrier.

"I took no real harm," I said defiantly. "A scraped knee, at worst. And how much time have I saved you? We could waste the entire summer up here, waiting for Mr. Gritelkin to come back—well, this way we can get on with our research."

"*If* this smuggler can help," Mr. Wilker said, not bothering to hide his doubt. "His trade may teach him a great deal about the mountains—but dragons?"

"You can hardly know the one without the other—not if you wish to avoid being eaten," I said.

Lord Hilford huffed thoughtfully, sending his moustaches fluttering. "I tell you again, they do *not* ordinarily attack people. But we stand to lose very little by following this lead. Mrs. Camherst has given her word that the men will be paid for her return; we cannot dishonor that. Furthermore, it sounds likely that the smugglers can tell us more about the dragons' sudden aggressiveness, which will be of value even without directions to their lairs. Yes, it will do," he said, with a decisive air. "Tomorrow we will go to meet them."

I had, during our journeys, seen Mr. Wilker argue with other men, and often with me; but never with the earl. "You can't be serious! Trusting these fellows—"

"Who said anything about trusting them?" Lord Hilford asked in surprise. "I intend to bring both of you with me, you and Camherst both, and you can argue about who gets to skulk in the bushes with a rifle. Not you, though, Mrs. Camherst, or your husband will have an apoplexy."

I think that a rather unfair word for Jacob's sentiments, but it is true that his nerves hadn't yet recovered from the scare. A part of me sorely wished to argue that I could mark the map, but any of the others could do that as well as me; only their marks would not be as elegant. And that argumentative part drooped its ears and tucked its tail between its legs upon seeing the look in Jacob's eyes. I am not the sort of lady for whom protectiveness sets her heart aflutter, but the incident had revealed an intensity of feeling in my husband that took me quite by surprise. I had thought us friends, and so we were; but the word fell short of describing all.

(Indeed, that same night we discovered one of the primary uses for that wakeful period between one's first sleep and one's second—the same use to which Reveka and her young lover had put their time.)

(Oh, for goodness' sake. I have already spoken about my fears when facing the smugglers; why should I not address the other side of that coin? It isn't as if the people reading this book are unlikely to be familiar with the activity. And if they are, I heartily encourage the adults among them to put the book down this instant and discover one of the simpler pleasures in life. I am a natural historian; I assure you, it is common to all species, and nothing to be ashamed of.)

So, for my husband's peace of mind, I agreed to be left behind.

By dawn the next day, I was just as glad not to be going out to the spring. My stockingless feet had been rubbed raw by the hike down from the smugglers' camp; I padded about our borrowed house in thick wool socks, a compromise between protecting my blisters and keeping my toes warm. I soon discovered, though, the downside to sparing my husband's nerves: I quite destroyed my own.

"What do you know of these smugglers?" I asked Dagmira as she beat out a rug on the slope behind our house. Her various looks were gradually becoming more familiar to me; I recognized this one as exasperation that I should ask so stupid a question. I clarified. "Are they violent men?"

Dagmira did not know the gentlemen had gone out to meet the smugglers—or rather, I *thought* she did not know; village gossips can uncover the strangest things. At any rate, she seemed to take my question as an aftereffect of my own experience. "They didn't hurt you, did they? They keep away from people, mostly. Unless people chase after them."

The barb sailed right past me. My attention was on her earlier words, so reminiscent of Lord Hilford's statement about the rock-wyrms. "Dragons have attacked people before, haven't they? I mean, in past years."

Clearly Dagmira had no idea why I had seemingly changed topics. "You hear stories," she said with a shrug. "A cousin's cousin, from the next valley over."

"Does it happen on any kind of cycle? Generationally, perhaps—" I stopped, for the exasperated look was back. *Teach a dragon to hatch eggs*, as they say nowadays. If the problem was anything like so regular, these people, dwelling in the mountains for centuries, would have noticed. "But it hasn't happened in Drustanev before, at least not for a long time. When did it start?"

She delivered a particularly vicious blow to the rug, sending dust flying. "Last autumn. Nebulis."

Mating season, perhaps? We knew very little about dragon mating habits. (We knew very little about dragon *anything;* hence this expedition.) But it would have taken Gritelkin some time to be sure of the problem, and by then, the mountains would be all but impassable. So he waited for spring—which I still was not convinced had arrived; I could see snow not a hundred feet from where I stood—and then sent his message. It was not his fault that the vagaries of travel and communication prevented him from warning us off.

Pulling my notebook from my skirt pocket, I asked, "What about injuries? Or deaths?"

The thwack of Dagmira's rug-beater punctuated her words, which came out terse with the force of it. "Two deaths. Don't know how many hurt. Half a dozen, maybe."

Plus Mingelo, the Chiavoran driver. Averaged across six months, it was not so bad—but of course that did not tell me how many had narrowly missed harm. Dagmira, however, had redoubled her efforts, and the noise prevented me from asking more. I tried not to calculate the odds of an attack on any given day—and refrained from asking whether a cousin's cousin from the next valley over had ever been killed by smugglers—and went back to pacing in my thick wool socks.

I nearly melted in relief when the gentlemen returned. My eyes went to Jacob first; he looked thoughtful. Mr. Wilker looked faintly sulky, and Lord Hilford, to my secret satisfaction, looked jubilant. "Well *done*, Mrs. Camherst," he said once we had all withdrawn to our workroom. "Tom, lay that map out on the table, so she can see. They do indeed know where the dragons are, and more besides."

Jacob had marked the various locations with a lead pencil, which told me Mr. Wilker must have been the one lurking in the bushes with the rifle. "We will have to adjust them as we go looking," he said when I clicked my tongue over the rough marks defacing my pretty map. "The smugglers knew a fair bit, but they say the dragons move around, so none of this is certain."

"*Some* things are certain," Lord Hilford said, settling into a chair. "Dragons lair in caves, and so do smugglers—or rather, their goods do. And Vystrani rock-wyrms have a fiercely territorial streak, it seems."

"Fierce enough to cause these attacks?" I asked, glancing up from the map.

Jacob shook his head. "If it were, incidents like this would be much more common, and the smugglers would know the cause."

"*But*," the earl said, holding up one finger, "the territorial response is not always the same. Rock-wyrms wishing to chase off an interloper most often breathe particles of ice. Sometimes, however, they attack more closely. And the accepted theory among smugglers is that this happens when the dragon is sick."

I immediately saw possibilities in this. "Illness might interfere with the operation of their extraordinary breath. Could it be the dragons are sick? But no—they aren't defending their territory, not unless one was lairing near the road by which we came."

"It depends on the size of the territory," Jacob said. "But from what the smugglers told us, the range for such attacks is fairly small."

I sat to take the weight off my complaining feet, and propped my elbows on my knees to think. "How *many* dragons have been attacking people, anyway? If it's only one or two, it might be something exceptional—some kind of degeneration, perhaps, that causes them to run mad. If it seems widespread, though . . ."

"Then the entire local population might be diseased," Lord Hilford said.

This grim possibility put us all into silence for a few moments. My experience thus far with dragons in the wild had given me no reason to feel kindly toward them, but I did not like the notion of so many falling victim to contagion.

Of course, we had no proof of the theory; only the speculation of smugglers. We did, however, have information that might let us proceed. "Now that we have the map," I asked, "what next?"

Lord Hilford levered himself out of his chair and went to study the map. "We confirm these reports—carefully, mind you—and then get on with the work we should have been doing a fortnight ago, if Gritelkin hadn't gone haring off. I think, under the circumstances, that we might turn our attention first to anatomical study."

Mr. Wilker frowned at him. "Observation? Or do you mean to hunt one of them?"

The earl tapped the map, frowning as he weighed one location against another. "Hunting, I should think; we can catch two wolves with one snare. We've brought an artist with us; well, she needs a specimen to draw, at closer range than on the wing. And if there *is* some kind of disease among them, we may find signs of it."

I was sadly slow to catch his meaning about the artist. "You mean—I am to help you?"

He gave me a conspiratorial smile. "It's why we brought you, isn't it? That and to file papers—but we don't yet have any, so there you have it."

Is it any wonder I developed such reckless habits later in life? Chase after smugglers in the middle of the night; achieve information and a chance to further my dreams. With rewards such as those, I naturally concluded that such behaviour was a splendid idea.

Blisters and scrapes forgotten, I stood, unable to contain my grin. "I should gather my materials, then."

ELEVEN

The dragon hunt — The application of my skills —
Conversations with a skull — An unexpected loss —
Carrion-eaters

Yes, we shot a dragon.

I find it fascinating that so many people take exception to this. Not simply in light of my later attitudes on the matter; no, the objections began long before then, as soon as the book detailing our research in Vystrana was published. People exclaimed over our "monstrous" actions, destroying a dragon simply so that we might understand how it worked.

These same people do not seem to care in the least that at the height of the Great Sparkling Inquiry, I had no less than six hundred and fourteen specimens in my shed—very few of them dead from natural causes. Entomologists trap insects in their killing jars and then pin their corpses to cards, and no one utters a single squeak of protest. For that matter, let a gentleman hunt a tiger for its skin, and everyone applauds his courage. But to shoot a dragon for science? That, for some reason, is cruel.

Mind you, these objections come exclusively from men and women in Scirland and similar countries, most of them (I imagine) extolling the sanctity of dragons from the comfort of their homes, far from any actual beast of the breed. Indeed, few of those letter-writers seem to have seen a single dragon in their lives. They certainly have not spent days among Vystrani shepherds, for whom dragons are neither sacred nor even likable, but rather troublesome predators who all too often make off with the shepherds' livelihood in their jaws. The men of Drustanev did not hesitate to shoot dragons, I assure you. We might even have waited for one of them to do the deed, at which point my letter-writers might have been better satisfied with our virtue. But Vystrani shepherds try very hard to *avoid* dragons when possible, and we were impatient to get on with our work. So the gentlemen of our party studied the map, shouldered their guns, and went out to find their prey.

And I went with them. It was not at all like my first journey out from Drustanev; this time I was fully dressed and properly shod, and the piercing mountain sun illuminated our path. This second expedition did much to improve my feelings toward the region: by my standards the air was still bitterly cold for the season, but the brilliance and life of my surroundings could not be denied. We saw eagles and thrushes, rabbits and deer, and even one bear lumbering down the far side of the valley. When I stepped apart from the men to take care of a certain biological matter, I startled a lynx, which stared at me with flat, unfriendly eyes before melting away into the trees.

We had chosen for our destination the nearest and most isolated of the dragon lairs the smugglers had identified, in the hopes of disturbing only one beast. (While we might have gotten a great deal of observational data from having three or four wyrms descend upon us at once, I feared it would all be lost to science ten minutes later.) With us came the servant lad Iljish and another, Relesku, to act as our porters; they carried food and tents, for this expedition was expected to keep us out for several days. The gentlemen carried their guns and other tools, and I had my artistic materials, which I insisted upon carrying myself.

I had studied the map a great deal before we left, and formed a private theory as to where the smugglers' camp was, based on my recollection of the climb down. Our hunt took us westward of that place, over a sharp ridge and into another valley, bisected by a snowmelt stream. Pausing for breath at the top of the ridge, I thought I saw something in the lower distance: a shape too far and too shrouded in trees to be made out clearly, but also too blocky to be mistaken for an ordinary mountain. I squinted, to very little effect; the field glass was in Lord Hilford's keeping. And the others had gotten ahead of me, so that there was no one nearby to ask about it. By the time I puffed my way down to them, I had grown too embarrassed by my slowness to ask any questions; but as it turned out, the answers came to me a few days later, and so I will return to the mysterious shape in time.

We were not going tremendously far—only seven miles or so. Lord Hilford stopped us mid-afternoon, in a steep little defile too narrow and overhung with trees for a rock-wyrm to stoop on us from above. "You will stay here, Mrs. Camherst, with Iljish and the tents," he said. "I trust we can leave the arrangement of the camp in your capable hands? Many thanks. We'll scout out the place before the light fades, and pick a location for our blind; then, with any luck, we'll nail the beast tomorrow morning."

Being no kind of hunter myself, I accepted this with grace. The men departed; Iljish began erecting the tents, and I set about making the camp, if not comfortable, then at least an efficient place from which to work.

Lord Hilford, Jacob, and Relesku returned shortly before sunset, with the news that they had found both the lair and sufficient sign as to persuade them it was in current use. Mr. Wilker had stayed behind to wait for the dragon's return, so as to forestall the possibility of the men watching an empty hole come morning.

The food—garlic-laden sausages, bread, and a spicy bean paste I was growing tolerant of—required little in the way of preparation, so I tugged Jacob's sleeve until he bent to listen. "Could we not see the dragon from here?"

"In the sky, perhaps—but there's more than one cave nearby, and we didn't have time to check them all," Jacob said, frowning. "That's why it was necessary to leave Wilker keeping watch."

I waved this away with an impatient hand. "No, I meant—*I* wish to see the dragon, Jacob. Before you've shot it and laid it out for me to draw. See that boulder up there?" I directed his attention to a rock I'd had my eye on since we arrived at the gully. "If we cut a few branches to hide ourselves, and sat *very* still . . ."

I expected him to protest. But Jacob gave me an amused look and kissed the top of my head. "I knew the moment I saw that rock that you would not rest until you could perch atop it and watch for dragons. Yes, as long as we take precautions, it should be safe. They say dragons see movement better than shapes, and pine boughs should hide our scent."

So it was that, when sunset came, I was seated on a lofty boulder, with the sharp bite of pine sap in my nose and my husband's arms encircling my shoulders. The fading light flamed across the tops of the ridges, sending the valleys into deep shadow, and the stark contrast was breathtaking.

And then the dragon came.

It flew in from the west, so that all I truly saw at first was a black silhouette against the fiery sky. Then it caught an updraft and skimmed up the mountain's slope, barely above the trees, and that gave me a better view: the blocky plates of the hide; the close-tucked legs and trailing tail; the enormous expanse of wings dwarfing the body they bore.

I did not realize I had stopped breathing until the dragon backwinged to land in some clearing hidden from my view, and Jacob kissed the top of my head once more. Then I let out my stale air in a wavering breath, drew in fresh, and leaned back to return my husband's kiss.

"Thank you," I said.

"Thank *you*," he murmured. "Were it not for your prodding, I likely would not be here."

Atop this boulder? Or in Vystrana at all? I didn't ask, because in the end it didn't matter. He had come—both of us had—and I felt a surge of emotion I can only describe as terrified joy at the thought of having missed this. Had we not met Lord Hilford—had Jacob refused to let me join the expedition—

I might have missed my chance at the life I was always meant to live.

I must have spoken that thought aloud, for Jacob's hands stilled on my shoulders, and then he said, "You truly mean that, don't you."

My mouth opened silently, as if hoping the right words would alight on my tongue, and give me some way of explaining the fierce, indescribable *thing* that swelled in my heart. No such happy incident occurred, but I tried anyway. "Ever since I was a girl. I want to understand things, Jacob; and we understand dragons so very little. We can't breed them, we can barely keep them in captivity—" I stopped, for my tongue was leading me down intellectual paths, when it was passion I needed to explain. "This will sound very silly."

He squeezed my shoulders, as if supporting me. "I promise not to laugh."

"It's—it's as if there is a dragon inside me. I don't know how big she is; she may still be growing. But she has wings, and *strength*, and—and I can't keep her in a cage. She'll die. *I'll* die. I know it isn't modest to say these things, but I *know* I'm capable of more than life in Scirland will allow. It's all right for women to study theology, or literature, but nothing so rough and ready as this. And yet this is what I *want*. Even if it's hard, even if it's dangerous. I don't care. I need to see where my wings can carry me."

I had reason to be glad that I was leaning back against Jacob; it meant I did not have to look in his face as I said these things, which sounded like pure foolishness to my own prosaic ears.

But it also meant I could feel the tension in his body, resisting my declaration of unconcern for danger. Our society did not only dictate the boundaries of my life; it also circumscribed him, saying he would fail as a man and a husband if he permitted me to risk myself in such fashion.

He was holding his breath, I realized, and a moment later released it in a long gust. "Oh, Isabella," he murmured. "I thought—at times, while we were planning this journey, I thought I was like an indulgent father, who could not bear to see a child unhappy. But that was a disservice to us both. You are no child. You—" Something shook his body. I was surprised to identify it as a suppressed laugh. "This will sound terrible."

"Tell me."

"Do you remember the Vystrani runt in the menagerie?"

"The albino? Of course." Lord Hilford's prize, and in so many ways, the reason both Jacob and I were here.

"You remind me of that dragon."

Now I sat up and twisted to face him, torn between outrage and hilarity. "I'm a pale, sexless *runt*?!"

He fended me off with his hands, laughter getting the better of him. "Not in the least. But Mr. Swargin always said it was surprisingly robust. I think if Hilford hadn't captured it, the creature would have lived a fine life somewhere in these mountains." Jacob sobered, hands sliding down my arms to grip my hands. "I don't want you to pine away, Isabella. If it's my job, as your husband, to take care of you, then I will do so—by giving you the life you need."

Something else swelled in my heart, then, that was not in the least dragonlike. I could not bring myself to let it free, though; it was too personal, with our companions so close. I swallowed down three different responses, and finally managed to say, "Thank you. I should not like to be neighbours with a Moulish swamp-wyrm."

We stared at each other for a moment, then burst into laughter that must have scared off every nonhuman animal for half a mile around.

Once we had regained our composure, we climbed back down, ate our sausages reeking of garlic, and welcomed Mr. Wilker when he returned bearing word that the dragon had indeed gone where expected. The men retired immediately, for theirs would be a very early rising, and if it were not for the exertion of carrying my artistic materials across miles of mountain terrain, I would not have slept a wink that night.

I certainly roused with ease when the men did, and chewed my fingernails to nubs after they were gone. Vystrani rock-wyrms are primarily crepuscular hunters, hunting in the morning and evening, but subsiding into wary sleep during the brightest part of the day. Catching one napping is extremely difficult; far easier to accost one in the awkward moment of leaving its lair, before it can take to wing.

The abrupt crack of a rifle a little over an hour later brought me whirling around to face the direction they'd gone. Before I'd completed half the turn, two more shots echoed the first; then a fourth. Then, as I held my breath once again, a fifth, much belated—as if to put a dying beast out of its misery.

"They got it," I murmured, staring toward the upper end of the gully as if my gaze could penetrate rock and tree to see the men. (In fact I was staring in the wrong direction; the cave lay about forty degrees westward of the way the gully pointed.)

If I thought I could find the location unaided, I would have gone charging off that instant, without pen or paper or anything else of use. Since I had to wait, I gathered everything up, and went to wait at the top of the gully. The moment I saw Jacob, I hurried to greet him, and to meet my dragon in person.

The carcass sprawled across a bare shoulder of limestone, whose scored surface gave testament to the dragon's leaps and landings. Its grey, plated hide blended very well with that backdrop, giving me a sudden jolt as I wondered how many of the stony outcrops we had passed the day before might have included drowsing dragons. The head had fallen more or less in the direction of our approach, and the mighty jaw gaped open, the green eyes already glazing over in death.

The memory of the attack we suffered on our way to Drustanev had not left me. Even knowing the beast was quite dead, I hesitated to approach the dragon. It seemed both larger and smaller than I expected; larger because I was so near, and smaller because it lay so still. I held my breath as I put one foot forward, and then the next, until at last I was close enough to lay my hand upon the grey hide, its warmth already fading in the chill mountain air.

A dragon. More than a badly drawn shape on the page; more than a sudden threat from above. Real, and in front of me—and now we would begin to learn its secrets.

Lord Hilford and Mr. Wilker were already busy taking measurements: wingspan, girth, length from nose to tail. (Ours was quite a good specimen, nearly five meters in total length, and very well proportioned.) Then smaller divisions: the head, the neck, the spread of its claws, and so on. We had no convenient way to weigh the beast, alas; only Mr. Chiggins's formula, which has since been proven woefully inadequate for calculating the mass of a dragon. But we did our best.

My job, of course, was to draw. I had given a great deal of thought to how I wished to approach this task, and so did not hesitate before giving orders. "Jacob, darling, could you spread

OUR DRAGON

out one wing? The right one will do very nicely, yes, across the stone there. Relesku may begin the task of skinning the other, for the muscular and skeletal drawings; I expect that will take him a little while. Best we do the more delicate parts before proceeding to the main body."

The exposed location was good for our purposes; it would receive sunlight for almost the entire day. We posted Iljish to keep watch for dragons, and set to work.

I laid out my drawing board, charcoal, ink, and pens, and clipped a sheet of paper into place. I half expected my hands to tremble: I was standing scarcely one foot from a dragon—albeit a dead one—and the time had come for me to justify my presence with the expedition; surely that was enough to make any young woman nervous. And so I was; but my hands knew their business, and carried it out without concerning themselves over the state of my brain.

The first priority, of course, was a rapid sketch of the carcass, providing suggestions of the surrounding terrain, and including Jacob for scale as he crouched to take a cast of the dragon's teeth. Although the drawings of details would be more useful to science, it was just as vital to depict the whole; most dragon illustrations at the time still held deplorable inaccuracies, showing the beasts with humanlike shoulder joints, or bodies far too thick, or wings far too small. My first sketch would be the frame into which we would fit the later details. But I could not take too long at it, and so once I had the most necessary lines, I bent to the task of drawing the wing.

Its structure is remarkable. The uninformed often say that dragons have "batlike wings," which is a gross oversimplification. It is true that the appearance of a dragon's wing (and here I speak of the most common terrestrial species) is more akin to that of a bat than a bird, with a membrane stretched between elongated phalanges. But it is more accurate to say there are four major types of wings extant in the animal kingdom: birdlike, batlike, insectlike, and dragonlike. The spacing of the phalangeal joints makes the fourth type entirely distinct.

But all of that thought came later, once I was in a more scientific frame of mind. That particular day, two things distracted me as I worked. The first, of course, was the periodic spurts of giddy joy: I was drawing a *dragon wing*! All my girlhood obsession had come to fruition in most spectacular fashion.

The second was less pleasant. Relesku had dutifully gone to work skinning the beast's other wing, adding to the blood shed by the hunt, and the odor rapidly grew from "noticeable" to "appalling." It occurred to me to wonder whether airborne predators posed the greatest danger after all; any number of creatures in these mountains would be drawn to the smell of fresh meat. Then again, most were leery of humans, and none were currently on a rampage against us. But the stench was very distracting, even for one as little squeamish as I.

There was no avoiding it, though. A tiger may be killed and preserved by a taxidermist, or defleshed and its skeleton studied at leisure; not so with a dragon. They did not fall to ash as sparklings did, but it was well known at the time that dragon bones rapidly became frangible postmortem, defying even the most careful padding to keep them intact. Even one day after death, simply picking up a bone in your hand could be enough to crack it, and the degeneration grew worse with time. This, of course, was one of the primary reasons we had so few accurate sketches; such work *must* be done in the field, and rapidly, before the decay progressed too far.

Relesku had not yet finished skinning the other wing when I finished drawing my own. I took a moment to lift the limb and study the underside. Despite common sense, I expected it to be heavy; a rock-wyrm's wingspan is often comparable to its length, and my brain was convinced anything so large must be correspondingly weighty. But of course a heavy wing would not permit flight. The humerus, radius, and ulna are hollow, and the phalanges consist of tough, lightweight cartilage. The membrane of the wing itself is shockingly thin, to the point where I expected it to tear in my hand. But it stretched over my fingers without rupturing, a smoothly pebbled surface.

At least, it felt pebbled when I drew my fingers from the bones toward the wing edge. As I slid my hand back in the other direction, though, intending to lift the wing higher, the membrane rasped at my skin like a cat's tongue.

"Lord Hilford," I said to the earl, who was taking a cast of a nearby taloned foot, "have you noticed this before?"

He came and ran his hand over the wing's underside. The roughness was only palpable there; the top surface felt quite smooth, if a little porous. "Hmm!" he exclaimed, bracing the wing higher so as to get a better look. "Indeed I have not. Mind you, I've only ever been within touching distance of my little runt, never a fully grown rock-wyrm. Is this a skin condition the beast is suffering, or a common feature my runt lacked? I wonder."

The earl retrieved a piece of hide from Relesku's work and slid his palm across it. "Same thing here. Tom, bring me the magnifying glass—" He examined it beneath the lens. "Hmm. It's clearly textured in some fashion, but I can't make out enough at this magnification. We'll have to try it under the microscope, back at the house. Damnation—your pardon, Mrs. Camherst—I knew I should have brought brandy. The skin and flesh don't degenerate in the same way as the bones, but they do decay. Well, cut a good sample, and we'll hope this chill works in our favor, for once."

His mention of decay recalled me to my purpose, and its urgency. I drew the body, sprawled inelegantly across the stone, and then the opposite wing was ready for me, stench and all. Dragon's blood is truly a pungent thing; I recommend avoiding it if possible. I ended up sacrificing dignity for comfort, cutting two pieces from my handkerchief and stuffing them up my nostrils for relief.

Thus protected, I sketched the musculature and skeletal structure of the wing. Then the true butchery began. Mr. Wilker, whose veterinary knowledge surpassed my own, was determined to dig for whatever organ gave rise to a rock-wyrm's extraordinary breath. This necessitated turning the carcass onto its back and thoroughly gutting it. (I caught a glimpse of the wishbone, and did not try to suppress my smile.) I had not yet drawn the feet in anything like sufficient detail, but since we had casts of those, it was decided that I should first devote my time to the skull. Mr. Wilker, in an oddly chosen attempt to protect my feminine sensibilities, had Relesku hack off the necessary bit and carry it a little distance away from the rest of the body.

There are undoubtedly stranger experiences in life than sitting cross-legged on an outcropping of stone with a severed dragon head facing you like the skull of Gortos himself—indeed, I have had my share over the years—but I must say that one ranks fairly high.

Especially when one begins conversing with the head. "This is most undignified for you," I confided to the staring eyes, their green filming over with grey already. "My apologies. You were on your way to find breakfast, and instead you found us. I don't suppose it would comfort you to know how much we are learning? No, I imagine not."

The jaws remained silent and shut. (A good thing, too, or I would have fallen to my death from that stone in shock.)

"Why are you attacking people?" I mused, turning the head so I could draw its profile. Relesku had helpfully cut through the spine several vertebrae down from the skull, leaving the ruff undamaged, like a proud fan of stony plates. I was surprised to find them stiffly flexible to the touch. "Of course, *you* may not have harmed anyone. But what about your kin? Not that you could have told us if you knew. Do you communicate with one another at all, beyond mating and territorial disputes? Do rock-wyrms have some way of signaling that there is a fat, unguarded flock of sheep the next valley over?"

"What *are* you doing?" Jacob asked from behind me. My pencil skidded across the paper as I squawked and nearly toppled over. "My apologies," he said, all contrition; but then—"Were you *talking* to the skull?"

"No," I said, and then, "Perhaps," which as responses go is not very good for covering up the truth. Jacob shook his head, but forebore to comment further. "Is there something you need?"

"Only to ask how long you think it will be before you're done with the skull. Lord Hilford wants to try defleshing it before the bones become too brittle."

The customary methods of defleshing, of course, involve boiling or leaving the material in a container with a large number of hungry insects. Neither is suitable for dragon bones; we would have to rely on knives. "I'll be done presently," I said, and bent once more to my work, this time without talking.

We worked until the light began to fail, leaving ourselves just enough time to return to our camp before it became too dark. With the exception of our Vystrani lads, none of us wanted to go; we knew very well that during the night, scavengers would be at the carcass, and the bones would continue their inevitable decay. But the location was far too exposed to be safe.

As soon as dawn came we clambered back up to our carcass— only to find it *gone*.

We stood in a ragged line, staring comically at the empty

expanse of stone. Blood yet stained the ground, and shreds of offal swarming with ants, but of the body itself, nothing.

Faintly, I said, "Bears . . . ?"

"Or wolves," Jacob added, as if wolves were capable of carrying off anything a tenth so large. Even for bears, it was too much.

Lord Hilford stirred himself and began to quarter the area, examining the ground. He had been a great hunter in his youth, I knew; for the first time, I could see it in him. "I don't think so," he said. "See here? Scratches in the stone—but they cut *through* the blood. These were made last night."

Mr. Wilker had joined him, and was frowning over the scene. "It looks like they tore the carcass to pieces before carrying it off. A fight, I suppose."

Dragons. "Do they *eat* carrion?" I asked, stammering slightly. "Their own *kind*?"

"As to the first, I imagine so," Lord Hilford said. "We may idealize predators as noble hunters, but the truth is that very few of them will turn their noses up at a meal that can't run away. As to the latter . . . it *does* happen among animal-kind. I have known lions to do it."

My readers may recall that I am the woman who, at the tender age of seven, dismembered a dove with my brother's penknife. I am not squeamish. But I must confess that the notion of dragons committing cannibal acts—tearing apart the body of their fallen brother, then carrying the pieces off to eat—made me sufficiently ill that I pivoted and went rapidly down the slope, stumbling and nearly falling as I went.

I did not, in the end, vomit into a bush. But I am glad I removed myself from the immediate vicinity of that smell, or my fortitude might have failed.

Jacob came and stood at my side. His expression was much like the one I'd seen the day our Chiavoran drivers went on to the boyar's house: he was regretting having brought me along. It was to banish that look from his face that I mustered my best smile and said, "Well. I don't imagine the carcass would have been useful for much further study anyway, and now we have learned something new."

I watched him very nearly say three or four things, discarding them all, before he settled on answering me in kind: with scholarly detachment. He had not forgotten our conversation before the hunt. "It may be related to the attacks. There are many legends telling of people sent mad by eating human flesh; the same might well be true of dragons."

If so, it answered one question and raised another. Why had dragons begun eating their own kind? For they must not do so habitually, not if what Dagmira had said was correct.

It was not a question we could answer that day. At Jacob's suggestion, I went back down to the camp and began packing things up; there was nothing more for me to draw at the kill site. The gentlemen investigated the now-abandoned lair, collecting droppings and other materials for later study. And so, much chastened, we returned to Drustanev.

TWELVE

The Feast of the Reception — New Vystrani words — Draconean architecture and inscriptions — Something unexpected in the grass — Something even more unexpected belowground

The village, of course, did not cease its usual activity simply because there were Scirling visitors present. The calendar followed its usual course, and not long after our dragon hunt the Feast of the Reception came around.

I have not discussed religious matters yet. (Not in this book, and my earlier publication is, again, not to be relied upon for this matter. Please do me the kindness of ignoring all references to religion in that work.) Vystrana, of course, was and is a land of devout Temple-worshippers. All of our Scirling party were proper followers of the Magisterial path, which made us very much the odd men (and woman) out in Drustanev. But we held a brief conference two nights before the feast and agreed that, although we were loath to interrupt the pace of our work—which had most recently produced evidence of the differences in male and female rock-wyrm anatomy—for the sake of harmony, we should at least make a nod to the local practice.

We did not enter the tabernacle and participate in their ceremony. But we stayed awake through the night—a harder job in the Temple calendar, I must say; they celebrate the feast a good fortnight earlier than we do, in late Floris instead of early Graminis—reading our scriptures, and then joined them outside the next morning for a celebration.

There would be no pleasant strolls through the surrounding countryside for flowers; snow had fallen during the night, though fortunately not very much of it. But the villagers set up trestle tables in what passed for the center of Drustanev, and there was singing and dancing, and everyone dressed in their finest. For that morning, Vystrana looked more like it does in the stories: yokes of colorful embroidery stretching across snowy-white shirts, men playing lively tunes on their violins, and so on.

In keeping with the generosity of the season, we Scirlings gave out small trinkets from among our belongings, such as we could spare, and received pipes and beads and a fine wool shawl in return. This latter I wore draped over my arms as I attempted to learn the local dances, which everyone else seemed to execute without the slightest trouble—even when so drunk they could scarcely stand. I wondered if some of the smugglers' brandy finished its journey in Drustanev, or rather in the bellies of its inhabitants.

One young fellow asked me in comically simplified Vystrani whether I had seen much of the surrounding countryside, and upon hearing I had not, brightened like the dawning sun. "No? You must go to the—" And then he said a word I did not know. When I shook my head, he said, "Building! Go down!" He gestured with his hands: something toppling, with a crash at the end. "Very old. Very old."

"Ruins!" I said in Scirling, and then all at once remembered the blocky shape I had seen during our hunt.

Draconean ruins are rare in Scirland—or rather, the ones that exist are none too impressive. I had seen one as a girl, shortly before the beginning of my grey years, but it took a scholar to recognize it for what it was; the remains had none of the distinctive art that gave the ancient civilization its name. I did not mind; the illustrations I had seen in books were enough to show me that fantastical dragon-headed gods were much less interesting than actual *dragons*. But my recent tastes of freedom had given me a hunger for more; I had much rather visit Draconean ruins than sit cooped up in Gritelkin's dark house, failing to have conversations with the incomprehensible Dagmira.

A blind man might have missed my sudden excitement; my interlocutor did not. "I show you! I take you!" Then he gave up on keeping his sentences simple enough for my poor ear, and let spill a flood of words, from which I gathered that he would be more than happy to guide me there and back at my earliest convenience—tomorrow, if I liked.

I extracted the young man's name from him—Astimir—and the location of his house, a shabby place he occupied with his ailing mother. Though he had said nothing about payment yet, I suspected that was his eventual goal. Well, so be it; by the standards of Drustanev we were absurdly wealthy, and could afford to share a bit of it with this energetic young man. "Not tomorrow, though," I said, laughing, when he tried to urge me onward. "A few days. We will go soon enough."

Whether the others would be interested or not, I could not say. Draconean ruins had very little to do with actual dragons, and our reasons for being here. But there was only so much paper-filing I could do; I was determined to go, even if I had to go alone.

For a time it seemed I *might* be going alone. "It's hardly worth our time," Mr. Wilker said. "We aren't archaeologists, and I hardly think anything in the ruins would shed light on why the dragons are attacking people—which is, you may have forgotten, a rather more pressing question. It leaves little time for sightseeing."

"*I* have a great deal of time, which I am permitted to spend on very little other than sightseeing," I replied sweetly. "Perhaps if you could arrange to produce more in the way of useful observations, I would have more work to do here."

That sounds cattish, and it was. Our research was at last making something like progress, and a good deal of that was owing to Mr. Wilker's effort. Indeed, it was one of the things about him that annoyed me, for I would gladly have taken on some of his labors, if he would only let me. But he was jealous of anything that might diminish his usefulness in Lord Hilford's eyes. I might have said as much, too—embarrassing all parties in the process, myself included—but Jacob intervened. "Wilker and I cannot both go to the ruins and do useful work, Isabella. And we *must* gather data, if we're to have any hope of stopping these attacks. Too many of the lairs we've visited so far have been abandoned; we need to find occupied ones, so we may examine the evidence of their eating habits. If they're eating their own kind, of course, the bones won't be there—but a *lack* of bones from other animals would tell us something."

Since we could hardly take the pulse and examine the tongues of the local wyrms, I had to concede that made sense. "But why can't I be spared? It will hardly end the world if your notes remain unfiled for a day or two."

My husband had the grace to look awkward. "It may seem a silly concern, but—I do not like you going alone. With that fellow, I mean. It would not look right."

I raised my eyebrows at him. I was kidnapped by smugglers in the night, and he worried about my reputation if I went sightseeing with Astimir? But Lord Hilford spoke up. "Eh, that's easily solved. My joints would never permit me a strenuous climb; that's a job for younger men. I'll go with your wife, and keep her safe. Unless you don't trust *my* intentions." He mock-leered, and I laughed; and that settled the matter.

It was a mark of the relaxed standards creeping upon us during this expedition that everyone accepted the propriety of this arrangement: Lord Hilford, though unmarried and not my husband, was judged a suitable enough chaperon, at least in comparison to a Vystrani villager. I have often found this to be true since, that matters which seem terribly important in the early days of such a journey (what *will* people back home say?) fade into triviality with the passage of time. It has the consequent effect of making one question how vital those matters truly are—which goes some way toward explaining my increasingly extravagant behaviour, as time went on.

We set out at the crack of dawn. No camping gear this time; it would take about half the day to reach the ruins, but there was a hut used by the boyar's huntsmen, Astimir told us, in which we could pass the night before returning to Drustanev.

Buoyed by the exciting prospect of our goal, we hiked quickly. After a few hours the overgrown, rectangular silhouettes of the ruins became visible on the opposite slope, but Astimir did not lead us directly toward them. Lord Hilford questioned him, but got enigmatical replies. "I've half a mind to leave him; we can find our way from here," the earl grumbled.

I persuaded him not to—if anything went wrong, I could *not* hope to carry Lord Hilford back on my own—and soon had cause to be glad. The reason for our roundabout path, it seemed, was Astimir's sense of the dramatic: he led us down into the valley, then back up again by another trail, so that we might approach the ruins by way of their great gate.

This stood cloaked in pines nearly as tall as the ancient stones, but the trees had no foothold on the gateway itself. The central figure strode out boldly on an outcropping of solid rock, its human feet planted on the ground, its draconic head staring through the clear mountain air toward Chiavora. Vystrani winters had

DRACONEAN RUINS

been harsh to the mighty sculpture; its features were so eroded as to be almost indistinguishable, and the lintel of the right-hand passage had fallen, leaving the unknown god with only one wing. The damage somehow made the figure more inspiring: nowadays we may carve as large as the Draconeans—the Archangel in Falchester is even larger—but no amount of artistic "weathering" can counterfeit the sheer weight of time.

I stood, awestruck, pinned as surely as if a rock-wyrm had stooped on me from the sky. My reverie was only broken by Lord Hilford's chuckle. "Never been to the ruins at Nedel Tor, have you?"

My gaze was still riveted to the statue, but the spell was weakened enough for me to respond. "Only Millbridge, and those aren't very impressive."

"No, they aren't," he agreed. "Nor is Nedel Tor—not compared with what one can find in the Akhian desert—too much looting of stone for later use. But the gateway is in moderately good condition, aside from the loss of the head."

He went on talking; I think he said something about double gateways, so characteristic of Draconean architecture, and theories as to their purpose. (My favourite is the one promoted by Mr. Charving, the great urban reformer: that the Draconeans regulated traffic into their settlements by guiding arriving riders and carts through the left gate, and those departing through the right. It is utterly fanciful, as no one has ever discovered evidence of sufficient traffic at these ruins to require such measures—but as Mr. Charving parlayed this into a very successful scheme for the regulation of traffic in Falchester, where it very much *was* needed, I cannot but applaud his rhetoric.)

I hardly attended to Lord Hilford's lecture, however, for I was already fumbling my sketch pad from the bag I carried. My hands found it and the pencil by touch alone, while my eyes gauged proportions and noted evocative details. There would not be enough time at these ruins to draw them properly—not on this trip, at least, though my subconscious had begun to plot a return— but I could at least compose a brief sketch.

Astimir was impatient with this plan; he could not understand why I wanted to stop out here, without even entering the ruins. "A moment more," I said absently, casting onto the page a rough outline of the fallen lintel stone, cracked in two. How long ago had it fallen? It had rolled forward when it did; the face pressed into the earth might preserve more detail of the wing than now visible in the one still standing. But it would take a crane to lift the thing, and so its mysteries would remain hidden, alas.

The promise of further wonders finally tore me from my work. I turned to a blank page and kept the sketchbook out as we walked beneath the surviving arch and into the ruins. That single day in Vystrana taught me more about working at speed than anything that has happened since: I threw down the most cursory lines, suggesting the perspective and decay of the structures we encountered, and spent days afterward filling in the details from memory. (You may still see the results in *Sketches from the Vystrani Highlands*, published when I began to acquire enough notoriety that anything from my pen could turn a tidy profit. I do not recommend them for scholarly purposes—too many of those "remembered" details are generic or downright fanciful—but they will give you a sense of the place.)

The Drustanev ruins are not extensive. Inside the gateway lay a large, open courtyard, now thoroughly choked with underbrush and trees. Lord Hilford scuffed at the ground in one exposed spot and uncovered the chipped corner of a paving stone, tilted up at a sharp angle by a root thrusting beneath. But we did not linger long, for Astimir was urging us onward, to the main temple ahead.

I call it a "temple," though of course the function of those places has been debated ever since the days of the Nichaeans. All Draconean structures are built on such an imposing scale as to inspire awe; we therefore naturally associate them with religion. Lesser edifices did not survive the thousands of years that elapsed since the dissolution of that ancient civilization; all we have now are the great works. And to what purpose would such buildings be raised, if not for the glory of their dragon-headed deities?

A little further inward lay the pylons of the temple's front wall, too massive even for time to collapse them. Like the right-hand half of the gateway, the lintel between them had fallen, and an accumulation of debris and dirt raised the passage to nearly a third the height of the wall. Astimir assisted Lord Hilford up this slope, then bent to aid me. My skirts caught on the undergrowth, and one wicked thorn tore a long rent in the fabric, but I did not mind. From the top of that passage I could see into the hypostyle hall, now open to the elements, the thin stones of its roof long since having relocated to the ground, where they lay nearly as buried as the paving in the courtyard.

Some of the columns themselves had toppled, leaning against one another like drunken gentlemen exhausted after a night's carouse, or rolling in hefty cylinders on the ground. The sun was now high enough to make the space within a warm shelter, secret and still. The proud figures of Draconean gods spanned the walls, flat and odd to an eye accustomed to modern conventions of perspective, but hinting at mysteries forgotten ages ago. I wished I were a painter, to capture the quality of the light as it poured across those weathered shapes; being only a poor woman with a pencil, I marshaled my sketchbook and did what I could.

That particular sketch included Lord Hilford bending to peer underneath one of the tilting pillars, pulling at the tall grasses that choked the space below. Before long, he called out to me.

"Mrs. Camherst! You must come look at this. Have you brought anything that might do a rubbing?"

I obligingly fetched out a charcoal stick and a large sheet of loose paper, then picked my way across the space to join him. "What is it?"

"Run your hand across this," he instructed me, as I had done with the dragon wing.

What greeted my fingers, however, was not the microscopic roughness of the rock-wyrm's hide. Instead it was deep grooves, somewhat softened by the passage of time, but still clearly perceptible.

I crouched, trying to see, but after the brilliance of the sun, the shadow defeated me. With the assistance of Lord Hilford and Astimir, one man on each side of the pillar, holding my paper in place, I rubbed the charcoal stick everywhere I could reach.

When we pulled it free, a white gap ran down much of the center, but to either side the charcoal's smear was broken by an arrangement of lines I had seen before, in books. "It's an inscription!" I exclaimed.

Even more than the art—whose strange, stylized nature had never really caught my interest—Draconean script excited a feeling of mystery and wonder. The markings were indubitably language, though men had once dismissed them as the scratchings of dragon claws. (This is largely owing to the poor preservation of ruins in Anthiope. Once our scholars became aware of less-weathered inscriptions elsewhere in the world, opinions changed—after a certain amount of hidebound resistance, of course.) What message they conveyed, however, was completely inscrutable. Draconean writing had frustrated all efforts to decipher it.

With that clear example to hand, I gazed about with new eyes, and saw the weathering on the other columns for what it was: the faint, nearly obliterated remnants of more writing. There had once been inscriptions all over the columns of the hypostyle, but the exposed surfaces had been badly degraded.

Lord Hilford ran his hand across the leaning column and brushed grit off his fingers. "Limestone. It hasn't survived well. The walls are marble; that does better. I wonder where they brought it in from, and how?"

My finger traced along one of the gaps in the charcoal, following its raking line. "Why is it that no one can read what this says? Do we not have enough samples yet?" If so, this one might be of some value.

But the earl shook his head. "That used to be the notion, but a fellow named ibn Khattusi made a concerted effort, oh, ten or fifteen years ago, to gather together all the known inscriptions, and encouraged people to document more. He published his findings in a great fat book, and a few years later the Akhian government offered a prize for the man who deciphered the language; but no one has claimed it yet."

"We don't even know what language it *was*, do we?" I asked. "That is—obviously it's Draconean, or rather, that is the name we've given it. But we don't know what languages Draconean might be ancestral to."

With a grunt for his stiff knees, Lord Hilford knelt at my side to study the paper. "Precisely. So we have no idea what sounds these symbols might represent, or indeed whether they *do* represent sounds; they may be ideographic, like the archaic script of the Ikwunde. Codes can be deciphered, but codes represent a known language, which means one side of the equation is already in hand. Draconean is a complete mystery." He smiled sideways at me. "Fancy taking a shot at it yourself, Mrs. Camherst? The Akhian declaration did say their prize was for the *man* who sorted it out, but I daresay you could argue them into paying out for a woman."

The notion had honestly not even crossed my mind. I laughed. "Oh, no, my lord. I wouldn't even know where to begin. You've heard me butcher Vystrani." I nodded in the general direction of Astimir, who, having brought us as far as the hypostyle hall, seemed to think his work was done—that, or he'd given up on the tedious Scirling scholars who kept pausing to examine things rather than continuing onward to new sights. "I am no linguist, much less an expert."

I folded the rubbing carefully, though, on the possibility that ibn Khattusi might want it for his collection, and we spent some time poking about the ruined stones to find other bits with inscriptions not too badly weathered to record. I tore several fingernails digging up a fragment mostly buried in the earth, but was rewarded with the clearest bit yet, once I'd brushed the dirt away.

The central chamber of the temple, unfortunately, had collapsed too thoroughly for us to enter. We instead toured the remainder of the small site, including the bit of wall I had glimpsed on our hunt; I clambered rather higher atop it than was likely wise, and spent some time attempting to guess which open bit of stone in the distance might be stained with that dragon's blood.

When I climbed back down, peering past my skirts to see where I should set my feet, a twinkle of vivid color caught my eye.

My foot, already descending, almost landed atop it; I swung wide and stumbled, but managed to avoid falling. As soon as my balance was secure, I bent double, searching for that glint of color.

The grass half buried it, such that I almost missed it. But my fingers, sweeping through the blades, touched something hard; and I lifted it to my eyes.

And promptly dropped it again.

This time the finding went faster; I knew what I was looking for. A firestone, the size of my thumbnail, and brilliant in the light. I cradled it carefully in my palm, marveling. There was no mistaking this for a piece of jewelry lost by some previous visitor: quite apart from the unlikelihood of anyone so wealthy coming here in their formal gems, it was raw, not shaped by any lapidary's tools.

What on *earth* was it doing in an obscure Vystrani ruin?

I dropped to my knees and cast around in the grass, stabbing my hands on every twig and turning over every pebble. I covered an area at least five feet in radius before I conceded that my find was a solitary one. But tremendously valuable; I had seen only a handful of firestones during my days in the marriage market, and those adorning the fingers or necks or ears of people *far* beyond my own class. This one, set into a pendant or ring, would be the finest jewel the Camherst lineage owned.

Do understand, I am not a covetous woman. Not for physical things, at least; where knowledge is concerned, I am as greedy as the mythical dragons in the stories, sitting atop their glittering hoards. (Though I, unlike those dragons, am not only willing but *eager* to share.) But the firestone entranced me, for it was the first I'd ever held in my own hands. I knelt there in the dirt, tilting it in my fingers so the fire within danced back and forth, until I became aware that I'd lost all feeling in my feet. Then I staggered upright, and realized my companions had gone missing somewhere during my ascent of the wall.

I wasn't unduly concerned. Astimir was likely relaxing in a comfortable spot, waiting for us to be done. As for Lord Hilford, I thought it most probable that he'd returned to the hypostyle hall, or the great double gateway. With my sketches of the site, I knew the most direct route back would be to go left, across a broken, ruin-less bit of ground.

Halfway across that ground, something snapped beneath my foot, and I plummeted into darkness.

Not far, but it does not take much of a fall to twist one's ankle— not when the fall is so entirely unexpected. I landed awkwardly and tumbled without grace to one side, fetching up at last on my rear, with one palm skinned and my cry of surprise still ringing from the walls.

I clamped my mouth shut before a second cry could escape my lips, because two thoughts occured to me in quick succession. The first was *cave*, and the second was *dragon*.

My surroundings were undoubtedly natural. The light spilling in from above showed me rough walls and a sloping floor, unshaped by human hands. The hole I'd come in by wasn't nearly large enough for a dragon, but such a passage might exist elsewhere; the cave extended into the darkness, well beyond my ability to see. I sniffed, thinking I might catch a scent that would at least confirm my mortal peril, but all I smelled was pine.

Pine—because those were the boughs that had been laid across the opening, and then covered in needles until they matched the surrounding forest floor. A convincing disguise, but not one that could support my weight, and so I had fallen.

A disguise implied a disguiser. Someone had gone to effort to hide the opening, and not out of concern for public safety.

I went very still. Only my ears moved, drawing back along my skull as if that would make any significant improvement to my hearing.

Eventually those muscles tired, and I rubbed them with my fingers, thinking. I'd heard nothing in the darkness, and only the wind and the cry of an eagle above. The *sensible* thing to do would be to shout for help; there did not seem to be any person here at present, and if this was a dragon's lair farther along, I would do well to vacate the premises before the owner returned.

But I am not always sensible.

My eyes had adjusted as far as they could. Peering into the gloom, I saw that I had fallen quite near one end of the cave; to my right, the floor sloped away into impenetrable blackness. But I thought I could make out some shapes at the edge of the void. Brushing my skinned palm clear of debris, I rose to my knees and made my way carefully toward those shapes.

(Crawling in a dress, for those gentlemen who have never had occasion to try it, is an exercise in frustration, all but guaranteed to produce feelings of homicidal annoyance in the crawler. But there was not enough room to stand without crouching, and I did not want to test my ankle just yet.)

The shapes, when I arrived at them, proved to be a pair of crates. I brushed my hand over the top of one, and realized with a mingled feeling of horror and disbelieving hilarity what I had found.

Stauleren smugglers, as I have noted before, make extensive use of caves in their work.

The two crates were empty, so I could not be sure of my conclusion. It seemed likely, though; they were shoved against the wall as if left there temporarily, not quite far enough out of sight. The cache, if there was one, undoubtedly lay deeper in the darkness.

I was not about to go looking for it. Already it was unlikely that I could hide the evidence of my fall; it might have been the work of a bear or deer, but then where was the animal? And to leave the cave without yelling for help, I would have to drag one of the crates over and stand on it, which a bear surely would not do. To hide my trespass, I would have to shout for Lord Hilford, and then there would be more questions. He might even feel honor bound to send word to the boyar, and it would all be a tremendous mess I did not want in the slightest.

The entire incident had me giddy with surprise. That giddiness made certain courses of action seem much more reasonable than they ought to be. With the firm convinction that I was thinking good sense, I dragged one of the empty crates into position beneath the hole, then retrieved my sketchbook, which I had dropped on landing. A quick thought led to a frantic search of my pocket, soon reassured: my firestone was still there.

Then I took my pencil and wrote a quick note in Eiversch.

My apologies for the intrusion. It was an accident, and I will speak of it to no one.

I didn't sign the note, figuring that my feminine handwriting would be identifier enough—and if it was not, then no sense helping Chatzkel and his men draw the right conclusion. I tucked the paper beneath the lid of the crate, leaving most of it visible, then took my sketch pad in my teeth and climbed grimly to my feet.

My ankle was not pleased with this decision. But although it complained, it would hold me. The only bad part was when I had to climb atop the crate, putting all my weight on that foot for longer than I would have liked. That done, however, my head and shoulders emerged once more into the open air, and from there I was able to drag myself onto the ground above.

(The penny dreadfuls that purport to relate my adventures would have had me braiding grasses together into a sturdy rope, or leaping ten feet in the air to grab the lip and haul myself out by the strength of one hand. My life would have been far easier if such things were truly possible.)

Outside once more, I permitted myself three heaving breaths of relief. Then I got up, found a stick that would support my weight, and hobbled off to find Lord Hilford, planning my lies as I went.

PART THREE

*In which scientific progress is made,
despite the obstacle of a demon
from the ancient past*

THIRTEEN

An unexpected greeting upon our return — The continued problem of Jindrik Gritelkin — A possible source of aid

The twisting of my ankle cut our trip to the ruins short, although I maintained that it would be perfectly easy for me to rest somewhere with my foot elevated, sketching, while Lord Hilford concluded his tour. He insisted he was quite finished, however, and that we should depart for the hunters' hut forthwith. I only just barely dissuaded him from making poor Astimir hike through the night back to Drustanev, so as to return with a rescue party at first light. "I've had quite enough of dawn rescue parties," I said tartly. "Let us at least see how my foot feels come morning, before you call in the cavalry."

We made the mistake of taking my boot off once we got to the hut; my ankle was swollen, and without the boot to restrain it, the swelling increased. But I bathed it in a stream—grateful, this once, for the frigid quality of mountain water—and got Astimir to select a fat log from the woodpile that I could use to elevate my foot for the night, so that in the morning it was close enough to its ordinary size that I could cram the boot back on. With that laced up as tight as it would go, I told Lord Hilford I would be fine, and off we went.

Before long I was regretting that choice but refusing to admit so to my companions. It's nasty business, walking on a twisted ankle—even one only mildly wrenched. You step carefully so as not to provoke the injury, but walking in that fashion is inconvenient enough that your body keeps trying to return to more natural patterns, which of course causes discomfort. And such awkward movements eventually cause their own discomfort, as your knees and hips and back begin to complain. Alas for my well-being, I was young, and therefore *far* too stupidly stubborn to admit to any of this; and so we trekked on.

By the time we reached Drustanev, I wanted nothing more than to collapse into bed, with Jacob to bring me a soothing drink. But I knew luck was not with me the moment I saw the people gathered in the center of the village.

I had names for only a few; we had, in the regrettable manner of Scirling travellers the world over, held ourselves almost entirely aloof from the locals. Dagmira was there, however, and with her, a distraught man I recognized as Menkem Goen, the village priest.

Even had I not seen him during the festival, his clothing would have identified him; he wore full religious garb—shawl, sash, embroidered headdress, and all—and even stood barefoot on the rocky ground, as if he were in the tabernacle. Furthermore, no sooner had we spied him than he raised both hands in the air and began, in a loud voice, to recite Scripture in our general direction.

Loudly—but not enough to be heard over the racket that immediately followed, as all the gathered villagers ran toward us waving graggers. Lord Hilford and I stopped dead, gaping, as their noise filled the air.

"What on earth?" I said, but I don't think Lord Hilford heard me.

I had only ever encountered the wooden rattles during the tale of the Casting of Lots, when they are used to drown out the name of wicked Khumban. That day I discovered they have another use in the superstitions of rural Vystrana: driving out evil spirits.

It took some time to discover this, however. Dagmira glared

furiously at me while Menkem continued to recite, and everyone else surrounded us such that we could not progress even a single step farther. We were not to be permitted in Drustanev, it seemed, until the prayers were done. I could not hear enough of Menkem's words to understand their meaning—then as now, the Vystrani conduct all religious matters in Lashon, rather than the vernacular—but Temple and Magisterial traditions both make use of the same blessing at the end, with the fingers divided. On the last words—"give you peace"—Menkem lifted and blew the sacred horn, and the rattles stopped.

Into the twitchy silence that followed, I said, "What is the meaning of this?"

Dagmira stormed forward. "You didn't tell me where you were going! I had to find out from that one's mother!" She jabbed a finger at Astimir, who flinched back as if her finger were a sword.

"What does that matter?" I asked, bewildered. The truth was that I didn't know the Vystrani word for "ruins," and didn't feel like undergoing the tedious circumlocutions necessary to find out; so I had just told her we were going for a walk.

My supposed maid spat on the ground, then kicked the wet spot for good measure. The priest, who had followed at a more sedate pace, laid a calming hand on her shoulder. He didn't look calm, though; he looked worried. "There is a *gorost* on the *isdevyit*," he said, giving me a good guess as to what the word for "ruins" might be. What *gorost* was, however, I couldn't guess.

Lord Hilford's Vystrani was better than mine, and he frowned. "What kind of *gorost*?" he asked skeptically.

The priest pronounced two more words, these with an air of doom. "It is a *milgri* place; the ancients practiced many *ovyet* there, and the effects remain. It is bad luck to go there, my lord. You should not have gone."

My limited vocabulary frustrated me, but I was beginning to

guess his general meaning. Ghosts or demons or some such, and disaster for whoever crossed them. There were many such famous legends associated with ruins in Akhia; I shouldn't have been surprised to encounter them elsewhere. "We saw nothing of the sort," I told him sharply.

"You may not see them," he said ominously, "but they are there."

By now my uninjured foot was hurting almost as much as the other because it had to bear the greater part of my weight whenever I stopped. The pain made me snappish. "Nonsense. Or if there are—*spirits*," I said, substituting the Scirling word because I could not spare the patience to remember what words he'd used, "then I'm sure your most excellent prayers have banished them. We thank you, and we'll be on our way."

Now it was Lord Hilford's turn to lay a calming hand on *my* shoulder. "My good man, I'm sure all will be well. But Mrs. Camherst has suffered an injury to her ankle, and needs to lie down. If you'll pardon us—"

They did not in the least want to pardon us; his words produced a great stir, as everyone began insisting my twisted ankle must be the work of demons. Lord Hilford told them I had not sprained it at the ruins—which strictly speaking I had not; I told him I twisted it on a slope behind them, and he elided the specifics even further—but that mollified no one. I forebore to tell them their "evil spirits" were only smugglers, as by then anything I said would have come out laced with generous amounts of Scirling profanity.

The white, pinched quality of my face at least persuaded Dagmira to help. Ignoring my protests, she slung one of my arms over her shoulder, and together we hobbled off toward the house.

Or perhaps her sympathy was merely a stratagem, allowing her to lambast me without interruption. "Idiot!" she said fiercely, dumping me into a chair so she could pull my boot off. "Drag-

ons, smugglers, ruins—is there any danger you *won't* go running
to meet?"

I said something extremely foul as the boot came off. My
ankle had swollen a great deal more with all that walking, and
she had to tug quite hard. When I had my breath back, I snapped,
"You never *tell* me about these dangers until afterward!"

"I expect a fancy lady from foreign parts to have the sense the
angels gave a babe in arms!" The other boot came off more easily, and was a blessing when it did.

"More fool you," I muttered in Scirling, thinking of some of
the brainless young things (not to mention middle-aged ones) I
had met during my Season. Before Dagmira could glare a hole in
me, I added, "Astimir suggested it, you know. Or don't Drustanev
men have the sense the angels gave a babe, either?"

She spat a few words I suspected were curses. Then, to my
surprise, she added something further, in a grim tone. "One of
the smugglers has been killed. A dragon attack."

It distracted me from the pain in my ankle. A fresh incident
did not explain all of the alarm in the village; there would be no
reason for Menkem Goen and the others to focus their attention
on our ruins trip, if what they feared was dragons. But it might
account for the vehemence of their response. Wetting my lips, I
asked, "Where?"

"Down."

From the perspective of Drustanev, that meant the sharp descent to Chiavora. The smugglers must have been taking a ship-
ment to the lowlands. "How far?" I asked, but Dagmira only shook
her head; she did not know.

Surely it could not be far. The dragons would never leave their
mountains. Or would they? These attacks were already unusual;
all certainties must now be questioned.

Chastened, I cooperated as Dagmira more or less carried me

up the stairs and deposited me in bed. There I lay in troubled thought until Jacob appeared.

After the scare over my disappearance with the smugglers, I was afraid of what his mood might be, but he came in grinning. "I hear you alarmed the locals," he said, perching on the edge of the bed and taking my hand.

"Lord Hilford did his part," I said, then grimaced as Jacob inspected my ankle. "That part is all my doing, I own. A foolish misstep." And that was true enough.

My husband shook his head. "Oh, Isabella. I know you crave the freedom to explore, but—"

"But you wish I could do it without spraining my ankle?" I coaxed him into lying down at my side, and fitted my head onto his shoulder. "I quite agree. At least I was not eaten by a dragon, though."

Jacob went still, then shifted out from under my head. "What aren't you saying?"

The question surprised me. "Have you not heard? About the smuggler?"

His frown made it clear that he had not. Was this something the mayor had been saving to tell Lord Hilford, rather than his men? Or had Dagmira spilled a secret not meant to be shared with the outsiders? I told Jacob what little I knew, reluctantly surrendering the pleasant moment in favor of more important matters.

"I'll talk to the others," he said when I was done. "We need to find out how far down this happened."

I heard the warning before he could voice it. "My ankle will keep me safely at home, filing papers like I'm supposed to." I could not suppress a sigh. "Mr. Wilker shall be pleased."

Our companion might be, but my husband was not. Frowning still, Jacob kissed the top of my head, then slid off the lumpy mattress and left me to my rest.

* * *

True to my prediction, I was completely housebound for several days. The first morning, I abandoned dignity and went down the staircase on my rump; the steps were narrow, dark, uneven, and prone to bending underfoot, and I did not like the prospect of pitching down them headfirst if my ankle gave out. I was certainly not fit to go anywhere. I occupied myself filling out my rough sketches of the ruins, but soon enough something else came along to engage me.

Our sample of hide from the dragon's wing had not well survived its journey back to Drustanev. Lord Hilford had examined it under the microscope, but was unable to make much out. I was quite surprised when, three days after the trip to the ruins, a boy came charging into the workroom and shoved a pottery jar into my hands.

Mystified, I picked apart the knotted string holding the lid in place. A powerful smell greeted me as soon as I opened the jar; it was mostly filled with the plum-based spirit they call *tzuika*, which is alcoholic enough to drop a mule in its tracks. But something floated inside, and I rose and hobbled carefully over to the window to see.

It was a piece of dragon hide, nearly fresh. "Where did you get this?" I asked the boy.

His broad smile showed missing teeth; I guessed his age to be about ten. "A dragon came after us," he said. "Tata shot him."

Another attack. It had been less than a week since the smuggler was killed; the pace, it seemed, was picking up. I bit my lip in worry.

The child in front of me was not obviously bleeding or bandaged, nor did he look terribly upset; still, I had to ask. "Was anyone hurt?"

The boy shook his head. "We were hunting deer. Hidden, you

know? Tata said the lord's man wanted skin, so he sent me back with that."

The lord's man? Mr. Wilker, I guessed. I hadn't been aware that he asked the locals for help. "Not a bad idea," I murmured under my breath, fetching a pair of tweezers and lifting the scrap of hide from its aromatic container. Many of the shepherds carried jars of *tzuika* with them; it was my pet theory for how they survived without anything one could call a proper summer. "Light more candles, if you wouldn't mind—"

The boy obeyed, then hovered to watch eagerly over my shoulder as I gently patted the hide into a semblance of dryness and laid it on the microscope. My familiarity with the device was minimal, but I dared not wait until the men returned. Biting my lower lip, I bent to look through the eyepiece.

Microscopes are fiddly things; it took endless minute adjustments of the knobs before I had a clear image. I held out my hand and called for a needle, several times, before the boy said, "I'm sorry, I don't understand," and I realized I'd been commanding him in Scirling. I surfaced long enough to point at my pincushion (I had been mending my much-abused ruins dress—*ruined* dress, rather—when he arrived), and he brought it to me. Instrument in hand, I returned to the microscope, and began to prod at the magnified hide.

What I discovered will be no surprise to those familiar with dragon anatomy; it has since been found in many different species. At the time, however, it was quite a revelation. The roughness on the underside of the wing comes from tiny scales, which are not present on the upper surface. These cover tiny holes that perforate the wing, and are hinged to form a sort of valve. When the wing lifts, the valves open, reducing the resistance the dragon's muscles must overcome. When it sweeps down again, the valves close, allowing the stroke to have its fullest effect.

I did not immediately understand the function of what I saw, but began drawing it nonetheless. When the epiphany came, I exclaimed out loud—quite startling the boy, who had wandered off in boredom as I drew, and was now aiming Jacob's rifle about the room. "Careful with that," I said absently, scribbling notes on my drawing.

(I have long been accused of having no motherly instinct. As near as I can tell, this instinct consists of attempting to wrap anyone below the age of eighteen in swaddling bands, so that they never learn anything about the world and its dangers. I fail to see the use of this, especially from the point of view of species survival; but I do confess that on this occasion I may have let my intellectual excitement distract me from the peril of allowing a ten-year-old boy to wave a loaded rifle about.)

Fortunately for all involved, the boy's boredom soon overwhelmed him. I flapped my hand in his general direction when he asked if I needed the jar of *tzuika* any longer; he collected it and departed, and I fetched out Gotherham's *Avian Anatomy* to assist me in my speculations on the mechanics of dragon-wing flight. When the sun began to set, I did not even notice, except to hunch closer over my sketches as the light failed; and thus did the menfolk find me.

I knew as soon as I surfaced that now was not the time to share my discovery. Jacob and Lord Hilford entered together, deep in worried conversation. "—haven't *been* any rains," the earl was saying, "nor enough snow, even up here, to justify it. Much less in the lowlands. It's been nearly a month; he should have returned long since."

"Who should have?" I asked, diverted from my work, and rubbing my fatigued eyes.

"Gritelkin," Jacob said, dropping with a frown into the nearest seat.

Our host, supposedly: the razesh who should have been our local guide in this work. To my shame, I had nearly forgotten him. "Returned from Chiavora, you mean," I said.

Jacob's face was grim. "If he ever went."

At this, I laid down my pen and sat straighter, hardly noticing the cramps in my shoulders from hunching so long. "You think someone lied to us?"

"*I* don't," Lord Hilford said, pacing along the creaking floor. "Your husband is a more suspicious sort. No, too many people agree that Gritelkin went to intercept us. I fear that something happened to him along the way."

In the gloom of our workroom, the suggestion was more than ominous; it was frightening. But I was determined not to behave like a nit. I made certain my voice was steady before I asked, "The dragons?"

Lord Hilford shrugged. "Any number of things can befall a lone man on the road. Illness, bandits—he might have been thrown from his horse."

"But you think it's the dragons," I said.

"A scientist must never reason ahead of his data, Mrs. Camherst."

We *had* data. We knew the local rock-wyrms were attacking human beings, and furthermore that although the bulk of the incidents had taken place higher up, at least two had occurred in the direction of Chiavora. But this, I was willing to concede, hardly constituted proof that Mr. Gritelkin had been eaten by a dragon. The question was, what would? "Should we send someone toward Chiavora?" I asked. "They could inquire along the way—see if anyone recalls him passing through." Though the land was peopled sparsely enough that our odds were not very good.

"Perhaps," the earl said, "but who? I'm loath to abandon our research."

The answer seemed obvious to me. "I could go."

"Absolutely not," Jacob said, coming bolt upright in his chair.

His vehemence was startling. "Were you not *encouraging* me to return to Chiavora, not long past?"

"When you could go with the Chiavorans," Jacob said. "Who would escort you now? I'm not concerned with propriety," he added, waving away my objection before I could speak it. "Rather your safety. All the things that can befall a lone man on the road can as easily befall a lone woman."

Perhaps it was due to the darkness of the room that I focused so much on his voice, rather than his expression. The latter, I expect, was fairly well controlled, but I heard real tension in the former. Even fear.

A thousand counterarguments rose to my tongue. I was a fully competent horsewoman; Dagmira could accompany me; better me than, say, Mr. Wilker, who was of far more use to the expedition. I voiced none of them. Because one thing was stronger than my argumentative streak, and that was my desire not to cause my husband distress. I had failed signally at that goal since coming to Vystrana; but I did not want to fail again right now.

I rose from my chair and went over to him. Wordlessly, I held out my hand, and wordlessly he took it; we gripped each other's fingers tight in the dark, and that touch communicated everything that was needed. We were in a foreign place, surrounded by more danger than either of us wanted to admit, and we had very little beyond each other, and our companions. But that might be enough.

Mr. Wilker arrived then, breaking the spell, and while Lord Hilford explained the situation I went around the room and lit candles, which I should have done long since. In their warm light, our circumstances seemed far less bleak than they had a moment before. "Could we ask some of the village men to go?" I said.

"I thought of that," Lord Hilford said, "and we may try—but it's a bad time to be asking. The shepherds will be taking their flocks up to the high pastures soon. They won't have anyone to spare."

For one brief, irrational moment, I entertained the notion of finding the smugglers and asking *them* to inquire. But Chatzkel would not want to see me; not after my reckless promise to him in the mountains that we could make the dragons stop attacking. A promise I was no closer to upholding now than I had been that night.

Then a better thought came to me. "Could we ask the boyar for help?"

I knew by the sudden quiet that I had hit upon a very real possibility. When I turned from lighting the last candle, I found the men exchanging looks. "You haven't met the man, have you?" Mr. Wilker asked.

Lord Hilford shook his head. "Gritelkin was to introduce us. They're a standoffish lot, the boyars of Vystrana; not a one of them is Vystrani himself, and they all look down on the peasantry. Half of them spend all their time at the tsar's court in Kupelyi and leave the actual running of their domains to their agents, the razeshi and so on. But Gritelkin said this one has taken to spending more time here. Out of favor in Kupelyi, maybe; or he just likes the mountain air. Iosif Abramovich Khirzoff is his name."

Though I had hardly ingratiated myself with the locals, I had overheard a few comments, which I hastened to share. "He isn't much liked in Drustanev, I'm afraid. He thinks himself too good for this place, even though he isn't rich—well, he's rich compared to the villagers, but it doesn't sound like much to me. He has a good friend from Chiavora, though, some kind of doctor or scholar, who's staying with him right now; we may hope from the evidence that he's friendly to foreigners."

"And who does *this* information come from?" Mr. Wilker asked.

"The women of the village."

He muttered something dismissive beneath his breath, from which I only caught the word "gossip," but Lord Hilford nodded. "I could believe it. Gritelkin said the man was ambitious, and not very loyal to the tsar. Whether that makes him amenable to helping us, I couldn't say."

"It's at least worth a try," Jacob said. "You'll have to be the one to go, though."

A Scirling earl should impress a boyar, at least enough to get Lord Hilford through the door. After that, we would have to see how helpful Iosif Abramovich Khirzoff was willing to be.

FOURTEEN

A noise outside the sauna — Further disturbances that night —
Footprints — Zhagrit Mat

Lord Hilford set off the very next morning, with a local man for escort; it was two or three days' journey to the boyar's hunting lodge. No sooner had he departed, though, than a new trouble reared its head.

It began while I was in the sauna. For those unfamiliar with the practice, saunas are what the Vystrani use in place of bathing. Rather than subjecting themselves to the ice-cold waters of their homeland, or heating water for individual use (a wasteful practice, when one considers it), they build structures in which they burn wood to heat stones. After the smoke has been released, one may sit inside and enjoy the warmth. This induces sweating, and when the moisture is scraped away it carries the dirt with it.

But as the mention of sweating may indicate, one uses the sauna completely naked. Because of this, the Vystrani strictly regulate who may use the building when. Women stoke the fires in the morning, then clean themselves while the men are out. In the evening, the men have their turn.

Each sex uses the building communally, though, and here my Scirling sensibilities put their foot down. I could *not* bring myself to sit naked with the village women while they exchanged gossip too rapidly for me to follow—or, more likely, sat in awkward silence. I imagine they preferred not to have me among them, either; the sauna is expected to be a time of convivial relaxation, and the presence of a stranger rather inhibits that. We had therefore arrived at a compromise, which was that I put up with the blistering heat and smoke-tinged atmosphere immediately after the sauna's airing in exchange for privacy.

I should have overcome my hesitation; it would have been better to socialize more with the people of Drustanev, and participating in such rituals of daily life is very effective in that regard. As it was, though, I preferred our arrangement. After the initial, smothering effect of the warmth—such a contrast to the crisp mountain air—I settled in comfortably, sweating out my tension along with my dirt. Lord Hilford had ridden away that morning to visit the boyar; Iosif Abramovich Khirzoff would send out men; Jindrik Gritelkin would be found; and all would be well.

A coughing, moaning, *snarling* noise brought me bolt upright on my wooden bench.

Initially, it was simple startlement. What had that been? I wondered. It sounded as if it came from outside. I listened, but heard nothing more, and moved to lean against the wall once more.

An instant before my back touched the warm planks, the noise came again.

This time, it sounded closer.

Every hair on my body tried to stand up—a difficult task, in the stifling heat. The noise, whatever it was, came from no human throat. Nor was it a sheep, or a wolf, or anything I was familiar with. The most likely candidates, my mind informed me in a rational fashion entirely at odds with the chill running down my spine, were bear . . . and dragon.

Fear gains particular force when one is naked. It doesn't matter whether clothing would be of any use in the situation; linen and wool would do nothing to protect me against the claws of whatever creature lurked outside. What matters is the psychological *effect*. I felt vulnerable, with only the wooden boards of the sauna to protect me. And yet, I wished the boards were not there, because they meant I could not see the source of the noise.

Could not see, and could not easily run from.

Silence. I held my breath, then forced myself to release it when the heat swiftly made me light-headed. The exhalation turned into a pitiful yelp as something scraped along the logs of the outer wall. Where were the villagers? The sauna stood a little distance apart from the houses of Drustanev, but not all that far, and surely a bear or a dragon or *whatever* was stalking me was too large to be overlooked. I thought about crying for help, but fear of provoking an attack paralyzed my throat.

A rasping, grating sound. Moving as silently as I could, I pressed myself to the far wall, and cast my gaze about for anything that might be used as a weapon. The hot stones could surely burn the creature, but I had nothing with which to lift them except my own tender hands. The benches? Could I swing one at the creature's head? Only if I first maneuvered it out the door—or the beast tore out one of the walls. Nonetheless, it seemed my best option, and so I wrapped my hands around the planks that formed the seat.

It was heavier than I expected, and I grunted a little as I lifted it. Then I stood, waiting, until my arms began to tremble and I had to put my makeshift weapon back down. But I remained crouching over it, ready to snatch it up once more.

Nothing.

And still nothing.

Then a knock at the sauna door.

I screamed. Every nerve in my body was drawn so tight, the slightest noise would have snapped them like harp strings, and this was a brisk, impatient rapping. "Others are waiting," Dag-

mira called through the door. Then, as my scream registered—
"Are you all right?"

"Yes, I—I'm fine," I called back, panting with fright. What a lie
that was! I stumbled over my own feet as I passed through the inner door into the dark little anteroom that kept too much heat
from escaping when people went in and out. I always disrobed
there, not quite trusting the village etiquette that made everyone
look the other way as their fellows stripped down outside, and
not willing to subject my flesh to the mountain chill, either. Hastily I shoved myself back into clothing and shoes, snatched up
my bonnet, and then tore the outer door open, to find Dagmira
waiting.

She peered at me closely. "What happened?"

I ignored her, plunging leftward to make a circuit of the sauna
hut. And here something impossible greeted my eyes: *nothing.* No
tracks, save those left by human feet as people went around the
building, taking firewood from the nearby pile, leaving their
clothes in baskets by the door. I was not much of a huntswoman,
to read the ground and know what had passed there, but surely
anything as large as that sound suggested *must* have left an impression.

Dagmira was waiting when I completed my circuit, with her
hands on her hips. "What are you looking for?"

Already doubt was beginning to creep into my mind. Had I
imagined it? Nodded off on my bench, perhaps, and been awoken
by a bad dream. The heat made me light-headed, I knew that;
I could have become delirious. It didn't seem *likely*—but no less
so than that sound, and the lack of evidence for its source.

But I didn't have the presence of mind to form a convincing lie
for Dagmira, either. (Not that it would have done anything to
change what followed later.) "Nothing," I said, then added, "I'm
sorry I took so long. If anyone is looking for me, I'll be in the

workroom." Cramming my bonnet back atop my head, I floundered up the slope toward Gritelkin's empty house.

I slept badly that night. When I awoke, though, I thought it only the usual pause between first sleep and second, and lay for a moment considering what I wanted to do with myself during that wakeful time.

Then I heard a sound outside, and knew what had woken me.

It wasn't the same sound as before, that moaning, rattling snarl. No, this was a more familiar sound—and more frightening for it, in a way.

The flapping of enormous, leathery wings.

If the rock-wyrms were attacking humans, might they go so far as to attack the *village*?

I rammed the point of my elbow under Jacob's ribs, unceremoniously rousing him. "Wha?" he mumbled, coming bolt upright in bed.

"Shhhh!" I hissed, as if I hadn't provoked his too-loud response. "Listen."

"Isabella, what—" He fell silent as the flapping sound came again.

The childish instinct in me wanted to curl up under the covers, as if those were proof against all monsters in the night. The part of me that remembered being naked in the sauna sent me on a hunt for shoes. If I had to do anything, I'd prefer not to be barefoot while I did it. In a quiet, tense voice, I related my thoughts to Jacob. "The rifles are downstairs," he said, his tone matching mine.

"Do you think we should go outside and shoot at it?" I whispered.

The bedroom windows were shuttered for the night, but a

small louver over them admitted fresh air and just enough light to make out the indecision in Jacob's face. His thoughts, I guessed, were much like mine: would that drive the beast off, or simply enrage it?

"Wake Mr. Wilker," he said at last. "I'll load the guns."

This I did with alacrity. Mr. Wilker, it turned out, was not an easy man to rouse, and I did not quite dare elbow him as if he were my husband. I don't think he was quite fully conscious when he stumbled downstairs to join Jacob, and in retrospect it might have been better to trust that ten-year-old boy with the rifle I pushed into his hands. Remembering the wolf-drake incident, I wasn't entirely certain *I* should have one, either; no one had taught me to shoot in the intervening years.

But I could at least aim the barrel skyward and make noise to frighten the creature off, so out I went with the men, gun in hand.

Fog had settled into the valley that cradled Drustanev, and its touch made my skin crawl. Of course it could not be a clear night: I was doomed never to see this threat properly. There was an unpleasant stink in the air, too, that made me wrinkle my nose. Then I glimpsed movement through the fog. "There!"

I bless the chance that made me point with my finger instead of the rifle. Jacob and Mr. Wilker both brought their guns swinging around, but they were seasoned enough men not to pull the trigger immediately; and so we avoided shooting Relesku, one of our porters from the hunt.

He, too, carried a rifle. "You heard it?" he whispered, hurrying to our side.

Many people had, it seemed. There were others outside that night, most of them armed. But, as with my fright in the sauna, the sound had stopped. Whatever had brought the dragon to Drustanev, it seemed to have gotten bored and flown away.

At least, I thought it was a dragon—until we heard a cry from behind our house.

Everyone rushed in that direction. The cry was human, though, and one of shock and fear rather than pain. We arrived on the slope behind the house to find Astimir pressed against the wall, eyes wide in horror and rifle dropped to the ground.

Some ten paces away, the grass was blackened and scorched as if with fire. In four places, I saw as I forced myself closer; and the unpleasant smell was strongest here. Jacob came with me, then went ahead and knelt alongside one of the marks. After a moment's study, he lifted his head and looked at me in confused alarm. "It—it looks like a footprint."

My hands wrapped tighter around the rifle. The print—if so it was—stretched nearly two feet front to back, and there were four of them. The size of beast that implied . . .

Mr. Wilker had joined Jacob. "It's almost like a dragon's print—but not quite. And it seems to be *burnt* into the soil, not pressed."

He spoke quietly, but not quietly enough. Murmurs sprang up among the villagers, and then Astimir shattered the tension by wailing, "*Zhagrit Mat!*"

A swift glance showed me the words meant nothing to either Scirling gentleman. The Vystrani, however, were murmuring prayers, and gripping their rifles as if no longer sure they would do any good.

I knew they would not like me asking, but I had no choice. "What, or who, is Zhagrit Mat?"

Everyone immediately spread their fingers against evil. No one answered. Astimir flung himself forward, though, and seized the nightshirt of a man toward the back of the group, who I realized was the village priest. "I'm sorry, I'm sorry," Astimir babbled, falling to his knees. "I should never have taken them. I thought it was just a story—something to keep the children from being hurt in the ruins—I've been there before! Nothing had ever happened!"

The ruins. I remembered the crowd that had greeted us on our return to Drustanev, the graggers and prayers. Evil spirits, or some such. At the time I had dismissed it as local superstition. But now . . .

Astimir suddenly wheeled on his knees to point at me. "Her! She must have done something! She wandered off, I don't know where she went—she must have roused him!"

The accusation did not banish my fear, but it gave me something else to feel as well: annoyance. "I roused nothing," I said sharply. "What is this creature supposed to be? Some kind of dragon? You have enough of those about; no need to go inventing demonic ones." Though no rock-wyrm had ever left its prints burned into the ground, that I knew of. Their extraordinary breath was ice, not fire, and even an Akhian desert drake did not have feet of flame.

"He was not—" Astimir began, but stopped when the priest gripped his shoulder.

"We should not speak of it here, now," the priest said, glancing about. Whether he meant at night, so near the prints, or when the beast might still be about, I do not know, but everyone spread their fingers again. "Tomorrow. You will come to the tabernacle—we may speak there safely—and I will tell you."

I stiffened at the thought of entering that idolatrous place. Recall, I was very young; to me, Temple-worshippers were pagans. I had not yet been to parts of the world where Segulism of any sort held no sway at all, and the various heathen rites I underwent later would have given my nineteen-year-old self indignant vapors.

But my desire for knowledge was stronger than my religious sensibilities, which after all were more a matter of unthinking habit than real conviction. I nodded. "Very well. But I sincerely hope what you have to say is not a waste of time."

FIFTEEN

The tale of Zhagrit Mat — An offer of help to Dagmira —
A chilly cure for our supernatural woes

I was young, and Scirling, born and raised in a pragmatic land where many of the more intricate points of religion had long since been discarded as unnecessary complications.

I'm afraid I gave very great offense to the priest of Drustanev by walking in the front door of his tabernacle.

Those among my readers who are Temple-worshippers have likely just dropped this book in horror. Alas, I was (and still am) a natural historian, not an anthropologist or a student of history, and although in these enlightened times we acknowledge men to be a higher order of animal, I concerned myself only with the nonhuman sort.

This is my grandiose way of saying: I hadn't paid the blindest bit of attention to the local tabernacle, even during the Feast of the Reception. I had not noticed that only men went in the front door, while women used one on the side. The Grand Magister of Scirland, after all, ended segregation by sex nearly two hundred years ago, though some Magisterial traditions in other countries maintain the practice in their Assembly Houses. Jacob, it seems, no more thought of that issue than I did, for he walked in along with me, and we were ten feet in before our brains figured out what the low wooden wall at our side was.

We stopped at the same instant, and exchanged looks of identical dismay. And that, of course, was the moment that the priest chose to enter and spot us.

Had I thought I could manage it gracefully in my dress, I might have tried to vault over the wall. (It only came to my waist.) Images of my skirts catching and sending me over face-first stopped me. Would it be better to retreat and come back in by the side door I had now spotted, much too late? Paralysis over this question resulted, as it so often does, in me taking a third, entirely unsatisfactory, route: I curtsied to Menkem Goen and offered a stammering apology. "I did not realize—it's quite different in Scirland, you see—"

He scowled at me. He had been scowling the night before, too; clearly my status as the bringer of evil spirits did not endear me to him in the slightest, and this error compounded it. I was not surprised to see him in full religious garb once more, though at least we were spared the racket of graggers. Wordlessly, he pointed at the door behind me.

Was I to leave permanently, or come back in the proper way? I decided on the latter, mostly because I refused to be shamed into scurrying away. If he wanted me gone, let him say so.

But when I came back in through the women's door, Menkem made no comment. He simply gestured for both of us to sit down on our respective sides—we both chose the frontmost benches—and then went through a routine not unlike the one he had performed upon my return from the ruins. Over both of us; perhaps Jacob was contaminated by virtue of our marriage.

I filled the time by studying the interior of the tabernacle. When I was six, we briefly had a nursery maid with very strong opinions on the goat-killing heathens (her phrase) that followed the Temple. To hear her talk, the interior of the building should have been a dank, foul place, liberally decorated with entrails, with perhaps a baby's skull rolling forgotten in some corner.

It was stuffy, but no more so than any other building in this freezing and near-windowless land. The priest had lit candles for this meeting—proper candles, not the tallow dips used by most Vystrani peasants. There was an altar, but its stone surface was ruthlessly clean apart from the scorch marks, and the air smelled of nothing worse than incense. Behind the altar, an oil lamp burned with a steady flame, carried from the sacred fire in the Temple itself; it would be used to light the fires for the sacrifices, and was never permitted to go out.

Menkem finished his prayers. He turned to face us, and then stopped, appalled anew, at the sight of me with my pocket journal braced against one knee.

"You're going to write this down?" he asked, disbelieving.

Confused, I glanced down at the journal. "Should I not?"

From across the dividing wall, I heard a muffled sound from Jacob that might have been a laugh.

It was, after all, a very Magisterial response. Ours is a religion of scholarship and intellectual debate, rather different from the sacrifice-and-purity concerns of the Temple. It baffled Menkem—or perhaps he simply did not expect such a response from a woman; I could not say. Either way, I had thrown him off his script, and he chose to ignore me in favor of recovering. "If I'd known you were going to the ruins, I would have forbade it, for your own sake. There is evil there."

"So you said, when we came back." Jacob sent me a quelling look across the wall, and I went on more temperately. "Where does this evil come from?"

Menkem cast a glance over his shoulder toward the altar and the eternal flame, as if looking to them for strength, or protection. Then he took a deep breath and began.

I will not attempt to reproduce his exact wording here. Between my imperfect Vystrani, the haste of my notes, and his tendency to punctuate every sentence with an invocation to the Lord, the result would be unreadable. Instead I will give you the tale as I understood it then.

"Zhagrit Mat" is the name the inhabitants of Drustanev give to the man who supposedly once ruled the kingdom surrounding the ruins I had seen, back in Draconean times. Such kings are invariably either well beloved by their subjects or complete tyrants; Zhagrit Mat, to my surprise, was the former. But it seems he had one ambition that led him badly astray: the desire to become a dragon.

For many years he prayed to the gods to transform him, but with no success. At last, unhinged by this obsession, he turned the other way, and instead made a pact with a demon.

But the demon, of course, did not properly fulfill his end of the bargain. Some error in wording on the king's part, or simple maliciousness on the demon's, led to a terrible result: the king became not a dragon, nor the man he had been, but a monstrosity, caught forever halfway between. And not in the manner of those heathen gods, either, Menkem was careful to tell us, with a draconic head on a more or less human body; he was four legged like a wyrm, but with human skin, and a half-human face, and human hands at the ends of his twisted wings.

Driven mad by this transformation, the king became a plague on his own people. He declared himself a god, and hoarded all the riches to be had, while his subjects starved; worse yet, he demanded humans for sacrifice, and the blood ran out the front door of his shrine like a river. His evil grew and grew, until one night he took flight in a storm, and lightning struck him; he fell atop the roof of his own shrine, collapsing it, and that was the end of both king and kingdom.

Those who have read David Parnell's *Reliques of Vystrani Wisdom* will recognize this tale. It is told in other parts of the mountains as

Zhagrit Mat

well, though the details differ; in some versions the evil dragon-king is slain by an angel of the Lord, or by a brave hero, or else the pact was for a limited time and afterward the demon claimed him. Even the notion of the monstrous king's spirit haunting a nearby ruin is not unique, though that epilogue is not as often heard.

I knew nothing of such tales that day, taking notes in the Drustanev tabernacle. And although the struggle to follow Menkem's account gave me some distance from what he said, the dim interior, and the memory of those monstrous footprints burned into the ground behind our house, made me shiver. Did I believe what the priest was saying? No, of course not; I prided myself on being a rational woman, and the notion that the spirit of a twisted dragon-human hybrid would lurk about for thousands of years after the downfall of his civilization, ignoring all visitors to his ruins (for certainly there had been some), only to latch on to me for no good reason—

Then I remembered the firestone.

Nonsense, my rational mind said again, once it had recovered from its brief stagger. True, we knew the Draconeans had valued the stones; many had been found in their ruins (which is why so many sites have been ransacked by looters). But the story Menkem told said nothing about treasure.

The part of my mind that remembered the noise outside the sauna, and the footprints in the grass, was not reassured.

Then— "Lord Hilford!" I said abruptly, interrupting the priest.

Menkem nodded gravely. "Yes."

I might have imagined the noise, but the footprints were undeniably real. Which meant *something* was out there—something that might, based on the evidence thus far, have an interest in me—and if that interest had anything to do with our trip to the ruins, then both Astimir and Lord Hilford might be in danger. The young man was here in the village, but the earl . . .

Jacob stood swiftly. "I'll go talk to Wilker."

I could tell he was not convinced. Neither was I, really—but I didn't have to be. I would far rather take the precaution of sending Mr. Wilker after Lord Hilford and feel a fool for it later than *not* take that precaution, and feel an even bigger fool if something did happen.

To my husband as much as the priest, I said, "I have a few more questions. If I may?"

Jacob's hand extended as if to grip my shoulder briefly in comfort, but the wall kept us too far apart, and it might have been a breach of etiquette to reach over anyway. His fingers curled into a fist that jerked once, a curiously masculine gesture that seemed to exhort me to strength. Then he went out.

The end of my pencil was between my teeth, I realized, as I glanced down at my notes. I removed it and said, "If this is some kind of . . . evil spirit." A little of my doubt crept into my voice, but I did my best to sound agreeable. "What would you recommend?"

"You must be cleansed," the priest said with an air of finality. "It should have been done when you came back from the ruins; I said so at the time. But we will do it now."

The Temple's obsession with washing had not been part of my nursery maid's tales—she was too convinced their followers were all dirty and foul—but I knew of it from other sources. Well, if this was the price for laying Menkem's fears to rest, then it was a small one to pay. Tucking my pencil into the journal, I held out my hands. "Where is your basin?"

It required rather more than a basin.

Menkem sent me to gather Jacob, Mr. Wilker, and Astimir; the latter certainly needed purification along with me, and it was judged best to give a scrub to the gentlemen as well, just to be on the safe side. Lord Hilford could be cleansed when he returned.

By the time I had done this, somehow the entire village knew what was afoot. (This might have been the Drustanev gossips at work, but I think it more likely Menkem had said something the night before.) Quite a crowd of them gathered outside the tabernacle, including Dagmira. "I'm told this is to be a full bath," I said to her. The notion was rather appealing; I never felt quite properly clean after using the sauna. "Will that be done inside the tabernacle?"

Her look was scandalized, as if she sincerely hoped I had botched my Vystrani and meant to say something else entirely. "Of course not! I'm surprised he let you in there, heathens as you are. No, it has to be living water."

Reciting Scripture in a loud voice, Menkem began leading the crowd forth. "Living water?" I repeated, unsure if I'd heard her correctly.

Dagmira nodded, but seemed uninclined to explain. I translated the words into Scirling for my companions, and Jacob stumbled over a rock. "Living water? Oh, surely they don't mean— Yes, they do."

I followed his gaze, and saw the icy stream up ahead.

No amount of protest would convince the priest to back down. His rural theology included nothing that would cover this situation, but he was determined to use what little he had. Jacob, whose scholarly interests had at one point included religious history, mustered some very learned-sounding arguments that lost half their force when translated into broken Vystrani; to no avail. Nothing would do but that we be dropped into the deepest part of the stream, where the water could cover every last inch of our bodies.

Every last inch. I realized, halfway through the argument, that

Jacob was less concerned with the cold, and more concerned with the spectating villagers who were about to see his wife stripped naked in front of them. And I had thought the sauna was bad! Menkem seemed to believe that this being a ritual affair meant it didn't matter who saw me; I could only chalk that up to rural practicality, since surely any religion that requires women to sit apart from men in tabernacle ought not to approve of nudity in mixed company.

My willingness to tolerate their superstition only went so far. "You have a choice," I told Menkem firmly. "You can bathe me publicly with my clothes on; you can bathe me privately with my clothes off; or you can bathe me not at all. But I am not removing a stitch out in the open like this, nor so long as any of these other men are around." My gesture took in everyone but Jacob and the priest himself. I would have excluded Menkem, too, except that I was fairly certain the ritual required him to be present.

The priest did not like it, but Jacob and I stood firm, with Mr. Wilker's support; I rather thought the latter less than eager to expose himself to the locals, either. Finally it was agreed that the villagers would be sent away, except for a few assistants; these would help Menkem bathe Astimir and my two companions, after which Jacob and Dagmira would bathe me under cover of one of our tents.

I accordingly gave them their privacy. Unfortunately, this left me to sit alone on a line of barrels with Dagmira, who glared at me. "You bring trouble."

Several possible responses rose to my tongue, all of them defensive. Menkem's story had placed a worm of doubt in my heart, though, and it gave me pause. Even without evil spirits in the picture, we were a disruption to this village.

For a good cause, of course; despite our awkward start, we had gathered a great deal of valuable information, ranging from simple matters like a reliable description of a mating flight to my observation of the tiny valves in the wing membrane.

But what did that matter to Dagmira? It would bring us acclaim in Scirland—well, it would bring the gentlemen acclaim, once they presented our findings to the Philosophers' Colloquium—and, of course, I had the satisfaction of the scholar, uncovering things never before known to man. That meant nothing in Drustanev, though.

They had our coin, I told myself; Lord Hilford had paid for any number of things in the course of arranging this expedition. Much of that, though, had gone to the missing Gritelkin, and this boyar above him. Was what remained sufficient compensation for all the disruption our presence caused?

These thoughts had occupied me long enough in silence that Dagmira made a disgusted noise and looked away. She turned back, however, when I said in a small voice, "I am sorry."

The surprise in her eyes would have made me laugh, had I been feeling less low. "What we're doing—well, I tell myself it is for the benefit of all mankind, and I do believe that's true. But the benefit to you is very distant, I must admit. Is there something that could make it better? Should I tell Lord Hilford to distribute more payment?"

The offer produced a wealth of conflicting reactions in her face, less than half of them positive. Finally Dagmira said bluntly, "Get rid of the dragons."

"Get rid of them!" I shot to my feet, appalled.

She flung one impatient hand at the sky. "They eat our sheep, attack the shepherds—what good do they do us?"

All my childhood obsession with dragons welled up in my throat, choking me. "But they're—they're—" I was not capable of having this conversation in Vystrani, where my vocabulary lacked the word for "magnificent." Perhaps it was for the best; the struggle to convey my meaning gave my brain time to catch up. Beauty and splendor are all very well, but they put no food on the table for a mountain peasant, nor do they keep the house warm in winter.

But I could hardly commit myself to their eradication, either. Suddenly fierce, I said, "I cannot do anything about the sheep; dragons must eat, just as wolves and bears and humans must. But we will find out what is making them attack the shepherds, and put a stop to it. That is one thing our science can do for you."

It was the same promise I had made Chatzkel during my night with the smugglers, and I had yet to fulfill it. But my words then had been driven by a desire to get away safely. This time, my motivation was quite the reverse; I did not want to go anywhere. Not when going would mean admitting defeat, and abandoning these people to further attacks, further deaths.

And so my promise carried a silent echo: I *would not leave* until I had made good on my word.

Even if it meant freezing to death in a Vystrani winter.

By the pursing of her lips, Dagmira was less than entirely confident, but she accepted it with a grudging nod. "That would help."

As would laying their minds to rest on the matter of this curse, whether it was superstition or not. Jacob came, wet-haired and irritable, to summon me, and together we went back to the stream, where one of our tents had been pitched across the flow.

It was not large enough that I could stand anywhere both sheltered and dry. Mouth set tight, I took off my shoes and stockings, drew a deep breath, and waded in.

The first touch of water against my bare foot was enough to persuade me that the sauna was a splendid device when the alternative was this frigid stream. It only got worse as I went deeper, my skirts plastering themselves against my calves like clammy hands, and my toes going numb enough to render my footing uncertain. I counted my blessings, though; the stream here was barely deep enough to submerge me lying down, and rose no higher than my knees while standing.

I ducked into the tent, crouching to fit under the stretched canvas. Dagmira followed me, and Jacob stood outside to receive my clothing. I would have preferred it the other way about, but Menkem insisted; we Scirlings were all heretics, after all, and could not be trusted to do the thing right.

Any shyness I might have felt was vanquished by my desire to finish this *quickly*. I stripped off dress, petticoat, stays, and shift in record time, while Menkem prayed outside. Dagmira stopped me, though, as I steeled myself to descend into the water. "Your hair," she said.

"What of it?" I snapped, my teeth chattering. Goose pimples had sprung up all over, until my skin felt as pebbly as a dragon's.

"The water must touch everything," she said, turning me about so she could drag the pins from my hair. It tumbled over my shoulders, a warm touch I was sorely reluctant to ruin. But delay only made things worse, and so the moment Dagmira's fingers finished their rough combing, I sucked in a deep breath and dropped.

The sheer, appalling *shock* of it caused me to lose most of that air an instant later. I think I yelled, though I cannot be sure. I know I surged partway up again, only to be met by Dagmira's hand, mercilessly forcing me back down. By then I had very little air, but rationality had managed to recover enough that I knew I needed to last only a few moments.

Without warning, a foot planted itself against my ribs, driving me against the hard rocks and slimy mud of the stream's bed. I clawed at it, and Dagmira caught my hands—no, just my right hand, and she was prying at my fingers. I would have screamed at her if my head weren't underwater. Just before I could be certain

she was trying to murder me, though, I realized what she was after: my wedding ring. The water had to touch *everything*.

That ring had not been off my finger since Jacob placed it
there. But right then, it was standing between me and the chance
to breathe again; I did not think he would begrudge its brief absence. I let Dagmira take the ring, and dropped my arms beneath
the water again.

Her foot vanished, and a moment later, when I truly could not
stay down any longer, I floundered to the surface. Air, blessed
air, rushed into my lungs. Then Dagmira helped me to my feet. I
needed the aid; every part of me seemed to have gone numb, and
I was shaking so badly that I surely would have fallen.

The clothing Jacob thrust into the tent was not my own. I
could not have gotten such closely tailored garments on just
then, and they had all gotten soaked besides. The robe Dagmira
flung over my head was soon the same way, but it was thick wool,
warm even when wet. She then helped me from the tent and back
up onto shore, where Menkem finished his prayers with the holy
gesture.

At that moment, I did not care in the slightest what spiritual
benefit I might have gained from the exercise. I was in sunlight,
and no longer in the stream—all to the good—but the wind cut
like a knife. The sooner I got indoors, the better. I stumbled badly,
trying to walk, until Jacob took the simple expedient of picking
me up and carrying me onward. "You d-d-d-on't have to do that,"
I said, my chattering teeth contradicting my body, which was
more than glad to curl up against his chest.

I felt the quick jerk of his laugh. "Nonsense. Carrying you helps
warm me up. We both benefit."

Who could argue with that?

My wet hair was the worst, holding the chill long after my

body had started to recover. Jacob and I huddled under the blankets in our bed until I had stopped shaking; then he went out again. I remained there a while longer, feeling like a small child in winter, reluctant to leave my cocoon. Finally I forced myself out, pinned my hair up in a messy knot that at least would not freeze my back, and went downstairs.

Jacob came through the front door as I did. "Wilker and Menkem are off, with Astimir to guide them," he said, to my questioning look. "Astimir has been to the boyar's lodge before, and knows the way. I will give the priest this much; when I pointed out that Lord Hilford would be on his way back by the time Wilker caught him, and then it would be days yet before they got back here, he immediately insisted on going with them." Jacob snorted with quiet laughter. "I should like to be there to see Hilford's expression, when Wilker tells him he must be dunked in a mountain stream."

Lord Hilford was not a religious man; he joined us in our studies on Sabbath night, but only because he would spend the night reading anyway. But I hoped, with the superstitious chill that had been plaguing me since the previous night, that he would cooperate.

"Will they be safe?" I asked, rubbing my arms for warmth. "I don't mean this Zhagrit Mat business—well, that, too—but from the dragons."

"They're armed," Jacob said, "and know to keep an eye out. It's as safe as they can be, short of hiding indoors."

He had a point. There had been no trouble in the village—perhaps because there were so many people; predators often prefer lone prey—but anyone who ventured beyond its boundaries was at risk. Mr. Wilker was likely safer than if he were going out with Jacob for research.

I was selfishly glad my husband would not be leaving the village. And yet, how could we answer our questions, and fulfill my promises to Dagmira and Chatzkel, without risking ourselves in the field? We would have to dare it eventually. And as much as I wished to pretend otherwise, we had to do it soon.

SIXTEEN

*Idle hands — An odd circle — Plans for investigation —
Dagmira's family*

With both of the other gentlemen gone, Jacob was at loose ends. He tried to talk to the villagers, but none of them wanted to come near him until they knew whether the evil of Zhagrit Mat had been banished. Back home in Pasterway, he would have passed the time answering his correspondence; but the difficulty of receiving mail in Drustanev meant no one was writing to us. I recognized the signs of frustrated idleness, and took steps to mitigate them.

I had, as originally advertised, been filing the gentlemen's notes. It was a more haphazard affair than I would have liked, though, because I had never done such work before, and had no system. Together Jacob and I went through the pages, discussing what we had learned, and writing fair copy of many things that had been jotted down in a messy scrawl.

It was tedious work, but at the same time, it gave me a deep, wordless pleasure. I remembered the naive girl that had stood in the king's menagerie, never dreaming that Jacob Camherst would become her husband, but hoping he would be her friend. My naivete had been vindicated; we *were* friends now, in what I thought of (at the time) as a queerly masculine way. Ladies did not have these sorts of conversations, speculating as to how the daytime torpor and winter hibernation of rock-wyrms allowed those enormous predators to survive without eating everything in sight—not with each other, nor with gentlemen either, who were not supposed to tax our minds with such weighty matters.

The Manda Lewises of the world will say that is not love, at least not of a romantic kind. I will grant that it certainly is not the sort one finds in plays and sensational novels—but that sort always seems to be causing trouble for everyone involved, and the occasional innocent bystander. (I thought so then, and I think so even more now, having seen that very principle in action.) I argue, to the contrary of Manda and her ilk, that such a deep and pleasant rapport *is* love, the common thread that may link friends and relations and spouses; and furthermore, the mightiest torrent of passion, without that thread woven into it, is mere animal lust.

Such were the thoughts filling the depths of my mind, while the surface occupied itself noting down changes on our map. Many of the lairs marked by the smugglers had proved to be abandoned; Jacob and Mr. Wilker, in the course of their explorations, had found a handful more with new inhabitants within. Clearly the dragons had moved house . . . but why?

I scowled down at the paper, for I had not thought to provide for alterations when I made my marks, overwriting Jacob's hasty pencil scratches in more careful ink. Finally I blacked out the X's of empty lairs until they were solid squares, and drew new X's where Jacob said they had found dragons unexpectedly in residence. "I should like to know how long ago they started migrating—and where the rest of them have migrated *to*," I said, and he murmured in agreement.

My eye drifted over the revised map. If migration *was* occurring, I wondered whether there might be an underlying pattern—a certain distance traveled, or a certain direction—which would help us understand the process, and to find the remainder of the dragons.

I did not see an answer to that question. But I saw something else.

My finger traced an arc of lairs, curving around from east to south. It continued, with interruptions, through the west and north, with a diameter of several miles. Not a perfect circle, but . . .

"Jacob," I said, "what's here?"

He leaned over to see where my fingertip rested, in the center of that circle. The map there was blank—entirely without lairs, so far as we had recorded. "There? Let's see—that's past the ravine . . ." He shrugged. "Nothing in particular, that I can think of."

"You've been in there?"

"Not yet," he said. "Those lairs you just marked are the farthest Wilker and I have been; it's a fair hike, getting up there."

"So there *could* be something there, that you haven't seen?"

Jacob sat back, frowning at me. "Such as what? I'll grant you it looks oddly regular, but our map is hardly perfect; some of our distances are wrong, and I'm sure we don't have all the lairs. There might be one right in the middle of that apparent circle."

"Which is one possible answer to your question," I pointed out. "We *think* that rock-wyrms are solitary, coming together only to mate, and that they have no hierarchy amongst themselves. What if we're wrong? There might be some kind of . . . oh, queen dragon lairing there, and all the others keep their distance."

"Or it could be there are no suitable caves there."

A fair point; the reason rock-wyrms are found in clusters, and fly such distances to hunt, is because not all parts of the Vystrani highlands have caves that meet the dragons' needs. But that circle seemed so very regular. Could it possibly be an accident?

(The answer, by the way, is yes. In this case it proved not to be, but such things happen all the time, when one's data is as scanty as ours was. The human mind is very good at imagining patterns where none truly exist. If you are reading this book because you have an interest in pursuing a science, whether natural history or some other, bear that warning in mind. It will save you a great deal of humiliation—I speak from experience. But that is a tale for a later book.)

I had enough sense to know I should not leap to conclusions. In fact, there was only one sensible way to proceed. "We must go and look."

Jacob's eyebrows rose at the word "we." "This is where I remind you that it will be at least four days, more likely five, before Wilker and Hilford return."

I gave him my most charming smile, and the reply he knew was coming. "And where I suggest that we need not wait for them."

"Isabella . . ."

"You took me on the hunt."

"Because it would have been inefficient to lug a dragon's carcass all the way back here for you to draw. And the attacks are coming more and more often."

"The fact remains that you *took* me," I pointed out. "The dangers were no less simply because you had reason. And you have reason now, too: it will be four days, more likely five, before Mr. Wilker and Lord Hilford return, which is four or five days wasted— not to mention four or five days in which the dragons might grow even more aggressive than they already have."

"You don't know how to shoot, Isabella."

A lack I was acutely aware of, these days. "But I can keep watch with the best of them. Truly, can we afford to delay, when we might learn something that could save someone's life?"

Jacob bit his lip; he was wavering. I pressed my advantage. "If you go out alone, you will certainly *not* be safe; think of the time you fell, when you and Mr. Wilker were mapping caves. What if you had hurt your leg? You need a companion, and I am volunteering."

"*You* are supposedly being haunted by the spirit of a dead monster," he said drily.

By that, I knew I was winning the debate. In all honesty, I cannot think of anything Jacob ever truly refused me—even things others would say he should have done.

I was bright enough not to say that myself, though. Instead I addressed his point, as if it were a genuine concern. "We'll see if anything troubles us tonight. If not, then we can trust that either Menkem Goen's ritual did some good, or it was some kind of chance occurence, not to be repeated." We could hardly have set out that day regardless; it was far too late. So it cost me nothing to wait.

Jacob, I suspect, performed the same calculation for himself, but he said nothing of it. "We shall see."

I must have woken up eight times that night, but I heard nothing, and neither did Jacob. And in the morning, the grass was clear of any new marks, though the ones behind the house remained.

Still, we didn't leave that day. I think Jacob was quietly looking for ways to dissuade me; we had a number of brief conversations on such matters as the weather (cold and relentlessly windy, as always, but otherwise fair) and the suitability of my clothing for such a hike (I told him I would borrow a pair of his trousers).

Jacob's own impatience settled the matter. I had not thought of him before as a restless man, but he had none of his usual hobbies to occupy him in Drustanev; and having spent the better part of a month going out nigh daily, he found himself chafing at this sudden inaction. He did not like any better than I did the thought of sitting idle when we might be learning something that could help the villagers.

"If tonight passes quietly," he said at last, "we'll go tomorrow."

I spent the afternoon in preparation, so that we would not waste any time the following morning. The area was a strenuous day's hike away; allowing a day to explore, that would be three days altogether. We would return when Mr. Wilker and Lord Hilford did, or possibly just before.

My preparations were hardly secret; it is no surprise that Dagmira guessed their general purpose. "Where do you think you're going?" she demanded, hands on her hips.

Before, I might have fobbed her off with some vague answer, not wanting to face the possibility of argument. Ever since our conversation, though, I felt guilty about the extent to which we ignored the villagers of Drustanev. I told myself we had reason; they'd been largely sullen and unhelpful where our researches were concerned, seeing us as a disruption and possibly a threat. But if Dagmira knew of any danger, she might unbend enough to warn me. "Come with me," I said, leaving off my packing, and led her downstairs.

Our map still lay on the workroom's one large table. I pointed to the center of the circle and asked her, "What's there?"

Dagmira frowned in puzzlement at the map. "On the paper?"

"No, in—" I caught myself. "Do you know how to read a map?"

I actually said "picture of the land"; although I knew the Vystrani term, it temporarily escaped me. Dagmira mouthed through my odd choice of words, even more puzzled. Then her brow cleared. "*Ulyin!* Mayor Mazhustin has one, and Menkem Goen keeps one of Akhia. They're pretty—much prettier than this."

Her casual denigration of my work, I surmised, amounted to a "no." Why should she know how to read a map? Drustanev was so isolated, she might never have been as far as another village. The people here navigated by landmarks, not drawings of them. I described the area to her, based on what Jacob had said of it, and then Dagmira nodded. "In the middle of that area," I said. "Is there anything there? Anything special, I mean."

The young woman shook her head. (As I write this, it occurs to me, for the first time, that Dagmira cannot have been much younger than I was. She was not yet married—they wed surprisingly late in the Vystrani highlands; she would not seek a husband until her dowry of weavings was complete—and perhaps that was part of it; but I suspect the larger part of it was simply that I saw myself as a worldly, sophisticated woman, and her as a rural child. What an unfortunate thing to realize, long after I could possibly apologize to her for it.)

"Too rocky," she said of the region in question. "There's no point in cutting or burning the trees; it wouldn't make good pasture."

"You don't have any legends about it? Evil spirits I should be wary of?" I could not undo my ruins trip, but I could at least try to prevent another one.

Dagmira looked at me sharply, to see if I was mocking her, but I was quite sincere. "Nothing," she said. "It's just more mountain."

When she heard that Jacob and I intended to go see for ourselves, she shrugged philosophically. By then she had resigned herself to the fact that I would behave neither like a sensible Vystrani peasant girl, nor like a fancy lady from foreign parts. But she laughed at the notion of me carrying a proper share of our supplies—not over the proposed terrain. "You wouldn't even make it halfway," she said, and was probably right. "I'll make my brother go with you."

"Your brother?"

She looked at me as if I were simple in the head, and soon I found out why. "Iljish?"

The lad who acted as the gentlemen's valet—though in truth he'd become more a man-of-all-work than manservant. I had not realized he was Dagmira's brother. They did not look much alike.

Stammering with embarrassment, I said, "Won't your parents mind?"

Dagmira shrugged with unconcern that was, I think, partially real, and partially a scab over an old wound I had just prodded without knowing. "They're dead."

My face heated even further. This young woman had been my maidservant for weeks, and I had not bothered to learn the first thing about her family. I had never thought of myself as particularly arrogant, or prone to ignoring the world around me, yet I had devoted far more thought to the doings of rock-wyrms than to the people who kept our house.

I managed to accept Dagmira's offer with something like grace, but the shame of my blindness stayed with me. How difficult was it for her, orphaned in this village, having to be both mother and sister to Iljish? No wonder she had taken this position, serving the strange foreigners. I was very quiet through supper that night, wondering if our placid cook had some sorrow in her own past I was ignorant of. She did not dress in a widow's weeds, at least, but beyond that I could not muster the nerve to ask. I did not know her well enough, and that was not the way to start.

But I could not dwell on that matter forever. At the crack of dawn the next morning, Jacob, Iljish, and I departed, on what surely must be accounted one of the more momentous hikes of even my adventure-filled life.

SEVENTEEN

The usefulness of Iljish — Adventures in abseiling — An enormous cavern — What we found there — Its implications

Talking to Dagmira about our journey was one of the better decisions I made in Vystrana, for she was absolutely right: I would not have made it even two hours into that hike if she had not sent Iljish along.

He had inherited none of his sister's robust build. But he was a wiry thing, far more capable of scrambling over the rough terrain than I, even with a pack on his back. Iljish scampered across the stones and hacked through the brambles with the boundless energy of a squirrel. I came second, and Jacob brought up the rear. In theory he held his gun at the ready, prepared to shoot at any dragons that might think to trouble us, but in practice he had to sling it across his back as often as not, needing his hands for balance on the broken terrain.

We set out in the direction the smugglers had taken me, but soon diverged from that course, into terrain where we need not fear running into them, or indeed anyone except the occasional hunter. The limestone bones of the mountains came to the surface in jagged blocks there, where the walls of steep valleys had collapsed downward in the not-too-distant past. The forest across much of this had reached the stage where it supported a dense undergrowth of flowering brambles, making our progress far more laborious than under the venerable fir.

We went up, and up, and up. Lowlanders that we were—I had

never lived more than a thousand feet above sea level—Jacob and I made heavy going of it, though nothing like so bad as we would have done on our arrival, before we had a chance to adapt. During one of our rare breaks, Jacob admitted that he and Mr. Wilker had been thoroughly blown by their first few explorations. "I thought myself fit enough," he said, "but this air is so much thinner; I had no idea it would make exertion so hard." He spoke in Vystrani, but Iljish still looked mystified. Having lived his entire life in the mountains, he found nothing odd at all in the quality of the air.

When I could spare the energy to think, I made up my mind to speak to Iljish about his family. He was, I judged, a bit younger than his sister, and I had no awkward history with him (though Dagmira might have shared her side of our own); these combined to make him seem more approachable, to my embarrassed mind. But by then he had begun ranging outward from our progress, snapping off shots at anything whose fur he might sell. The rifle was ours, and better than any in Drustanev; the use of it was as much a payment to him as whatever Jacob had offered.

Iljish came back at last with a pair of rabbits slung over his shoulder. Jacob and I had paused for breath in a congenial spot, where sunlight broke through the trees to warm the air, and an edge of limestone formed a handy bench. Nerving myself, I began, "I was talking with your sister, Iljish, and—"

"Hush!" Jacob hissed, in a low, urgent voice.

My husband had never once spoken so peremptorily to me. I hushed, more out of surprise than obedience; and then I heard what he had.

A single flap of wings. And then, just when I thought I might have imagined it, another.

We recoiled back from the sunlight, so inviting a moment before, so dangerous now. A shadow passed overhead. Through the trees, I caught a glimpse of the dragon, banking on a warm up-draft of air to continue its exploration of the area. Had the beast spotted some animal prey? No, it wasn't nearly close enough to sunset; no rock-wyrm should be hunting at this hour.

I dared not pull out my notebook to jot the line *aggression linked to disturbance in sleep patterns?* But I thought it, and even while I crouched at the base of a tree, trying not to feel too much like one of the rabbits over Iljish's shoulder, I wondered if there was any way to test the theory.

Jacob had slid his rifle free, and now knelt with the barrel pointed at the ground. I met his gaze, and saw the hesitation there. Should he shoot to defend us, and risk failure, which would almost certainly bring the full threat upon us?

I shook my head, a tiny gesture, as if the dragon would hear my face moving through the air. Under cover, Jacob would be shooting half blind. And he dared not go into the open for a better angle.

The dragon coughed out a noise that sounded, to my excitable ear, like annoyance. A moment later we heard the renewed flapping of its wings fading into the distance; nevertheless, it was several long minutes before any of us could move.

"That," I said at last, "was not Zhagrit Mat."

Jacob let out the breath he had been holding. "No. An ordinary dragon—perhaps." He ran his left hand through sweat-damp hair, then said, "I know why we argue so rarely. I can predict enough of what you will say that there isn't much point in starting it. We're far enough along that it hardly makes sense to turn back."

The point was debatable. But I was hardly going to argue Jacob's side for him, if he would not. "Let us continue on, then, and get out of that dragon's range before sunset."

We did not make it quite so far after that as any of us had

hoped, but Jacob, in consultation with Iljish, decided it was best to stop where we found a defensible campsite, and cover the last bit the following day. I forced myself through my share of the work in setting up that camp, but fell on my nose as soon as I could, and slept so deeply a dragon could have eaten my legs for a snack and I would not have discovered it until morning.

The next day, we began our exploration.

No more the headlong marching of the previous day; now we picked our way carefully, one eye on the sky above, one on the ground ahead. Approaching from Drustanev sent us through one of the gaps in the circle I had noted; there were, so far as we knew, no lairs in the immediate vicinity. But once inside the circle, who knew what we might find?

It was wildly beautiful terrain, if you have the spirit within you to appreciate *true* wilderness, rather than the groomed version that appears in romantic paintings. I have never liked Vystrana so much as I did on that journey, though how much of that was the scenery and how much my circumstances—stretching my wings, with my husband at my side—I cannot say. The stone here was quite porous, so that we heard a steady soft rushing from snowmelt flowing along below the ground, and here and there found a small waterfall cascading from the broken rock. (For once my exertions were strenuous enough that I was actually *glad* for its icy touch upon my face, though it still left me gasping.)

"I expect there are caves," Jacob said, peering up one of the cracks from which water issued forth, "but they may not be large enough for lairing."

I retied the laces of my boots and shoved errant strands of hair back beneath the Vystrani kerchief with which I had restrained their fellows. "Whatever accounts for the circle—if indeed there is any such thing—will be found at the center." We forged onward.

Until we found our way blocked by another ravine, even more forbidding than the one we had traversed on our way here. This one looked like the mountain had been split open by a giant's axe: a steep crevasse, too wide to be bridged by a fallen tree, too long to be conveniently circled. "Have you ever been here before?" I asked Iljish.

He shook his head, peering over the edge in a way that made my muscles twitch with the desire to pull him back. "What do you think is at the bottom?"

More brambles, in all likelihood, but I did not say it; I heard in his voice the buoyant energy of a young man who cannot see a challenge like that ravine slope without wanting to conquer it. I shared his impulse, in more feminine form. This was not precisely the center of the circle I had marked, but perhaps the secret lay here. Our map was not exact, after all, and dragons might be less than entirely precise themselves.

Jacob had caught the same enthusiasm. He grinned at me and said, "I once climbed Matherly Crag, without ropes, on a dare. But I think we will use ropes here."

I was glad of that, as I had never climbed anything more challenging than a tree, and that in skirts. Fortunately, this slope was not quite vertical—at least not on our side. The far wall was a different matter, overhanging the base of the ravine and casting it into shadow. If we had to go up that side to continue our search, I suspected our exploration would end here.

We tied our first rope around a sturdy tree, and then Jacob used it to steady himself as he descended. Once he found a suitable place to stop and attach another, I began to follow him. The disadvantage to this method, I discovered, was that I must face the cliff; not all portions of the slope required me to cling to the line, but if I turned to see where I was placing my feet, it put me in a bad position for those times when I *did* require it.

The final stage of our descent was even steeper; in the end, Jacob had to teach me how to abseil, which I was not very good at. I cracked my knees repeatedly against the stony wall, and my ribs were quite bruised from the constriction of the rope by the time I reached the comparatively level floor of the ravine. Once Jacob had extricated me, I staggered off a few steps to lean against a boulder and nurse my pains in private while he guided Iljish through the process.

The sheer *quiet* of the place struck me. The curve of the ravine was such that it blocked the wind rather than channeling it; I had not realized just how ever-present that sound was here until it faded. The verdant undergrowth rose around me like some kind of enchanted jungle, until I almost expected a talking fox to walk out of it, like in one of my old nurse's tales. I did not fancy the notion of climbing that rock face again, even with the ropes—but it was worth it, and so were my bruises and scrapes, for the sheer pleasure of this place.

And for the sight that greeted my eyes, when I looked around the curve to what lay beyond.

The overhanging wall on the far side of the ravine concealed an enormous black opening, easily fifty feet across, and deep enough that I could see nothing of what lay inside. A cave, most definitely, and far larger than any we had seen used as a lair . . . but I remembered my half-serious comment about a queen dragon, and my mouth went very dry.

"Isabella!" Jacob called out. I nearly jumped from my skin. Swiftly I turned to wave at him, both to show him where I'd gone, and to silence him.

He frowned in puzzlement at my urgent gesture, but did not argue; moving as quietly as he could across the rough ground, he joined me, while Iljish unwrapped himself from the rope. "What is—" Jacob began.

He never finished the question. His gaze fell upon the cave opening, just as mine had, and I suspect I had gaped in much the same way. "I haven't seen anything moving," I said in a murmur that went no farther than us.

Jacob shook his head. "No, you wouldn't . . . they are crepuscular hunters, after all. At this time of day, any rock-wyrm would be sleeping in the sun. Any healthy one, at least. But they prefer their lairs far smaller."

To be precise, they preferred their lairs a bit bigger than themselves. "You haven't seen anything that large in the sky, have you?"

Of course not; he and Mr. Wilker would have fallen over their own feet to come tell us. Jacob frowned. "I don't see how anything that large could *fly*. Granted, we don't understand very well how it works even with the dragons we've seen; we don't know enough about their anatomy yet. But surely there must be a limit."

"A limit to what?"

I took some comfort from the fact that Jacob, too, leapt a foot in the air at Iljish's question. The boy was far quieter across the ground than either of us, but spoke far more loudly. He looked taken aback when I frantically hushed him.

"Nobody's *ever* seen a dragon that large," he said, in a lower tone, once we had explained. "Not outside of stories."

Stories like those about Zhagrit Mat? I was *not* going to calculate what that creature's wingspan might supposedly have been. He was associated with the ruins, anyway, not with this cave. Assuming Dagmira was correct.

Jacob straightened, looking back to where he'd dropped the supplies we brought down with us. "Well. Now would be the safest time to explore; we gain nothing by delaying."

Thinking back, I suspect him of a degree of bravado, not

wanting to show fear in front of his wife. It had the salutary effect of inducing a similar bravado in me, though, which may not have been what he intended. "I couldn't agree more. Do we have torches of any kind in that pack?"

Bravado or no, we approached the cave carefully, skulking along the base of the overhanging wall until we reached the mouth. There we paused, all three of us listening mightily for any sound within.

The only things we heard were the steady drip of water, and the echoing silence of empty space.

Jacob went first, followed by Iljish, both of them gripping rifles tight. I remained outside for the moment, unlit torch in hand. They kept close to the wall, not wanting to silhouette themselves against the brightness outside. The ground sloped down before them, and I realized what had seemed like a low ceiling—serrated with stalactites like a dragon's maw; an image I could not shake— was nothing of the sort; the cavern broke through to open air near its top, and the men were now descending toward the depths.

Down they went, Jacob drawing ahead of Iljish, farther and farther until I could scarcely make him out at all in the darkness.

Then he moved, and a moment later Iljish turned to beckon me. Jacob had seen nothing, heard nothing; we could risk light.

I struck a match and lit the torch. We had lanterns, too, but those would not make the slightest difference in this enormous, black void. Even the blazing light of the torch created only a small island of light, bobbing nervously around me as I picked my way down to join the men.

"Stay behind me, Isabella," Jacob murmured, not turning. "I don't want the torch to blind me."

In case he had to shoot something. But the cave had a dead feeling about it; the subconscious mind hears breathing, tiny movements, all the little sounds of life, and here we heard none.

Nor, as we began to examine our surroundings, did we see any of the castings or marks we associated with a dragon's lair. The stone all about us was formed into queer shapes, stalactites and stalagmites and things I didn't have names for, flowing sheets of stone I would not have believed until I saw them for myself.

What we did note, faintly near the entrance, and more strongly the farther we went, was the smell. "Faugh!" I whispered, wishing, for the first time in my life, that I had one of those ridiculous little nosegays young ladies carry around and sniff from every time they want to politely imply an insult. "What *is* that? Are there dragon eggs down here that have gone rotten?"

"Sulfur," Jacob murmured back. Our sibilants rebounded from the stone, whispering off into the depths of the cavern. "There must be a source of it here somewhere."

Neither of us was a chemist, so I will annotate my husband's comment with a detail from Mr. Pegshaw's excellent geological treatise, *Methods of Cavern Formation in a Variety of Environments*, which will become quite relevant later. The rotten-egg smell came not from deposits of sulfur, but from hydrogen sulfide gas seeping up from some source far below. (We were fortunate in the extreme that its concentration was not high enough to pose an incendiary risk—and that we did not go deep enough into the cavern to encounter the stronger pockets.) When this gas meets water, it forms sulfuric acid, which created the cave system whose topmost chamber we were now exploring. The Drustanev Caverns, as they are now called, have been the object of mapping efforts by later speleologists, and as I understand it their more accessible parts have become something of a tourist attraction in recent years; but the full extent of the system is still unknown, and the mighty void we had entered is off-limits to all.

We certainly felt like trespassers. But as the floor leveled out for a time, Jacob ventured outward from the wall; we had no fear of becoming lost, not so long as we could see the pale oval of the cavern mouth at the top of the slope. And, before we had gone very far at all, we found something entirely unexpected.

I thought at first it was another rock formation. The light glistened off it oddly, though, and I realized—first with curious surprise; then with an unpleasant jolt—that it was a pile of rotting meat.

A pile in which a limb could be discerned.

To be precise, the hind leg of a dragon.

Had the sulfur stench not obliterated the competing smell, I suspect I would have felt very ill. As it was, my thoughts leapt instead to my original, nearly discarded hypothesis: that this was, in fact, the lair of a mighty rock-wyrm, and furthermore one that ate its own kindred. *That*, not the rot, was what turned my stomach.

Iljish was morbidly fascinated, going forward to inspect it. Jacob turned, quite incautiously, to stare straight at me and the torch. "Isabella—" he said.

My own logic had followed the same trail. The leg had not been eaten; it had been dropped here, perhaps in rather battered condition to begin with, and then left. I could not guess at rates of decay, not in this environment, where even flies would not come . . . but I only knew of two rock-wyrms that had died so recently. And one of them I had examined in quite a bit of detail before its body vanished.

This was, I was certain, the hind leg of our own missing dragon.

Nor was it alone. Farther up, we discovered what I could only surmise were the remaining pieces of the beast, though by then it was far enough gone that I was not eager to conduct a tally. We could discern enough to be sure that it had indeed been torn apart, as Mr. Wilker indicated that shocking morning; but it had not been carried off as food. Instead the dragons had borne the remains here.

Why?

We had been long enough about our explorations that my torch was beginning to gutter. The noxious air, too, took its toll on us. Collecting Iljish, we fled back to the green quiet of the ravine, and there collapsed on handy bits of stone to stare at one another and conduct a discussion the boy could not follow in the least, for we spoke Scirling. Neither of us was in any state of mind to force our ideas into Vystrani.

"Have you ever heard of elephant graveyards?" Jacob asked.

"Only in very sentimental tales," I said, wiping sweat from my brow. The sun now stood overhead, bathing the still air with heat, but I could not say with honesty that was the cause of my perspiration. "I thought them a cloying notion invented for children."

Jacob rinsed his mouth with water and spat into the underbrush, trying to clear away the sulfuric tinge. "They may or may not be real. Hilford would know. But dragon graveyards . . . no one has even speculated as to those."

"We don't know it *is* a graveyard," I pointed out. "One burial—or deposition, or whatever I should call it—is not a pattern. But if there were others, they will have disintegrated by now."

Because I am a practical woman, the thought *did* cross my mind that we could test the graveyard theory by killing another dragon, and seeing if his fellows carried him off in the same way. But although I am not above shooting creatures for science, I balked at doing it so callously, to answer only a single question.

Indeed, I was rather less sanguine about having done it at all, now that I faced the notion of dragons actually *caring* what happened to their brethren. It seemed such a peculiarly human thing to do—something that set us apart from the beasts. If they mourned their own kind . . .

At least we no longer feared the return of a hypothetical queen dragon, though we kept one wary eye out in case dragons of ordinary size were to visit the ravine. Indeed, I found myself wondering if the reason our dead beast had been torn to bits was because he was otherwise too heavy for his fellows to carry here. Without a tame dragon to try with different loads, I couldn't be certain. Or perhaps if we observed one in the act of carrying off a bear . . . I dragged my thoughts back to the present question. Was this an aberration, or a pattern?

Mindful of the need to climb back out of the ravine before it grew too late, we could only explore a little farther. Torches in hand, we went back into the cave, finding once more the rotting pile (we had not imagined it, then), and branching out from there.

We almost overlooked the evidence. There were, as I have said, many peculiar rock formations in that cave; an additional knob or stick here or there hardly attracted the eye. I am embarrassed to say we might have missed it entirely had I not quite literally tripped over it.

My torch skittered across the ground, and Iljish picked it up. Jacob came to help me to my feet, and stopped halfway through the act of pulling me up. My heels slid across the slick stone, dropping me hard on my rump, and I made an indignant sound. "If you are going to offer, then kindly do not—"

Then I saw what he had already spotted.

It stuck out from the side of a lumpy pile, encrusted with needle-like crystals (those I had not shattered with my foot), but still recognizable as the epiphysis of a long bone. Deformed and half buried as it was, I could not identify it precisely; the femur of a small dragon, perhaps, or the brachial humerus of a larger one. Too large to come from a bear—that much was certain.

In a low voice, Jacob said, "Why has it not disintegrated?"

All in a rush, my brain started working again. I had been so

THE GRAVEYARD

distracted by the wonder of a dragon graveyard that I had clean forgotten the simplest fact of dragon osteology: their bones did not long survive their deaths. Even the one we had hunted should have long since deteriorated to the point of collapsing under its own weight. This one had clearly been here long enough for stone to form around it; by now, it should have been dust.

Jacob and I exchanged wide-eyed stares. Scrambling to my feet without his hand, I seized my torch from Iljish and ran back across the cavern floor to where we had left the dragon carcass.

Rotting meat could not deter me now. I plunged my hand into the mess, seeking. Sure enough, some of the bone crumbled beneath my fingers—but not all. I shouted toward Jacob, my voice echoing madly off the stone. "It should be entirely gone by now, should it not? Lord Hilford said."

"Yes," he shouted back. "Isabella, come see! I think all of this is bone!"

Once more across the cavern; how I did not fall and break my neck, running on that slick and uneven surface, I will never know. Jacob had given his torch to the mystified Iljish, and was hammering at the lumpy stone with the butt of his rifle. Soon he had cracked a bit off, and I realized what he meant: what I had taken for a cave formation was in fact a layer of accretion over a pile of dragon bone.

There could be no question now; any bone that had been there long enough for such a process to occur should have been dust ages since. "It's somehow . . . *petrified*," I said, dumbfounded.

Jacob raised his rifle again, then lowered it abruptly. "No, I'm just destroying it. We need—"

He stopped, helpless. What we needed was a stone carver's tools, something delicate enough to chisel these remains out of their stony matrix without damaging them. But we had brought nothing of the sort with us—not to this cave, and not to Vystrana. Who would ever have thought we would need them?

"There are bound to be more samples here," I said, though I shared his frustration. "What's important is that we bring something back for Lord Hilford and Mr. Wilker to see. Get a few more chips, and we'll break off this long bone; we don't have all of it, but some is better than none."

With a pained look on his face, Jacob smashed his rifle down where the long bone vanished into the pile, cracking it clean through. We collected all we could, and might have gone looking for more, save that Iljish tugged at my sleeve. "Please, ma'am—"

I looked where he was pointing, and saw the light beginning to dim at the cave mouth. If we were to climb out of the ravine before it got dark, we needed to go soon.

Reluctantly Jacob and I bundled up our prizes and left the cavern. Even with our ropes, getting up the ravine wall was no easy matter; I could manage the partially walkable bits, but that bottom twenty feet, purely vertical, defeated me. I had not the first clue how to climb a rope, nor the arm strength with which to follow Jacob's well-meant advice. I finally allowed Iljish to go before me, then clung to the line while the two of them hauled me up by main force. (Between that and the abseiling, I think I left enough skin behind on those rocks to cover an entire second person.)

With our bone fragments packed away as carefully as we could manage, we ate a hasty meal, then lay down to sleep. Or to try; Jacob took the first watch, and I knew it was because he was as wakeful as I.

Curling up on my side to regard him, I said, "Jacob—do you think this has anything to do with the attacks?"

He had, of course, been considering the same thing. He crossed his arms over his knees. "At first I thought it might—when we found the carcass. It might have been some change in the dragons' behaviour, them bringing their dead here, and showing aggression to people. But with those new bones, or rather the older ones . . . those must have been there for years, Isabella. Who knows how many. Long before the attacks began."

"Unless it comes and goes. Dragons might have been attacking people when those older bones were placed there, too. If there *were* people in the region; as you say, who knows how old they are."

"But what's the logic, then? Why should dragons start bringing their dead here, then stop, then start again—and why should that have anything to do with this aggression? No, it makes more sense that it's a disease."

Not one brought about by eating their own kind, though. I picked up a twig and stabbed at the ground beyond the edge of my blanket. "Perhaps it's something to do with this Zhagrit Mat."

Jacob's eyes glittered with the last flickers of the fire. He did not answer at first; then he shook his head, bowing it until it nearly rested on his folded arms. "I should say that's superstitious nonsense. But I'm not certain of anything any longer."

"Zhagrit Mat didn't start haunting the village until after I went to the ruins," I said. "The attacks started far earlier. But that doesn't mean there isn't some connection that I'm missing."

The last log-end collapsed into a heap of embers with a muffled sigh. Jacob said, "You won't figure it out by fretting. Get some rest, Isabella."

And hope for answers in the morning. I drew the blanket closer around my shoulders and waited for sleep to come.

EIGHTEEN

*Lord Hilford's answer from the boyar — More trouble
in the night — Consequences in the morning — Return to the
ruins — What Dagmira and I saw there*

The hike back to Drustanev was quicker (though more punishing to the knees) as we descended toward the village, and blessedly undisturbed by dragons. We had a splendid view of Gritelkin's house as we came in, and I saw the telltale signs of activity that said *someone* had returned.

It proved to be both Lord Hilford and Mr. Wilker, each of whom must have pressed quite hard on their journey for them to be back so soon. Unless— "Did you manage to see the boyar?" I burst out as we came into the workroom, suddenly worried that something might have turned Lord Hilford back.

"I did, and where the devil have you two been?" the earl said. He went on before I could answer him, making it clear the question had been rhetorical. "Really, Camherst—for a man who was so reluctant to let his wife come to Vystrana in the first place, you're remarkably willing to drag her all over it now that she's here."

Jacob looked shamefaced at the accusation. For my own part, I was taken aback; it was unlike Lord Hilford to speak that way, when he had been so readily agreeable before. "Jacob dragged me nowhere," I said with asperity. "We went for a lovely hike and discovered something completely unknown to the science of dragon naturalism—but you will not hear it until you say what has put this burr in your brain, that you should accuse my husband like that."

Mr. Wilker had been seated on a stool by the window, his face in his hands; now he sat up and said, "The creature was stalking him."

I blinked. "What?"

All my thoughts had been bent upon the wonderful news we had to tell them once they returned; I had quite forgotten what had sent Mr. Wilker after Lord Hilford in the first place. "We found more prints burned into the ground," he said. "Along the path toward the boyar's lodge."

"Did you see it?" I asked Lord Hilford, with perhaps a touch more eagerness than was polite. I suppose I should have asked first if he was well, but I could see with my own eyes that he was; the other had to be asked.

"No," the earl said, "and I wasn't about to let that priest drown me in a stream, either. But that night . . ." He harrumphed into his mustache. "Well, I don't know what I heard. Menkem declared I wasn't coming back to Drustanev, though, unless I let him do his little ritual. It seemed more politic to agree."

Jacob admitted, "We've had no trouble—not of that sort—since we let him, ah, 'purify' us."

"Neither did we," Mr. Wilker said.

"That's settled, then," I said briskly. "No more hauntings—and we can show you *this*."

In the interests of not misleading the reader, I should admit that more than scientific rationality led me to dismiss the specter of Zhagrit Mat so quickly. I had managed to half forget the sounds I heard, and the footprint burned into the slope behind our house; I did not deny the evidence, but I did trivialize it, for it had not been repeated. Hearing that Lord Hilford had been stalked by the beast—or whatever it was—unnerved me badly, and I responded by ignoring it.

This is not, of course, a terribly profitable response, and I do not recommend it to the reader. Problems rarely go away because you ignore them, and this one would prove no different.

But the choice was made, and the samples from our cave expedition laid out. These distracted Lord Hilford on the spot. He snatched them up, exclaiming, and Mr. Wilker was not far behind. The earl's assistant, however, withheld his acclaim, examining the fragments closely.

"It's a damned shame you could not get anything intact," he said. I bristled at his critical tone, which seemed to imply that the shortcoming was due to sheer laziness on our part, and not a lack of suitable equipment. "With pieces this incomplete, and so crusted with minerals, I can't agree that they are certainly dragon bone. More likely some other large predator—a bear, perhaps."

"It is *not* a bear," I said sharply before Jacob or the earl could respond.

Mr. Wilker gave me a pitying look. "On what do you base your declaration, Mrs. Camherst?" He laid the faintest stress on my title of courtesy, which put my back up as if I had been laced into the most severe of corsets. "What are the skeletal characteristics which mark ursine anatomy? Unless you have been studying a great many books we have not brought with us, my knowledge of such matters is far more complete than yours; it is my judgment we shall be trusting in this matter."

"And *my* knowledge of what we saw in the cave is far more complete than yours, Mr. Wilker," I shot back. "I saw with my own eyes the carcass of our slain dragon, whose bones should have fallen to dust long since; and on that I base my judgment of these fragments."

It was not kind of me, but I laid my own stress—not nearly as faint—on his own form of address. He heard my implication very clearly. Mr. Wilker was not a gentleman by birth, and in those days I did not understand what effort had been required for him to lift himself above his humble birth, obtain an education, and bring himself into the circle of a man as socially and scientifically exalted as Lord Hilford. I therefore did not understand why he should resent me, and my presence on this expedition. But the blame must be shared equally; neither of us behaved very well toward the other, as I was in the process of proving.

Mr. Wilker reddened. "*Your* judgment, Mrs. Camherst? I was not aware that you had any authority in this expedition, except that of which pencil to choose in your drawing. But as you seem to have adopted your husband's trousers, perhaps I was wrong."

"Now see here—" Jacob said, his voice rising.

"I should hardly—" I began.

"Enough!" Lord Hilford slammed one hand down on the table before we could answer the question of who was about to say the more unforgivable thing, me or my husband. "For God's sake, Tom; you know these aren't bear bones. Even with the mineralization, they aren't nearly heavy enough. Mrs. Camherst, Tom Wilker's birth may be below your own, but he has raised himself up by his own brilliance and effort, which is something I should expect *you* of all people to respect."

He paused long enough for shame to secure its grip on me. Then, in a more moderate tone, he said, "Now, if someone will fetch me a magnifying glass—"

Mr. Wilker leapt to do so, caught halfway between scowling and red-faced embarrassment. My hands went by reflex to straighten my skirts, encountered the trousers, and sprang away as if burned; my own face heated. But I bit down on the impulse to excuse myself and go change.

Lord Hilford accepted the magnifying glass and spent a long moment peering at the various fragments, murmuring excitedly to himself. "How I wish we had brought a bone saw!" he said. "If we could cut a thin enough slice of this—" Then he recalled our presence, and looked up. "It's difficult to be certain; the bone has become saturated with all manner of minerals. But I've long speculated that dragon bone, where not hollow, is spongy, far beyond what we find in other creatures' skeletons; in fact, a crystallographer of my acquaintance thinks the material may be arranged quite regularly, to provide strength while minimizing weight. We may at last have a sample with which to answer that question! Where did you say you found this?"

I left it for Jacob to explain. Lord Hilford was, of course, correct; but his insight did not go far enough. I *envied* Mr. Wilker, for the simple fact that our society made it easier to transcend class than sex. Which was not only unfair of me, but in some respects inaccurate: there is sometimes a greater willingness to make an exception for a woman than a man, so long as her breeding is good enough. But at the tender age of nineteen, I had not yet seen enough of the world to understand that.

Fortunately, Mr. Wilker seemed as eager as I to sweep the matter under the rug, at least for the moment. I sent Dagmira to roust up our cook; our group of four talked animatedly all the time we waited for supper, and all the way through it. "I should set out tomorrow morning to see it for myself," Lord Hilford said, "except these old feet demand a rest. The day after, perhaps."

I had nearly forgotten about his own journey, and its purpose. "What did the boyar say?" Jacob asked.

"Ah, that's right; Tom's heard, but you haven't." The earl laid his napkin aside, looking sober. "It didn't go as well as we might have hoped. Khirzoff didn't come out and say this—it would have made him look rather foolish—but I don't think Gritelkin's arrangements with him were nearly so extensive as I'd been led to believe. Arrangements concerning our visit, that is. He seems to have expected us to be Scirling tourists."

"Not natural historians on an expedition," I said.

The earl nodded. "He knows *now*, of course; some gossip carried word to him, no doubt. He's not unfriendly to science, mind you. That guest of his, Gaetano Rossi, is a scientist himself. But our welcome was chillier than I might have hoped for."

Jacob had been picking at his remaining food; now he laid his knife down. "So he will not help us?"

"Oh, he will," Lord Hilford said. "The man is a razesh of his, after all, and can't be permitted to simply vanish. Khirzoff's guess is that Gritelkin fell prey to a dragon; his people have had quite a bit of trouble with the attacks. But he has promised to mount a search, and someone will come around to inform us if they find anything. Or, for that matter, if they don't."

It should have reassured me, but it did not. Very few things since our arrival had made it quite so clear to me how isolated we were here: Gritelkin was more than an ordinary villager, and still, his absence had managed to go unremarked for all this time.

The natural thought, following on that, sprang from my mouth without waiting for permission. "Did none of the villagers report the disappearance to him?"

Lord Hilford frowned, shaking his head. "This was the first Khirzoff had heard of it."

"A villager would not have got in to see the boyar himself. Perhaps they reported it, but no one wanted to trouble Khirzoff himself with the matter," Mr. Wilker said. He did not sound as if he was even convincing himself.

"I can ask the mayor tomorrow," Jacob said. Then he sobered. "If the man will help us. The villagers haven't been fond of us at any point, and these strange troubles have soured opinion even worse."

"Would you like me to ask Dagmira?" I offered. "I would not go so far as to say that she *likes* me, but I think she would answer."

Mr. Wilker did not make the disparaging comment he might have indulged in before. Lord Hilford said, "You may as well try, Mrs. Camherst, and if that fails we can approach the mayor." The gentlemen then agreed that they should spend the next day studying the bone fragments and asking about for delicate stone-cutting tools (though for the latter, they did not hold out much hope), and so we all went to bed.

But as so often happened during this expedition, nothing went as we had planned.

I did not hear any sounds in the night. But others did, and even had their neighbors doubted their word, the remainder of the evidence was plain for all to see.

There must have been a dozen prints burned into the ground, all around the village. Perhaps more; I did not count. I might have—as before, scientific modes of thought provided me with some refuge against fear—but we were not permitted to go in search.

We were not permitted past our front door.

I would not term them a *mob*, precisely. As Mr. Wilker said, rather sourly, there were not enough people in Drustanev to get up a proper mob. Nor, it being daylight, did they have burning torches. But there were various tools in their hands, from shepherd's crooks to hoes to, yes, a couple of pitchforks, and there was a great deal of angry shouting.

Menkem did not lead the charge, but he was up among the leaders, just behind Urjash Mazhustin, the mayor. When Lord Hilford stepped out to speak with him, the man held up one hand, looking regretful, but also frightened and determined.

"You must leave," Mazhustin said. "All of you. Gather your things and go, and take the demon with you."

"Come now, man," Lord Hilford answered him, with poorly concealed impatience. "Your priest there dunked me in the stream; wasn't that to wash this 'demon' of yours away?"

That was when we heard of the disturbances elsewhere in Drustanev. Not in any orderly fashion; despite the fact that Mazhustin had clearly been nominated to speak for them, the villagers called out a dozen accusations, each more panicked-sounding than the last. I was standing behind Lord Hilford, on the bottom step of the stairs, with my robe clutched around me; Jacob drew me back with one careful hand on my arm and bent to speak in my ear. "Isabella—it might be best if you go upstairs."

"Will that protect me if they decide to break in here and thrash us all?" I whispered back.

Jacob's jaw tightened. "No—but I would just as soon you not be where they can make an easy target of you."

Guilt twanged in my heart again. Though Jacob was too polite to say it, the ruins expedition had happened because of me; I was the one who had leapt upon Astimir's suggestion, and persuaded Lord Hilford to join me. Some out there might remember that. I wondered, with brief bitterness, whether anybody was mobbing Astimir's house—and then, with much less brief fear, whether they had already dealt with him in some fashion.

It might be better after all if I were not where the villagers could see me. The mayor's voice pursued me as I went up the stairs. "This creature is beyond Menkem's strength to conquer. You carry Zhagrit Mat's corruption with you now, and for the safety of my people, I cannot allow it to remain in my village!"

My toe caught against the edge of the top stair, and I nearly measured my length on the floor. Mazhustin's words echoed in my ears: *You carry Zhagrit Mat's corruption with you.*

Dagmira was in the bedroom Jacob and I shared, throwing my

dresses into a chest without any attempt at folding. "What are you doing?" I demanded.

"Better if you go now," she said. "There are donkeys that can carry your things. Some of them, at least," she added doubtfully, as if thinking of Lord Hilford's beloved chair.

She seemed willing to arrange the donkeys for us, which was more charity than I expected, given the mood outside. But it was a different favor I needed from her now. I crossed the room with quick strides and addressed her over my shoulder as I rummaged through a pile of my stockings. "Dagmira, do you know how to get to the ruins?"

By her stare, she thought I had gone completely mad. "Why would you go there?"

The object I was looking for fell into my palm, out of the stocking I had concealed it in. "To return this."

Even in the wan light coming through the louver, the firestone glimmered. Dagmira's jaw sagged. "Where did you—" She caught herself before the foolish question could make it the rest of the way from her mouth. "You've had that, all this time?"

"Is there anything about firestones in the legend of Zhagrit Mat?"

"No. Well, he was very rich, they say."

It was good enough for me. "This and some drawings are all I carried away from the ruins. A rubbing, too. Unless you think one of those is responsible for this trouble, it must be the stone."

Dagmira backed away, shaking her head. "I cannot go there. It would only make things worse."

"You needn't go *into* the ruins," I said impatiently. "Just bring me within sight of them—or not even that far, if you prefer. I can find it well enough, if you bring me most of the way. But if we are going to do this, we must do it soon." I threw off my robe and reached for the nearest shift.

I had not intended to put her friendship to the test in such fashion, not when I was still uncertain whether I could even call it "friendship." It might only be grudging neutrality. But she had unbent enough to send Iljish with us to the cave, and now, after a moment's hesitation, she came forward and helped me dress.

"I know a quicker path," she said. "But it's hard."

After the journey to the cave, I no longer felt so daunted by the prospect of a strenuous hike. And even if Lord Hilford managed to talk the mob down—which, by the sound of it, he was making some progress at—the sooner this was settled, the better.

It almost made sense . . . so long as I did not let myself think about danger from the dragons.

I tore a page from my notebook and scribbled a quick message on it, then nodded at Dagmira. "Lead the way."

Dagmira's way was indeed quicker than Astimir's—and far, far harder. Rather than curving south into the gentler part of the valley, and then back up again toward the ruins, we went at them straight, along a path better suited to deer than women, and very nearly vertical.

My legs complained mightily after their exertions of the previous days, but I clamped my jaw shut, refusing to let my voice do the same. At least we had packed very light; since I had no intention of sightseeing this time, Dagmira promised we would be back before dark.

I'd thought to ask her about Gritelkin as we went, but I had no breath to spare for it as I picked my way down one side of the valley, then hauled myself back up the other side, puffing like a bellows all the way. I managed only one brief, regretful curse that I had not thought to put on trousers again. Not for the first time in my life, I envied dragons their wings.

Dagmira's path at least had the virtue of being heavily sheltered by trees, which reduced the risk that we might attract draconic attention. And if my calculations were correct, it would bring us up to the back of the ruins, which suited me entirely. It seemed best to leave the firestone where I had found it, and the less time I spent in that accursed place, the happier I would be.

Just when I thought I might have reached the limit of my strength, Dagmira stopped and turned to wait for me. "We're nearly there," she said, while I tried to slow my breathing enough to drink water without aspirating it. "I will not go with you," she added fiercely, as if I might have forgotten.

I nodded and wiped away the water dribbling down my chin. "I understand. Just show me which way to go."

"You can see them from up here," she said, gesturing to a large outcropping of rock. I withheld my sigh; if she was willing to come within eyesight of the ruins, it was more than I had expected, and surely climbing a boulder was not such a large price to pay.

After casting a wary look around for dragons, Dagmira scrambled up it like a mountain goat. I followed with much less agility, splitting one of the seams of my skirt with a noise like breaking wood. I half expected her to frown at me for the sound, but Dagmira, I realized as I achieved a better foothold, was lying flat on the stone, and staring unblinking toward the ruins.

Had she seen a dragon? I eased myself up alongside her, and found that she had not.

We had a fine view of the back end of the ruins, the place where I had fallen through into the little cave below. The slope there was crawling with men: only a dozen at most, but busy as ants on a hill that's been kicked. We were not so far from them that I could not make out their yellow hair. The Stauleren smugglers were visiting their cache.

"Damnation," I swore under my breath, in Scirling. Why had they not moved on yet? This would make it a great deal harder to return the stone. Did I dare circle around to the front of the site, and throw it down any old where? But I had no certainty they were not keeping watch, or that there were more men where I could not see.

I opened my mouth to ask Dagmira what she thought, and stopped.

A dozen men there, not just behind the ruins but in them; I could see one man on the same bit of wall I had climbed, who I thought might be Chatzkel, their leader. They had surely been there before. And why in heaven's name should Dagmira know of a quick path to the ruins—one direct enough to allow an energetic hiker to go and return in a single day—if no one ever went there, for fear of Zhagrit Mat?

"You've been here before, haven't you," I whispered.

Dagmira flushed and did not meet my eyes. "Children do stupid things. But we all know better than to disturb the demon!"

So none of them had ever carried anything away from the site? Not a firestone, I would wager; that would be unimaginable wealth in Drustanev. Such a tale would be as famous as that of Zhagrit Mat. But I was increasingly unconvinced the stone had anything to do with it.

I was about to press her further when she made a small, startled noise. Following her gaze, I saw a new man moving through the trees, one with dark hair cut to just above his collar, and a fur-trimmed hat on his head. Not Stauleren, and by his finer clothing, not a smuggler of any race. "You recognize him?" I asked, still keeping my voice low. They could not hear us, not at this distance—at least, I did not think they could—but my nerves demanded it.

"No," Dagmira murmured, still staring. "But—"

She paused. "But?" I prompted.

Dagmira flattened herself even more against the stone, as if newly afraid of being seen. "He's one of the boyar's men."

The fellow in question carried a rifle, but was not pointing it at the smugglers; rather he strolled among them with the attitude of an overseer as they lifted bags from the hole. Small bags, but apparently heavy. What was in them? Not brandy; that much was certain. Opium? I knew almost nothing of it, except that the plant had been brought over from Yelang, and was now grown widely in certain parts of Bulskevo; addicts smoked it, and doctors used it for medicine. But its form was unknown to me. It might be carried in sacks.

An entirely new explanation for the haunting incidents was taking shape in my mind. This one had very little to do with ancient demons, and a great deal more to do with the note I had left on the smugglers' crate.

I pounded my hand against the stone, cursing my stupidity. I had honestly forgotten about that note. A lie is most plausible when the teller believes it; I had so rehearsed the false tale of how I hurt my ankle that it had all but painted over the truth in my memory. Now that I remembered—

Dagmira's hand landed atop my own, trapping it. "Stop that!" she hissed. "Do you want them to see us?"

No, I most certainly did not; the smugglers might think of something worse to do than strange sounds and alien footprints. Gritting my teeth, I wriggled backward down the boulder until I could no longer see the men, then turned and dropped to the ground. The breeze through my split skirt felt very cold indeed, and woke up my mind. Jacob and Lord Hilford should hear of my theory first, before I went babbling it to anyone in the village; but that meant securing Dagmira's cooperation. "Never mind returning the stone," I said. "I must tell my companions about this, as soon as possible. But I must also ask you to keep silent, at least until we have had a chance to confer."

She gave me a withering look. "We know better than to talk about the smugglers' business. Or the boyar's."

Did that apply also to Reveka, I wondered, with her smuggler for a lover? But it seemed a great many things could go on in Drustanev without anyone talking about them. My skirt flapped annoyingly; I tore it the rest of the way, then knotted the free ends, so that it was kilted up like some hoyden's dress. At least it would be easier to move in, and there was no one here to see.

The valley gaped before me, looking nearly as steep as the ravine of the dragon graveyard. Sighing, I put myself to it. Even the steepest path was preferable to going anywhere near those men, and I could not wait to tell what I had seen.

NINETEEN

My theory — Keeping watch in the night — A stroll around the village — Incriminating bottles — A surprise encounter — The truth of Zhagrit Mat

I half expected Jacob to rage at me when I returned, and went into the workroom alone so I might have a modicum of privacy while he did it. My husband, however, did not move from his seated position at the table. Wearily, not raising his head from his hands, he said, "I suppose they could not make an easy target of you if you were not here at all."

"Was there violence?" I asked, glancing around. The other men were not there, but I saw no signs of a disturbance, nor were our things packed to leave.

"No," Jacob said, sitting up at last. "They're in the sauna," he added, seeing my curiosity. "They should be back soon. Did you dispose of your stone?"

I dropped into the chair opposite him. "No, and for good reason—but I should wait until the others return, so as not to repeat myself. What happened after I left?"

Jacob sighed. "Hilford promised we would all attend a service in their tabernacle, next Sabbath. It was like pulling teeth for him to agree; he scarcely has any patience with our own religion, let alone anyone else's. But the general consensus was that this trouble came about because we are all heathens. Hilford bargained Mazhustin down from conversion to a simple service, which I call quite a feat."

I had not considered the religious aspect, when I realized that smugglers and village children went to the ruins without bringing back a demon. But the spell of our various terrors had been broken; I found it far more likely that they had a human origin than a supernatural one. Impatience made me bounce in my seat, wishing the other two men would return. Jacob raised one eyebrow at this, mouth lifting at last into a hint of a smile. "You seem excited."

"Does it have anything to do with what this girl says you have to tell us?" Lord Hilford came into the room, Dagmira between him and Mr. Wilker like a prisoner being marched to the bar. He would be feeling none too charitable toward the locals, I imagined, after this morning's strife.

"Yes," I said, rising to rescue Dagmira. "I think our problems may actually be quite ordinary."

I outlined the situation in broad strokes, partly for the sake of brevity, and partly because I spoke in Vystrani, so that Dagmira might understand me. She confirmed my observations readily. And she alone was not astonished when I admitted the truth of how I'd hurt my ankle; that girl was too clever by half. Of the note, I said, "I didn't see any better solution; they would know *someone* had been there, and if I made it clear it was the mad Scirling woman, they might not see any danger in it. Chatzkel had been agreeable enough, when we met before. But it seems I was wrong."

"It was damned stupid of you," Mr. Wilker said, not bothering to hide his fury. "You endangered this entire expedition! All because you could not do as you were told, and *stay here!*"

Jacob shot to his feet. "Now see here, Wilker. Isabella has been an asset to our work. It is *my* business, *not* yours, to decide whether she should be kept on any kind of leash, and I have told you already that I will not do it."

He was ready to go on, and a part of me wished he would; I had no idea he'd been defending me to Mr. Wilker, and was childishly

eager to hear what more he had to say. But as it would not serve
the greater purpose, I stopped him with one hand on his arm.
Addressing Mr. Wilker, I said quietly, "You're right. It *was* stupid
of me, and it *did* endanger the expedition. They want to scare us
off, or provoke the village into driving us out; if they don't succeed, they may try something more direct. I can't do anything to
change what happened. But if we can prove this is mere trickery,
it may all yet be well."

Mr. Wilker had prepared himself for an argument; my capitu-
lation left him at a momentary loss. The resulting silence was
awkward in the extreme. Jacob, drawing in a steadying breath,
sought to resolve it by changing the subject. "*Could* anyone fake
the events?" he asked, slipping out from under my hand to pace.
"I mean—I'm certain they could. But how?"

I snapped my fingers at a sudden thought. "Dagmira. The day
I seemed so uneasy, coming out of the sauna—before the first footprint appeared. Did you see anyone hanging about as you approached?"

She shook her head, but it proved nothing either way; the
trickster would have wanted to stay hidden. "Some kind of device
to make the sound," Lord Hilford said, from where he slouched in
his favourite chair, hands steepled before him. He'd been very
quiet through my entire tale, brows drawn close, eyes staring into
the middle distance as if watching a scene no one else could see.
"It sounds rather like a bullroarer, perhaps. The footprints . . .
it's hard to be both controlled and subtle with fire."

Mr. Wilker also snapped his fingers; I had not realized we shared
that habit. "Not fire—acid! A strong acid could burn the grass like
that. It would be easy to pour out in the appropriate shape. I
smelled something around the print, I thought; that could be it."

"Means and motive," Lord Hilford said, sounding like a bar-
rister. "Opportunity . . ."

"They're sneaky bastards, smugglers," Mr. Wilker said. "Begging Mrs. Camherst's pardon." This puzzle, once entered into, seemed to have distracted him from his annoyance with me.

"Sneaky enough to be in and out of the village without being seen? In broad daylight, even?" Jacob asked dubiously.

Dagmira spoke up, startling us all. "Reveka's lover, maybe."

No one would think anything of seeing him skulking about at night, after all. "Can you ask her if he's been about lately?"

That earned me a frown. I had overstepped my boundaries again, meddling in village business. I raised my hands to placate her. "We must do *something* to stop it; guessing isn't enough. If Reveka will help us, we can simply speak to the man; otherwise we must—oh, lay in wait, I suppose."

The phrase was calculated to conjure suitably alarming images. Dagmira's nod was grudging, but there. "I will go now."

She suited actions to words without delay. Once she was gone, Jacob turned to me. "You say one of the boyar's men was with the smugglers?"

"Supervising them," I confirmed. "Lord Hilford, do you think the man was acting on his own behalf? Collaborating with the smugglers, as it were."

"Corruption among the boyar's guards," Jacob said. "He might be grateful to us for informing him."

Lord Hilford blew out his mustaches with a thoughtful sigh. "Perhaps. But think of what we know of Khirzoff: he is ambitious, and connected in Chiavora. The man might have been there to make certain the boyar got his fair share."

"Would he *do* that?" I asked, scandalized. (Recall: I spent my youth reading scientific works, not sensational novels. Manda Lewis could have told me all about the motif of corrupt noblemen.)

The earl shrugged. "I wouldn't be half surprised. If he stops the smugglers, he can usually confiscate everything they had—but then no others will follow them along this route. He'd kill the goose that lays the golden egg, so to speak. By letting them carry out their business, for a modest bribe, he can enjoy a continuing profit, with no effort on his part. And that's presuming he's not an opium-eater himself."

"You met him," Mr. Wilker said. "Did he seem like one?"

It earned him a snort. "How many opium-eaters are there in my acquaintance, that I should know the signs? That companion of his might be an addict—Gaetano Rossi. But they go hunting a great deal, from what Astimir said, which sounds rather more active than I'd expect from an opium-eater."

Dagmira returned before long. We knew by her frown that it hadn't gone as we'd hoped. "Reveka hasn't seen him since this one went chasing after them," she said with a jerk of her hand at me.

Hadn't I once been determined to teach her the proper manners of a lady's maid? Well, too late for that now, and not much use. "That doesn't mean he hasn't been here," Mr. Wilker said.

Lord Hilford snorted. "You're a young man yet, Tom. If you were skulking about the village, on orders to scare the visitors away, would *you* pass up a chance to visit your pretty young widow?"

Mr. Wilker flushed, gaze darting at me as if trying to decide how to use my presence to make the earl stop speaking so coarsely. He neither received nor needed a chance; Lord Hilford continued on as if unaware he'd said anything inappropriate. "Right, then. We need to catch our culprit in the act. It's better that way, regardless. Will he—or they; can't discard the possibility of there being more than one—will they wait until after we've attended this damned Sabbath, to show it's done no good? Or will they try to force us out faster?"

Privately I suspected there was only one; it would explain why Jacob and I had that period of quiet after our purification in the river. The fellow had to chase off after Lord Hilford instead. And it would be harder to keep multiple men out of sight. But I agreed with Jacob when he said, "It doesn't much matter either way. The obvious thing to do is keep watch, every night until we catch somebody. But how shall we do it?"

I let the gentlemen discuss the logistics of it; they were far better at planning such things than I. The difficulty, of course, was that we could not look to the villagers for help: they were convinced Zhagrit Mat haunted the night, and the only way we could persuade them otherwise was to bring proof of fakery.

My gaze fell upon Dagmira. Rising and going to her side, I murmured, "Do you believe us? That it isn't a monster?"

She shrugged and answered in a pragmatic tone. "If it *is* a monster, you'll see it soon enough. If it isn't . . . either way, I want this to end."

For once, she and I were in complete accord.

We were none of us spies, nor detectives either. The final plan—if I may call it that without laughing, which I confess is rather difficult to do—depended primarily upon the use of strong coffee: one gentleman would stay up each night, keeping watch for miscreants, and would rouse the others as soon as he heard anything. Mr. Wilker would take the first night, and Jacob the second. Judging by the way I saw them whispering to each other, they were already plotting how to divide all the nights between their two selves, and spare Lord Hilford the duty of standing watch.

(I, of course, had already been exempted, on account of my sex. Though I suspect Jacob feared I would go charging after the perpetrator myself, without first calling for aid. Privately, I calculated the odds of Mr. Wilker doing just that as roughly eighty per cent.)

Whether this would have succeeded in time, we never had the chance to discover.

Have you ever awoken in the morning with a thought in your head that seems to spring full-grown from nowhere? I am told this comes about because the mind ruminates upon a topic while asleep, and presents its conclusions when you wake, without any of the intervening steps. As such, it almost feels as if the thought comes from a source outside yourself—an enlightening or unnerving sensation.

Either the mind is capable of exercising the same process while the body is awake, or mine is a terrible sluggard, quite tardy in the presentation of its overnight conclusions.

When I awoke the next morning, a bleary-eyed Mr. Wilker reported hearing nothing in the night; but Dagmira, coming in a moment later, told us there were footprints all around the village, as if the creature had been pacing a circuit of the place. This, of course, did not endear us to the locals. I feared the smugglers might achieve their aim and drive us out before we even had a chance to make good on our Sabbath promise.

The gentlemen went out—even the exhausted Mr. Wilker—with guns in hand, to at least give a show of trying to address this supernatural threat. I gathered my things and went to use the sauna, for it was bathing-day (or rather steaming-day), and Dagmira had promised to keep watch while I was inside, in case someone tried to haunt me again.

But when I opened the sauna door, I found three withered old Drustanev aunties already occupying the place.

It was no accident; they knew, for we had arranged it, that I always used the sauna first—and alone—before the air cleared to the point where it was pleasant to breathe. Their glares dared me to protest, or to join them.

Even had I been accustomed to using the sauna communally,

the atmosphere of hostile defiance would have dissuaded me. I took refuge in the manners of a Scirling gentlewoman: I murmured the politest Vystrani apology I knew and closed the door, for all the world as if it had been a simple misunderstanding. Then, fuming, I put my clothes back on, and went back out into the bright air.

At least I didn't have to explain to Dagmira. She had already found the aunties' clothing in the baskets outside. Seeing me emerge so quickly, she scowled and muttered something under her breath that was not, I think, a polite apology. Together we began the trek back to the house.

Partway there, my brain offered up its conclusion, quite without warning.

I stopped dead on the path. The thought that had just occurred to me, seemingly out of nowhere, did not fit the chain of causality we were taking for granted. But that did not mean it was wrong. Carefully, step by step, I reviewed what I knew, half hoping to find something that would prove me wrong, almost entirely certain I would not.

"Are you *sick*?" Dagmira hissed, stepping in front of me and stooping to peer into my blank face.

I came back to myself with a jerk. "Dagmira. You know where everyone in the village lives, don't you?"

Suspicion drew her brows together. "Why?"

The girl was clever; I ignored her question and gave her the name, and it was enough. Her eyes narrowed. "What do you think you're going to find?"

"Let's keep walking," I muttered, suiting action to words. The weather was developing quite fine—by Vystrani standards, anyway—and many of the village women were in their yards, tending the chickens and geese or spinning wool into thread, or gossiping at their front gates. They were already staring at me because of Zhagrit Mat, but I didn't want to give them additional reason.

Dagmira followed me. "That many tracks would take quite a bit of acid," I said quietly to her. I used the Scirling word, not knowing how to say it in Vystrani, but my meaning was clear enough. "And where it came from is a good question—but there must be bottles of it on hand. If I can find those, it will be proof enough."

"I'll look for you," she offered.

It was kindly meant, and I appreciated it, but— "With two, one can keep watch," I said. I judged that less likely to put Dagmira's back up than the suggestion that she would not recognize acid if she saw it. There was not much call for such things up here (as they tanned their furs by vegetable means), and though I was no chemist, I knew enough to be worried about her safety. Any acid strong enough to burn the grass could badly damage skin.

One bit of luck, at least, was in our favor: my target's mother was bedridden, and according to Dagmira spent most of her time asleep. So long as we were quiet, we could slip in and out with relative secrecy.

We opted for disguise over skulking. Returning to the house, I collected my art supplies, and Dagmira and I sallied forth again in quite the wrong direction, as if looking for something suitable to draw. I sketched a view of Drustanev—something I should have done long since, regardless—then wandered toward the edge of the village, pausing for a flower, a rock, an interesting tree. I started to sketch a house, but got no more than three lines in before the woman charged up to her gate and sent me on my way with a harangue. Bit by bit, looking as if we were headed everywhere but our destination, Dagmira and I worked our way over to the right house. Once she had darted a quick glance inside to make certain it was clear, she kept watch at the door, and I slipped in.

For this to be properly mysterious, I should tell you about a secret panel hidden in the wall, or a trapdoor concealed beneath a rug, discovered only after an arduous search. But the truth is that I found the box shoved under a bench, and it took me no more than two minutes.

Bottles of sulfuric acid, labeled in Chiavoran. Several of them empty, and surrounded by charred straw where dribbles had tracked down the sides.

The noise was faint—no more than a tap of foot upon floor. My nerves were so tightly wound, though, that I shot upright . . . and found Astimir standing in the door to the inner room.

It is hard to say who was more horrified, him or me.

He certainly broke the paralysis first. Astimir flung himself at the outer door before I could even think to shout, racing past a startled Dagmira and vaulting the low fence in one long-legged hurdle, scattering chickens everywhere. "Catch him!" I bellowed, but it was too late; by the time I reached the door myself, he was off down the slope, drawing plenty of perplexed stares, but no attempts to halt his flight.

Of course not. Why should the villagers stop him? They had no idea he was the man behind the so-called haunting.

"*Damn* it!" I kicked the doorpost, which at least had the salutary effect of hurting badly enough to bring me to my senses. From within the house, a querulous voice arose; Dagmira shoved past me to reassure Astimir's mother with some kind of empty lie.

Astimir, all along. I should have seen it. He'd guided Mr. Wilker to find Lord Hilford; that must have given him opportunity to plant signs of "Zhagrit Mat." No wonder Jacob and I had enjoyed a few days of peace while he was gone. Come to that, Astimir had "found" the first print, behind our house; he'd even been the one to cry out the monster's name, setting everyone's thoughts in the proper direction.

But he'd also taken Lord Hilford and me *to* the ruins in the first place. And that did not fit with our smuggler theory at all.

People were beginning to look toward Astimir's house. I could not blame them; we *had* made some amount of noise. Or rather, I had. And it was far too late to duck back inside and hope no one had seen me.

I marshaled my Vystrani vocabulary (woefully inadequate though it still was), preparing a speech to explain matters to everyone. Fortunately, before I opened my mouth, I thought the better of it. Ducking my head back inside, I said, "Dagmira? I'm afraid they'll think I've—" Why did travellers' phrasebooks never include useful words like "framed"? "Made it look like Astimir did this." (One would think my weeks in Drustanev would have inured me to my own awkward phrasings, but no; I winced at the clumsy circumlocution.) "It might be better if you explained matters."

After a moment—a tense moment; in which I could hear the suspicious whispers growing behind me, and the skin between my shoulder blades itched as if expecting something to hit it— Dagmira appeared in the inner doorway. She gave me a sour look, which I translated as meaning that she knew I was foisting an unwelcome duty off on her, but could not argue with my logic. I pointed at the box of acid bottles, trying to be helpful. Muttering curses under her breath, she picked it up and went outside.

She spoke far too rapidly for me to follow, of course. I concentrated more on the replies from the gathered crowd; they were the important part, after all. People did not seem convinced. I resisted the urge to prompt Dagmira; she could figure out for herself, and tell them, that the test would come tonight. If it passed peacefully, then it would prove our point—or at least start to.

They wanted more than that, though. The mutters were still ugly. I bit my lip, thinking of what Mr. Wilker would say . . . then stepped up to Dagmira's side.

In my best, most careful Vystrani, I said, "If Dagmira is wrong—if the village is troubled again—then we will leave. I give you my word."

It was, I thought, a reasonable gamble. I did not think Astimir would return; he had seen me with the bottles, and would know I had exposed him for a fraud. Not to mention that without his acid, he would be hard-pressed to burn any more mysterious prints into the ground. But it was nevertheless a gamble, and I held my breath after I finished speaking.

The mutters sounded more promising, at least. I caught Mazhustin's name once or twice, and Menkem's. "Lord Hilford would be more than glad to talk to them," I offered. Inwardly I began formulating plans for how to ensure that I talked to Lord Hilford first—then discarded them. It might be better if the gentlemen were not forewarned. Their surprise at hearing Astimir accused would help allay suspicions that the Scirling outsiders had colluded to frame a Drustanev lad.

"Come on," Dagmira said under her breath, shoving at me with the box of acid. "Let them think it over—*without* you."

I could only trust her judgment of her neighbors. Belatedly, I ducked inside to retrieve my art supplies, and then we made our way toward the gate—villagers parting around us like a reluctant sea—and back to our house.

PART FOUR

In which many answers are found,
not all of them pleasant,
and some carrying an unfortunate price

TWENTY

The consequences of my bargain — An invitation from the boyar

In most cases I believe the phrase "tearing his hair out" is meant metaphorically, but I'm fairly certain I saw a few strands caught between Mr. Wilker's fingers when he took them away from his head.

"Are you *mad*?" he demanded. I took the question as rhetorical, but he answered himself. "Of course you are. That much has been obvious since before we left Scirland. I knew it then; no sane woman would demand to be involved with this. But since you've gotten here—!"

"Once there's been a quiet night or two, people will begin to accept it," Jacob said. "Isabella is right; Astimir will certainly not come back. Not tonight."

Mr. Wilker made an inarticulate noise of frustration. "He doesn't *have* to. The villagers don't want us here, and never have; now they know that all they must do to be rid of us is cause trouble tonight."

Pleasure over my cleverness had been glowing warmly inside me; his words were like a bucket of cold water dashed over that flame. I had thought about Astimir. I had not thought about everyone *else*.

"Then we'll just have to keep watch," I said, trying to sound confident.

"*We?*" Mr. Wilker's eyes were bloodshot. He had not gotten any rest the night before, I remembered; that might have some bearing on his volatility now.

I lifted my chin. "Yes, *we*. I am not too delicate to go a night without sleep. I will stand watch alone or with someone else; Dagmira might join me. Or Iljish. There are *some* people here sympathetic to us."

From Jacob I heard a grim murmur of "Not many," but I paid it no heed. "Science will triumph, Mr. Wilker. I will not be driven out of Drustanev by peasant superstition."

His murmur was rather more audible than Jacob's. "No, by peasant pitchforks and torches." But apparently he considered the argument at an end, for he stormed out of the workroom. I wondered if I had won or lost.

Jacob sighed and dropped into a chair. After a moment, he asked, "*How* many bottles did you say he had?"

"Half a dozen."

My husband shook his head. "Where in heaven did he *get* them?"

The bottles in question were with Lord Hilford and the mayor, but I remembered them well enough. "The writing on the labels was Chiavoran. Jacob, I'm wondering if the plan to drive us away was formed even before we *came* here."

The specter of the missing Gritelkin hung over us, more ominous than ever. Jacob said, "Then why wait so long? Why not cause trouble as soon as we arrived?"

"We hadn't been to the ruins yet. Astimir needed a justification for his haunting."

"He could have invited you sooner, though."

That was true. I thought back through our time in Drustanev. The invitation had come after my misadventure with the smugglers; perhaps it had something to do with them after all. They might have provided Astimir with the acid, though why they would have it on hand themselves, I could not guess. They had not killed me—but then, killing a Scirling gentlewoman would have brought a great deal of trouble down upon them. Scaring her off, on the other hand, would not. But why not threaten me *then*?

Too many questions. I fingered the firestone in my pocket. Acid. Smugglers. Rock-wyrm attacks. Gritelkin missing. This charade with "Zhagrit Mat." The dragon graveyard. The ruins. I could not tell if we had too little data or too much; I was convinced at least *some* of the pieces belonged together, but I could not tell which ones, and they all stubbornly refused to form a clear picture.

I told myself to take one problem at a time. This is not always useful advice; one does not always have the leisure, and some problems are best tackled together. But at the moment, I could see no useful course of action except to make certain we were not driven out of Vystrana in the morning. That must come first.

And—once again, addressing the nearest problem first—it might be best if we all got a little sleep that afternoon, so as to be fresh for the night. (Mr. Wilker particularly.) I drew breath to say as much to Jacob, when a knock at the workroom door forestalled me.

Back home in Scirland, of course, we would have had servants to receive any visitors, inquire of their business, and then interrupt our conversation in as graceful a manner as possible. Here in Drustanev, we had Dagmira, Iljish, and our cook, whose name I had never learned. The first two were somewhere in the village, talking of Astimir's treachery, and the cook came only twice a day. Jacob and I therefore found ourselves blinking at a total stranger, without the faintest clue who he was or why he had decided to walk into our house without invitation.

He was rather more finely dressed than your average Vystrani peasant. His heavy coat, hanging to the knees, was of fine wool, and the leather boots below shone beneath their dusting of dirt. It was a style of attire I had seen before, and as soon as I placed it, the words leapt from my mouth. "You're one of the boyar's men!"

The bow he executed looked foreign, to my inexperienced eye, and when he spoke even my ear could detect a different accent in his Vystrani. "I am Ruvin Danylovich Ledinsky, stolnik to the boyar, yes." He glanced past me to Jacob. "You are one of the Scirling companions to the Earl of Hilford?"

Jacob gathered his wits and came forward. I did not mind a little more time to gather my own; my first, nonsensical thought was that this man—this *stolnik*, whatever that was—had come to evict us from Drustanev where the locals could not. "Yes, I'm Jacob Camherst, and this is my wife."

This was not, I thought, the same man I had spied upon at the ruins, overseeing the smugglers' work. Ledinsky was older than that fellow, with grey salted into his hair; the fur-trimmed cap the man at the ruins had worn might have concealed that, but I did not think so. Which removed, or at least weakened, one of the *other* possibilities for why he might be there.

"I come bearing a message from Iosif Abramovich Khirzoff," Ledinksy said. "He regrets the unfriendly welcome he gave to your lord, which was a consequence of his surprise. Iosif Abramovich did not know Gritelkin was bringing such honored visitors to this village, and was displeased to learn his razesh had been so inconsiderate. But he wishes to make amends now. He invites all of your party to visit his hunting lodge and enjoy his hospitality." A dubious glance cast around our workroom spoke volumes as to Ledinsky's opinion of the low conditions in which we had lodged all this time.

Those low conditions had (mostly) ceased to bother me, but the prospect of a few nights in the boyar's lodge did appeal. Time away from the hostility of the villagers—which I suspected would persist even after we had made our point regarding Zhagrit Mat—

and a chance to put the matter of Astimir and the smugglers to Khirzoff; possibly even news of Gritelkin. When I glanced at Jacob, I saw him thinking much the same. "I will have to speak to Lord Hilford, of course," he said, "but your master honors us with the invitation. When would he like us to come?"

"I have brought horses for you all," Ledinsky said.

Neither of us understood right away. Jacob said, not quite believing, "You wish us to leave *today*?"

Ledinsky nodded. "The cook is preparing a feast in your honor."

In our honor, perhaps—but this Vystrani boyar had some cheek, expecting Lord Hilford to leap at his command. I knew from Lord Hilford's comments that the boyar class had many distinctions within it; where the Vystrani ones ranked, I did not precisely know, but given the client-state condition of Vystrana, I doubted it trumped the status of a Scirling earl. Jacob's frown mirrored my own. "I will let Lord Hilford know," he said, his tone hinting at cool disapproval.

Whether Ledinsky heard it or not, I could not tell. He said, "I will send a boy to help you pack your things," and bowed himself out of the room.

Jacob held up a cautioning hand when I would have spoken. "You should fetch Dagmira and Iljish; we'll want them with us, at least for the journey there. No doubt Khirzoff has servants of his own to wait on us once we're arrived. I'll send Wilker back in, and go tell Hilford."

Very well; I would not say what I thought of such a peremptory invitation. If we were going to tell Ledinsky to wait, it would be better coming from the earl.

In the meantime, I was not going to let some stranger pack our things. I hurried outside and saw Dagmira in the distance, arguing with two women at their front gate. Cupping my hands around my mouth, I called her name, and beckoned for her to come. "Fetch your brother," I said with a sigh as she drew near. "It seems we may be guests of the boyar for a few days."

We did not refuse the invitation. Urjash Mazhustin had, it seemed, had quite enough of the trouble we were causing in his heretofore quiet village, be it supernatural or otherwise. He was not quite vexed enough to run us out of town, but when presented with such an ideal chance to be rid of us for a few days, he spoke volubly in favor.

Ledinsky seemed to think we could depart immediately, but of course it was not so easy. The lodge lay three days' ride away, even on horseback; the beasts had little advantage over donkeys or our own feet, along such tracks as the mountains afforded. We would need to pack clothes for that journey, and then better clothes for our time at the boyar's lodge, and of course the stolnik was unhelpful as to how long that time might be. "It will depend on his master's pleasure," Lord Hilford said, resigned. "Which might be anything from a day to a month."

"We haven't the clothes with us to look fine for a month," I said, "even with laundry. But I will do what I can. At a minimum, I suppose we want enough to be respectable for a week; that will give enough time for someone to come back here and fetch the remainder, if it falls out such that we stay there longer." I did not like the thought of staying there longer; the lodge was quite in the opposite direction from the cavern graveyard, which we'd had no chance to show to the other two men.

The panniers on Ledinsky's horses were not enough to hold everything we wished to bring. But he had not brought horses for Dagmira and Iljish, either; they would have to ride donkeys, and so we might as well bring a third for the remainder of our baggage. Sorting all of this took the better part of what remained of the day, with the stolnik frowning impatiently over us. When it became apparent that we would not be able to make any distance worth mentioning, Lord Hilford insisted we stay in Drustanev one more night.

Jacob stepped aside with the earl and asked quietly, "What will that mean for our situation here?"

Lord Hilford shrugged, looking philosophical. "We may as well sleep, if we can. Mazhustin was quite adamant that we would not set even a toe beyond our door tonight; he and a few of his fellows will keep their own watch. They'll do a better job of it than we could, anyway."

"*If* none of them decide they'd rather have us gone."

"The mayor is a fair-minded man," Lord Hilford said, unperturbed. "He admitted, when I put it to him, that the local children dare each other to visit those ruins all the time. They may not want to consider that Astimir would fake such a thing, being that he's one of their own—but if this *is* a trick, then Mazhustin is determined to pillory whoever is responsible."

With that, we had to be content. And it seemed to suffice, at least for one night, for when we rose the next morning, there were no new disturbances to report. So it was, with a feeling of vindication, that we rode to meet Iosif Abramovich Khirzoff.

TWENTY-ONE

Iosif Abramovich Khirzoff — Gaetano Rossi — Opinions of Jindrik Gritelkin

The term "hunting lodge" had led me to expect something small and on the rustic side: the sort of place a gentleman or peer might retire for a week or two of shooting before returning to the comforts of a less isolated residence.

Whatever else might be said of Khirzoff's lodge, it was not small.

The fence that surrounded it was no wattle-and-daub affair, but sturdy planks of wood, with a shingled roof over the gateway, which had doors sized to admit both carts and people on foot. For our distinguished party, the larger was unbarred and swung open, admitting us to the spacious courtyard beyond.

Above us reared a three-story dwelling of roughly dressed stone walls that, as Mr. Wilker muttered under his breath, might have been dropped there by a dragon migrating from Bulskevo. I had little eye for such things, but the crude scallops of decorative woodwork along the edges of the roof and the octagonal bay at one end certainly resembled nothing I had seen in Drustanev. The place would have been charmingly rustic, were it not for an unpleasant smell in the air. I hoped the odor did not originate in the kitchens, or the promised feast would be difficult to choke down.

Someone must have been keeping watch for our arrival, as a man stood on the steps of the lodge, ready to greet us. It took no great deductive mind to guess that this was Khirzoff himself. His knee-length coat was of imported silk, and held more embroidery than all of his followers' clothing combined. The man beneath all that splendor I judged to be about fifty or fifty-five, with a beard gone mostly grey springing magnificently from his jaw.

He remained at his post while we dismounted from our horses, but spread his arms wide and said in a voice that boomed across the courtyard, "Welcome, honored guests, welcome!"

To my surprise, he spoke in Chiavoran. That country's favorable trade position in Anthiope has made its language known to many, of course, and all within our party spoke it more fluently than we did Vystrani. (Also, as I later learned, few of the boyars of Vystrana actually speak the language of their own subjects; they hold instead to Bulskoi, the language of the tsar, relying on underlings to communicate with the locals, and in this Khirzoff was no exception.) But I suspected the reason for that choice stood at his right hand: a man whose olive complexion and manner of dress marked him as Chiavoran himself. This must be his scholar friend.

Taking his cue from this, the earl returned the greeting in kind. "We are honored to be welcomed in your home, Iosif Abramovich," Lord Hilford said, climbing the stairs. He could not suppress a wince as he went; even with the fine tent Ledinsky supplied, the journey had taken its toll on the man's aching joints. "I am Maxwell Oscott, Earl of Hilford." He introduced each of us in turn. I suffered Khirzoff to kiss both of my cheeks in the Bulskoi manner, wishing he had forgone the friendly gesture of greeting us as we arrived in favor of the more civilized Scirling practice of allowing guests to freshen themselves briefly first. There was sap in my hair where a tree branch had knocked my bonnet askew.

Our host then introduced us to his friend. Gaetano Rossi bowed over my hand with perfunctory courtesy, for which I was grateful; my mind had chosen the most inopportune moment to remind me of my facetious comments to Jacob back home, about Chiavoran dancing girls.

"But come, it is late," Khirzoff said, when the introductions were done. "I have servants waiting for you inside; you may send your peasants on their way."

It was, I think, the dismissive manner in which he delivered those words that raised my hackles. Dagmira might have been a terrible excuse for a lady's maid, but I was suddenly determined not to be parted from her. Had anyone demanded a rationale from me, I would have said I saw no sign there were any other women at this hunting lodge. Khirzoff was a widower, according to Ledinsky, with two sons both grown and trying to curry favor in the tsar's court, and of course he could not possibly have fetched anyone in time for our arrival. If I was going to have a ham-handed Vystrani woman doing up my buttons, at least it would be the ham-handed woman I knew, rather than a stranger.

But my response was not rational. I simply did not like the fact that he was attempting to separate us from Dagmira and Iljish. I only barely managed to avoid saying so outright, which would have been unpardonably rude. I resorted instead to a silly carica-ture of some women I had known at home. "Oh, I could not *possibly* be without Dagmara," I said, deliberately erring on her name. "She's been my only companion all this time; we've come to know each other quite well. I would feel quite *lost* without her. And of course her brother must stay, too . . ." I let that trail off, gesturing vaguely in Iljish's direction in a manner calculated to suggest that I had forgotten his name entirely.

(Oddly, although I have grown more liberal-minded with time, as my travels brought me into contact with many strange-nesses to which I had no choice but to adapt, on this one point I have instead grown more inflexible. As a young woman I was willing to be thought quite brainless when it suited my purposes, for that was, all too often, the assumption of those around me. The more I encountered such assumptions, though, the less patience I had for them, and the more assertive—some would say "unpleasantly opinionated"—I became. At that tender age, however, I had no compunctions about behaving in a manner my current self would smack silly.)

Jacob gave me a peculiar look, which I hoped the boyar did not see. What reports the man had of me I did not know, but any quick summary of my activities in Vystrana could well make me look fluff-brained. (The harmless sort of fluff-brained, I mean; not the sort I actually *was*.) I thought I saw Khirzoff's lip curl in disdain as he looked over our two companions, but the concealing mass of his beard and mustache made it hard to be sure. "Very well," he said at last, not quite as graciously. "Rusha will find a place for them."

Lord Hilford had tried to coach us on the journey regarding the subtleties of Bulskoi names, but it still took me a moment to realize that "Rusha" must be our guide, Ledinsky—a diminutive of "Ruvin." He gestured for Dagmira and Iljish to follow him. In the meanwhile, two of Khirzoff's men hurried to open the doors of the lodge, and those of our party who were not servants went inside.

We were shown to our rooms—one apiece for the earl and Mr. Wilker, and a shared room for myself and Jacob. The chief extravagance of this place seemed to be the abundance of chambers, and the willingness to squander wood in heating them; our bed was certainly an improvement over our accomodation in Gritelkin's house, but nothing on the comforts of a Scirling mattress, and the decorations were scanty. The serving boy who brought up a basin of water spoke no Chiavoran, and either lacked equally in Vystrani or was afraid of me; he just shrugged at my question about Dagmira and hurried out of the room.

"Why do you want her?" Jacob asked, once we were alone. "I thought you detested the girl."

"Less than I used to, and besides, it's a friendly sort of detestation," I said. "It's just—" I lowered my voice. Inside, the lodge was less charmingly rustic, more grim and dark. I had, at Manda Lewis's insistence, once read *The Terrible Thirst of Var Kolak*. The terribleness of that novel lies more in the overwrought prose than the monster Var Kolak, but standing in this place, I understood at last what had inspired Mr. Wallace's pen. "We have few enough friends in this place, and I don't think Khirzoff is one of them."

I expected Jacob to chide me out of that view; it was easy to imagine my uneasiness a simple fancy, brought on by the isolation. But Jacob nodded, and answered in the same low tone. "We may be his guests, but I don't think we're welcome. The question is, why did he invite us here?"

I had no answer. We washed our faces in the cold water and went down for supper with the boyar. Gaetano Rossi was not present, and after the first course had been laid—a style of service which, I reflected, we had acquired from the Bulskoi in the first place—Lord Hilford asked after the man.

"He is occupied with his work," Khirzoff said, attacking his soup as if he, not we, had been riding for three days.

"Work?" Lord Hilford repeated, with an inquiring tone. "He is not here for leisure, then?"

Was it my imagination, or did Khirzoff hesitate? It might only have been that the slice of beet in his spoon was too large and overbalanced back into the bowl. He cut it with the edge of the spoon and said, "Leisure, yes, but we have been hunting. The preservation of our trophies is his task."

The conversation went on to bear, wolf, and other game, while I listened in silence. A young lady, of course, could not be expected to take much interest in such talk, but in truth I was glad for the chance to observe. Khirzoff's friendliness and good cheer was distinctly forced, I thought. It might be explained away by saying his razesh had not warned him sufficiently about us; now the boyar felt obligated to play host, against his own wishes. But my uneasiness grew.

Khirzoff did pause long enough to assure us that this was not the promised feast; that would come the following night. I wondered if it would be an improvement over what we faced now. Our dishes were odd, as if the cook were trying too hard, or unsure of his work. He did not stint on expensive spices—I could not even recognize some of them—but the application was peculiar and sometimes less than successful, as with the venison dyed a most off-putting shade by aggressive use of turmeric. I left most of it on my plate, politeness be damned.

Lord Hilford did tell the boyar of our "supernatural" difficulties in Drustanev, and their source. "You say the lad ran?" Khirzoff said, and frowned through his beard. "My men will hunt him down. Or he will go back to his village; either way, we will find him."

I was hardly well-disposed toward Astimir after everything he had done to disrupt our work, but I found myself hoping the young man was not taken up by Khirzoff's followers. It sounded as if his punishment might be harsher than I would wish.

From his seat across the table from me, Jacob said, "I suppose there hasn't been time yet to find traces of Jindrik Gritelkin."

He could count the days as well as I could; the boyar's men could scarcely have returned yet, even if they found the man almost immediately. Ledinsky must have been sent to Drustanev practically on Lord Hilford's heels. No, I thought—my husband had spoken simply to watch Khirzoff's reaction.

The man's lips thinned inside his beard. "No, there has not."

Gritelkin was supposed to be this man's agent. Even if his primary duty was to collect the village taxes twice a year—which was the description Lord Hilford had given of a razesh—surely his title meant something. "I'm astonished the villagers did not send to you when Gritelkin went missing."

The boyar snorted, picking up his glass of wine. "Likely they got drunk in celebration. They hate Gritelkin there, you know. The razeshi are rarely liked, but every time he came to me with the taxes, more complaints."

By the expressions around the table, my companions' thoughts were the same as mine. We had heard nothing of such conflict, and yet, it explained a great deal—including the general miasma of hostility that had surrounded us since our first moments in Drustanev. Living in the house of the hated razesh, expecting him to be our local guide, must have tarred us with his brush.

I wondered how much of that had been due to Gritelkin himself. As I had told the men, village gossip had made it clear that Khirzoff himself was not much liked, either. Few of the Vystrani boyars were; they were Bulskoi interlopers, reminders of Vystrana's subject status. But Khirzoff made no attempt to hide his own disdain for the villagers of Drustanev. Everything about his establishment, even here at this summer hunting lodge, was Bulskoi, with no concessions to local habits.

Gritelkin, though . . . his was a Vystrani name. How did that figure into this web of tension?

"We will speak more of it tomorrow," Khirzoff said, rising from the table. "And also of what you have been doing here, this research of yours. The servants will show you to your rooms."

He did not even offer brandy as an after-meal courtesy. Lord Hilford murmured to Jacob and Mr. Wilker, "I have some in my pack," and the men went off to cleanse their palates.

I found Dagmira in my room, turning down the covers, scowling fit to light the bed on fire. I had meant to ask her far sooner, but everything from the mob onward had distracted me. I wondered how badly I would regret that delay. "Tell me about Gritelkin. Your people don't like him, I'm told."

I received a glare of the sort that told me I was prying into village business, where I did not belong; but Dagmira answered me nonetheless. "Why should we?" she muttered, keeping her voice low, as if she, too, felt the oppressive weight of this place. "He made himself the boyar's creature. Too much reading put ideas in his head; he said it would be better for Drustanev if he was razesh. But he was just as bad as the one before him."

I worked through this with lamentable slowness, hearing what she did not say. "Was Gritelkin *born* in Drustanev?"

"Of course," she said, once again filled with scorn for my ignorance.

Had Lord Hilford ever mentioned that? He'd called Drustanev Gritelkin's village, but I had assumed the association a political one. A Vystrani man, somehow positioning himself as the boyar's administrator, with grand dreams of benefiting his village. It made sense; a local man would be more sensitive to local issues, more willing to advocate on their behalf to the foreign overlord. But it had done no good—no wonder, with Khirzoff as he was— and worse, it had rebounded to ill; the people of Drustanev felt betrayed by his failure. It was truly unfortunate that Lord Hilford had chosen this of all places to conduct our research.

It raised an unpleasant specter in my mind. "Dagmira—would anyone *kill* Gritelkin? Anyone in Drustanev, I mean."

For once, her fury came as a relief. "What do you think we are? Just because Astimir is an idiot, playing those tricks—but you're outsiders; half the village would say you deserved it. If he hadn't been scaring us, too."

Again, I had to listen to what she did not say. "Gritelkin was *not* an outsider, then. Even though he worked for the boyar." I paced around the small room, the spring of my mind wound too tightly for me to rest, even though my body was tired. "We're fair certain he's dead, Dagmira. He's been missing for too long, and—there's just too much going *on* here. What about the smugglers? They're outsiders, Stauleren; have they been known to kill people?"

"No," she said, but the word came out uneasily. Enough strange things had been happening that I could understand why.

Lord Hilford had told me that a scientist must never reason ahead of his data. He thought the dragons had done it, and maybe they had; I knew well that it was my own partisan inclinations that made me not want to believe it. But there was another prospect in my mind, growing stronger each time another possibility was eliminated or reduced. "Would the *boyar* have any reason to kill him?"

Dagmira's response was incredulous. "Why would he?"

"Gritelkin claimed he'd made arrangements for us to visit, but it doesn't seem to have been true. Khirzoff isn't happy we're here." That was hardly motivation for murder, though. My thoughts progressed further. "And Gritelkin sent a message saying it was a bad time to come. What if he meant more than the dragon attacks?"

"If the boyar didn't want you here," she said, "he could just order you to leave."

That was true. However, its being true did not rule out other factors that might make Khirzoff reluctant to send us away. I just could not imagine what those might be.

I must have paced for some time without speaking, because Dagmira gave me a pointed attempt at a curtsey. "Do you need anything else?"

"Oh, don't be like that, Dagmira," I said, distracted. "I wanted you here because something about this place sets me on edge, and I trust you. But no, I don't need anything else; rest well, and I'll see you in the morning."

She kissed my hands and went out. I lay down in bed, but it was a long time before I managed to sleep.

TWENTY-TWO

A ride, with awkward conversation — Draconic provocation — The contents of Khirzoff's cellar

The next morning, as I went in search of breakfast, I encountered Rossi on the ground floor, emerging from some kind of cellar. He gave me an unfriendly look, though I nodded a polite good morning to him. "Will you be joining us on our ride today?" I asked, for Khirzoff had made mention of an excursion the night before.

"No," Rossi said curtly. "I have work to do."

"Yes, so the boyar said. Taxidermy." It no doubt accounted for the unpleasant smell that wafted along with Rossi. "Would you be so kind as to show me where breakfast is laid?"

I asked mostly to annoy him; breakfast, given the layout of this lodge, would be in the same room where we had taken our supper the night before, but I wished to make him behave like a gentleman. As the words left my mouth, though—the Chiavoran words—a thought came to mind that jolted me where I stood.

The bottles of acid had been labeled in Chiavoran.

Under most circumstances, I would call it meaningless coincidence. Drustanev lay on the southern side of the mountains, facing into Chiavora; much of their trade went across that border. Naturally any such exotic thing would be brought into Vystrana from the south. And Rossi's nationality could hardly be considered proof of guilt.

Except that the man was also, by reports, a scholar of some

kind. He might be doing taxidermy for the boyar—but that required a knowledge of chemicals.

Had Astimir's sulfuric acid ridden with us in the carts from Sanverio, destined for the boyar's lodge?

I ate very little breakfast, sorting rapidly through the details of this possibility. Khirzoff discovered the Scirling visitors to Drustanev were natural historians—from the villagers? Or from the smugglers? Chatzkel's men were working with at least one minion of the boyar; they, wishing not to rouse curiosity by ordering us away, arranged the charade with Astimir, intending that it should cause us to be driven out. Or Rossi might have done that, but he was not a known figure in the village. When it failed—no, he sent Ledinsky before we discovered Astimir's perfidy. When Lord Hilford came inquiring into Gritelkin's disappearance, then. At that point, Iosif Abramovich Khirzoff resolved to deal with us more directly.

I had no proof, but I had more than enough suspicion to make me very worried indeed. The only thing preventing worry from becoming outright panic was the unlikelihood of Khirzoff wishing us dead. If *that* were the case, I reasoned, Ledinsky could have done away with us any time those three days from Drustanev, or upon our arrival here.

It was not much to comfort myself with as we rode out on the boyar's horses, around mid-morning. Khirzoff's own mount was a stallion that he controlled with a hard grip, but the rest of the horseflesh was uninspiring; my own gelding made heavy weather of some of the slopes, lurching up or down them such that a lesser rider might have lost her seat. As it was, I found myself glad my divided skirts permitted me to sit astride.

I feigned difficulty, though, so as to draw Jacob to my side. In brief snatches as he steadied me or chivvied my horse on, I related my fears. I had no sooner finished than Mr. Wilker reined in at our side. He nodded toward Lord Hilford and Khirzoff, who were then turning their horses to continue on through a stand of fir, and spoke to Jacob in quiet Scirling. "I don't like it."

"Like what?" Jacob asked. He and I had kept toward the back, followed at a discreet distance by one of the boyar's men, but my shoulders tensed, fearing we made a suspicious group.

"He's been asking endless questions about our research. But I don't think he's *interested* in it," Mr. Wilker said. "The earl is being his usual self—you know, holding back most of it because he hasn't yet presented to the Colloquium, but hinting all over the place that we've discovered incredible things. And yet, Khirzoff doesn't show the slightest bit of intellectual curiosity."

I knew what Mr. Wilker meant about holding back. Lord Hilford had told us a lengthy story once about von Grabsteil, the fellow who had developed the theory of geologic uniformitarianism; he unwisely shared it with a like-minded colleague before he was ready to make public his conclusions, and that colleague, someone-or-another Boevers, had published a book on the topic first. It was a terrible feud at the time, though considered old history by the time I was a young woman, and of course it's all but forgotten now; its effect, however, lingered in the paranoia of many scientists, who feared others would steal a march on them.

Frowning, Jacob said, "I thought you said he's been asking 'endless questions.'"

"He *has*," Mr. Wilker replied, frustrated. "But—oh, Khirzoff isn't a scholar; surely you've gathered that. I don't think he cares in the least about the science. He only wants to know what we've been doing."

Jacob and I exchanged worried looks. "I thought it had to do with the smugglers," I said, even more quietly than before. "But could it somehow be related to our *research*?"

Mr. Wilker's gaze sharpened. "What do you mean?"

I did not want to draw attention. Nodding to Jacob, I prodded my horse forward, and let him give Mr. Wilker a précis of our suspicions—even more abbreviated than the one I had given Jacob, by the rapidity with which it concluded. Mr. Wilker's horse, choosing its path, detoured to the side of me, and the gentleman and I met each other's gazes.

That wordless moment ended the minor war between us that had waged since I was added to the expedition back in Scirland. If I was right—if the boyar had killed his own razesh for uncovering something he should not, and it had anything to do with our own work—then the points of friction between us were trivialities, not worth so much as another second of our time. Mr. Wilker was not certain I was right, and neither was I; but the possibility was too grave to dismiss for lack of certainty.

The three of us were in accord, then. It only remained to inform Lord Hilford, and to devise some response. I left the former to the gentlemen, while all three of us considered the latter. Soon, however, Khirzoff and the others began hunting, bringing down several pheasants for our feast that night, and the crack of the rifles only added to my tension. How easy would it be for someone to suffer an "accident" out here? I flinched when Lord Hilford fired without success at a fleeing bird, and found myself wishing the pheasant success in escaping.

Behind the pheasant's line of flight, a little distance above us, a stony promontory stirred.

With menacing and predatory slowness, it expanded to either side; and because I had been thinking of the pheasant and its madly flapping wings, my first reaction was—hard though it may be to believe—to think anatomically, watching how the outer "fingers" of the wing spread first, before the upper structure stretched out to catch the air.

Then, belatedly, the rest of my mind pointed out that a dragon was about to stoop upon us.

I cried out a warning, all the more frantic for being delayed. Two of Khirzoff's men brought their guns to bear on the looming figure, but held their shots until it came into closer range. My gelding shied: he might not have been born to the mountains, but he recognized the approach of this predator just the same. I swiftly weighed the likely outcome if I were on his back, and flung myself from the saddle, diving for cover in a thick stand of trees.

Because of that action, I failed to see what ensued; I could only hear and feel. Several shots rang out. By the cursing that followed, they had done no good. A shriek from above then heralded the dragon's attack; branches snapped like kindling as it tried to seize its prey, but I heard no cries to suggest that it had met with any better luck. Khirzoff bellowed orders in Bulskoi, probably for his men to keep shooting—and then a gust of wind raked through my pitiful cover, bringing with it a shower of needle-sharp ice fragments.

If you must be the victim of a dragon's extraordinary breath, I recommend the rock-wyrm. Its ice shards are capable of cutting the skin, but not deeply; the chief danger lies in the body's instinct to curl up tight against the sudden, bone-aching cold. This renders one more vulnerable to the dragon's subsequent dive.

Further gunshots told me that at least some of the men were still in a position to defend us. I forced my reluctant body to uncurl and peered out above a fallen branch. Jacob was alive—I sucked in a great gasp of relief—and there were Mr. Wilker and Lord Hilford; after them I spotted Khirzoff and his two men. All seemed intact, and one final volley of shots brought a cry from above that might have been either frustration or pain. Whichever it was, it seemed to persuade the dragon to seek easier prey, for after a few tense moments, we emerged from cover.

All our horses had scattered, with the exception of the boyar's stallion; for a wonder, none had broken their legs or necks, though Jacob's mount had gone lame. My idiot gelding surprised me by being perfectly fine, and I patted his neck soothingly. He might not have been pleasant to ride, but I was glad he had not been killed.

Khirzoff was spitting words in Bulskoi that I doubted were fit for a lady's ears. Lord Hilford asked him a question in the same tongue, and got a curt answer. Translating for us, the earl said, "This isn't the first attack they've seen, of course. He's quite vexed they failed to bring the beast down, though for my own part, I feel it's just as well. We haven't any of our equipment with us; such observations as we could make would hardly be worth the effort."

One of the Bulskoi men gave Jacob his horse, and led the lamed one on foot; it seemed we were going back to the lodge. Though I dreaded the place, I would be glad to have a roof over my head, concealing me from a dragon's gaze.

The beast had done me the service, though, of breaking my thoughts away from fears of conspiracy, toward other matters of equal—or perhaps greater—importance. *Sotto voce* to my husband, and in Scirling so the foreigners would not understand, I said, "Could it be the gunshots roused the dragon to such fury? It did not stir until after Lord Hilford had fired."

"As an immediate cause, perhaps," Jacob mused, glancing back at the place where the rock-wyrm had been napping. "But if you mean an ultimate cause for the attacks, I doubt it. The locals shoot game all the time. If that upset the dragons, these incidents would be a constant thing, all over Vystrana."

True—and yet, one of our drivers had shot at a wolf not long before the attack on the road. Iljish had been shooting rabbits. Even the boy who brought me the sample of skin had said he and his father were hunting deer. It was not enough to constitute proof; as Jacob said, there were many other shots fired in this region, and not all of them brought down draconic wrath. It was, however, the closest thing to a common factor we had observed, and might be significant.

Back at the lodge, we had little opportunity to speak privately. Mr. Wilker must have managed to say something to Lord Hilford, though, because shortly before supper, Jacob conveyed a message to me. "We'll look for an excuse to leave. If there *is* a danger, though, that may provoke him. For now, we stay."

My first instinct was to protest. I had spent the entire afternoon dwelling more and more obsessively on my desire to escape this place; to have that prospect drawn back felt cruelly unfair. And if there were danger, should we not leave *sooner*? Yet I immediately saw Jacob's point about provocation. So far, Khirzoff had offered no violence to us. The violence I suspected him of, moreover, was purely theoretical.

I am—and was, even then—a scientist. When I find myself with an uncertain theory, my impulse is to gather evidence that will prove or disprove it.

Jacob is capable of sleeping under any circumstances; I am not. I lay awake quite late that night, and finally could endure the uncertainty no longer. Moving quietly, I rose and stuffed myself into the most easily donned of my dresses, tucking my notebook into my pocket. Working by touch alone, I located the candle and matches at the bedside, which I would light once I was safely away. Then I lifted the latch on the bedroom door and stepped out into the corridor.

Where I promptly fell over something on the floor. It was a soft-but-bony something, and it swore as I kneed it in the stomach; the voice was Dagmira's. Extricating myself from the girl and her blankets, and wondering if my heart was going to pound its way right out of my rib cage, I hissed, "What in Heaven are you doing there?"

"Sleeping—or trying to," Dagmira hissed back. I scrambled to my feet and dragged the bedroom door shut before we could wake Jacob. By the time that was done, I understood. For all my airs about needing "Dagmara," I had not asked where she and Iljish were being housed. It seemed that Khirzoff had no room for them, or else was fond of the old ways, where a servant slept outside his master's door, or at the foot of his bed. This gave me entirely new reasons to detest the man.

Dagmira, for her own part, quite rightly demanded to know what *I* was doing. "Snooping," I said. "Will you help me?"

She knew me well enough by then to take my bluntness and audacity in stride. We collected the fallen candle and matches and went downstairs, where we discovered that despite the late hour—I judged it to be midnight, or nearly so—someone else was also awake. We heard noises from the vicinity of the kitchen, and stole quietly in the other direction, toward the cellar door from which Rossi had emerged that morning.

It proved to be locked. I lit the candle and examined the latch, unwilling to be thwarted so easily. From what I could see, the lock was of a simple sort; the key acted to pivot a narrow bar on the other side. The gap was just large enough to admit the cover of my faithful notebook. With nary a tinge of remorse, I tore the cover off, and with its length was able to reach through and lift the bar, allowing the door to swing open.

Stairs led downward, into a veritable sink of Rossi's distinctive and unpleasant odor. Dagmira followed me with the candle, its light bobbing and dancing with each step. And then, when we reached the bottom, the flame reflected off a hundred glassy surfaces.

The cellar was no taxidermist's workshop. It was a chemical laboratory, the likes of which I had never before seen, and have only seen since on the premises of a university. I lacked the proper names for most of the things I saw: bottles and beakers and retorts, rubber tubing and large, shallow tubs. Poor judge of such things though I was, the entire array must have cost a fortune, in transport costs alone.

Dagmira touched the candle flames to a pair of lamps, brightening the room so I could see further. The light played over a well-used notebook on the table, crates of chemicals underneath. I knew their labels would be familiar before I even looked: Chiavoran make, most of the names unknown to me, but the sulfuric acid immediately recognizable. So Astimir had indeed gotten it from here. But *why*?

The answer, or at least part of it, lay at the far end of the room.

There was no question of mistaking the bones for ursine or lupine. I had drawn their like in the open air, hurrying for fear that they would disintegrate before I could record all the details. I had seen mineral-encrusted samples preserved by some trick of chemistry in the great cavern near Drustanev. Here they lay in an enormous pile: uncounted numbers, *far* too many to come from a single beast, not with that stack of femurs against the wall.

Dragon bones. Processed in this laboratory so that they would not break down—my breath stopped at the thought. With what Rossi had developed, we could study them with vastly greater accuracy; we could answer mysteries of anatomy and osteology that had puzzled dragon naturalists since the founding of the field.

But he did not want them for study; of that, I was sure. Had he intended to sell them to collectors, he would have kept each individual's skeleton separate, and he would have preserved *all* the bones. I saw none of the smaller, more irregular components, and only one skull, placed atop a table in the manner of a trophy. The rest were roughly sorted, and they were long bones all: femurs and humeri and great, curving ribs.

ROSSI'S LABORATORY

My hand trembled as I reached out and picked up a rib. Even in those days, with my limited experience of animal physiology, I marked the extraordinary lightness of the thing. It was necessary; the weight of ordinary bone would never have allowed something so large as a dragon to fly. And where the bones of birds were delicate, these were tremendously robust for their thickness, or they would have collapsed under the burden of muscles and organs. Acting on sudden suspicion, I gripped the rib and tried to snap it across my knee. It did not give.

Dragon bones, perfectly preserved, as if they were still within the body of their dragon.

How many had Rossi and Khirzoff killed, to achieve this success?

Behind me, I heard Dagmira gasp. It broke me from my stunned contemplation of the bones. I turned and found her standing, candle holder almost slipping from her nerveless fingers, staring into the palm of her other hand, where something small gleamed.

I went quickly to her side. "What is it?"

Wordlessly, she extended her hand to me. The object was a ring: a small, cheaply made signet. The emblem, when I examined it, bore words abbreviated in a manner I recognized as Chiavoran. In a voice made tight with fury, Dagmira said, "That is Jindrik's ring."

Gritelkin. "You are sure?"

"That is the school he went to, in Chiavora, after he ran away from Drustanev."

It *did* look like a university ring. And when I turned it over in my fingers, I found letters engraved on the underside of the face: *J.G.* Not Rossi's own ring, then. It was proof enough.

We had to leave the lodge as soon as possible. *All* of us.

But when I slipped the ring over my thumb and turned with

Dagmira to go, we found a new light descending the stairs. A moment later, it emerged into the cellar, and it was borne in Gaetano Rossi's hand.

His surprise, I think, was for finding two women in his laboratory. Our lights would have long since given away that *someone* was prying about in his things. I wondered, briefly, whom he had expected. Jacob? Lord Hilford?

In his other hand he carried a plate of sausage, cheese, and bread. A midnight snack, I supposed, to fortify him in his work. He laid it down atop his notebook, not taking his eyes off us, and then said, "Well. What do I do with you two?"

He spoke Chiavoran, of course, which Dagmira would not understand. I imagined she could make out his tone well enough, though: speculative and threatening. Licking my lips, I answered in his own tongue, hoping to flatter our way out of this cellar. "Your work is remarkable. Men have tried to preserve dragon bone before, but so far as I know, you're the first to succeed. It's a tremendous discovery for science."

Rossi dismissed that last word with a sneer. "Science is for withered-up old men in dusty rooms. We have better plans for those bones. Stronger than wood, and lighter than steel; what could we not do with that?"

It was not at all what I had expected him to say. "You—you are talking about *industry*?"

"I'm talking about wealth," he said. "And power. The nations of the world already squabble over iron; that will only grow worse with time. The man who can offer them an alternative will be able to name his price."

Despite the circumstances—which should have held my attention very firmly indeed—I could not stop my mind from leaping to consider Rossi's point. Stronger than wood and lighter than steel, yes; as braces or struts, dragonbone would be worth—well, far more than its weight in gold. But you could not build an engine out of it, not by riveting ribs or ilia together. Unless he had some notion of how to—

That was as far as my thoughts got before Rossi put down his light, and picked up a knife.

"But never mind what I'm doing with the bones," he said. "The real question is what to do with a pair of spies."

I had thought myself frightened when that rock-wyrm attacked us on our way to Drustanev, or when I believed us stalked by an ancient demon. It was nothing, I discovered, to facing a man who might be about to murder me in cold blood.

Threats from natural sources I can handle calmly; threats from humans bring out the most foolish impulses in me. The next words from my mouth were very ill considered indeed, from the standpoint of wanting to survive, but I could not stop them. "You killed Gritelkin. Why? Because he learned about this?" I gestured toward the dragon bones.

Rossi's mouth twisted. "No. Because he was sniffing around the smugglers too much." Knife reflecting gold in the light, he advanced a step toward me.

"Wait!" I flung my hand up to stop him—the hand bearing Gritelkin's ring; not a very wise choice. But there was the faintest chance that my scientific conclusions might do some good. "Please, you must listen. You saw the bones in the cave, didn't you? Or Khirzoff did. That's how you knew it was possible to preserve dragonbone after death. You *must* know they use that cave for a graveyard—the dragons do—they mourn their dead, don't you see?"

"And what if they do?" he said impatiently.

I doubted a moral argument would sway him, but a pragmatic one might. "That's why they're attacking people! I'm sure of it. Because you've killed so many of them, and likely because you haven't let them carry off their dead; it has made them angry. If you continue on like this, *more* people will die."

His lip curled, and he answered with disdain. "Peasants."

His next words were cut off by footsteps, coming in a staccato rush down the stairs. I had never before heard that sound in such a panic, but even so, I recognized my husband's step.

I opened my mouth to call out—with what words, I will never know—but Rossi had no more patience with intruders. As Jacob came off the stairs, the Chiavoran turned and plunged the knife into his gut.

The horror of that sight paralyzed me, from my hands to my voice. I could not even shriek. But Dagmira was not thus frozen; she had been waiting for Rossi's distraction, and when it came she moved without hesitation, snatching up a jar and smashing it over the man's head.

Rossi went down like a felled tree. The chemical that spilled over his head and shoulders was soon joined by more, as he collapsed sideways into the table and then to the floor, taking glassware and the lamps with him.

His fall broke my paralysis at last. Jacob had staggered backward against the wall; I rushed to his side, one hand hovering over the crimson stain that flowered across his shirt. I knew how to draw the body. I did not know how to fix it.

Jacob fumbled in his pocket, came up empty-handed. The motion roused me to my own search; I found a handkerchief and, after brief hesitation, pressed it to the wound. Jacob covered my hand with his own and met my gaze. What he saw there must have alarmed him, for he put on something like a smile and said, "I will be all right, Isabella."

I would have liked to believe him. But the blood seeping through the handkerchief was hot against my fingers.

From behind me, Dagmira spoke in an unsteady voice. "He is the one who killed Jindrik?"

Rossi. We'd spoken in Chiavoran; she would have understood nothing but the name. I turned enough to put the fallen man in my field of vision, but he showed no sign of rousing. "Yes." Him, or someone else involved with this scheme. He was the one who had stabbed Jacob, though, and that was more than enough guilt for me.

I had spoken of there being a dragon inside me. For the first time, I felt it not just in the yearning for freedom, but in the predator's desire for the kill.

Could I have done it? Could I have slipped my hand from beneath Jacob's, picked up the knife or a shard of glass, and murdered Rossi where he lay?

I do not know. I would like to think not; there is something dreadful about believing one's nineteen-year-old self could cut the throat of a fallen man, whatever his crimes might be. But I never made the choice: Jacob spoke before I could, and the moment slipped past. I wonder, sometimes, whether he sensed my thoughts in the rigidity of my hand, and intervened before I could resolve myself one way or the other. "Dagmira. Go rouse the others; we must be out of here tonight, before Khirzoff can discover that we have learned his secrets. We'll meet them at the stables. Isabella, is there anything with which to bind Rossi?"

Dagmira went. Moving like a Hingese automaton, I found a length of rubber tubing, and used Rossi's fallen knife to cut it into lengths suitable for binding his feet and hands. A few sheets of paper and a third bit of tubing sufficed for a gag. Jacob remained against the wall, not moving to help, and I tried not to think of what that meant. Would he be able to ride?

He must. My task done, I moved to help him up the stairs, but stopped as we reached the bottom step. "Wait—"

Jacob steadied himself as I turned back. Jumping over Rossi's prone body, I snatched up the Chiavoran's notebook, and then fetched the first portable bone that came to hand: a wishbone. Proof of what he had done. "*Now* we can go."

TWENTY-THREE

*Departure, Without Farewells — Searching for Shelter —
A Detour to the Ruins — More Answers There, Many of
Them Unpleasant — The Arrival of the Dragons*

I almost turned back at the beginning of our flight, when we had saddled some of Khirzoff's horses and ruined the tack of the rest, and were set to put that place behind us forever—because a glimmer of light caught my eye.

Steadying my husband in the saddle, I said, very quietly, "Jacob? There is a fire."

The others heard. Dagmira growled something that might have been "let them burn." For my own part, I did not realize I'd begun to move until Jacob clutched desperately at my arm. "Isabella—you cannot—"

"There are innocents in there!" I said, too loudly. Softer, but with no less intensity, I went on. "Khirzoff and Rossi may be monsters, but what of their servants?"

Guilt prodded me as much as altruism. I saw my husband's white, drained face in the night, and knew our hope of survival depended on fleeing straightaway; and yet I could not sacrifice all those men on the altar of our own preservation.

Mr. Wilker growled and flung himself from the saddle, running for the stable, where he had left a watchman—a boy, really—tied up while we stole the horses. A moment later he was back out, setting his gelding into motion even as he spoke. "He'll rouse the household. You realize this means they'll be on our trail faster."

He realized it, too; and yet he had gone. None of us wanted that atrocity on our heads.

It made the nightmare of our flight even worse, though. We could not ride at speed through the mountain night, even with the half-moon to light our way, and although we had done what we could to hamper pursuit, we knew Khirzoff's men would be following us. No, not even following; they knew where we would go.

Or so they would think. Dagmira and Iljish consulted in quiet whispers too rapid to follow, and then proposed that we go where Khirzoff would *not* expect: to the ruins. There was the huntsmen's hut, where Astimir, Lord Hilford, and I had spent the night after our visit, or we could attempt shelter in the ruins themselves. Iljish volunteered to slip into the village on his own, to gather up what he could of our more valuable possessions. Then, I supposed, we would go south. Back to Chiavora, back to Scirland, leaving behind our notes and equipment and Lord Hilford's beloved armchair—and the people of Drustanev.

It would mean breaking my vow. Dagmira and her brother could spread word of my theory, explaining to their neighbors why the dragons were attacking humans—but what good would it do them? They had no capacity to stop Khirzoff and Rossi, no recourse to any higher authority. Nor did we, not from where we stood. We could perhaps write to the tsar, once we had returned home, but it was a poor excuse for aid. And as little as that would do for their village, it would do even less for Dagmira and Iljish, unless I could persuade them to go with us. Surely Rossi, if he survived, would remember the peasant who broke a jar over his head. They would not be safe anymore.

All of that was a distant hypothetical, though, soon lost behind the immediate necessity of our flight. The world narrowed to the simplest, most primitive of tasks: find water. Find food, what little could be got while making forward progress. Cover our tracks. Keep watch for dragons. Stay in the saddle, or put one foot in front of the other when the terrain made riding all but impossible.

Pray for Jacob.

Mr. Wilker was the closest thing among us to a doctor, and he could do nothing except bind the wound. It would have been dreadful enough, were Jacob lying in a bed; three days of grueling, cross-country flight made his condition dire. All the blood leached from his lips, and his eyes acquired a staring, blank quality, as every ounce of effort he could spare went into clinging to his saddle, and to life. I writhed with helplessness, my mind racing in futile, exhausted circles, trying and failing to find some way to help him. If I had entertained the slightest shred of hope that Khirzoff would take pity on us, I would have sent the others onward and waited with my husband for our pursuers to come. But I did not, and so the only thing to do was to press on, praying that we would make it to the ruins, and that rest there would restore my husband's strength.

My prayer was doomed to failure, and I knew it.

We struggled at last up the back slope of the ruins, with the shattered wall rising before us. There, with shelter in sight, Jacob slid bonelessly from his saddle and crashed into the ground.

I cried out even before his sleeve had slipped from my grasp. Jerking my mount to a halt, I lurched down without grace and fell to my knees at my husband's side. So sure was I that Jacob had died, I could not even speak his name.

But the touch of my hand on his cheek roused him. For one instant, I felt hope; he was *not* dead, and we had reached the ruins, and surely all would be well. The delusion, however, could not survive for long. He would not move from this place: Jacob knew it, and so did I.

I caught up one of his hands, clutched it in my own. He responded with the merest twitch of his cold fingers. The only words I could find were pitifully inadequate. "I'm so sorry."

His white lips shaped the word "no." Jacob closed his eyes, then opened them again, and mustered enough strength to speak in a bloodless whisper that went no further than my ears. "No regrets. Be strong, Isabella. Stop them."

I had spared enough energy during our flight to tell the others what Khirzoff and Rossi were doing to the dragons, what I had found in that charnel house of a cellar. But how could I stop them? All I could do was flee.

The others had dismounted, forming a silent ring around me. The sun baked the silent ruins, a gentle blessing of warmth. I bent and kissed my husband's lips, pressing my mouth to his until I felt the faintest trace of pressure in return, tears slipping down my face to wet his. When I drew back at last, Jacob's eyes had closed for the last time, and a moment later his breath stopped.

You will think me inhuman for saying this. But even in the face of the worst grief I had ever experienced, grief piled atop mortal exhaustion and shock, my mind would not grant me the mercy of ceasing to work. It persisted in ticking along, like a soulless collection of gears, and so when—after how long, I do not know—I lifted my head to regard the others, the words that came from my mouth were nothing to do with my dead husband, stretched before me on the ground. I said, "I'm going to search the cave."

It lay not twenty feet from where I knelt, covered once more by branches. I nodded toward it, and saw the others realize what I meant. In a tone half bewilderment, half groan, Mr. Wilker said, "The smugglers. Mrs. Camherst, with all due respect—do they truly matter?"

"Yes," I said sharply. "They are part of this, Mr. Wilker—part of the same damnable conspiracy that has just killed my husband. Rossi said as much. I do not think it is opium they are smuggling; it is something else, and I am determined to find out what. Jacob told me to stop them, and I intend to honor his last words."

The entire picture had *almost* come together in my head. Only a few pieces were missing. Khirzoff was an ambitious man, cultivating connections to the south, seeking to make a fortune for himself with Rossi's work on the dragon bones. He feared our research on account of that. But Gritelkin did not die because of the dragons; he died because of the smugglers. And Khirzoff already *had* a fortune, at least a small one, with which to buy Rossi's chemical laboratory, not to mention rich clothing and spices for himself. But he had come to it recently, or the rest of his surroundings would be better.

The keystone that would hold it all together lay here. I was sure of it.

Mr. Wilker accompanied me, because we had no rope, and he could lift himself from the cave where I could not. He could have gone alone, but I was determined to see with my own eyes. We struck a light on a fallen pine branch, which would do for a short-lived torch, and Mr. Wilker lowered me down, following a moment later.

The crates I had seen before were gone. It was possible the smugglers had emptied the entire place out the day I'd come here with Dagmira, leaving no evidence behind; but the only way to be certain was to look. Torch raised against the darkness, I went farther into the cave.

The way was cramped in places, but not enough to force us to crawl. And it did not go nearly as far back as I had feared: no more than two hundred feet, I judged. At that point, the cave ended in a wall of solid earth and stone.

Mr. Wilker brushed his hair from his face with one filthy hand and sighed. "I'm sorry, Mrs. Camherst. Whatever they were storing here, it's gone."

My gaze swept over the dirt, trying, in a most unscientific fashion, to deny its blank uselessness. There *must* be something. I would not allow there to be nothing. "Assuming what they did here was *store*," I murmured, going forward another few steps.

The signs were there, in the uneven shape of the earthen wall, the spots that might have been sharp gouges before the edges crumbled into softer slopes. Someone had been digging there, and not many days ago, either.

I dropped to my knees, jamming the narrow end of the torch into the ground, and began to scrabble at the dirt. The rigors of rock climbing and cave exploration had already roughened my hands beyond what befitted a lady; now I sacrificed the last bit of delicacy, tearing my nails as I clawed lumps of earth and stone away. And, as Mr. Wilker reached out to stop me, my persistence was rewarded.

It glimmered even before I wiped it clean on my sleeve and held it up to the light: a fragment of firestone, larger even than the one I had found in the grass above.

"This isn't a cache," I whispered. "It's a mine. Khirzoff has found a source of firestone."

Mr. Wilker took the stone from me, lips pursed in a soundless whistle. His Niddey accent came through strongly as he said, "If Bulskevo's laws are anything like Scirland's, by all rights this belongs to the tsar."

For such a glorious find, Khirzoff might well receive a reward from his master. But how much more wealth could be gained by smuggling the stones across the border and selling them in Chiavora? He would have to do it slowly; a sudden glut of firestones would be noticed, even if they were sold in secret. But it would not take many at all to fund Rossi's efforts, and pay for some new luxuries in the bargain. Given enough time, the stones and the innovation of dragonbone—lightweight, all but indestructible; better even than steel—could make Khirzoff one of the wealthiest men in the world.

"You know more of politics and law than I do," I said, my voice tight. "What might the tsar do, if he discovered his vassal was stealing from him in this fashion?"

It was a rhetorical question; we could both guess perfectly well. Mr. Wilker nodded. "It will be enough to bring him down, yes. Let's go tell the others."

The discovery put new life into our limbs, hurrying us back toward the ragged spill of light that was the cave's entrance. But Mr. Wilker, without warning, dragged me to a halt, one hand going over my lips to muffle my startled question.

A rope dangled down from above. We had brought nothing of the sort with us from the boyar's lodge.

With his mouth by my ear, Mr. Wilker whispered, "You didn't see another way out of here, did you?"

I shook my head, hand tightening on the dying torch. The passage might continue beyond the dirt wall—my guess was that the ground above had collapsed at some point in the distant past, as this whole place lay very near the surface—but that was of no use to us. The only exit was that opening, into the arms of whoever waited above.

It was a mark of our dire situation that I found myself *hoping* it was the Stauleren smugglers.

Mr. Wilker drew in a deep breath and squared his shoulders. "Stay hidden," he murmured near-soundlessly, "and snuff out that light. I will go. With any luck, they'll think I came down alone."

It was the gentlemanly thing to do. It was also the one thing that might win us the slightest advantage, if only I could think how to use it. Iljish had left us already, diverging toward Drustanev in the hopes of snatching up our money; only Lord Hilford and Dagmira waited above. What use I could be, separate from them, I did not know, but it was worth a try. My jaw tight, I nodded to Mr. Wilker and doused the torch in the dirt.

The drop was not a large one; with jumping, he could have caught hold of the edge and dragged himself out. With the rope's aid, he was gone from my sight in mere seconds.

From above, I heard muffled voices.

Then a voice, speaking Bulskoi-accented Chiavoran, that I recognized all too well. "We know you are down there. Come out now."

I kicked myself inwardly as I remembered the horses. If Khirzoff had snared my companions—as I had to assume he had—then he would have seen an extra riderless mount; even the best liar would have been hard-pressed to make him believe I had lain down somewhere for a nap, or fallen over a cliff, or any such thing.

Gritting my teeth, I went forward, and took hold of the rope.

They dragged me up without ceremony and dumped me to the ground. When I climbed to my feet, I saw it was quite as bad as I had feared. Khirzoff had brought with him half a dozen men: the sort of odds that may be entirely manageable in a drunk man's boast, but which are rather more difficult in real life, especially when the half dozen have guns, and the two gentlemen and two women those guns are pointed at do not. In addition, there was Khirzoff himself—and with him, Gaetano Rossi.

When the man had lain helpless at my feet, I had felt compunctions about the desire to see him dead; now that he stood before me, and my husband was the one lifeless on the ground, I wished with foul, poisonous rage that I had cut his throat while I could. It was scant satisfaction to notice the bruising from Dagmira's jar, and the discoloration where the chemicals had spilled over his skin.

Our captors looked tired—they must have ridden hard to catch us—but nothing like so exhausted as we were. Khirzoff mostly looked angry. "When I invited you to my lodge, I was considering whether it might suffice to order you out of my lands," he said. "Had you not been so determined to pry, it might have done. If you had been content to remain ignorant."

"We would have been suspicious," I said, too foolish to keep my mouth shut. "That's why you tried the ridiculous charade with Astimir."

The boyar shrugged. "Yes—but what could you do? Complain to the tsar? He would not care. Not if all you had were suspicions."

But now we had proof. Or rather, enough specifics to give the tsar reason to investigate. Theft, smuggling, murder—even if no one cared that the boyar's scheme was causing the dragons to attack people, the rest would be enough to cause him trouble.

I retained enough sense not to point that out, if only barely. The most likely case was that he had followed with the intention of killing us, but if not, there was no sense in encouraging him.

Lord Hilford said, "You forget, sir, that I am a Scirling peer. And your man there has murdered a Scirling gentleman." The way he pronounced the word "sir," it might have been the vilest insult he knew.

Khirzoff seemed entirely unconcerned. "With the feuds between Bulskevo and Scirland? That only gives the tsar more reason to ignore you."

"Perhaps," Lord Hilford said, drawing himself up, "but it gives others more reason to pay attention. If anything should happen to me, or to my companions, it will go very hard for you."

Rossi laughed outright, a harsh, ugly sound. "What if you met with an accident? Chasing around the mountains, trying to pet the dragons—there have been so many attacks lately, after all. Who could be surprised if it ended badly?"

As covers for murder went, that one was unfortunately plausible. And even if the villagers or our families back home could raise suspicion regarding our deaths, it would not do *us* much good.

I had little hope that it would be any use, but I had to try. "Didn't your tame chemist there tell you, Iosif Abramovich? All these attacks—you're causing them yourself. The more you pursue this course, the worse it will get."

As I feared, Khirzoff only shrugged again. "Dead dragons will attack no one. And we can protect ourselves better than the peasants can."

He would not keep talking forever; sooner or later, and likely sooner, he would decide to end at least one of his problems by ending *us*. I glanced toward Mr. Wilker, hoping he might see some way to make use of our firestone discovery to persuade Khirzoff to spare us—but he seemed entirely distracted, squinting into the late afternoon sun.

Late afternoon.

I squinted, too, wrinkling up my face so that our captors might think me about to cry. With my lashes filtering the light, I could make out what Mr. Wilker had seen: a large shape in the air, winging its way home for the night, but too distant to be any threat.

Unless we happened to provoke it.

There are proverbs about frying pans and fires that I might have quoted to myself, but I preferred to adapt a different one to my purposes: better the devil that would attack everyone impartially than the devil specifically looking to kill *us*. At the very least, it would create chaos, and we might be able to take advantage of that.

Or rather, the others might. What I had in mind to do might leave me in no state to take advantage of anything at all.

I could not let myself think about it; if I did, my nerve might fail me. I simply looked at Rossi and said the first offensive thing that came into my head: "By the way, I burned your notebook."

Then I hiked up my skirts and took off for the ruins.

For the first few steps, I thought it would do no good. One of the soldiers would just chase me and drag me back, with nothing gained. But then I heard Rossi's enraged sputtering, which resolved at last into words: "*Shoot her!*"

Even when you are exhausted beyond any previous experience of the word, adrenaline has the marvelous ability to bring life to your limbs. I ducked and wove through the thin trees, praying desperately that I might make it to the wall where I had found my firestone; the first shot came close enough that splinters rained across my face. It was soon followed by more, and then I flung myself to the ground behind the stone, gasping for air.

How many shots was that? Eight? Ten? Would they carry clearly enough in the mountain air to draw the rock-wyrm's attention to this place?

I had certainly occasioned a great deal of shouting. I wanted very badly to look whether the others were all right, but my respite lasted only a few seconds; then I scrambled once more to my feet and looked for a hiding spot, knowing someone would be after me, if they weren't already.

Gunfire broke out again, this time more sporadically. My heart was torn; every shot, I hoped, increased the odds that a dragon would take offense, but it also meant my companions were in danger. Already I was cursing the impulse that had made me run: it seemed such a hopeless gamble. And yet, what better chance did we have? Run and be shot, or stay and do the same.

I plunged through a concealing screen of brush—and found myself mere feet from a terrified and very dirty Astimir.

More precisely, from the barrel of his rifle. But I had passed through fear to a region on the far side, where I could without hesitation do things that would have seemed unthinkable risks in the light of saner contemplation. I seized the gun's muzzle and wrenched it aside, and either my conviction that he would not shoot me was powerful enough to convince him, too, or Astimir was paralyzed with his own fear, for he did not resist.

"The boyar is going to *kill* us," I snarled, and grabbed him by the collar of his shirt. "He has already killed my husband. You helped create this disaster; you will damn well do something to fix it. Get out there and *help*." Upon that last word, I hurled him bodily toward the fight.

I honestly cannot tell you whether I remembered to speak in Vystrani or not. It may be that my tone sufficed all on its own. Astimir stumbled through the brush, and then I sallied after him, driven by grief and rage past the bounds of rationality, into a soaring state wherein I had lost all capacity for fear. My husband lay dead on the ground. I must do *something* more than run.

As if to give voice to my rage, from above came a furious, inhuman scream.

I had indeed managed to attract a dragon—and a very angry one at that.

The ruined wall blocked my view of what happened on the ground. I saw only the penultimate stage of the dragon's stoop, and heard shots ring out from below. The wyrm screamed again, this time in pain.

Either none of the boyar's men had made it this far in pursuit of me, or they had already gone past in their search. I swarmed up the wall, thinking the unexpected vantage point would give me a degree of protection from any guns, and looked down to the ground beyond.

The dragon was thrashing about, too wounded to regain the air. Its blood seemed to be everywhere, and the frantic beating of its wings, the quick whipping of its head and tail, made it almost impossible to parse the scene. I saw one of the soldiers, half behind a tree, taking aim for the dragon once more; then I spotted Mr. Wilker across the way, crouching for cover. A sudden twist of the dragon's body revealed Khirzoff lying motionless, and my heart gave a savage leap; but it turned to pain a moment later as the soldier shot and the beast suddenly collapsed into the dirt, dead.

A banshee howl from just below me dragged my gaze downward. Heaven only knows what had gone through Astimir's head during those days hiding in the ruins; I think it had rather unhinged him. I doubt it was any sort of vengeance for the fallen dragon, or even for us, that made him aim for the soldier and shoot. Whatever motivated him, the bullet struck true; the boyar's man cried out and toppled backward down the slope. But there were still others now emerging from cover; and then I heard a snarl from behind me.

I twisted to see Rossi halfway up the wall, his discolored face contorted into an expression of animal fury. He was close enough to snatch at my foot, braced against the stone; I drew it up just in time. But he caught a handful of my skirt, and only a desperate clutch at the wall kept me from falling.

I kicked out, twice, three times, and struck his hand hard enough against the rock to make him swear and let go. Then I scrambled higher, drawing myself fully onto the top of the wall, less afraid in that instant of the men with the rifles than of the one pursuing me with single-minded madness. But there was nowhere to go; if I leapt off the wall, I should certainly break something, and be left easy prey.

The stone crumbled beneath Rossi, giving me a fleeting moment of hope. He caught himself, though, and clawed for a new handhold, after which it was the work of mere seconds for him to attain the top of the wall. I retreated as far as I could, but it put me barely out of arm's reach, and there was nothing more behind me except a steep angle of broken rock and air.

Rossi paused, securing his balance. The mountain wind tried to make a sail of my skirt; soon it would carry me off my own precarious footing, and he would not get the satisfaction of killing me after all.

My attention was so fixed on him that I did not realize those tearing gusts of air were not solely from the wind until a shadow fell across us both.

TWENTY-FOUR

*The price of our victory — My reluctance to write — Rossi's
notebook — Its possible consequences — Our departure from
Vystrana — Jacob — Lord Hilford's offer*

Y ou may say it is pure fancy to think that the second dragon
took Rossi and spared me because it somehow knew which
of us was the enemy, and which a friend. I will agree with
you. Vystrani rock-wyrms are intelligent enough to
carry their dead to rest in that great cavern, but they have not the
slightest shred of affection for humans, nor any care to distinguish friend from foe. But fancy or not, I have no other explanation for how, when that shadow beat flapping off from the wall,
Rossi was screaming in its claws, and I was left untouched.

(Even fancy cannot explain how I managed to avoid falling,
either. That, I must attribute to divine providence.)

The chaos left Khirzoff and Rossi both dead, along with two
of their men; the others had fled. We were, in the end, saved by
the dragons: a fitting revenge for their fallen brethren. And the
boyar and his chemist were stopped. But the price of that victory
had been so very high.

I sometimes think it has taken me this long to write my memoirs
because I knew I could not avoid speaking of Jacob's death.

The grief, of course, has faded. The Vystrani expedition was
decades ago; I no longer weep into my pillow every night for his

loss. But coming to terms with one's sorrow is one thing; sharing it with strangers is quite another. And given how many of the events that led to his death can be laid at my feet, I was deeply reluctant to invite the sort of criticism that would—and still perhaps will—inevitably follow.

I will not attempt to lay before you the pain I suffered then. I have said what I can; it is insufficient, but then I am a scientist, and not a poet. My feelings are as strong as any woman's, but I lack the words to express them. It is not true, what some said of me, that I never loved him: I have already refuted that argument. If it lacks the grand passion some demand, I will not apologize; I am who I am, and the sincerity of my affection, the worthiness of my marriage, are not things I care to debate.

Let us speak instead of what followed.

We would not leave the bodies for the scavengers, not even those of our enemies. The horses bore those to the hut, where we passed the night. The next day we returned to the village, and there Lord Hilford, Mr. Wilker, and Dagmira took on the unenviable task of explaining matters to everyone.

The reactions ranged from doubt to anger. The boyar was not loved, but we Scirlings were even more strangers to the people of Drustanev than he was; no one was in a hurry to believe us, and furthermore the explanation for the dragon attacks was not one that could be easily proven. Many people were also worried—very understandably—for what consequences might fall upon them as a result of Khirzoff's death.

I attended to none of it. The rock-wyrms of Vystrana bear their dead to the great cavern; we humans have our own rites, and those began upon our return. The old women of Drustanev left their sons and daughters to argue over worldly matters, and quietly went about the business of washing and shrouding the bodies of my husband and my enemies. We buried them all the

Jacob

next day, with ceremonies that would have offended a Magisterial purist; but those ceremonies were all the comfort I had, and I was grateful for them.

For all the differences of religion that lay between us and the Vystrani, I will say this for them: when it came to mourning, we were not treated as outsiders. I think everyone in the village came to visit while we sat shiva, even if only from a sense of obligation. Nor did we hold ourselves apart: when the Sabbath interrupted our mourning, we attended Menkem's service in the tabernacle, with nary a murmur of protest, even from Lord Hilford.

It's possible we offended them by our behaviour after our shiva ended. We felt we owed certain obligations to the village, though, and in discussion amongst ourselves, Lord Hilford, Mr. Wilker, and I agreed that it would be no insult to Jacob's spirit if we brought our work to a proper conclusion, rather than leaving at the first opportunity. It was different than it had been, of course; there was no tramping around the mountains, collecting samples from dragon lairs. But while Lord Hilford rode off to handle the matter of Khirzoff's death, Mr. Wilker and I confirmed that the dragon carcass had been taken from the ruins to the graveyard, and we documented the latter as thoroughly as we could. We could not apologize to the rock-wyrms for what had been done to their kin, but Mr. Wilker held a sober conference with Mazhustin and the village elders, and we hoped that would lay a foundation to prevent such difficulties in the future.

We also studied Rossi's notebook, as fervently as if it had been Scripture. (I had, of course, lied to the man about its fate; I would never destroy knowledge so recklessly.) Mr. Wilker had enough chemistry to grasp the general outline, but I was entirely baffled by his attempts to explain why adding a solution of sulfuric acid to dragonbone, however slowly, whatever it was mixed with, could *preserve* anything. Upon one point, though, we were in perfect agreement.

"This knowledge is dangerous," I said to him one night as we sat by the light of a few candles in our workroom.

Mr. Wilker's face was drawn and weary in the dimness. "The things that could be built with dragonbone . . . Rossi was not wrong. There have already been minor wars over iron, and there will be more; we have too much technology that needs it, and a hunger for more. Anything that could replace iron, much less improve upon it, is priceless. But harvesting the bone, if you will pardon the phrase, makes the dragons angry, which makes them attack people."

"To which the only solution is to hunt them more," I said. "Between that and the demand for their bones . . . they will be driven to extinction." Khirzoff and Rossi had already made progress toward that, in this region. No wonder so many lairs had been empty.

Mr. Wilker paged slowly through Rossi's notebook, as if brighter thoughts might leap from it. "It may only work on rockwyrms. We know too little of dragon biology to be sure."

Even if the process, or the mourning behaviour, was specific to only the one breed, the effect would be catastrophic. People would pursue all dragons, in the hope of getting something useful from their bones. Big-game hunters would want trophies; engineers would want bones for their inventions. It was bad enough when animals were wanted only for their pelts or ivory. This had the potential to be vastly worse.

I hated the thought of destroying knowledge—but what if the alternative was even more unbearable?

Mr. Wilker caught me looking at the book, and must have read my thoughts in my expression. "It wouldn't do any good," he said warningly. "Men have been trying to find a way to preserve the bones for some time. Rossi figured it out; someone else will, too."

"What are you saying?" I asked sharply. "That I should accept this as inevitable? Allow you to publish the contents of that notebook in the *Proceedings of the Colloquium of Philosophers*, and get it over sooner rather than later?" A discovery of this sort could do what he so clearly craved, and lift him above the the limitations of his birth.

"No, no, of course not," he said, his own anger and helplessness so evident that they calmed my own. "Concealing it at least defers the problem, and perhaps . . ."

"Perhaps?" I prompted when he trailed off.

Mr. Wilker sighed and laid his hand atop the notebook, staring as if sheer force of determination could make its contents more clear to him. "Perhaps, in the interim, an alternative could be found."

An alternative. A different process would not eliminate the base threat to the dragons. He must therefore mean— "Some method of, oh, what is the word—"

"Synthesis," Mr. Wilker said. "Artificially producing a substance that would have the *properties* of preserved dragonbone, without any need to kill a dragon at all." He grew more animated as he spoke, sitting up in his chair and gesturing energetically enough that he almost knocked over a candle. "Whatever it is that gets precipitated by the acid titration—it *must* be the major component of dragonbone, but we could never analyze it because it breaks down so quickly in air. With a preserved specimen to work from, we can determine what elements the molecule consists of, and attempt to re-create them in a laboratory—"

"Do you think it's genuinely *possible*?" I asked, partly to stop him before he sank into a babble of chemical jargon I could not follow in the slightest.

He sank back in his chair with a sigh. "I'm sure of it—someday. Whether we can do so *now*, with the knowledge and tools we have . . . you would have to ask someone more qualified than I."

It was reason enough to preserve the notebook. Without that, our hypothetical chemist would be set back by months, if not more. This way, we at least had a head start on anyone else rediscovering Rossi's process.

Neither of us knew, that night in Drustanev, how vital the issue would eventually become. The Aerial War and similar matters lay years in our future. But I do not claim undeserved foresight when I say that we saw trouble coming, and did what little we could to prevent it.

"We speak of this to no one," I said, "except Lord Hilford and whatever chemist you recommend."

Mr. Wilker nodded. "Agreed."

The tsar of Bulskevo was distracted enough by the deposit of firestones in Vystrana—of those mined so far, there were nineteen of sufficient quality to be set in jewelry, and dozens of smaller chips—that he forgave Lord Hilford for the tragic loss of a boyar in a dragon attack.

I thought nineteen more enough for any one man to acquire at a single stroke. He did not need a twentieth, or a twenty-first. The stone I dug out of the ground beneath the ruins was sold discreetly later on, and the money sent by even more discreet means back to Drustanev, sometimes as coin, sometimes in the form of items useful for the village. It was one part apology, one part compensation for the temporary suspension of hunting (lest it attract angry dragons), and one part incentive for them to say nothing about Rossi's research.

Also, if my husband must be buried in a foreign land, I wanted some form of tie to bind me to his resting place.

The stone I found during my first visit to the ruins remained in my pocket, a reminder of too many things to count.

We made our farewells in late Messis, packing up our belongings and loading them onto the cart of a trader we had paid to come to Drustanev just for us. Not everyone was sorry to see the backs of us, of course; the villagers were more than ready to return to normalcy. Urjash Mazhustin bid us a stiffly formal farewell, with Menkem at his side. Astimir apologized for the hundredth time; he had initially thought the boyar's suggestion a great joke, scaring the foreigners with the specter of Zhagrit Mat, but he had not reckoned with the fear it would evoke from his neighbors. I repeated the same forgiveness I had given him a hundred times before. The rote words became less heartfelt every time I spoke them, but there was nothing to be gained by railing at him for his stupidity.

Dagmira . . . I will not say she was reluctant to see me go. But she and I had achieved a kind of equilibrium, and I realized, to my surprise, that I would miss it. "Thank you," I told her, and if I could not quite put into words what exactly I was thanking her for, she understood me regardless.

"I hope you at least got us a better boyar," she said with the straightforwardness I had come to expect. "He'll probably be just as bad, though—another damned Bulskoi stranger. And Iljish, the idiot, wants to go to school."

There was a stone for Jindrik Gritelkin, in the same field where Jacob and the others were buried, even though his body had never been found. By now it would be anonymous bones, I supposed, stripped of the one item—his ring—that might have identified it. Although I had never met the man, I found myself in sympathy with him. "It isn't necessarily a bad idea," I said. "Having someone educated to speak on behalf of Drustanev, whether as razesh or not—there could be a great benefit in that." What I did not say was that she and Iljish were already on the fringes of village life; schooling would not mark him out much more, and it could give him something of value to bargain with.

Dagmira only shrugged, kissed both my hands with perfunctory Vystrani courtesy, and walked off.

And then, by slow stages, we made our journey back to Scirland.

I did not suspect a certain change until we were on the ship, and was not sure of it until after we arrived back at home. The symptoms might, after all, have been a simple consequence of the stress of mourning and travel.

But they were not. I gave birth to a son in late Ventis of the next year, and named him Jacob, after his father.

Of him, I will say much more in future volumes. For now, I will limit myself to this unlovely admission: that there were times, both during my pregnancy and after his birth, when he was less a source of joy and more a painful reminder of what I had lost. I risked falling once more into the depression that had gripped me after my miscarriage, and took comfort in intellectual work. I corresponded often with Mr. Wilker, making arrangements to find someone to study our samples of dragonbone, and I spent long hours transcribing our notes, finishing my sketches, and otherwise preparing the results of our expedition for public consumption. My marriage contract provided for me generously enough to live on, but not enough to pay for the book's publication; Lord Hilford kindly undertook a subscription on its behalf. One afternoon, some four or five months after my son was born, the earl paid me a visit in Pasterway and presented me with a finished copy.

My fingers trembled as I brushed them over the green leather cover, then opened it to the title page. *Concerning the Rock-Wyrms of Vystrana*, it read, and in smaller letters, *Their Anatomy, Biology, and Activity, with Particular Attention to Their Relation with Humans, and the Revelation of Mourning Behaviour.* And then, a short distance below the title, *by Jacob Camherst and others.*

"It ought to have *your* name on it," Lord Hilford said bluntly. "Alongside his, at the very least."

I shook my head. I had not taken much care in dressing that morning; my hair was only hastily pinned up, and a hank of it fell forward at the motion, half obscuring Jacob's name. "This is all the scholarship that will ever be credited to him; I have no desire to claim it as my own."

"Claim it or not, it's still yours, at least in part." Lord Hilford dropped into a chair without first asking permission, but I did not begrudge it. If I was going to receive him in a shabby old gown with my hair falling down everywhere, I could hardly stand on formality. He said, "If we're ever going to get those old sticks at the Colloquium to let you present to them, we must start laying the groundwork now."

"Me? Present?" I stared at the earl. "Whyever would I do that?"

He snorted through his mustache. "Come now, Mrs. Camherst. Books are all well and good, but if you intend to be a scholar, you must have the acquaintance of your peers."

With careful hands, I closed the book and laid it aside, then tucked my hair behind my ear. "Who said I intend to be a scholar?"

"I did," he said bluntly. "You aren't going to give this up. Right now you're grieving; I understand that. I'm not here to chide you out of it. But you have a shed full of sparklings out back, and a book you wrote even if your name isn't on it; any woman who puts in that kind of effort is not a woman who could simply turn her back on intellectual inquiry. You're dragon-mad, Mrs. Camherst, and sooner or later you'll be keen to have another chance at it. When that day comes, let me know."

Having pronounced those odd words, he levered himself up out of the chair, nodded a polite farewell, and headed for the sitting room door.

It was swinging shut behind him when I found my tongue. "What do you mean? What 'other chance'?"

Lord Hilford caught the edge of the door and peered around it, his whiskered face all studied innocence. "Oh, didn't I mention? It so happens that— But no, if you intend to give all this up, then it's of no interest to you."

I had risen from my chair without realizing it. "Lord Hilford. I will thank you not to play games with me. If you have something to say—as you so obviously do—then stop hanging about in the doorway, come back in here, and tell me."

He complied, a smile beginning to break his casual facade. "A little matter concerning the Scirling colony in Nsebu. His Majesty's government is sufficiently pleased with the progress there that, as of next year, they will grant visas for citizens to travel there."

Nsebu. I knew of it only from the papers, and not much even then; something about establishing a colony to protect Scirling interests in Erigan iron, and to oppose Ikwunde aggression. "Are there dragons there?"

"Are there dragons! Mrs. Camherst, I must remedy your lack of cartographical knowledge at *once*. Nsebu lies scarcely across the border from Mouleen."

Moulish swamp-wyrms. Ugly beasts, with an extraordinary breath of foul gas—but two hundred years before, the great traveller Yves de Maucheret had written of peoples in the swamp who worshipped dragons as the ancient Draconeans had. His claims had never been verified, or even investigated.

"Some identify three major breeds of dragon within the region," Lord Hilford added. "Others say there are no fewer than seven. It wants a proper study, truly."

For one glorious moment, the bleakness of grief lifted from my spirit. To go to Eriga, and to see the dragons there . . . but then practicality reasserted itself. Mr. Wilker could not pay for chemical experimentation himself; between that and my son, I had scarcely enough money left to run my household. An expedition was out of the question, even if I had the first notion how to organize one.

I said as much to Lord Hilford, then added politely, "But I would be grateful to hear of what your expedition learns."

"*My* expedition! My dear Mrs. Camherst, I cannot go to Nsebu. The heat, the humid air—my health would never permit it. Let me phrase this in a way you cannot misinterpret: I intend to *fund* an expedition, and if you wish to join it, all you need do is say so."

Fortunately, my blindly groping hand found my chair again before I attempted to sit where it was not. Once I was securely planted, with no risk of falling, I said, "But—"

Lord Hilford put up one hand. "You needn't say anything *now*, one way or another. The expedition won't happen tomorrow. But I wanted you to be aware of it. You can make your decision later."

"Thank you," I said faintly, and so he departed.

After what seemed an eternity of staring blankly at the wall, I picked up the green-bound volume of Jacob's and my work and went to set it on my desk. There I paused, staring at the slim spine of Sir Richard Edgeworth's *A Natural History of Dragons*—the volume I had read so many times as a child, the one my father had given to me upon my marriage to Jacob.

Life without dragons was grey and empty. Sparklings had led

me out of the grief that followed the loss of my first, unborn child; might not their larger cousins do the same for the loss of my husband?

The mere prospect of it was already lifting my spirits. To define myself first and foremost not as a widow, but as a *scholar* . . .

The dragon within my heart stirred, shifting her wings, as if remembering they could be used to fly.

Tucking errant strands of hair behind my ears, I took *A Natural History of Dragons* off the shelf and curled up in the window seat to read.

THE MEMOIRS OF LADY TRENT CONTINUE IN

THE TROPIC OF SERPENTS

AVAILABLE AT ALL BOOKSELLERS OF REPUTE.

Lady Trent has graciously shared an excerpt from the manuscript for your enjoyment.

ONE

My life of solitude—My sister-in-law and my mother—
An unexpected visitor—Trouble at Kemble's

Not long before I embarked on my journey to Eriga, I girded my loins and set out for a destination I considered much more dangerous: Falchester.

The capital was not, in the ordinary way of things, a terribly adventurous place, except insofar as I might be rained upon there. I made the trip from Pasterway on a regular basis, as I had affairs to monitor in the city. Those trips, however, were not well-publicized—by which I mean I mentioned them to only a handful of people, all of them discreet. So far as most of Scirland knew (those few who cared to know), I was a recluse, and had been so since my return from Vystrana.

I was permitted reclusiveness on account of my personal troubles, though in reality I spent more of my time on work: first the publication of our Vystrani research, and then preparation for this Erigan expedition, which had been delayed and delayed again, by forces far beyond our control. On that Graminis morning, however, I could no longer escape the social obligations I assiduously buried beneath those other tasks. The best I could do was to discharge them both in quick succession: to visit first my blood relations, and then those bound to me by marriage.

My house in Pasterway was only a short drive from the fashionable district of Havistow, where my eldest brother Paul had settled the prior year. I usually escaped the necessity of visiting his house by the double gift of his frequent absence and his wife's utter disinterest in me, but on this occasion I had been invited, and it would have been more trouble to refuse.

Please understand, it is not that I disliked my family. Most of us got on cordially enough, and I was on quite good terms with Andrew, the brother most immediately senior to me. But the rest of my brothers found me baffling, to say the least, and my mother's censure of my behaviour had nudged their opinions toward disapproval. What Paul wanted with me that day I did not know—but on the whole, I would have preferred to face a disgruntled Vystrani rock-wyrm.

Alas, those were all quite far away, while my brother was too near to avoid. With a sensation of girding for battle, I lifted my skirt in ladylike delicacy, climbed the front steps, and rang the bell.

My sister-in-law was in the morning room when the footman escorted me in. Judith was a paragon of upper-class Scirling wifehood, in all the ways I was not: beautifully dressed, without crossing the line into gyver excess; a gracious hostess, facilitating her husband's work by social means; and a dedicated mother, with three children already, and no doubt more to come.

We had precisely one thing in common, which was Paul. "Have I called at the wrong time?" I inquired, after accepting a cup of tea.

"Not at all," Judith answered. "He is not at home just now—a meeting with Lord Melst—but you are welcome to stay until he returns."

Lord Melst? Paul *was* moving up in the world. "I presume this is Synedrion business," I said.

Judith nodded. "We had a short respite after he won his chair, but now the affairs of government have moved in to occupy his time. I hardly expect to see him between now and Gelis."

Which meant I might be cooling my heels here for a very long time. "If it is not too much trouble," I said, putting down my tea-cup and rising from my seat, "I think it might be better for me to leave and come back. I have promised to pay a visit to my brother-in-law Matthew today as well."

To my surprise, Judith put out her hand to stop me. "No, please stay. We have a guest right now, who was hoping to see you—"

I never had the chance to ask who the guest was, though I had my suspicions the moment Judith began to speak. The door to the sitting room opened, and my mother came in.

Now it all made sense. I had ceased to answer my mother's letters some time before, for my own peace of mind. She would not, even when asked, leave off criticizing my every move, and imply-ing that my bad judgment had caused me to lose my husband in Vystrana. It was not courteous to ignore her, but the alternative would be worse. For her to see me, therefore, she must either show up unannounced at my house . . . or lure me to another's.

Such logic did little to sweeten my reaction. Unless my mother was there to offer reconciliation—which I doubted—this was a trap. I had rather pull my own teeth out than endure more of her recriminations. (And lest you think that a mere figure of speech, I should note that I *did* once pull my own tooth out, so I do not make the comparison lightly.)

As it transpired, though, her recriminations were at least drawing on fresh material. My mother said, "Isabella. What is this nonsense I hear about you going to Eriga?"

I have been known to bypass the niceties of small talk, and ordinarily I am grateful for it in others. In this instance, however, it had the effect of an arrow shot from cover, straight into my brain. "What?" I said, quite stupidly—not because I failed to understand her, but because I had no idea how she had come to hear of it.

"You know perfectly well what I mean," she went on, relentlessly. "It is *absurd*, Isabella. You cannot go abroad again, and *certainly* not to any part of Eriga. They are at war there!"

I sought my chair once more, using the delay to regain my composure. "That is an exaggeration, Mama, and you know it. Bayembe is not at war. The mansa of Talu dares not invade, not with Scirling soldiers helping to defend the borders."

My mother sniffed. "I imagine the man who drove the Akhians out of Elerqa—after two hundred years!—dares a great deal indeed. And even if *he* does not attack, what of those dreadful Ikwunde?"

"The entire jungle of Mouleen lies between them and Bayembe," I said, irritated. "Save at the rivers, of course, and Scirland stands guard there as well. Mama, the whole point of our military presence is to make the place safe."

The look she gave me was dire. "Soldiers do not make a place safe, Isabella. They only make it less dangerous."

What skill I have in rhetoric, I inherited from my mother. I was in no mood to admire her phrasing that day, though. Nor to be pleased at her political awareness, which was quite startling. Most Scirling women of her class, and a great many men, too, could barely name the two Erigan powers that had forced Bayembe to seek foreign—which is to say Scirling—aid. Gentlemen back then were interested only in the lopsided "trade agreement" that sent Bayembe iron to Scirland, along with other valuable resources, in exchange for them allowing us to station our soldiers all over their country, and build a colony in Nsebu. Ladies were not interested much at all.

Was this something she had attended to before, or had she educated herself upon hearing of my plans? Either way, this was not how I had intended to break the news to her. Just how I *had* intended to do it, I had not yet decided; I kept putting off the issue, out of what I now recognized as rank cowardice. And this was the consequence: an unpleasant confrontation in front of my sister-in-law, whose stiffly polite expression told me that she had known this was coming.

(A sudden worm of suspicion told me that Paul, too, had known. Meeting with Lord Melst, indeed. Such a *shame* he was out when I arrived.)

It meant, at least, that I only had to face my mother, without allies to support her in censure. I was not fool enough to think I would have had allies of my own. I said, "The Foreign Office would not allow people to travel there, let alone settle, if it were so dangerous as all that. And they *have* been allowing it, so there you are." She did not need to know that one of the recurrent delays in this expedition had involved trying to persuade the Foreign Office to grant us visas. "Truly, Mama, I shall be at far more risk from malaria than from any army."

What possessed me to say that, I do not know, but it was sheer idiocy on my part. My mother's glare sharpened. "Indeed," she said, and the word could have frosted glass. "Yet you propose to go to a place teeming with tropical diseases, without a single *thought* for your son."

Her accusation was both fair and not. It was true that I did not think as much of my son as one might expect. I gave very little milk after his birth and had to hire a wet-nurse, which suited me all too well; infant Jacob reminded me far too much of his late namesake. Now he was more than two years old, weaned, and in the care of a nanny. My marriage settlement had provided quite generously for me, but much of that money I had poured into scientific research, and the books of our Vystrani expedition— the scholarly work under my husband's name, and my own inane bit of travel writing—were not bringing in as much as one might hope. Out of what remained, however, I paid handsomely for someone to care for my son, and not because the widow of a baronet's second son ought not to stoop to such work herself. I simply did not know what to do with Jacob otherwise.

People often suppose that maternal wisdom is wholly instinctual: that however ignorant a woman may be of child rearing prior to giving birth, the mere fact of her sex will afterward endow her with perfect capability. This is not true even on the grossest biological level, as the failure of my milk had proved, and it is even less true in social terms. In later years I have come to understand children from the perspective of a natural historian; I know their development, and have some appreciation for its marvellous progress. But at that point in time, little Jacob made less sense to me than a dragon.

Is the rearing of a child best performed by a woman who has done it before, who has honed her skills over the years and enjoys her work, or by a woman with no skill and scant enjoyment, whose sole qualification is a direct biological connection? My opinion fell decidedly on the former, and so I saw very little practical reason why I should not go to Eriga. In *that* respect, I had given a great deal of thought to the matter of my son.

Saying such things to my mother was, however, out of the question. Instead I temporized. "Matthew Camherst and his wife have offered to take him in while I am gone. Bess has one of her own, very near the same age; it will be good for Jacob to have a companion."

"And if you die?"

The question dropped like a cleaver onto the conversation, severing it short. I felt my cheeks burning: with anger, or with shame—likely both. I was outraged that my mother should say such a thing so bluntly . . . and yet my husband had died in Vystrana. It was not impossible that I should do the same in Eriga.

Into this dead and bleeding silence came a knock on the

door, followed shortly by the butler, salver in hand, bowing to present a card to Judith, who lifted it mechanically, as if she were a puppet and someone had pulled the string on her arm. Confusion carved a small line between her brows. "Who is Thomas Wilker?"

The name had the effect of a low, unnoticed kerb at the edge of a street, catching my mental foot and nearly causing me to fall on my face. "Thomas Wil—what is *he* doing here?" Comprehension followed, tardily, lifting me from my stumble. Judith did not know him, and neither did my mother, which left only one answer. "Ah. I think he must be here to see me."

Judith's posture snapped to a rigid, upright line, for this was *not* how social calls were conducted. A man should not inquire after a widow in a house that wasn't hers. I spared a moment to notice that the card, which Judith dropped back on the salver, was not a proper calling card; it appeared to be a piece of paper with Mr. Wilker's name written in by hand. Worse and worse. Mr. Wilker was not, properly speaking, a gentleman, and certainly not the sort of person who would call here in the normal course of things.

I did what I could to retrieve the moment. "I do apologize. Mr. Wilker is an assistant to the earl of Hilford—you recall him, of course; he is the one who arranged the Vystrani expedition." And was arranging the Erigan one, too, though his health precluded him from accompanying us. But what business of that could be so urgent that Lord Hilford would send Mr. Wilker after me at my brother's house? "I should speak with him, but there's no need to trouble you. I will take my leave."

My mother's outstretched hand stopped me before I could stand. "Not at all. I think we're all eager to hear what this Mr. Wilker has to say."

"Indeed," Judith said faintly, obeying the unspoken order woven through my mother's words. "Send him in, Londwin."

The butler bowed and retired. By the alacrity with which Mr. Wilker appeared, he must have sprang forward the instant he was welcomed in; agitation still showed in his movements. But he had long since taken pains to cultivate better manners than those he had grown up with, and so he presented himself first to Judith. "Good morning, Mrs. Hendemore. My name is Thomas Wilker. I'm sorry to trouble you, but I have a message for Mrs. Camherst. We must have passed one another on the road; I only just missed her at her house. And I'm afraid the news is unfortunate enough that it could not wait. I was told she would be visiting here."

The curt, disjointed way in which he delivered these words made my hands tighten in apprehension. Mr. Wilker was, quite rightly, looking only at Judith, save a brief nod when he spoke my name; with no hint forthcoming from him, I found myself exchanging a glance instead with my mother.

What I saw there startled me. *We're all eager to hear what this Mr. Wilker has to say*—she thought he was my lover! An overstatement, perhaps, but she had the expression of a woman looking for signs of inappropriate attachment, and coming up empty-handed.

As well she should. Mr. Wilker and I might no longer be at loggerheads the way we had been in Vystrana, but I felt no romantic affection for him, nor he for me. Our relationship was purely one of business.

I wanted to set my mother down in no uncertain terms for harboring such thoughts, but forbore. Not so much because of the sheer inappropriateness of having that conversation in public, but because it occurred to me that Mr. Wilker and I were engaged in *two* matters of business, of which the Erigan expedition was only one.

Judith, fortunately, waved Mr. Wilker on before I could burst

out with my questions unbidden. "By all means, Mr. Wilker. Or is
your message private?"

I would not have taken the message privately for a hundred sov-
ereigns, not with such suspicions in my mother's mind. "Please,"
I said. "What has happened?"

Mr. Wilker blew out a long breath, and the urgency drained
from him in a sudden rush, leaving him sagging and defeated.
"There's been a break-in at Kemble's."

"Kemble's . . . oh, no." My own shoulders sagged, a mirror to
his. "What did they destroy? Or—"

He nodded, grimly. "Took. His notes."

Theft, not destruction. Someone knew what Kemble was working on, and was determined to steal it for their own.

I slumped back in my chair, ladylike dignity the furthest thing
from my mind. Frederick Kemble was the chemist Mr. Wilker
had hired—or rather *I* had hired; the money was mine, although
the choice of recipient was his—to continue the research we ourselves had stolen in the mountains of Vystrana, three years ago.
Research that documented a method for preserving dragonbone:
an amazing substance, strong and light, but one that decayed
quickly outside a living body.

The Chiavoran who developed that method was not the first
one to try. What had begun as a mere challenge of taxidermy—
born from the desire of hunters to preserve trophies from the
dragons they killed, and the desire of natural historians to preserve specimens for study—had become a great point of curiosity for chemists. Several were racing to be the first (or so they
thought) to solve that puzzle. Despite our best efforts to maintain
secrecy around Kemble's work, it seemed someone had learned
of it.

"When?" I asked, then waved the question away as foolish.
"Last night, and I doubt we'll get any time more specific than

that." Mr. Wilker shook his head. He lived in the city, and visited Kemble first thing in the morning every Selemer. This news was as fresh as it could be, short of Kemble having heard the intruder and come downstairs in his nightclothes to see.

I wondered, suddenly cold, what would have happened if he had. Would the intruder have fled? Or would Mr. Wilker have found our chemist dead this morning?

Such thoughts were unnecessarily dramatic—or so I chided myself. Whether they were or not, I did not have the leisure to dwell on them, for my mother's sharp voice roused me from my thoughts. "Isabella. What in heaven is this man talking about?"

I took a measure of comfort in the irreverent thought that at least she could not read any hint of personal indiscretion in the message Mr. Wilker had brought. "Research, Mama," I said, pulling myself straight in my chair, and thence to my feet. "Nothing that need concern you. But I'm afraid I must cut this visit short; it is vital that I speak to Mr. Kemble at once. If you will excuse me—"

My mother, too, rose to her feet, one hand outstretched. "Please, Isabella. I'm dreadfully concerned for you. This expedition you intend . . ."

She must be concerned indeed, to broach such a personal matter before a stranger like Mr. Wilker. "We will speak of it later, Mama," I said, intending no such thing. "This truly is a pressing matter. I've invested a great deal of money in Mr. Kemble's work, and must find out how much I have lost."

TWO

Frederick Kemble's—Synthesis—The symposium—
Lord Hilford—Natalie's prospects—Two weeks

Being a recluse is not good for one's conversational agility. I was accustomed to thinking over my words, revising them, and writing fair copy before sending the final draft of my letter to its recipient. My comment accomplished its intended purpose—she let me go at last, with Judith's polite farewells to fill in the awkward gaps—but my satisfaction faded rapidly as I went out into the street. "I fear I will regret that," I admitted to Mr. Wilker, pulling on my gloves.

"I don't think you've lost much of your money," he said, raising his hand to signal a hansom on its way to the nearest cab stand.

Sighing, I drew his arm down. "My carriage is across the street. No, I don't mean the investment; I don't regret that in the least. Only that I said anything of it to my mother. She is determined to see bad judgment in everything I do nowadays."

Mr. Wilker did not respond to that. Although we were on more cordial terms by then, we were not in the habit of sharing our personal troubles with one another. He said, "All is not lost, though. Kemble took his current notebook upstairs with him last night, so that he could read over his thoughts as he prepared for bed. His wife may deplore the habit, but in this instance it's been a godsend."

(To those of my readers who flinch at minor blasphemies of this sort: I must warn you that there will be more ahead. Mr. Wilker restrained his language around me in our Vystrani days, but as we grew more comfortable with one another, he revealed a casual habit of naming the Lord. If I edited his language here, it would misrepresent his character, and so I pray you pardon his frankness, and mine. We were neither of us very religious.)

Mrs. Kemble was no resentful housewife; she worked along-side her husband, handling the practical matters of ordering and measuring chemicals, while he spent hours staring at the wall and chewing on the battered tail of his pen, mind lost in theoreti-cal matters. But she believed in a separation of work from daily life, and I—who, you may have noticed, am more of Frederick Kemble's mind—blessed her failure to break him of his habits.

I said as much to her when we arrived at Kemble's house and laboratory in Tanner Fields, and got a dry look that did not en-tirely hide the nervous aftereffects of the intrusion. "I appreciate that, Mrs. Camherst, but I'm afraid it didn't save the glassware."

"May I see?" I asked. Mrs. Kemble led us into the cellar, pres-ently in a state of half gloom, the only light coming in by the street-level windows. It was enough to show the destruction: shattered glass everywhere, measuring instruments bent and smashed. A chemical stink flooded the air, despite the open win-dows and a boy outside cranking a device to ventilate the room. They had not merely taken Kemble's notes; they had also done what they could to delay his further progress.

I held my handkerchief over my nose and said, "Mrs. Kemble, I am so very sorry. If you send a letter to my accountant, I'll see to it that you're reimbursed for what you've lost. It can't restore your peace of mind, but—" I gestured helplessly. "It can at least replace the glassware."

"That's very good of you, Mrs. Camherst," she said, mollified. "Kemble is upstairs; I needed him out from under my feet while I sort out what's broken and missing. Lucy will make you some tea."

Mr. Wilker and I went obediently up to the parlour, where we found Frederick Kemble scribing furiously onto a loose sheet of foolscap. Others like it were scattered across the table and the floor, and Lucy, the Kembles' remaining unmarried daughter, was trying to find a clear space to set down a tray containing not only tea but a stack of blank paper. She saw us come in and touched her father's elbow. "Papa—"

"Not now—let me—" He jerked his head in a motion I thought was meant to stand for a wave of his hand, his actual hands being occupied in note-taking.

Lucy retreated to our side. "What is he doing?" I asked, not daring raise my voice above a murmur.

"Writing down as much as he can remember," she said. "From the notebooks that were taken."

After three years' work, the process for preserving dragonbone must have been engraved on the inside of his eyelids; *I* had it memorized, and I was not even chemist enough to understand what most of it meant. As for the rest—"Mr. Wilker said the most recent notebook was not taken, yes? So long as we have that, the older notes do not matter half so much." Most of them were obsolete by now, documenting failed experiments.

Lucy spread her hands. "He says even the old notes are important—that he likes to look over them from time to time."

She went off to fetch more teacups, and then Mr. Wilker and I settled in at the far end of the parlour to hear Lucy's account of the break-in and the investigation thus far. By the time she finished, Kemble was ready to pause in his work and acknowledge the rest of the world.

"If they'd come before the Sabbath . . ." he said, clearly grateful they had not. His daughter presented him with a cup of tea, which he took and drained absently. "I was looking back through the old notebooks during lunch on Eromer, and something there caught my attention. Last year, I—"

Mr. Wilker, who had long since learned to recognize the warning signs, cut him off before he could descend into a thicket of scientific language I would not understand in the slightest. The body of our collective knowledge has grown so rapidly in my lifetime that although I am accounted an extremely learned woman, there are whole fields I know very little of; chemistry is one such. It was not a part of young ladies' curricula in my youth, and my self-education had gone in other directions. Mr. Wilker therefore diverted our chemist to the points he knew I would care about. "You said something about that this morning, yes. It gave you an idea?"

"I think so," Kemble said. "It's only a thought so far; it will take a great deal of testing. But I may have an idea for synthesis at last."

Had that not been the fifth time I heard those words from his mouth, I would have been more excited. It was, after all, the purpose for which we had hired Kemble. We knew how to preserve dragonbone; that was no longer a challenge. But Mr. Wilker and I, discussing the matter three years ago, had seen the peril in that knowledge.

Quite apart from the desire of hunters to preserve their trophies, and the desire of natural historians to study their subject at leisure *post mortem*, the qualities of dragonbone made it attractive to other kinds of person. Its mechanical properties were far superior to those of iron and steel, being both lighter and stronger—and as the easily accessible iron deposits in Anthiope and other parts of the world began to run dry, the value of any alternative grew by the year.

I could enumerate at length the drawbacks to the industrial use of dragonbone. Indeed, I had an article already prepared on the subject, ready to send at a moment's notice to all the reputable publications. Dragons were even rarer than iron, and while it

was true that they reproduced (which ore was not known to do), any widespread demand for their bones would lead to mass slaughter, perhaps even to extinction. The irregular shape of many bones rendered them less than ideal for the construction of machines, which would result in a great deal of waste. The expense and hassle of harvesting them from dead dragons (many of whom lived in locales as foreign and distant as those still rich in iron) rendered the prospect less than entirely profitable. It went on for pages, but the entire thing was flawed in its basic assumption, which was that people would consider the matter rationally before making their decisions.

The truth was that the idea would bring speculators flocking like vultures to a dead horse, ready to pick the bones clean. And if I tried to persuade myself that I was exaggerating—that such a doom-filled scenario would never come to pass—I had only to consider the Erigan continent, where the lure of iron had led several Anthiopean states to involve themselves in the affairs of the nations there. If Thiessin was willing to conquer Djapa, and Chiavora to encourage revolution in Agwi, and Scirland to insert itself between the Talu Union and the military might of the Ikwunde, for the sake of being able to build new steam engines, we would not hesitate to sacrifice a few dumb beasts.

I sighed and drained the last of my tea. "With all due respect, Mr. Kemble, I would almost welcome another set of eyes on the matter. I have every confidence that you can solve this riddle, given sufficient time—but that, we may not have. Sooner or later *someone* will figure out Rossi's method, even without your notes. If we are to avert chaos, we need a way to satisfy the demand for this substance that does not involve butchering dragons."

"I doubt we'll be that lucky," Mr. Wilker said, sounding bleak. "With the eyes, that is. How many people will go to the amount of effort you and I have, just to spare animals? We already butcher

elephants for their ivory and tigers for their skins, and those are only decorative."

He was likely right. Sighing, I said, "Then we had best hope the police recover the notebook—small hope that it is. Do we have any notion who took it?"

By the grim silence that fell, the answer started with "yes" and got worse from there. Mr. Wilker replied obliquely. "You know about the symposium, I think."

A gathering of scholars, hosted by the Philosophers' Colloquium, the preeminent scientific body in Scirland. Mr. Wilker had not been invited to attend, because he was not a gentleman. I had not been invited to attend either, because although my birth was gentle, I was not a man.

But we knew someone who met both of those requirements. "If it was one of the visitors, Lord Hilford might be able to find out."

"He won't have much time," Kemble said, coming out of the reverie into which he so frequently lapsed. "Doesn't that end this week?"

It did, and the scholars would be returning to their homelands. "Indeed. Then I suppose I know what I am doing with my afternoon."